Night Fall

Night Fall

Simon R. Green

ACE
NEW YORK

ACE
Published by Berkley
An imprint of Penguin Random House LLC
375 Hudson Street, New York, New York 10014

Copyright © 2018 by Simon R. Green
Penguin Random House supports copyright. Copyright fuels creativity, encourages
diverse voices, promotes free speech, and creates a vibrant culture. Thank you for
buying an authorized edition of this book and for complying with copyright laws by
not reproducing, scanning, or distributing any part of it in any form without permission.
You are supporting writers and allowing Penguin Random House to continue to
publish books for every reader.

ACE is a registered trademark and the A colophon is a trademark of
Penguin Random House LLC.

Library of Congress Cataloging-in-Publication Data
Names: Green, Simon R., 1955– author.
Title: Night fall / Simon R. Green.
Description: First edition. | New York : Ace, 2018. | Series: Secret histories ; 12
Identifiers: LCCN 2017050541 | ISBN 9780451476975 (hardcover) |
ISBN 9780698407459 (ebook)
Subjects: LCSH: Drood, Eddie (Fictitious character)—Fiction. |
Paranormal fiction. | BISAC: FICTION / Fantasy / Urban Life. |
FICTION / Fantasy / Paranormal. | FICTION / Fantasy / Contemporary. |
GSAFD: Fantasy fiction. | Occult fiction.
Classification: LCC PR6107.R44 N53 2018 | DDC 823/.92—dc23
LC record available at https://lccn.loc.gov/2017050541

First Edition: June 2018

Printed in the United States of America
1   3   5   7   9   10   8   6   4   2

Cover art by Paul Young/Artist Partners

Night Fall

THE NIGHTSIDE

London has a hidden heart and a secret soul, packed full of sin and shadows. Where gods and monsters go clubbing together, aliens and angels go fist-fighting through alley-ways, and you can find your heart's desire and your worst nightmare in the eyes of the same woman. Where it's always night and the dawn never comes, where it's always three o'clock in the morning and the hour that tries men's souls. On the packed streets and rain-slick pavements, where hot neon burns bright and gaudy as Hell's candy, you can rub shoulders with heroes and villains, brighter buccaneers and twilight souls . . . but there's only one man you can depend on. John Taylor, who started out as a private eye specialising in lost causes, and ended up as Walker, the man who runs the Nightside.

Inasmuch as anyone does, or can.

THE SECRET HISTORIES

For countless generations, the Drood family has guarded Humanity from all the weird things that threaten it. Demons, aliens, secret organisations . . . and the occasional invasion from other worlds and dimensions. Drood agents move between the pages of the history books, doing what needs to be done, never noticed by the people they protect. To help them do this, the Droods have a golden armour that makes them very strong, very fast, and very hard to say no to. They fight secret wars to keep us safe, and ensure we never need to know . . . that sometimes monsters are real. Eddie Drood is the finest field operative the family has ever had. While working under-cover, he uses the name Shaman Bond; because in his line of work you have to take your laughs where you can find them. He walks through the shadows of the world, the ghost in the machine of history.

The very-secret agent.

The Droods are all about control, making people do what they're told for the greater good. The Nightside is all about choice: good and bad and everything in between. The Droods want to make the world behave. The Nightside wants to party.

They were never going to get along.

For years almost beyond counting, a strict set of Pacts and Agreements have kept the Droods out of the Nightside.

But that is going to change.

CHAPTER ONE

When the Gods Are Afraid, Be Very Afraid

They say that home is where, when you have to go there, they have to take you in. The Nightside is where you go when the rest of the world wants to shoot you on sight. Usually with good reason.

The Nightside; it's one hell of a town. The jig is up and the hammer is down. Where it's always the hour of the wolf, and you should never look back for fear of what might be gaining on you. From Rats' Alley, where homeless monsters and forgotten heroes live in cardboard shelters and beg for spare change; to the Adventurers Club, where legends from all over Space and Time come to the long night to hunt the really big game . . . The Nightside is where you go to find everything you ever dreamed of, to save your soul or damn it. Your soul, or someone else's.

You get to Strangefellows, the oldest drinking hole, conversation pit, and scumbag attractor in the history of mankind, by walking down streets where hot neon burns like souls on fire, then slipping furtively down a side alley that isn't always there.

The wall that blocks off the end of the alley has a single door, a flat slab of steel set flush into the grimy brickwork, with no bell or handle. If you're the right sort, the door will open for you; and if you aren't, it's open to bribes. Above the door a small but dignified neon sign spells out the name of the place in ancient Sanskrit. Strangefellows has never felt the need to advertise.

Beyond the door lies an entrance foyer that doesn't even try to appear welcoming. The furniture usually looks like it's been recently used in hand-to-hand combat, apart from where people are slumped across it, doing their best to sleep off some of the hangover before they have to head out again into the unforgiving night. The precious Persian rugs are soaked with old blood and other less reputable stains. The walls are covered in obscene murals, by any number of Old Masters. The air is heavy with the smell of excitement, opportunity, and all the more dangerous kinds of sex. Music beats on the air like the heart-beat of a possessed teenager, calling you on. And if you've got this far, you probably feel like you've come home.

A metal stairway leads down into the bar itself, so everyone can hear you arrive. (It's not paranoia when people really do want to hunt you down and stick your head on a spike.) And in the wide stone-walled pit at the bottom of the stairs, the bar's patrons gather to drink and carouse, plot their angry schemes against an uncaring world, and slip a knife between the ribs of their best friend.

The atmosphere in Strangefellows can best be described as determinedly non-judgemental. Anyone can get in, though getting out can sometimes be a problem. The sign at the bottom of the stairs reads ABANDON ALL HOPE. Anywhere else, this would be a joke. To get to the long wooden bar at the far end of the room, you have to respectfully negotiate a maze of tightly packed tables and chairs, cheerfully mismatched because they're always being smashed in some dispute or another. Strangefellows is a boisterous kind of place, and its clientele wouldn't have it any other way.

On the night when it all began, John Taylor was leaning on the bar chatting with Strangefellows' owner, bartender, and celebrated pain in the arse, Alex Morrisey. John was in his late thirties and in pretty good shape considering the perilous nature of his chosen career. Back when he was the Nightside's only private eye, he used to wear a heavy white trench-coat because it helped to reassure his clients if he looked the part: the last of the knights-errant, in tarnished white armour. Now he was Walker and needed everyone to believe he was the man in charge, he wore a perfectly cut suit of neutral grey, a rich burgundy waistcoat, and a bowler hat. Partly in tribute to his former best enemy and mentor, the previous Walker, but mostly because that particular look had always represented authority in the Nightside.

John Taylor, a good man in a bad place. Because someone had to be.

Alex Morrisey, on the other hand, was born in a bad mood and probably punched the doctor. Now heading reluctantly into his late thirties, Alex was tall, pale, and malevolently moody. He acted like the whole world was out to get him because he honestly believed it was. His permanent scowl had etched a deep notch above his nose, and on the rare occasions when he did smile, it usually meant someone was about to have a really bad day. He always wore black, in one style or another, topped off with designer sun-glasses and a snazzy black beret tilted at a rakish angle. To hide the fact that he was prematurely bald. Proof, if proof was needed, he was prone to saying bitterly, that God hated him personally. People who knew Alex thought that was only to be expected. Wiser customers counted their change carefully and avoided the bar-snacks.

"It's surprisingly quiet tonight," said John Taylor. "Perhaps I can get some important lounging around done without being interrupted, for a change."

"Want to try one of our special offers?" said Alex. "I'm offering very reasonable rates on some glowing champagne, from the Holy Order of Saint Strontium. Complete with a depleted uranium swizzle-stick. Or there's the Timothy Leary Special, for people who want to get really out of their minds."

John gave Alex a hard look. "Are you trying to kill me? Is there a new bounty on my head that I haven't heard about?"

"Of course not!" said Alex. "I don't want you dead. Not till you've settled your bar bill."

John glanced around the bar. "It is unusually quiet . . . I mean, yes it's noisy as all hell, and the general ambience is just short of distressing, but that's just business as usual. No one's tried to open a gateway to Hell, or entice me into a conspiracy all evening."

"It's just the calm before the storm," Alex said wisely.

John raised an eyebrow. "Have you heard something?"

"No, that's just the voice of experience."

"Pour me another glass of Ponce de Leon sparkling water," said John. "With an adrenaline chaser."

He put his back to the bar while Alex poured, taking in the sights. There was a lot to be said about Strangefellows, most of it offensive and bordering on the obscene, but it was never boring.

Alex slammed John's drink down on the bartop, with a little extra emphasis to make it clear he didn't approve of non-alcoholics, and John turned back to accept it. The magician's top hat standing upside down on the bar rocked briefly from side to side, and a human hand emerged, brandishing an empty martini glass. Alex refilled it, and hand and glass disappeared back inside the top hat. Alex shook his head.

"That rabbit really was mad at him."

"He should have known better than to play Find the Lady with a Pookah," said John. "Though he has been in there for some time now . . . Maybe we should try to get him out."

"You leave him be," Alex said firmly. "He says he feels a lot safer where he is."

John nodded and turned away. It was just another long night in Strangefellows. A group of minor Norse deities was playing poker with Tarot cards, which meant the supernatural weather was going to be more than usually troubled for a while. And certain unfortunate individuals were about to discover their previously fixed destinies were now up for grabs. Sitting opposite each other at a nearby table, the bar's muscle-bound bouncers, Betty and Lucy Coltrane, were engaged in a flex off, while they waited for someone to get drunk enough or dumb enough to start something. The Coltranes were always ready to put a stop to something, usually with broad grins and excessive violence. One of the more glamorous of Baron Frankenstein's creations, in a black leather bustier that contrasted nicely with her dead white skin, was taking advantage of open-mike night to murder the old standard "Anyone Who Had a Heart."

Hecate's Handmaidens, a coven of apprentice witches out on a hen night, were dancing upside down on the ceiling and singing a very rude song about broomsticks. Something from a Black Lagoon was muscling its way between the packed tables, looking for signatures on its petition to save the Amazonian Rain Forests. Two Men in Black were crying into their gin-and-tonics because no one took them seriously any longer; and a handsome Time Agent in a World War II greatcoat was arm-wrestling with the Nightside's very own costumed super-heroine, Ms Fate. She was winning.

Just the usual crowd, enjoying a night out.

"I haven't seen Suzie in a while," said Alex, and John nodded.

"She's off in the border-lands, taking care of some last bounty-hunter business. While she still can."

"How long before the baby's due?" said Alex, spitting into a glass before polishing it with a dirty rag.

"About five weeks," said John.

"And you let her go off chasing dangerous fugitives?"

John gave Alex a look. "This is Shotgun Suzie we're talking about. The nearest thing to sudden death on two legs you're ever likely to meet in this life. Besides, do you really think I could stop her?"

"Any idea yet whether it's going to be a boy or a girl?" said Alex, just a bit too casually.

John grinned. "Leaving it a bit late to get your bet down, aren't you?"

Alex shrugged. "The longer I leave it, the better the odds. Though given some of the unnatural forces the pair of you have been exposed to on some of your cases, I could probably get really good odds on how human it's going to be."

"Suzie was very firm that she didn't want to know," said John. "And after she shot that hole in the hospital wall, the staff stopped trying to persuade her. I'm hoping for a boy, but . . ."

They were interrupted by some frankly unpleasant sounds from farther down the bar. Alex's pet vulture, Agatha, was squatting on her perch by the old-fashioned cash register, brooding over the night-dark egg she'd laid some months previously. The egg had grown steadily until now it was bigger than the vulture, but there was still no sign of its being ready to hatch. People who had studied the egg closely all ended up saying the same thing: *My God, it's full of stars* . . . The vulture rubbed her vicious beak against the gleaming black surface of the egg and made some more of what she fondly considered to be maternal sounds.

"Why did you choose a vulture for a pet, Alex?" said John.

"Suits my personality."

"And why name the obnoxious thing after your ex-wife?"

"You've met her," said Alex.

"I take your point," said John.

A vicious crack of lightning blinded everyone for a moment. Wild electricity stabbed down from ceiling to floor, crackling loudly and raising everyone's hairs before shutting off abruptly. When everyone could see clearly again, a young man was crouching in an open space in the middle of the room. People stood up everywhere to get a better look at the man who'd ridden the lightning in from some other place.

The young man rose slowly to his feet and glared around him with deep-set, haunted eyes. He looked half-starved, his face all hollows and shadows. He wore a battered black leather jacket over ragged jeans, and his bare feet were caked with filth and grime. The young man's terrible gaze finally found John at the bar, and he stabbed an accusing finger at him.

"John Taylor! It's all your fault!"

"Possibly," said John, entirely unmoved by the new-comer's arrival or his accusation. "What am I supposed to have done this time?"

"You murdered the world," said the young man.

He lunged forward, an open straight razor suddenly in his hand. The long steel blade flashed supernaturally bright as it leapt for John's throat. John grabbed hold of the young man's wrist at the last moment, then twisted it until he cried out and was forced to drop the razor. The young man hauled himself free and fell back, still glaring at John, who didn't allow himself to appear in the least disturbed. He watched the young man carefully, and when the new-comer went to snatch up the razor again, John threw his drink in the young man's face, blinding him.

"That's enough!" John said sharply. "We don't have to do this. Tell me what the problem is. Maybe I can do something to help."

The young man shook his head fiercely, drops of water flying in all directions, his terrible gaze fixed on John again.

"You've already done too much."

He produced a glowing knife from inside his jacket. The serrated blade shone with a nasty, unhealthy light, the essence of poison given shape and form and a cutting edge. He closed with John again, cutting and hacking viciously. John ducked and dodged, the knife always getting closer, until finally he had no choice but to grab the young man's arm again and turn it suddenly around, so he impaled himself on his own blade. He cried out once, in shock and outrage rather than pain, and fell backwards. Blood soaked the front of his jacket. The glowing blade disappeared. John knelt beside the dying man.

"It didn't have to come to this," John said. "Why wouldn't you listen to me? Who are you?"

One hand came up to grab John's lapel and pull his face down to the dying man's. He smiled horribly, his teeth slick with blood. "My name is Henry. Just like you planned."

"I don't understand," said John. "I don't know you."

Henry struggled to force out his last words, spitting them into John's face.

"I came all the way back from the future. The future you made! The time of ruins and monsters and the death of Humanity. You thought you'd avoided that timeline, made it impossible for those things to happen. You should have known better. The war is coming, and what you'll do to end it will make that future inevitable. I had to stop you . . . Damn you, Father. It's all your fault . . ."

His hand fell away from John's lapel and dropped to the floor, and just like that, the young man stopped breathing. Hate still seemed to glare from his unseeing eyes. John didn't know what to think, what to feel. He'd been meaning to tell Suzie that if they did have a son, he wanted to call him Henry, after the previous Walker. John reached out with a steady hand and gently closed the young man's staring eyes. This couldn't be his son. His future son. He couldn't have just killed his own child, who hadn't even been born yet. He'd been through so much, lost so much; he couldn't have lost the one thing that gave him hope. John looked away. The straight razor was still lying on the floor next to the body. He picked it up, and studied the familiar pearl handle. And then he got to his feet, to show the razor to Alex.

Because he had to do something practical or go mad.

Behind him, the bar's patrons went back to minding their own business, drinking and laughing and talking, as though nothing out of the ordinary had happened. Because this was Strangefellows, after all.

"Why are you looking at me like that?" said Alex. "I'm not the one who tried to kill you."

"I thought you had shields in place, to keep out undesirables!"

"Are you kidding? That's all we ever get in this place. What have you got there?"

"One of Razor Eddie's weapons," said John. "Only the Punk God of the Straight Razor carries a blade like this."

"How could anyone take a blade away from Razor Eddie?" said Alex. "I can't think of anyone I'd back against him."

"Unless he was dead . . ." said John.

Alex lowered his sun-glasses so he could stare over them at John. "Do you know something I don't?"

"More than you could possibly imagine," said John. Because some burdens can't be shared.

"You want me to have Betty and Lucy throw the body out?" said Alex. "There's bound to be something in the alley that will eat it."

"No!" said John, then stopped himself until he was sure he was in control of his voice. "No. I want the body treated with respect."

"You had no choice, John," Alex said carefully. "He would have killed you. Do you have any idea why . . . ?"

"I didn't know him," said John. Quietly, and bitterly. He turned to look back at the dead man and found that the body was gone. Not even a drop of blood on the floor to show where it had been. John glared around the bar. "Who moved the body?"

A chorus of voices rose up quickly, reacting to the anger in John Taylor's voice, protesting that they hadn't touched the body and hadn't seen anyone who had. Because nobody wanted Walker mad at them. John looked at his hand and found that the straight razor had disappeared too.

"I hate Time-travel events," he said. "You always end up with more questions than answers."

"At least this one cleaned up after itself," said Alex. "What did he say to you, right at the end?"

"That the world and everything in it will be destroyed," said John. "Because of something I will do."

"Oh come on!" said Alex. "Even you couldn't bring about the end of the world, all on your own!"

John didn't say anything. Alex looked at his empty glass.

"You want a refill? On the house?"

John managed a small smile. "The end of the world really must be coming if you're offering free drinks."

"Get out of my bar," said Alex, not unkindly. "If there's a problem, do something about it. That's your job, Walker."

John nodded and moved off through the crowd, and everyone moved back to give him room, without actually looking like they were. John didn't notice. He was too busy remembering the future he'd once encountered in a Timeslip: one of those arbitrary doorways that open up in the Nightside, to give glimpses of things that were and may be. He'd spent some time in the future world his son had claimed to come from. An awful place, all ruins and rubble, where monsters and abominations lurched through deserted streets in search of the last few surviving humans. A world where civilisation had been torn down, and only the insects thrived. He'd been told that was down to him, but he'd thought he'd done everything necessary to make sure that terrible future could never happen. Now he had to wonder if he'd done enough. Or if his whole life had been for nothing.

What war had Henry been talking about? There was nothing serious happening in the Nightside. He would have heard. What could he be about to do, that his own future son had fought his way back through Time to try to stop him? A cold hand closed around John's heart as he remembered the future version of his wife, Suzie, who'd also come back through Time to try to kill him, to prevent the awful future she'd known. Merlin had ripped the Speaking Gun grafted onto her right elbow right off her, in a spray of arterial blood, and she'd disappeared back to the future. John had been so sure he'd saved his Suzie from having to become that person. But now . . .

He wondered what, if anything, he would tell her the next time he saw her.

John had just reached the entrance lobby when his phone rang inside his jacket. He thought about turning it off because he already had enough to worry about, but he couldn't. He was still Walker, with Walker's responsibilities. He took out his phone. It was playing the theme from the old *Twilight Zone* television series because when John found a joke he liked, he tended to stick with it. He checked for caller ID, but nothing was showing. Which was not unusual in the Nightside, where most people preferred not to admit anything. He answered the call anyway because anyone who knew his private number knew better than to bother him for anything less than a real or unreal emergency.

"This is Walker," he said. "What do you want?"

The voice that answered was as cold and implacable as rocks grinding together. "This is the Lord of Thorns. You must go to the Street of the Gods."

"Why?" said John.

"Because something has happened."

It was turning out to be a night full of surprises. Not least because John hadn't thought the Lord of Thorns would ever do anything so ordinary as use a phone.

"Why would you care what happens on the Street of the Gods?" said John. "I thought you were above such things. Literally."

"Who else would I talk to? Who else could I have anything in common with?"

John supposed he had a point. "All right," he said resignedly. "What's happened on the Street of the Gods, that I need to get involved?"

"The beginning of the end," said the Lord of Thorns.

"The end of what?"

"Everything."

The phone went dead. John scowled as he put the phone away. Now he had to go.

Outside Strangefellows, the air felt hot and close, and the cobbles were slick and shining from recent rain. John looked up, but the storm had passed on, and the dark vault of the sky was packed with stars in unknown constellations. Some spun madly, like celestial Catherine wheels, throwing off comets like multi-coloured sparks, while the full moon, so much larger and closer than it had any right to be, looked down on the Nightside like a great watchful eye. Suggesting that the Nightside wasn't necessarily where or even when everyone thought it was. John tried not to let that bother him. The longest night of all was full of mysteries that were never going to be answered to anyone's satisfaction.

He glanced casually up and down the alley-way, to make sure he wasn't being observed, then retrieved his gold pocket-watch. He'd inherited the watch from the previous Walker, and it remained one of his most useful secrets. The watch contained a portable Timeslip, allowing him to jump directly from one part of the Nightside to another. Which, given the frankly dangerous nature of much of the transport in the long night, was just as well. The streets were full of things that only looked like cars and trucks, many of which were known to run right over slower-moving vehicles. The taxis ate their passengers as often as not, the buses frequently came unstuck in Space and Time, and the horse and carriages were really expensive. Most people walked. Or ran.

John did a lot of footwork in his time as a private eye, and got through a lot of shoes. Now he was Walker, the one sane voice in a crazy place and the only authority everyone would listen to, he needed to be on the spot and on top of things as quickly as possible. He opened the gold watch, and the darkness inside leapt out to engulf him. When it fell away again, he was where he needed to be.

The Street of the Gods is aggressively weird, even for the Nightside. On this strange and thankfully very separate Street, you can find anything and everything that people have ever worshipped. All the gods that ever were or may be, all the beings and entities and anthropomorphic representations, crammed together in row upon row of churches, temples, sacred places, and eldritch grottos. Towering spires stand next to golden minarets, and do their best not to notice the dark and dangerous edifices on the opposite side of the Street, into which not one ray of light has ever entered. Pilgrims and penitents come to the Street of the Gods from all over the worlds, searching for the kind of answers that can't be found anywhere else. No one ever actually says *Believer beware*, but it is strongly implied. On the Street of the Gods, prayers are heard and answered.

Powerful beings and unknowable creatures parade openly on the Street, sometimes stopping to chat with their worshippers and pose for selfies. There are glories and wonders, penances and punishments, premonitions of doom and good news for all. The tourists eat it up with spoons, especially when gods come together to dispute points of theology, compare the weekly take, or argue over who performed the best miracles recently. Though it's a wise tourist who knows to start running before the smiting starts.

The smallest and least important of the gods huddle together in cheap accommodations at the bottom, and the various churches and meeting-places become gradually grander and more impressive as one progresses up the Street. It's all about location. Some of the more important temples and cathedrals are so huge they contain entire worlds within them, while others present such an enigmatic or abstract appearance, their priests have to hang around outside so they can lead people in. Wherever you look, doors are always open, ready to admit new worshippers, though getting out again with a full wallet and your soul still attached might prove a little more difficult. In this place, gods walk like gun-slingers.

Normally, if such a word can be used with regard to the Street of the Gods, you would expect the night air to be full of chants and songs, the practiced patter of supernatural confidence tricksters and the half-hysterical come-ons from shills and barkers, competing to lure in any wavering passers-by; for their own good, of course. Bells toll and voices summon, and choirs send up a joyous noise to drown out the screams of more or less willing sacrificial victims. Wide-eyed prophets struggle to out-shout one another over which particular End is Nigh, and up and down the Street of the Gods, crowds of worshippers and tourists and seekers after truth chatter happily and boast about the things they've seen, like bird-watchers ticking off names on their list.

The noise is rarely short of deafening, with no room for the small, quiet voice of conscience.

But when John Taylor appeared on the Street of the Gods, the first thing that struck him was the hush. All around him, and for as far as he could see, all the places of worship stood empty and abandoned, their doors left hanging open, as though no one cared any more.

Worshippers and tourists were milling back and forth, frightened and confused. The priests in gaudy robes had no words of wisdom for their flocks, abandoned by the beings they served. Even the prophets of doom had been struck silent, huddling together like lost children. John made his way through the dumb-struck crowds, doing his best to look assured and in charge, dispensing calm words and reassuring counsel as he went. But while people were more than ready to pluck at his sleeve or ask him the same things over and over again, none of them had anything useful to tell him about what had happened.

The Street of the Gods had seen turf wars, miracles and damnations, and all manner of exhibitionist supernatural behaviour on a daily basis, but never before had the gods taken to their heels en masse, deserting their churches and their followers.

John finally spotted a familiar face and forced his way through the crowds to join him. Dead Boy was lounging in the open doorway of the Church of Rotwang, god of automatons, regarding the general chaos with a broad grin. Dead Boy was seventeen. He'd been seventeen for more than forty years now, ever since he was mugged and murdered on a Nightside street for the spare change in his pockets. He made a deal he still wasn't prepared to talk about to come back from the dead, so he could hunt down his killers and avenge himself on them. And after everything he did to them with his cold, dead hands, they were probably glad to escape into death.

It was only afterwards that Dead Boy discovered he should have read the small print. There was nothing in the agreement he made about being allowed to lie down again afterwards. And so he continued, a returned spirit possessing his own corpse, a ghost that couldn't die in a body that wouldn't rot. He was philosophical about it, on the whole.

Tall and adolescent thin, Dead Boy wore a long, deep-purple coat over black leather trousers and shining calf-skin boots, and a large floppy hat crammed down on his dark, curly hair. He sported a black rose in his lapel, which had to be replaced on a regular basis because he was prone to snacking on them. His long, pale face had a debauched, pre-Raphaelite look, with burning fever-bright eyes and a disturbing smile. He deliberately left his long coat hanging open so he could show off the Y-shaped autopsy scar on his torso, along with various other wounds that would never heal. He stitched up the worst ones himself, plugged the bullet-holes with builder's putty, and occasionally resorted to lengths of black duct tape to hold everything together.

John was surprised to see Dead Boy on the Street of the Gods, since it was widely known he didn't worship anyone but himself. John nodded gravely to him, and Dead Boy grinned cheerfully.

"Hello, John. Welcome to the Street of Runaway Gods."

"Do you know what happened here?" said John.

"I know the what, if not the why. The Street of the Gods shut itself down, just a few hours ago. Everyone on the Street, priests and worshippers and gawkers alike, all found themselves suddenly and unceremoniously dumped outside. And when they tried to get back in, all the ways that normally gave access to the Street of the Gods suddenly didn't go there any more. At which point there were a great many raised voices, and not a little gnashing of teeth and tears before bedtime. I just happened to be passing, so I joined the gathering throng, ready for a spot of free entertainment, and just like that, all the entrances suddenly opened up again. The flocks surged back in, crying out for answers and reassurances, only to find that their gods had done a bunk."

"No signs of violence?" said John. "Nothing to suggest a god war, or a nasty outbreak of atheism?"

"No sign of anything," said Dead Boy. "It's like the *Mary Celeste* of godly dwelling-places. The priests have been going out of their minds, and the worshippers aren't far behind." He stopped, to smile wistfully for a moment. "I was worshipped, once. As someone who had clearly and demonstrably risen from the dead. I could have had my own church . . ."

"What happened?" said John.

Dead Boy grinned. "They met me."

"Of course," said John. He looked up and down the Street of the Gods, where crowds of the faithful were huddling together like sheep in a thunder-storm. Even the tourists were starting to look worried, perhaps fearful that what they'd come so far to see was going to be a no show. John frowned. "If all the gods have left, does that mean the end of the world really is nigh?"

"Don't look at me," said Dead Boy. "It's getting so you can't go for a stroll through the long night without bumping into one sign or another of the apocalypse. If you ask me, the Nightside is just one big drama queen."

John set off up the Street, and Dead Boy sauntered along at his side, for want of anything better to do. And because experience had taught him that wherever John went, trouble would inevitably find him. Dead Boy was always on the look-out for some new trouble to get into; it helped keep his mind occupied. Doors lay open to every side, offering free access to what had once been fiercely guarded secret sanctums and holders of the mysteries. With the gods departed, their various buildings seemed sullen and drab, for all their eccentric architecture.

"I might move into one of these very desirable properties," said Dead

Boy. "Stake a claim, just for the hell of it. That should upset all the right people."

"Not necessarily a good idea," said John. "The gods could still return, and they've always taken a very dim view of squatters. And I hate having to organise the clean-up after rains of frogs; they block up the guttering."

"To hell with them all," Dead Boy said happily. "Bring it on, that's what I say. Smite and be damned. I'm already dead; what more can they do to me?"

"You really want to find out?" said John.

And then they both stopped and looked around sharply, as an unexpected sound issued from a nearby door. Laughter, dark and disturbing, came drifting out of one of the more unusual buildings on the Street. The stout stone structure had clearly started out as an archetypal Victorian church, but someone had splashed bright and gaudy colours all over the stone frontage. The church looked like a Day-Glo rainbow had crashed into it or someone had dipped the place in ice-cream and allowed it to go off. The church now looked sweet and tempting and frankly unwholesome. The pigments in the stained-glass windows had melted and run, like Technicolor tears, but the bright pink front door stood invitingly open. The spiritual equivalent of the witch in her candy cottage.

Beyond the door there was only darkness. The laughter died away, ending on one last sardonic chuckle, like a hungry troll under a bridge who'd just heard dinner approaching.

"Well," said Dead Boy. "Someone sounds pleased with the way things are. Positively amused, in fact. I think it behooves us to go in there and investigate. And kick things around, just on general principles."

"It's a trap," said John.

"Of course it's a trap!" said Dead Boy. "But it's the first church we've found that's still occupied, and so much laughter on such a solemn occasion has to mean something. I vote we go in, and your vote doesn't count. Ready?"

"After you," said John.

Dead Boy nodded happily. "Wouldn't have it any other way."

He strode confidently through the open door, and John followed on behind, shaking his head resignedly and bracing himself for the inevitable unpleasantness ahead. Dead Boy didn't know the meaning of the word *fear.* He also had trouble with similar concepts, like *caution* and *self-preservation.*

The moment they both passed through the door, the building stopped even pretending to be a church. Vivid lights flared up, and John Taylor and Dead Boy were suddenly standing in the middle of a sawdust-covered circus-ring, surrounded by rows and rows of empty bleachers. There were ugly stains in the narrow aisles, and the air smelled of over-worked animals, stale pop-corn and staler urine, and candy-floss that had turned. Striped canvas walls shot up all around, arching towards a ceiling that was so high up it was lost in the gloom.

"A circus?" said John. "On the Street of the Gods?"

Dead Boy shrugged. "Why not? People have worshipped everything else, at one time or another."

The sound of approaching footsteps came clearly, from one particularly gloomy aisle between the bleachers. There was something very wrong about them. Dead Boy planted both fists on his hips and addressed the darkness defiantly.

"Get a move on, we haven't got all day! Get in here and face us! Come on; give me your best shot! Violent as you like! I can take it!"

"This is why no one ever wants to partner with you," said John.

"Bunch of wimps," said Dead Boy, cheerfully.

A colourful figure emerged from the gloom and stepped into the ring, dressed in a patchwork motley of rags far too big for the figure within. He might have looked amusing if both sleeves hadn't been dripping with fresh blood and other less pleasant stains. Instead of a row of buttons down the front of his costume there were small skulls, with bits of meat still clinging to them. The shoes were freakishly elongated, which explained the odd footsteps; but something about the shoes suggested they'd been made to fit the feet within. The figure's face had been painted in the traditional gaudy patterns over basic white, but it only took John a moment to realise that underneath the crimson grin the real lips weren't smiling at all. And the unblinking eyes were full of a terrible, spiteful malevolence.

Dead Boy clapped his hands delightedly. "It's a clown! I love clowns!"

"You stand alone in that," said John. "What the hell is a clown doing on the Street of the Gods?"

The clown spread both baggy arms wide, in a parody of welcome. His voice was loud and cheerful, like the con man who cheats your mother out of her life's savings. "I am Mockery: the god of clowns. Laughter is a form of worship, after all. What else does a laugh say, except: *Rather you than me.* Or *Please don't hurt me.*"

"If you're the god of clowns," said John, "why aren't you funny?"

"I laugh," said Mockery. "I don't get laughed at. I celebrate the insanity of the world, the futility of life, the great joke on Humanity that is existence."

Dead Boy pouted. "I hate all this post-modern stuff. He'll be deconstructing the custard pie in a minute."

"Why are you still here, Mockery?" said John. "Why didn't you leave, along with all the other gods?"

"I stayed behind to watch you all die," said Mockery. "To watch blood surge down the Street of the Gods in a tidal wave. And laugh and laugh and laugh."

"I'm going off you," said Dead Boy.

"I knew there was a reason why I never liked clowns," said John. "You shouldn't have to paint your face to look happy. Why did all the other gods leave, Mockery?"

"Because they didn't get the joke," said the god of clowns.

"Okay . . ." said John. "We've satisfied your curiosity, Dead Boy, and I hope you think it was worth it. Time we were leaving."

"You're not going anywhere," said Mockery. "You're in my domain now. And everyone knows there's nothing funny about a circus at midnight. You belong to me now because every clown needs a stooge or two. Oh the things I'll do to you, and the things I'll make you do! We'll have such fun together; while you last. You won't laugh much, but I will."

John looked at Dead Boy. "The things you get me into."

"You love it," said Dead Boy. "And I love a challenge." He showed Mockery his own dark and disturbing smile. "I am Dead Boy! Returned from the houses of forever with a song on my lips and violence in my heart. I come and I go and no one tells me otherwise. I love the smell of grease-paint in the morning! It smells of victory!"

He charged straight at the god of clowns, laughing breathlessly at the prospect of striking down someone who'd annoyed him. John stayed where he was, curious to see what would happen when a dead man fought a god.

Mockery waited until Dead Boy had almost reached him, then laughed in his face. Dead Boy slammed to a halt, as though he'd run face-first into an invisible barrier. Mockery laughed at Dead Boy, and he shuddered at the sound of it. The horrid power in that laughter denied everything he was and ridiculed everything he'd done. It was full of scorn and derision, vicious and unrelenting. Dead Boy dropped to his knees under the weight of it.

John wanted to clap both hands to his ears to keep out the awful sound, which made his whole life seem worthless. The god of clowns mocked John Taylor and Dead Boy on a spiritual level, his laughter eating away at their souls like acid. And then Dead Boy stood up suddenly, perfectly composed, his calm voice breaking easily across the laughter.

"Nice try, clown. But I lost all my illusions long ago. There's nothing like dying to put everything else in perspective."

Dead Boy suddenly punched Mockery right in his painted grin, and the god of clowns cried out in shock. He staggered backwards, covering his face with his gloved hands. He wasn't laughing any more. John was immediately himself again, unable even to remember what it was about the laughter that had affected him so strongly. But he remembered enough to be really angry about it. He stepped forward to stand beside Dead Boy.

"Nice punch."

"Beats a pie in the face every time," said Dead Boy. "For my next trick, watch me kick him in the crotch so hard his balls fly off in different directions."

"No," said John. "It's my turn now."

Mockery lowered his gloved hands from his painted face and glared at John and Dead Boy. "I am the god of clowns! I will make you the butt of my jokes for all eternity!"

"You have the gift of laughter," said John. "But I have a gift for finding things."

He reached deep inside himself, and his gift unfolded in his mind. Opening up his third eye, his private eye, until he could see all the things that were hidden from everyone else. He looked at the world with an unflinching gaze until he found what he was looking for: the man behind the painted mask, the human conduit Mockery was manifesting through. And having found that link, it was the easiest thing in the world for John to break it. And just like that the god of clowns was gone, leaving behind just a man in stupid clothes, with tears streaming down through his patchy make-up. Dead Boy laughed at him.

"You're not the god of anything; you're just a very silly boy."

"You can't leave me like this!" the man said. "Bring him back! Please . . . If he's not here, nothing's funny any more."

"Oh, I'm sure Mockery will find his way back," said John. "You can't keep gods out of the Nightside; they're worse than cockroaches."

"None of them are coming back," said the clown. "We're all going to die." He tried to laugh but couldn't manage on his own. "The other gods thought they were so important . . . but in the end they couldn't face what's coming. They're just gods, and what's coming is worse. Isn't that funny?"

"You know what's always funny?" said Dead Boy. "A kick in the pants."

He grabbed the clown by one shoulder and threw him in the direction of the door. Encouraging him on his way with a good hard kick up the arse. He kept on kicking the clown's backside, all the way out of the church and back onto the Street of the Gods. John followed, smiling slightly. He would have liked to contribute a kick or two himself, but he had his dignity as Walker to consider. Once they were outside, Dead Boy bestowed one last and particularly emphatic kick on the clown, then let him run away. The clown quickly disappeared into the baffled crowd, crying his eyes out.

John looked at Dead Boy. "Bully."

"He deserved it," said Dead Boy. "Well, that was fun, but I can't say I'm any clearer as to what it is that's coming, or why the gods took to their heels rather than face it. What could be more powerful than a whole Street full of Gods?"

"I think I'd better find out before it gets here," said John.

"You do that, John," said Dead Boy. "Off you go and do your investigating thing, while I busy myself with sex, drugs, and rock and roll till whatever the bad thing is has finished."

He swaggered off down the Street of the Gods, and everyone else hurried to get out of his way. Because Dead Boy, like the gods, was known to move in mysterious and occasionally incredibly violent ways.

John considered his options and finally decided that if you wanted information on the gods, the best person to ask was another god. Which meant contacting the only one in the Nightside he considered a friend:

Razor Eddie, Punk God of the Straight Razor. The homeless god, who slept in shop doorways, scavenged in bins for day-old food, and existed on the kindness and occasional intimidation of strangers.

Razor Eddie usually steered well clear of the Street of the Gods. He had no church on the Street, partly because he frightened the other gods but mainly because he refused to be worshipped. He spent most of his time going after the bad guys no one else could touch and doing terrible things to them. In penance for the many sins of his youth, when he was still human.

John took a conch-shell out of his jacket pocket, looked at it, and sighed quietly. Razor Eddie wouldn't be caught dead using anything as ordinary as a phone. It wouldn't go with his carefully cultivated outsider image. And besides, he'd made it very clear in the past that most of the time he just didn't want to be bothered. But in a moment of sentimental weakness, he'd presented the conch to John as a wedding gift, so that the new Walker could call on him when faced with a real or unreal emergency. John raised the conch to his mouth and spoke into it, just a little self-consciously.

"Razor Eddie?"

A dry, ghostly voice whispered in his ear. "What do you want, John?"

"How did you know it was me?" said John. "Does your conch-shell have caller ID?"

"You're the only one I ever gave a shell to."

John paused a moment, honestly touched, but knew better than to say anything. He moved on. "There's a problem with the Street of the Gods."

"I know," said Razor Eddie. "Good news spreads quickly."

"All the gods have disappeared," said John.

"I know. What do you want me to do about it? Lead the applause?"

"My concern is over what might have driven them off," John said patiently. "What if something is coming our way that's worse than them?"

"You had to spoil my good mood, didn't you?" said Razor Eddie. "All right, just let me finish this bit of dismemberment I'm in the middle of, and I'll be right with you."

His voice cut off and was replaced with the sound of the sea, complete with sea-gulls. John put the conch-shell back in his pocket. Razor Eddie might have been joking, or he might not. He was that sort of god. Some people are born scary, some have it thrust upon them, and some grab hold of the scary with both hands and hug it to them like a favourite toy. John looked around sharply as something unnaturally sharp cut a ragged rent through Space itself, opening up a door through which Razor Eddie could pass. Even the laws of physics threw up their hands and slouched off to sulk in a corner when faced with Razor Eddie's glowing blades. The Punk God of the Straight Razor stepped casually through the open rent, and it immediately sealed itself behind him, as though the universe were desperate to forget the awful thing that had just happened to it. Razor Eddie closed his pearl-handled straight razor and made it disappear about his person. The same kind of blade John's future son had brought back through Time, to kill him. He decided he wasn't going to think about that, for the moment.

A painfully thin presence wrapped in an oversized grey raincoat apparently held together by accumulated filth and grease, Razor Eddie had a hollowed face, dirty grey skin, and a disturbingly thoughtful gaze, as though he were quietly considering all the ways he could take you apart with his supernaturally sharp razors. He smelled awful, though whether that was him or the places he lay down in when he was sleeping rough, no one had ever wanted to get close enough to find out. Flies had been known to drop dead out of the air when they got too close. Razor Eddie wiped some fresh blood off his hands with a dirty rag and nodded briefly to John, who nodded back. The two of them were sometimes friends and sometimes enemies, but then, that's the Nightside for you.

"Do you have any idea what might have frightened off the gods?" said John.

"It wasn't me," said Razor Eddie, in his ghostly voice. "I've been good. Mostly."

"Have you heard anything?"

"You know I don't give a damn about what the gods get up to," said Razor Eddie. "But I might know someone who does. The only god I have any time for. I don't think he would have left without telling me . . . Let us go and see."

He started off down the Street, without even looking back to see if John was following. Because he honestly didn't care, one way or the other. John quickly caught up, and they strolled along together. People jumped out of their way, turned and ran, and occasionally prostrated themselves on the ground so Razor Eddie and John Taylor could walk right over them if they felt so inclined. And mostly they did, because it would be a shame not to. Standards must be upheld. Worshippers and tourists alike watched wide-eyed as the two of them passed by. Some made the sign of the cross, while others made the sign of the pants-wettingly terrified. John couldn't tell whether they were more scared of him as Walker or of Razor Eddie as an implacable force of justice, but he thought he could make a pretty good guess.

"Where are we going?" he said, after Razor Eddie had passed a whole bunch of deserted churches and temples without even glancing at them.

"All the way down to the lowest end of the Street," said Razor Eddie. "To see Dagon. An old-time god who fell from grace after his worshippers deserted him. He only recently returned to the Street of the Gods, to work his way back up again. He's all right for a god."

John didn't know what to say in response to that, so he didn't say anything. The ways of gods are not the ways of men.

They passed the dilapidated churches of such has-been gods as The Speaking Stone, Soror Marium, and the latest incarnation of The Carrion In Tears. All of which were clearly deserted. Until finally, right at the farthest end of the Street, there was Dagon's church. A pleasant little residence, its white stone walls scrubbed spotlessly clean. Lengths of bottle-green seaweed hung from the windows. Razor Eddie stopped before the perfectly ordinary door. It was closed, with a sign carved into the stone above that John didn't even recognise. He looked to Razor Eddie, who smiled faintly.

"It dates back to the Pharisees, who were the first to worship Dagon. Not many of them around these days, which may be why Dagon is currently just a man."

"Does he have any godly attributes?" said John.

"I'm told he can hold his breath underwater for a really long time," Razor Eddie said solemnly. "For anything else, ask him."

He pushed the door open and strode into the church. John hurried in after him. Razor Eddie called out to Dagon, his ghostly voice echoing across a much bigger open space than the small church could possibly have contained, but such small miracles came as standard on the Street of the Gods. It was the only way to fit everything in. The walls had been painted a deep, dark green, and the air was heavy with the smells of the sea. Strange creatures from the deepest part of the ocean swam freely in the green, in such detail they seemed almost to move on the edges of John's vision. He licked his lips and tasted salt. He looked at Razor Eddie and gestured expansively with both arms.

"Why?"

"It makes Dagon feel at home."

There was no sign of the god, or any of his current worshippers. Rows of crude wooden pews stood empty, with not even a hymn-book on show. The simple stone altar at the far end of the room held nothing but a single candle, unlit. Razor Eddie stopped in the middle of the aisle, and John stopped with him.

"Dagon!" said Razor Eddie, and his voice seemed to echo on and on, gathering strength and power on the quiet. "You know I'm here. This is John Taylor, the new Walker. Come out and talk to us, or I'll tie knots in your seaweed."

"Don't do that," said a calm voice. "How will I tell what the weather's going to be?"

A slim figure emerged from the shadows by the altar. A quite ordinary-looking man in dark priest's robes, with a bulging back-pack slung casually over one shoulder. He came forward to join Razor Eddie and John Taylor, and smiled pleasantly on both of them. He had the kind of face John knew he would have trouble remembering later, but there was an undeniable presence to the man. Razor Eddie looked at the back-pack and raised an eyebrow.

"Travel light, travel fast," said Dagon. His voice seemed to reverberate across the whole room, a god in his church.

"Knock that off," said Razor Eddie. "We're not tourists."

Dagon smiled, and when he spoke again, it was a perfectly ordinary voice. John thought the first voice had probably been more honest.

"Possessions only slow you down," said Dagon. "Never own anything you can't bear to leave behind. I'm always ready to get the hell out of Dodge, before the raging mob turns up. You learn things like that in the god business when you've been around as long as I have. First rule of religion: Nothing lasts."

"I thought you were in the eternity business," said Razor Eddie.

"Eternity isn't what it used to be," said Dagon.

"Is that why all the other gods have left the Street?" said John.

"There's something in the air," said Dagon. "Gods can smell trouble like a horse scenting a coming storm. Something bad is coming."

"Why didn't you leave with them?" said Razor Eddie.

"You know me," said Dagon. "Always the last to hear anything. And I stayed because I knew you were coming."

Dagon and Razor Eddie exchanged a quick smile: two men who were more than men, easy in each other's company. John felt a little left out.

"Do you know what's going on?" John asked, just a little brusquely.

"It's not only the gods who've disappeared," said Dagon. "All the Transient Beings, all the confidence tricksters with their big names and bigger promises, all the elementals and spirits and avatars, all the unnatural flotsam and jetsam thrown up by popular culture . . . Gone, all gone. And they shut the Street down when they left because they didn't expect to be coming back."

"So who opened it up again?" said John.

"The Street," said Dagon. "I think it felt lonely. Fill a Street with enough weird stuff, and you're going to end up with a pretty weird Street."

"I can never tell when you're joking," said Razor Eddie.

"To be fair," said John, "you have a hard time telling when anyone is joking."

"True," said Razor Eddie. "Now guess whether I give a damn."

John gave Dagon his full attention. "Where have the gods gone?"

"Some went back to where they came from," said the priest who used to be a god. "Some have gone to sleep, in the deep-down places under the Nightside. And some have taken refuge in higher and lower dimensions, to wait out the storm."

"What storm?" John asked, allowing his voice to rise just a little because he felt he'd been polite long enough. Razor Eddie stirred at his side, but Dagon seemed untroubled.

"The storm that's coming," he said steadily. "Powerful enough to uproot everything we know and sweep it all away. I haven't heard a name yet, or at least, not one I trust."

"Where have most of the gods gone?" said John.

"To the Sundered Lands," said Dagon. "The world King Arthur found in another dimension, to be a new home for the exiled elves. Or to Shadows Fall, and the Unseeli Court of King Oberon and Queen Titania."

"Of course," said John. "The only places gods could feel at home because elves have always behaved like little gods anyway."

"How did the gods know this storm is coming?" asked Razor Eddie.

"Gods exist outside of Time," said Dagon. "They see the Past, the Present, and the Future equally clearly. They saw something bad coming to the Nightside and decided not to be here when it arrived."

"I haven't seen anything," said Razor Eddie.

"Neither have I," said Dagon, smiling kindly. "We're too human."

"Given some of the crises the Nightside has already weathered," John said slowly, "from the angel war over the Unholy Grail . . . to the return of Lilith, the long night's original creator . . . What could be so bad that the gods themselves are frightened of it?"

"I don't know," said Dagon. "But I'm not sticking around to find out."

"You didn't tell me you were leaving," said Razor Eddie, and John thought he heard something in the ghostly voice that might have been reproach.

"I knew you were coming," said Dagon. "So I could tell you now."

"Are you going to the Sundered Lands?" said John.

"No," said Dagon. "I'm too human to fit in there. I think it's time for me to go to Shadows Fall."

"The elephants' graveyard of the supernatural?" said John. "Where legends go to die, when the world stops believing in them? Are things really that bad?"

"I should have taken the hint when my divinity was taken from me," said Dagon. "It was the last sign that I'd outstayed my welcome."

"Don't go," said Razor Eddie.

Dagon smiled warmly. "Don't look so sad. You could always come and visit."

"I don't think I'd be welcome there," said Razor Eddie.

"They take everyone," said Dagon. "That's the point."

"I can't go," said Razor Eddie. "I have too much work here, cleaning up the Nightside."

Dagon looked to John. "I thought that was your job?"

"I do what I can," said John. "And Razor Eddie does everything I can't."

Dagon nodded understandingly. He looked around his church one last time and settled his back-pack more comfortably on his shoulder.

"Time to go."

He led the way out of his church. John kept an eye on Razor Eddie. He was scowling, which was never a good sign. The Punk God of the Straight Razor was prone to taking out his frustrations on those who deserved it or those who just happened to be around at the time. They stepped out of Dagon's church and onto the Street of the Gods. Dagon didn't look back, even to shut the door, and when John looked, neither the door nor the church were there any more. Dagon sighed wistfully.

"I was just starting to be worshipped again . . ."

All three of them looked around sharply as they heard shouts and screams from farther up the Street of the Gods. John headed quickly in their direction, taking on his mantle as Walker, the man whose job it was to do something when he heard screams. Razor Eddie and Dagon shared a look and went after him. Soon enough they were having to force their way through packed crowds, gathered together before a particularly gaudy establishment. John noticed immediately that most of these people looked upset rather than frightened. They fell silent and quickly gave room as they recognised Walker. And then fell back even more when they realised who was with him. John studied the church before him, a garish sight, with flashing neon, psychedelic murals, and two frankly obscene statues standing on either side of the door. It was standing open, and from deep inside the church came a terrible, broken-hearted weeping.

"Oh, this is bad," said Dagon.

"I don't know," said Razor Eddie. "I've seen worse. Though this is pretty tacky."

"I meant the crying," said Dagon.

"I don't know this church," said John. "But then, they come and go so quickly . . ."

"It's home to the most recent incarnation of a rock god," said Dagon. "The Thin White Prince. An avatar of an attitude, the rock and the roll made manifest. For fans who don't just love the music; they worship it."

John strained his eyes against the gloom beyond the open door but couldn't make out anything.

"I'm getting a really bad feeling about this," he said quietly.

"Are we still going in?" said Razor Eddie.

"Of course," said John. "It's the job."

"I'll stay here," said Dagon. "And watch the door."

John led the way in. A sudden light flared up as he crossed the threshold, glorious and dazzling. The vast hall ahead was lined with two long rows of classic juke-boxes, all gleaming metal trim and snazzy colours, all of them silent as the grave. The towering walls were paved with golden discs, with no names or details. Psychedelic murals splashed across the walls and up onto the ceiling, as wild and extravagant as those outside; but here the colours were fading, dimming, like the last of the light before a bulb burns out.

John pressed on, his footsteps echoing loudly. Razor Eddie stuck close by his side, making hardly any sound at all. They followed the sound of the weeping until finally they came to a crowd of worshippers, the fans and the faithful on their knees before an altar piled high with slowly melting vinyl discs. Most of the fans had stopped crying because they'd exhausted their tears if not their grief, and now they just clung to each other for what little comfort they could find. They all had the same devastated look. For the lost music they knew they would never hear again.

John knelt beside a teenage girl in New Romantic silks. He spoke to her kindly, and she turned to look at him. The heavy make-up on her face had deteriorated under the strength of her emotions into long, smudged streaks. And slowly, she told him what had happened.

The worshippers of the Thin White Prince had returned to the Street of the Gods to find that the door to their god's church was locked. Not left open, like the others, which suggested he might not have deserted them after all. They milled around outside for a while, beating on the locked door and calling out. When they got no answer, they broke down the door and went inside to search for their god. The girl broke off, because she couldn't say any more, and gestured with a trembling hand at a nearby alcove. John looked at Razor Eddie, and the two of them moved over to where a single spangly curtain covered the entrance to the alcove. Razor Eddie wrinkled his nose.

"Something smells bad."

"You should know," said John.

"I mean, it smells of death in there."

"You'd definitely know."

John took a firm hold on the curtain and jerked it aside. And there was the Thin White Prince, hanging from a noose. The chair he'd kicked away still lay on its side on the floor. The rock god's handsome androgynous face was perfectly composed, even in death. The eyes stared sightlessly, but the mouth was clamped shut, as if to make it clear all his songs were at an end.

"He killed himself?" said John. "I didn't think gods did that. I didn't think they could die. In fact, I always thought that was rather the point."

"He was never a god, as such," said Razor Eddie, calmly studying the dead body. "Just a manifestation of the music. Though I doubt you could get his fans to believe that."

"Don't think I'll try," said John. "Should we cut him down?"

"No need," said Razor Eddie. "It's only the last vestiges of the fans' faith that's holding the body together. Once they finally accept he's dead, and leave, the body will just disappear. It was never real in the first place."

"Even so," said John. "He was real enough to be really scared. What kind of danger could drive a god to do something like this? Have you ever seen anything like this before?"

"No," said Razor Eddie. "Not even when Lilith came here, to strike down all the gods who wouldn't worship her."

"What could be on its way that's scarier than my mother?" said John.

"I've been wondering that," said Razor Eddie. He smiled faintly. "I do love a challenge . . ."

"You're getting as bad as Dead Boy," said John.

"Now you're just being nasty," said Razor Eddie. "Let's get out of here. Unless you feel like a game of divine piñata?"

"Go," John said firmly.

As they made their way past the grieving worshippers, one young man reached out to tug tentatively at John's sleeve.

"You're Walker. Can't you do something?"

"I'm sure he'll be back," John said kindly. "Rock gods always make come-backs."

When John and Razor Eddie emerged from the front door, there was no sign of Dagon anywhere. Just a large crowd who were clearly waiting just for them. Forty or fifty very upset men and women, wearing all kinds of military uniforms from all kinds of armies and periods. Complete with a great many medal ribbons they almost certainly weren't entitled to. All of them had guns in their hands, though they weren't actually pointing them at anyone, just yet.

"Followers of Mithras, the soldier's god," Razor Eddie said quietly. He didn't seem in any way impressed, by the crowd or their guns. "The god of the week-end warrior."

"You ever met him?" said John.

"I've kicked his arse a few times, just on general principles."

"Probably not the best time to mention that," said John.

One of the soldiers stepped forward to confront John and Razor Eddie. A middle-aged man with a shaved head and a deep scowl, he was trying hard to look impressive and not quite managing. His military uniform had been carefully tailored to conceal his paunch and was doing the best it could. He pointed his machine-pistol at John, ignoring Razor Eddie.

"Walker! I am the Major. I command these noble warriors of Mithras. You must know what's going on here. Hell, you're probably responsible for it. We demand you give us back our god! Or else!"

"Or else what?" asked John politely.

There was a loud clatter as all the soldiers locked and loaded and took aim at John and Razor Eddie.

"You had to ask, didn't you?" said Razor Eddie.

"You're not worried, are you?" said John.

"Only for you."

"You're too kind."

"No," said Razor Eddie. "I'm really not."

Some of the week-end warriors were starting to look distinctly unhappy. No one had mentioned they might have to go up against the infamous John Taylor and the notorious Razor Eddie. And they really didn't like the way Walker and the Punk God of the Straight Razor were looking at them. Some had already quietly lowered their weapons and were trying to edge back into the crowd, but the soldiers behind them were having none of it. The front row did not feel like the safest place to be. The Major realised something was going on behind him, glanced back, and all but stamped his foot in frustration.

"Stand your ground! You are soldiers of Mithras! Be worthy of him!"

More worshippers were streaming in from the rest of the Street, to watch the show from a safe distance. Anticipating imminent gun-fire and free entertainment. Voices were already encouraging both sides to stop messing about and get stuck in. Because there's nothing a crowd likes more than: *Let's you and him fight.* Bets were already being laid, mostly on which direction the soldiers would fall once Walker and Razor Eddie got sufficiently annoyed. All of which was doing nothing for the soldiers' morale. John could sense fingers tightening on triggers. And, of course, no one would intervene to help John or Razor Eddie because this was the Nightside, after all. John felt a responsibility to defuse the situation, before any innocents got hurt. Assuming any of those rare creatures had wandered onto the Street of the Gods when he wasn't looking.

He smiled easily at the soldiers of Mithras and slowly, so as not to panic anyone, he raised one arm. And then he opened his hand and a steady stream of assorted bullets fell from his open palm. The soldiers watched the falling shells, mesmerised, until the last round had bounced and tinkled on the ground; and then they hefted their guns and didn't like how light they suddenly felt.

"I have just removed the bullets from all of your guns," John explained pleasantly. "Now get the hell out of here before I decide to show you a similar trick involving some of your less important organs."

The Major looked back at his troops, saw their morale disappearing in front of his eyes, and raised his voice again.

"It's just one of his tricks! We have to make him give us our god back! Come on; he can't take all of us!"

"You ready to bet your lower intestines on that?" said John.

The week-end warriors lowered their guns and turned away, ignoring the jeers of the onlookers, and headed off down the Street of the Gods, muttering dejectedly to each other. That was the problem with John Taylor; he might not look like much, but you could never be sure just what he could and couldn't do. Until he did something really nasty right in front of you, then promised to do something even worse. The Major was left standing on his own. He called after his men, threatening, then pleading, but not one of them looked back. This was the Street of the Gods, and the soldiers knew a power when they saw one.

The Major turned back to face John and Razor Eddie. He raised his machine-pistol and pointed it at John's face. John smiled at him politely. The Major pulled the trigger, and nothing happened. He tried again and again, refusing to believe his gun was empty until he had to. The Major put it away and produced a glowing dagger. The thick steel blade glowed with a fierce, foreboding light. John regarded the knife thoughtfully, as the Major brandished it at him.

"Come on then! Let's see you make this disappear!"

Razor Eddie looked to John. "Would you like me to do something unpleasant to him? It wouldn't be any trouble. I've got this marvellous new trick that combines circumcision and origami."

"Thanks," said John. "But Walker has to be seen to take care of business himself." He fixed the Major with a steady gaze. "We are standing on the Street of the Gods, Major. Heaven and Hell are very close. Where do you think I'm considering sending you?"

The Major hesitated. He didn't really believe John Taylor had the power to do that, but . . . The Major lowered his glowing dagger and put it away. He looked suddenly older, and very tired.

"He was our god," said the Major. "He wouldn't go off and leave us without saying anything. He just wouldn't."

"I will find out what happened here," said John.

But the Major was already walking away, pushing his way blindly through the silent crowds.

"Were you bluffing?" Razor Eddie said quietly.

"I'll never tell," said John.

"Are you really intending to try to find out what is so powerful and so terrifying that the gods themselves have run away rather than face it?"

"Of course," said John. "That's the job."

Razor Eddie smiled faintly. "Where angels fear to tread and devils hide under the bed, John Taylor goes rushing in with a song on his lips. Call me if you need backup. I have to go practice my origami."

The last god on the Street of the Gods cut a hole in the world with his straight razor and disappeared through it. Leaving John Taylor to stand alone and wonder what to do next.

CHAPTER TWO

The Nightside Isn't What It Was

E veryone who matters knows about the Drood family, who they are and what they do, but no one knows where to find them. The location of Drood Hall, home to that most ancient of families, is one of the best-kept secrets in the hidden world. Partly because a great many people, and some things that couldn't pass for people even in the darkest of back alleys, would give everything they have for just one chance at revenge; but mostly because the Droods don't like to be bothered. They protect Humanity, covering every country in the world, which means they're always very busy. The Droods guard their privacy with extreme prejudice, and people who go looking for them tend not to come back.

Drood Hall is where all the decisions that matter are made, how to change the world and save it. It stands alone and unnoticed behind all kinds of protective shields, deep in the heart of South-West England. You get there by heading down roads that aren't on any map, taking turnings that don't exist, and finally by driving through a stone wall that is extremely solid to anyone who isn't a Drood. The Hall itself is a great sprawling manor-house that dates back to Tudor times, with four great Wings in the Regency style, added over the years as the family expanded. Set in the middle of extensive and magnificently cultivated grounds, vast and imposing, Drood Hall stands firm, Humanity's last best hope against all the forces that threaten it.

The roof rises and falls like a grey-tiled sea, complete with gables and gargoyles, observatories and eyries, and a whole bunch of landing pads for vertical-take-off planes and experimental helicars, steam-powered autogyros and winged unicorns. The roof also sprouts more ariels and antennae than you can shake something shakeable at because the Droods like to keep themselves informed. They watch the world closely, to protect it and to make sure it doesn't do anything they wouldn't approve of.

Drood Hall contains marvels and mysteries, secrets and horrors, and more history than any one family should have. Or have to cope with. The Droods have been around for a very long time and done a great many things, not all of which have the decency to stay in the past.

The Hall is surrounded by acres of open grounds, with wide lawns and impressive flower-beds, a fiendishly complicated hedge maze, and an artificial lake that comes complete with its own undine. A place of rest and peace, for soldiers home from the secret wars, and woe betide anyone who dares invade it. Drood Hall and its grounds are protected in endlessly inventive and often downright-unpleasant ways. Which is why a whole bunch of alarms went off when Eddie Drood and Molly Metcalf teleported in out of nowhere.

The grounds echoed to bells and sirens, alarms and excursions, and one very loud shriek from a young couple who happened to be picnicking on the lawns that evening. They took to their heels and bolted for the Hall, not even pausing to check who the intruders were because they really didn't want to be around when the grounds' hidden defences opened up. Eddie glared about him and raised his voice.

"Knock it off! We're expected!" He glanced apologetically at Molly. "They ought to recognise the energy signature on your teleport by now."

"They probably would," Molly said cheerfully, "if I didn't keep changing it, just to keep them on their toes. I like being greeted by panic, alarms, and open hysteria; it means they're still taking me seriously. And that they're still scared of me."

"Of course they are," said Eddie. "They've met you."

Molly smiled at him dazzlingly. "You say the sweetest things. Sometimes without my even having to remind you."

The alarms cut off abruptly, and a cautious hush fell across the grounds.

The prodigal son and the proverbial free agent stood together facing Drood Hall, wondering why they'd agreed to come back to the one place they put so much time and effort into trying to stay away from.

At first glance Eddie Drood seemed like just an ordinary guy, with a forgettable face and an easy manner. But that was because he'd been trained as a field agent to look like no one in particular, to make no impression so that he could move back and forth in the world and not be noticed. To do what needed doing. And if he'd done his job properly, no one would ever know he'd been there. Eddie was dark-haired and dark-eyed, and wore a nicely anonymous three-piece suit. The only thing that stood out was the golden torc around his neck. The mark of the Droods. The golden circlet hid its wearer from the world, and only a major-league psychic could catch even a glimpse of it. Or the seventh son of a seventh son, but there aren't many of those around these days. Blame family planning.

Molly Metcalf was an entirely different matter. She was born to stand out and be noticed, and if she wasn't, she kicked up one hell of a stink until she was. Molly Metcalf: the legendary wild witch of the woods. Supernatural terrorist or freedom fighter, depending on which side she happened to be supporting at any given moment. She wore a long gown of ruffled white silk, with ruby-red slippers, and looked like a delicate china doll with big bosoms. Though she was perfectly capable of punching out a stone golem if she felt like it. She picked fights, encouraged insurrections, and went through a phase of abducting aliens just to tell them knock-knock jokes. Molly had bobbed black hair, huge dark eyes, and a rosebud mouth red as sin. She was quite remarkably beautiful, in a threatening and disturbing way.

Eddie and Molly had spent many years on opposite sides and had made several determined efforts to kill each other. For what seemed like perfectly good reasons at the time. Until one day Eddie was declared rogue and apostate by his own family and had to go on the run in order to survive. With no one left to turn to but his old enemies, he discovered the world wasn't nearly as clear-cut as he'd been told it was. Eddie and Molly took on the whole Drood family, terrorised them into submission, then unleashed the Droods on all the bad guys and organisations of the hidden world. Somewhere along the line, Eddie and Molly fell in love; and it would be hard to say which of them was the more surprised.

Sitting at their feet, taking a great interest in everything, was Scraps.2, the robot dog. Built by the late Armourer, after his original pet was exploded in a lab accident, Scraps.2 was built to survive explosives and all other extreme possibilities. An Artificial Intelligence housed in a lean steel body, with a sculptured canine head and glowing red eyes, Scraps.2 was packed full of powerful armaments and nasty surprises. But he still insisted on being a dog first. He scratched at his steel side with a steel paw, making a loud clattering sound. Eddie winced. He always found it a little unnerving when Scraps.2 did things he knew were completely unnecessary.

"Must you?" Eddie said loudly.

"Yes!" said Scraps.2, just as loudly. "It's instinct."

"You're artificial," said Molly. "You don't have any instincts."

"All right then," said the steel dog. "Programming. What's the difference?"

Eddie looked at Molly. "He's got a point."

"I also have this terrible urge to chase rabbits," Scraps.2 said wistfully. "Even though I know shooting them would be far more efficient."

"Not all dogs have built-in guns, like you," said Eddie.

Scraps.2 sniggered loudly. "If they did, they'd get a lot more respect."

He broke off and looked around sharply. "Brace yourselves, people. According to my sensors, all the grounds' defences have just come on-line. And if I'm reading them correctly, they've been upgraded to respond to all sudden appearances with lethal force."

"But we're expected!" said Molly. "The Matriarch summoned us back from what should have been our Christmas break."

"Yes," said Eddie, "but you're still you. That's always been enough to make the defence systems nervous."

"Oh well," said Molly. "That's all right then. I like to think they respect me."

"Hello!" Scraps.2 said loudly. "Did everyone take in the bit where I said *lethal force?*"

"We heard you," said Eddie. "But I'm a Drood, this is Molly Metcalf, and you're made out of steel. Unless they've upgraded to nuclear bullets and cold-fusion grenades, I think we'll be okay." He stopped to think about it. "No . . . they couldn't have. No way they could get a budget hike pushed through that quickly."

"You'd better be right about this," said Scraps.2.

A robot gun rose from its emplacement under the lawns, long barrels swinging around to target the new arrivals. Its computer systems hesitated as they recognised the torc around Eddie's neck, then the gun opened fire anyway. Heavy shells pumped out of the long barrels, powerful enough to knock a tank on its arse, but the hesitation had given Eddie all the time he needed.

He subvocalised his activating Words, and golden strange matter shot out of his torc to cover him from head to toe in a moment. He stood on the lawns like a gleaming golden statue, placing himself between Molly and the robot gun. Heavy gun-fire slammed into his chest, and the armour soaked up and absorbed every single shell. Eddie didn't even feel the impacts. The gun kept firing until it ran out of shells, then stopped. There was a moment of quiet embarrassment, and the robot gun sank sulkily back into its underground bunker.

"What the hell was that all about?" said Molly, emerging from behind Eddie. "Not that I needed you to protect me, of course."

"Of course," said Eddie. "Scraps.2, what is going on? Drood defences opening fire on one of the family? That's unprecedented. I'll have someone's balls for this."

"According to my sensors, all the defences have gone into full panic mode and are currently contacting the Hall for new instructions," said Scraps.2.

Eddie armoured down, the golden strange matter disappearing back into his torc. "That gun couldn't hurt me inside my armour, and my family would have more sense than to shoot at you, Molly; so I don't think we were deliberately targeted. The family must be on really high alert."

"It was still very rude," said Molly.

"Oh yes," said Eddie. "Absolutely."

A pair of gryphons came lurching across the lawns to greet the newcomers and see if they had any food on them that they weren't actually using. The ugly beasts were low-level precogs, able to see a short distance into the future, which made them perfect guard dogs. They knew Eddie of old, and in particular they knew a soft touch when they saw one. The gryphons were great lumpy things, with scaly grey bodies and long, morose faces. They were the only ones who looked forward to intruders because they got to eat them. They made low, coughing sounds of welcome as they approached Eddie, and nuzzled his hands with their soft mouths as he fed them a few biscuits. They were friendly enough creatures, but given that their favourite pastime was rolling around in dead things, they were never allowed inside the Hall.

"It's your own fault for encouraging them," Scraps.2 said severely to Eddie. "Get out of here, you free-loaders!"

Searing energy beams blasted from his crimson eyes, driving the gryphons off. They loped away across the lawns, easily dodging the eye beams because they always knew where they were going to hit. All the steel dog ended up doing was blasting charred holes in the lawns. Eddie cleared his throat meaningfully.

"I hate precogs!" Scraps.2 said loudly. "I'm going to have to upgrade my targeting systems again."

Molly looked around the wide-open grounds and frowned. "You know, apart from us, it all seems very peaceful here. From the way the Matriarch sounded when she contacted us, I was half expecting open war to have broken out."

Eddie nodded and raised his voice. "Ethel! Will you please explain why the Hall has gone into full panic mode?"

A voice answered him from out of nowhere. The disembodied entity that insisted on being called Ethel, for no reason she had ever made clear, sounded unmistakably feminine, whilst at the same time distinctly inhuman. A visitor from another reality, Ethel had downloaded her consciousness into this dimension sometime back and taken on the role of patron and protector to the Droods. She supplied the torcs and armour that made their work possible, and had never got around to explaining why. The whole family was waiting for the other shoe to drop. You can't police the whole world for as long as the Droods have without becoming institutionally suspicious.

"Hello, Eddie! Hello, Molly!" Ethel said cheerfully. "Good to have you back! Did you bring me a present?"

"You always ask that," said Eddie. "And the answer is always going to be no. You are very difficult to buy for. What do you get the otherworldly entity who is everything?"

"But it's Christmas!"

"What's all this nonsense about the Nightside changing its boundaries?" said Molly, refusing to be side-tracked.

"I don't know," said Ethel. "And I'm not used to that. It's all very peculiar, and I really don't like it."

"The Nightside doesn't change," said Eddie. "It is what it is, and what it's always been. That's the whole point of the Nightside."

"It's certainly worrying," said Ethel. "People all around the world are going out of their minds trying to come to terms with what it all means, what it portends, and most important of all, who's behind it."

"We should have shut the Nightside down long ago," said Eddie. "Dreadful place."

"I like it!" said Molly.

"You would," said Eddie.

"It's fun!" said Molly. "It's wild, and free from authority, and always open to new possibilities. All the things your family disapproves of on general principles."

"Usually with good reason," said Eddie.

"You just don't know how to have a good time," said Molly.

"You like to think of the Nightside as one big party," said Eddie. "But people get hurt and killed there every day. They get robbed or cheated, or have the soul ripped right out of them, because there's no one in the Nightside willing to do anything about it."

"There's Walker," said Molly.

"One man," said Eddie. "And I'm not sure I trust him farther than I could throw a wet camel."

"The long night exists because no one has ever been dumb enough to take it on," said Molly. "There are things in the Nightside even Droods should have enough sense to be wary of."

"Hello!" said Ethel. "I am still here, you know."

"You must know something!" said Eddie. "Is the Nightside actually bigger than it was? It's not just a mistake or a rumour?"

"No," said Ethel. "It's true. And Eddie . . . Something bad has happened."

Eddie and Molly looked at each other.

"What's happened?" said Molly. "What could be so bad that we had to be dragged back here in such a hurry?"

"The Matriarch and her Council are waiting to talk to both of you in the Sanctity," said Ethel. "They should be the ones to tell you."

"Oh, it's never good when they want to talk to both of us," said Molly. "Given that they usually move Heaven and Earth to try and keep me out of their meetings."

"That's because you like to sit at the back and heckle, and throw things," said Eddie. "And you never agree with anything they want me to do for them."

"Exactly!" said Molly. "Someone's got to stand up for you! Whatever they want, you can bet it's never going to be in your best interests. You should know that by now."

"Of course I know," said Eddie. "But it's not about me. The family exists to protect Humanity. They come first. That's why the Drood motto has always been: *Anything, for the family.*"

"Shouldn't that be *Anything, for Humanity*?" said Molly.

"Actually," said Eddie, "now you come to mention it . . ."

"The Matriarch and her advisory Council are waiting for both of you to join them," said Ethel. "Increasingly impatiently."

"How can you be so sure?" said Molly.

"Because I'm there with them too," said Ethel. "I am large and complicated, and I get around."

Molly scowled. "What are the odds they'll find some way to blame everything on me?"

"What do you expect?" said Eddie. "You're Molly Metcalf."

She grinned at him. "Damn right."

"You go on without me," said Scraps.2. "I don't give a damn about the Matriarch or her Council. Never have. They keep looking at me, as though they think I should be wearing a leash. Or a muzzle." His sudden bark of laughter was a harsh and frankly disturbing sound. "Like that's ever going to happen. Think I'll go down to the Armoury. If there is going to be some action, the lab rats could use my advice."

He trotted off across the lawns, metal head held high. Eddie and Molly watched him go.

"I know my uncle Jack designed that dog," said Eddie, "but it still spooks me that Scraps.2 sounds just like him."

"His master's voice," Molly said vaguely.

"See you inside," said Ethel.

And just like that she was gone. There'd never been anything to show she was there, but Eddie and Molly could feel the difference. They looked at each other, shrugged pretty much in unison, and set off towards Drood Hall.

As they drew closer, they could make out all kinds of activities concentrated around the landing pads on the roof. Flying saucers came hurtling in, bright plasma lights discharging around their edges, while short-range teleporters bounced in and out in puffs of smoke. Black helicopters landed and took off again in such thick flurries they were doing everything short of engaging in butting contests over precedence. There were people balanced on gravity sleds, teenage girls riding winged unicorns, and someone clinging desperately to a broomstick that had got caught in an updraught. When a family has been around as long as the Droods, they have a tendency to accumulate things, and to never throw away anything that works.

"What are they all doing up there?" said Molly.

"Bringing in fresh information," said Eddie. "And probably doing regular fly-overs of the grounds, just in case. Something extraordinarily bad must have happened to cause this much excitement."

"But it's the Nightside!" said Molly. "Nothing that happens to the long night has any effect on the outside world. That's the point!"

"Unless that's changed," said Eddie.

They looked at each other and walked a little faster.

They slammed through the front door, bracing themselves for more security confrontations, but one glance at the packed entrance-hall made it clear the family was far too busy to bother with them. A large and airy expanse, the entrance-hall was usually deserted, apart from the odd messenger hurrying through. Nothing to see but antique furniture, wood-panelled walls and waxed floor-boards, and a grandfather clock that ran backwards, courtesy of the last Time War. Along with a whole bunch of accumulated tributes from grateful governments or loot from intimidated politicians, depending on how you looked at it. Statues that should have been in muse-ums, any number of Old Masters on the walls, and so much gold and silver and brass it had to be polished in relays.

But now the entrance-hall was packed with Droods rushing back and forth, faces tense with purpose and worry. Everyone had a job to do, so it was all eyes front, get a move on, and get out of the way.

Eddie tried several times to stop someone, so he could ask what was going on, but they kept avoiding his eyes, intent on their missions. Eddie tried being polite, and he tried shouting. He even tried standing directly in front of people, but they just darted around him and kept going. Molly finally picked one at random, snapped her fingers, and froze the poor Drood in his tracks. His eyes rolled wildly as he realised he couldn't move. Eddie and Molly strolled over to confront him.

"Oh shit, it's you," said the Drood.

"Got it in one," said Eddie.

"You're not going anywhere till you talk to us," said Molly. "Tell us what we want to know, or I'll turn you into something squelchy."

"What the hell is going on?" said Eddie.

"Speak," said Molly.

"I don't know!" the Drood said desperately. "No one's telling us any-thing. All I know is the shit has hit the fan so hard it broke the fan and just kept going. The whole family's under orders to gather information."

"What kind of information?" said Eddie. "About what's happening in the world?"

"Mostly about the family," said the Drood. "How strong we are, how prepared we are for an attack, what resources we have, how ready we are to do . . . whatever the Matriarch decides is necessary. Everyone's got their own assignments, but no one is telling us what it's all for."

Eddie looked to Molly. "I don't like the sound of that."

"None of us do!" said the Drood. "But when the Sarjeant-at-Arms says jump, you ask how high while clinging to the ceiling. Can I go now? Only I'm pretty sure I can hear some clean underwear calling my name."

Molly snapped her fingers. "Get out of here."

"Gladly," said the Drood. He hurried off and was quickly lost in the crowd. All of whom were now giving Eddie and Molly lots of room. And then the Sarjeant-at-Arms came striding through the crowd, which parted before him like a bow-wave. Eddie and Molly stood together, shoulder to shoulder, presenting a united front in the face of the enemy. The Sarjeant-at-Arms slammed to a halt right in front of them and bowed briefly to Eddie. Large and muscular and openly threatening at all times, the Sarjeant was wearing his usual formal butler's outfit, in stark black and white, a guise that fooled no one. The Sarjeant was in charge of Hall security and internal family discipline, and he looked what he was: a thug in uniform with a licence to commit violence.

"The Matriarch is waiting for you," the Sarjeant said flatly. "I've been sent to escort you to the Sanctity."

Eddie glared at him balefully. "One of the robot guns shot at me!"

"I know," said the Sarjeant. "I wanted to be sure the grounds' defences were on their toes."

"Which part of *shot at me* are you having trouble grasping?"

"And me!" said Molly, adding her glare to Eddie's.

The Sarjeant met Eddie's gaze calmly. "I knew you'd armour up in time. You were never in any real danger."

"Molly could have been hurt," said Eddie.

"You say that like it's a bad thing," said the Sarjeant. "Joke. The Matriarch is waiting for you."

"We know," said Eddie. "We're on our way."

And then he stopped and studied the Sarjeant-at-Arms thoughtfully. Behind the man's usual poker face, the Sarjeant looked troubled. Which wasn't something the Sarjeant usually did. He didn't get worried; he worried other people. So if the Sarjeant-at-Arms was troubled, Eddie felt he should be too.

"You both need to come with me," said the Sarjeant.

He turned on his heel and led Eddie and Molly through the entrance-hall and on into the depths of Drood Hall. People everywhere hurried to get out of the way. The crowd didn't get any thinner; it seemed like the whole family had been mobilised and set to work. After a while, Eddie cleared his throat meaningfully.

"This isn't the way to the Sanctity."

"I know that," said the Sarjeant-at-Arms, not looking back.

"Then where are we going?" said Molly, not even trying to hide her suspicions.

"The Ops Room," said the Sarjeant.

"Why are we going there?" said Eddie.

"The Matriarch is getting ready to commit the entire family to a singular course of action," said the Sarjeant. "And I'm not sure she's up to it. You need to understand the situation we're in before you see her."

"Nothing's ever straightforward in this family, is it?" said Molly.

"Not if we can help it," said the Sarjeant-at-Arms.

The Operations Room was way over in the South Wing, a high-tech centre dedicated to overseeing all the Hall's defences. Ops had control over short- and long-range scanners, scientific and magical protections, and all the interior and exterior weapons systems. And if anyone did get past all of that, Ops had even nastier surprises in store. The Sarjeant led Eddie and Molly right up to the great steel door that sealed off the Ops Room from the rest of the Hall. A huge circular plate some ten feet tall and six inches thick, it rolled silently aside as the Sarjeant approached. Eddie raised a mental eyebrow. Normally there would be a whole series of security protocols to get through before they'd be allowed anywhere near the door. It was turning out to be a day full of surprises, and Eddie was liking it less and less. The guards on duty stared straight ahead, as though nothing out of the ordinary was happening. The Sarjeant strode straight past them, and Eddie and Molly followed after, sticking their noses in the air, as though they were used to such treatment.

The massive steel door closed itself the moment they were inside, and the general din from the rest of the Hall shut off abruptly. The Ops Room was calm and quiet, a reasonable-sized space packed full of computers and assorted high-tech, manned by a dozen technicians under Howard, the Head of Operations. There was no hurry or sense of urgency here, just experienced men and women sitting quietly at their workstations, carrying out their duties with calm efficiency. They kept their heads in a crisis because that was drilled into them long before they were allowed anywhere near the Ops Room. On the rare occasions when Drood Hall came under direct attack, Ops was responsible for organising the defences and protecting the family. They took their duties very seriously.

Holographic displays snapped on and off in mid air, showing shifting views of everything that was happening in and around the Hall, including all of the grounds and quite a bit of the surrounding country-side. Eddie looked quickly from screen to screen, but couldn't see anything obviously worrying, let alone threatening. Molly studied everything with great interest. She wasn't normally allowed in such a high-security area.

"Your family has the best toys, Eddie."

"Perk of the job," said the Sarjeant. "Please don't touch anything, break anything, or slip something into your pocket."

Molly looked at Eddie. "Why is he saying these things to me?"

"Because he knows you," said Eddie.

"Howard," said the Sarjeant-at-Arms. "A moment of your time."

There was the sound of a deep sigh, suggesting much-tried patience being stretched to the breaking-point. The Head of Operations was standing with his back to them, studying the displays with fierce concentration. It was clear he didn't want to be interrupted, but no one says no to the Sarjeant-at-Arms. Apart from Eddie. And Molly. Howard turned around and fixed each of them in turn with a challenging stare. A large and blocky man in a button-down suit, his face was permanently flushed and deeply lined, partly from the strain of his responsibilities, mostly from a constant sense of outrage that anyone would dare threaten his family. Howard took such slights personally and punished all would-be home invaders with his own version of the wrath of God. Most of his hair was gone because he had a tendency to tug at it. He looked like he wished there was enough left to tug now, but he made himself nod respectfully to the Sarjeant-at-Arms.

"I brought Eddie and Molly here so you could tell them what's happening, Howard," said the Sarjeant. "Before they talk to the Matriarch."

"Does she know about this?" said Howard.

"Of course not," said the Sarjeant.

"You don't approve of what she's planning," said Howard.

"It's not my place to have an opinion," said the Sarjeant.

"No," said Howard. "That's why you're setting up Eddie to say it for you, so he can take the blame instead."

"I'm used to that," said Eddie. "It's what I'm for."

Howard gave Eddie his full attention, frowning as he chose his words carefully. And Eddie wondered just what the Matriarch could be planning, to upset so many experienced family members. He knew why they wanted him to be the one to raise objections. He was the only one in the family who'd butted heads with the Matriarch in the past and got away with it.

"The Matriarch has ordered a Code Red Ten," said Howard. "Which is usually only issued when the family is in immediate danger of attack. I've had my people scanning the whole of the grounds, and most of the surrounding country-side, for some hours now . . . and we can't see anything. We've even checked out adjoining dimensions and looked for signs of tachyon displays that would suggest approaching Time travellers. The boards are clear, nothing showing anywhere. The Matriarch wants everyone ready to react at a moment's notice, but she hasn't even hinted who our enemy might be."

"So what is she afraid of?" said Eddie.

"You ask her," said Howard. "She won't talk to me. I'm just Head of Operations, with responsibility for the safety of the entire family. I need to know what she's so worried about if I'm to serve her properly." He gave Eddie a calculating look. "You've always been better informed than me when it comes to the big picture. Should we be anticipating an attack from anyone in particular?"

"Not as far as I know," said Eddie.

"Who would dare?" said Molly.

"Exactly," said Howard. "Who?"

He turned his back on them to give his full attention to the displays again.

"We should go," said the Sarjeant. "Howard has work to do. And if he gets any more tense, he might start crushing his internal organs."

He led the way back through the steel door, which almost seemed to hurry to get out of his way. Not one of the men and women at their workstations so much as lifted their heads to glance after them.

"That's it?" Molly said to the Sarjeant, as the door rolled shut behind them. "You brought us all the way here, just for that?"

"Isn't it enough?" said the Sarjeant. "I thought Howard made his point very succinctly."

"Yes," said Eddie. "He did. So, Sarjeant, what is the Matriarch planning to do, that you don't approve of, that you want me to talk her out of?"

"I couldn't ask you to do any such thing," said the Sarjeant. "That would fall well outside my area of authority."

"Are we going to see the Matriarch now?" said Molly.

"No," said the Sarjeant.

"Imagine my surprise," said Molly.

"We need to make another stop first," said the Sarjeant. "The War Room."

"I'm getting a really bad feeling about this," said Eddie.

"You're not alone," said the Sarjeant.

He led them all the way through the Hall to the North Wing, home to the War Room. By now word had got out that the Sarjeant-at-Arms was on the prowl, and everyone hurried to get out of his way the moment they saw him coming. Some actually disappeared into adjoining rooms, just to be on the safe side. The Sarjeant took this as his due.

They reached the heavily reinforced steel doors at the back of what used to be an old ball-room, and the guards on duty snapped to attention the moment the Sarjeant appeared. It occurred to Eddie that they would never do such a thing for him, and wondered if he cared. He didn't think he did. The heavy doors opened slowly on their own, and the Sarjeant led the way down a steep stairway that had been cut into the outer wall of a vast cavern. There was no railing, nothing at all to stand between anyone on the stairs and the intimidatingly deep drop on the other side. The Sarjeant strode down the rough stone steps without hesitation. Eddie pressed his shoulder against the cavern wall, just to make sure he didn't wander too far from it. Molly tripped happily along behind him, humming tunelessly.

The electric lighting was almost painfully bright to make sure no one could hide in the shadows. Or sneak in by using them as doorways. Glowing force shields and shimmering magical screens opened and closed before and behind the three of them as they descended, triggered by the presence of Drood DNA. Molly Metcalf got a free pass because she was Molly Metcalf, and even automated security systems had enough sense not to annoy her. Goblins sat on guard in comfortable alcoves in the wall: squat ugly things with bodies no bigger than a football, and long, spindly arms and legs. They didn't look particularly dangerous, but Eddie once saw them run down and eat a werewolf, and you don't forget things like that. The goblins kept themselves busy with crosswords, and weren't at all averse to begging plaintively for help with the harder clues.

At the bottom of the stairs, more heavy steel doors opened onto the massive vault that held the War Room. A gorgon was sitting just inside the door, wrapped in great leathery wings like an enveloping cloak. Its hooded head was hanging down, as though it was sleeping, but Eddie was pretty sure it wasn't.

"What is she doing here?" said Molly.

"Penance," said the Sarjeant-at-Arms. "For sins against the family."

"You mean she's a prisoner?"

"It volunteered," said the Sarjeant.

Molly gave him a hard look. "What do you mean, *it*? I thought all gorgons were female?"

"Not in any way that would make sense to us," said Eddie. "Gorgons are pan-sexual creatures with unlimited orientation."

"What?" said Molly.

"Exactly," said Eddie.

They moved on. The gorgon didn't stir. Though Eddie was almost sure he could hear something very like giggling.

A vast auditorium carved out of the solid rock underneath Drood Hall, the War Room's walls were covered with state-of-the-art display screens, showing every country in the world. Coloured lights blinked everywhere, indicating matters of interest to the Droods. A green light meant a successfully completed mission, problem taken care of. A blue light stood for a person of particular interest or worrying capabilities. Purple for a major cock-up, meaning more help was urgently required; while potential trouble spots glowed amber. High-level threats were red. The countries of the world looked like so many Christmas trees, sparkling with lights. There was an awful lot of amber and red.

Men and women sat in long rows, concentrating on the information in front of them. Farseers with scrying balls, murmuring into hands-free headsets, sat next to technicians hunched over computer monitors. Together they covered the work of hundreds of Droods across the world. Some were field agents, protecting the innocent by doing things to the guilty, while others made up the support teams, supplying the field agents with whatever they needed and keeping them hidden from the worldly authorities. Still more stuck to the shadows, gathering useful information. It takes a lot of hard work to keep the world safe, without the world's noticing what it is they're being kept safe from.

A steady buzz of low voices filled the War Room, almost like being in church. Once again there was no sense of panic or even urgency, just hard-working men and women doing what they'd been trained to do. The War Room ran on strict discipline. And lots of hot, sweet tea and Jaffa cakes.

Messengers hurried in and out, bearing new information, vital updates, and the latest orders or queries from the Matriarch. The messages piled up on the main mission desk, where Callan, Head of the War Room, greeted them all with the same deep scowl. The Droods believed in writing things down, partly because you can't hack paper but also because it's so much easier to destroy. Does a secret still exist when there's no evidence left to support it? Having to ponder questions like that was just one of the many reasons why Eddie preferred not to come home.

Callan glowered at the three new arrivals, then gestured curtly for them to join him. The Head of the War Room was overweight, harried, and in the kind of bad mood you only got through years of hard practice and harbouring grudges. His broad, perspiring face was topped with thinning blond hair, and he had the kind of look that suggested you shouldn't get too close in case he tried to bite you. He started talking before the three of them had even reached the mission desk.

"Yes, I know why you're here, Sarjeant, and I'm not interested. I don't care, and you can't make me. I am up to my lower lip in bad news, and the tide is coming in. With sharks in it. The Nightside's sudden and entirely unanticipated expansion caught everyone in the world off guard, and they're all not at all happy about it. Even we didn't get any warning, despite our so-called information-gathering people. And don't even get me started on our precogs. We haven't had a decent psychic in the family for generations." He glared around him at the massive display screens. "No one heard anything! Not a clue, not a whisper, and you can take it from me that there will be a great many questions asked about that."

"Breathe, Callan," said Eddie, not unkindly.

"And as if things weren't bad enough, the Sarjeant's brought you and the wicked witch of the woods down here to bother me. Don't touch anything! Don't get too close to anything. What do you want from me, Cedric?"

"Tell them what's happening," said the Sarjeant-at-Arms, entirely unmoved by anything he'd heard.

Callan sniffed loudly and sat back in his chair, which groaned as his weight shifted.

"All the secret groups and organisations across the world, good and bad and everything in between, which covers a hell of a lot of ground, have gone batshit mental because the Nightside has overflowed its long-established boundaries. That wasn't supposed to happen. It isn't supposed to be possible. All of these groups are tearing their hair out, and each other's, trying to figure out what it means, while sending their own operatives out into the field in search of answers. Which, of course, complicates things even further. But as far as we can tell, no one knows what's really going on or why this totally unprecedented change happened in the first place. And the why is far more important than the what."

"Have any of our field agents turned up anything useful?" said Eddie.

"The Matriarch has tasked some of our most experienced agents to approach people who usually know things and persuade them it might be a really good idea to tell us everything they know," said Callan. "It was made clear to these agents that they shouldn't take *no, I don't know,* or *please stop hitting me* as acceptable answers." He gestured at the screens. "Conrad is in Uganda, Kathleen is in Peru, Bernard is in Australia, and Luther is in Los Angeles. We haven't heard back from any of them yet."

"Why are they spread so wide?" said Molly, looking at the flashing lights in a way she hoped indicated she knew what she was looking at.

"We're working on the assumption that whoever is behind this isn't any of the usual unusual suspects," said Callan. "We make it a point to keep every major bad guy and weird organisation under constant surveillance, so we know it isn't any of them. We're searching for someone or something we don't know about. We cover the whole world, so some things are bound to fall through the cracks. We can only do what we can do." He stopped to glare at a new messenger as he dumped a whole pile of papers on the mission desk. "You're not making any friends here!" Callan said dangerously, and the messenger fled. Callan reluctantly turned his attention back to Eddie and Molly. "Look, why don't you go talk to the Matriarch? She must know you two have returned by now. Why did you bring them down here to annoy me, Cedric?"

"Because Eddie needs to know what you know," said the Sarjeant. "Tell him, Callan."

"Tell me what?" said Eddie, immediately suspicious. "What am I not being told for my own good, this time?"

"Yeah," said Molly. "What he said, only louder."

Callan looked quickly around, to make sure everyone else was concentrating on their work, and when he did finally speak, he lowered his voice significantly, so that the others were obliged to lean in close.

"It looks to me like the Matriarch is getting ready to commit the family to open aggression against whoever turns out to be responsible for the Nightside changing its boundaries. She believes the whole world is under threat from the long night. And from everything I'm seeing and hearing, I'm not sure I disagree. But you have to understand, we're not talking about the Matriarch's authorising some quiet assassination, or even a mass attack on some subterranean organisation; she's getting ready to launch a pre-emptive strike with all the resources of the family behind it."

"You're talking about starting a war . . ." said Eddie.

"Can she do that?" said Molly.

"Of course," said the Sarjeant. "She's the Matriarch."

"Let's hope it doesn't come to that," said Callan. "When the Droods go to war, it makes a lot of mess, and the cleaning up afterwards can take decades. Sometimes we have to go to great lengths to keep things out of the history books, and that always leaves gaps. Gaps are bad. They raise questions."

"How long before the Matriarch makes her decision?" said Eddie.

"God knows," said Callan. "She's only held off this long because we haven't identified a target yet."

"And you don't approve," said Molly.

"Not unless it proves necessary," said Callan. "Such measures can be easy enough to start but a hell of a lot harder to stop."

"And if it should prove necessary?" said Molly, when it became clear Eddie was thinking too hard to raise the question himself.

"Then it's *Anything, for the family*," said Callan. "If you're going to fight a war, fight to win. Now get the hell out of my War Room, all of you. I have some important paper shuffling to be getting on with."

He leaned forward over his mission desk and gave the most recent report his full attention, so he wouldn't have to look at them any more. Because he didn't know what else to say. The Sarjeant-at-Arms gathered up Eddie and Molly with his eyes and led them back to the steel doors. The gorgon was still sitting in place, head down. She wasn't laughing any more.

"I needed you to see how things are," said the Sarjeant. "The position we're in and the position we could be in."

"You're not usually this underhanded, Cedric," said Eddie. "Or this subtle."

"Yes, I am," said the Sarjeant. "I just never let you see it before. Things are bad now, but they could get a lot worse."

"What do you expect me to do about it?" said Eddie.

"Help the Matriarch make the right decision," said the Sarjeant.

"Which is?" said Molly.

"I don't know," said the Sarjeant. "Or I'd be helping her make it. All I can see are bad choices and worse consequences."

"So naturally, you thought of me," said Eddie.

"Of course," said the Sarjeant.

They climbed the long stairs back up to the Hall, paused to get their breath back, then headed for the Sanctity. Walking in silence, not even looking at each other, occupied with their own thoughts. It wasn't until they started down the long corridor that gave onto the Sanctity that Eddie finally raised his voice.

"Given that the Matriarch has gone back to holding her Council meetings in the Sanctity, can I assume the really stupid argument between her and Ethel is finally at an end?"

"You'd have to ask them that," said the Sarjeant. "But they are working together now, for the duration. Nothing like a world-threatening crisis to bring people together. Even if one of them isn't people."

Two Droods in their armour guarded the huge double doors to the Sanctity. They stood on either side of the doors like gleaming golden statues, their armour moulded into fierce martial attitudes, all spikes and thorns and demonic face masks. It wasn't the stylings that spooked Eddie; it was that he didn't expect to see fully armoured Droods inside the Hall. The one place where the family was supposed to feel safe and secure and protected. What kind of threat was the Matriarch afraid of that she felt the need for armoured guards? He glanced at the Sarjeant-at-Arms, but he was staring straight ahead, saying nothing. So Eddie just increased his pace a little, to take the lead. He needed to get to the Matriarch and hear what she had to say. So he'd know what to say.

The armoured guards didn't even wait to be asked; they already had the doors open by the time Eddie reached them and stepped quickly back out of the way to let Eddie and Molly and the Sarjeant pass. Eddie gave them both a hard look. Demonic-faced Droods weren't supposed to impress that easily. Once inside the Sanctity, Eddie was quietly pleased to see that the full advisory Council had turned out to attend the Matriarch. It didn't necessarily mean that she had any intention of following their advice, but it did suggest she was prepared to listen to them.

The Matriarch was sitting bolt upright in a sensible chair behind a simple table, right in the middle of the great open chamber. The table was covered with phones and lap-tops, and a few pieces of comm tech Eddie immediately recognised as being of alien origin. But even though lights were flickering insistently on most of her devices, demanding her attention, the Matriarch ignored all of them to fix her gaze on Eddie.

He met her gaze steadily as he crossed the chamber. Molly had already slipped in beside him, supporting him with her presence, while the Sarjeant-at-Arms had dropped back a little. Distancing himself, for public purposes. Eddie wasn't impressed by the huge and awe-inspiring setting. He'd been here before, trying to figure out how to save the world from some dire threat, with a quite literal dead-line hanging over everyone. The trick was to focus on what was in front of you and not let yourself be distracted by personalities or politics. Or an increasing need to punch certain people in the head until they stopped arguing with you and talked sense. The Matriarch gave Eddie a wintry smile as he finally crashed to a halt before her, and he gave her his best unimpressed look in return.

She'd started out as Capability Maggie, in charge of looking after the Drood grounds and gardens. She'd loved her job, and only reluctantly gave it up to take charge of the family after the old Matriarch was murdered. She did seem to be growing into the job, and in recent times had become just as decisive, cunning, and convinced she knew better than anyone else as any of her predecessors. Though Eddie had heard gossip that she was just the same as when she only had the gardeners and groundsmen to boss around. She was wearing a dark blue power suit of almost brutal style and impact, and her determinedly serious face was topped with a blonde buzz cut. Short and stocky, the Matriarch always acted like she was ready to walk through walls to get what she wanted.

Eddie and Molly stood together in the narrow aisle between the wooden seats set out for the Council. Nothing too comfortable, of course, to make sure nobody nodded off during the longer meetings. The Matriarch nodded to Eddie and ignored Molly, indicating with a wave of her hand the empty seats set out before her. Eddie took out a handkerchief and dusted one of the seats thoroughly before he sat down. Molly dropped into the seat beside him, crossed her legs and folded her arms, and fixed the Matriarch with a stare that dared her to start something. The Sarjeant-at-Arms took up his usual position standing at the Matriarch's shoulder. Her guardian, her right hand, and occasionally her personal attack dog.

Eddie deliberately turned his gaze away from the Matriarch and looked around the Sanctity. The vast, open chamber was the physical and spiritual heart of Drood Hall, the place where policy was decided and the fates of countries and individuals were settled, to ensure the world went on turning as it should. Eddie would have been more impressed by that if he hadn't run the family himself for a time and known just how close to the wind the family could sail, on occasion. He looked thoughtfully at the Council members, sitting patiently on their uncomfortable chairs.

William the Librarian looked passably turned-out, for a change, in a heavy tweed suit, a clean white shirt, and a peach cravat held in place by a diamond pin. His bushy grey hair had been brushed and beaten into submission, and he'd shaved recently. He was still wearing fluffy white bunny slippers, with fierce pink eyes that seemed to follow you around the room. His mouth was firm and his eyes were clear, but there was still a worrying air of vagueness about him, as though his current state was only a temporary aberration, and he might slip back into his usual confused condition at any moment. William was a first-class Librarian, but that was mostly because he got along with books a lot better than he did with people. Still, there was no denying he'd come a long way from the broken man Eddie had found in the Happy Daze Asylum for the Criminally Insane, where William had been hiding from his family. With good reason.

William realised Eddie was looking at him and smiled uncertainly. "Hello, Eddie. And Molly! Well, well . . . What are you two doing here?"

"We're here for the same reason you are," said Eddie.

"Oh good . . ." said William. "Then you can tell me why I'm here. I'm never going to get the Index to the Old Library finished if people keep interrupting me. The current Index isn't worth the vellum it's written on . . ."

The woman sitting at his side leaned in close. "It's the Nightside, dear. You remember."

"Oh! Yes!" William nodded briskly. "Well remembered, dear. Don't know what I'd do without you."

William's wife, and the real reason he'd improved so much in recent years, was Ammonia Vom Acht, widely believed to be the most powerful telepath in the world. She'd spent a lot of time inside William's head, putting things back in order. She had a face like a bull-dog licking piss off a thistle, with a temperament to match. Short and dumpy in a baggy grey suit, she made an imposing and even frightening figure. Ammonia could not only make you believe you were a chicken, but get a really good price for your eggs. She and William were devoted to each other, even though they practically defined the phrase *What do they see in each other?*

A jolt of surprise and even shock ran through Eddie as he realised Ammonia was holding William's hand. Which meant she was physically there, in person. Normally she only sent a telepathic image to Council meetings because of the toll it took on her to keep everyone else's thoughts outside her head. For her to put up with a Hall full of Droods, things must be even worse than he thought.

On the opposite side of the aisle sat the Armourer, Maxwell and Victoria. They still looked almost indecently young for such an important post, responsible for providing the family with the very best in guns and gadgets. Looking impressively intelligent in their pristine white lab coats, Max was tall, dark, and handsome, while Vicky was tall, blonde, and beautiful. Together, they were love's young dream personified. Always hand in hand, never separated, and prone to sickening levels of lovey-doveyness. They smiled quickly at Eddie and Molly, in perfect unison, then looked away again. They didn't say anything because they were waiting for the Matriarch to speak first. They'd always had too much respect for authority figures, even now that they were one.

Ethel was there too, manifesting as a rose-red glow that permeated the whole of the Sanctity. Just being in Ethel's presence was enough to make you feel warm and cared-for and protected. Eddie had never been sure he trusted that feeling. Even though Ethel had saved his life on more than one occasion, he found it hard to entirely trust someone who refused to explain themselves. But then, that was what being a Drood did to you.

"Welcome, welcome, Eddie and Molly!" Ethel said loudly. "I do so love to see the family together. Deciding things."

"If we could get started," said the Matriarch, in her cold level voice. "We have a lot to discuss and even more to decide, and not much time to do it in."

"Of course," said Eddie. "Situation entirely normal."

He folded his arms and stared right back at the Matriarch. Because long experience with his family had taught Eddie that if you didn't fight them for every inch, they'd walk right over you.

"All right," he said flatly. "We're here. Now, will somebody please tell me exactly what has happened with the Nightside? How has it expanded? Where has it gone? And why do we care so much?"

He expected the Matriarch to bludgeon him into submission with a series of cold, implacable facts, but instead she looked to the Sarjeant-at-Arms to answer for her. Eddie smiled internally. One of the first lessons every Matriarch had to learn was how to wrong-foot people, keeping them off balance so she could dominate the meeting. Eddie had done a lot of that, in his time running the family. One of the reasons he'd stepped down so soon was because he decided he didn't like what that was doing to him.

"It all started with a series of increasingly scared and desperate reports from psychics all over the world," the Sarjeant said heavily. "Claiming that part of our reality had been invaded and overwritten. Changed and replaced by the Nightside. The Matriarch commanded the family psychics to focus their attention on the long night, and they quickly confirmed this to be true."

"Hold it," said Eddie. "Why didn't our psychics pick up on this at the same time as everyone else?"

"I've got people looking into that," said the Sarjeant. "It's possible our psychics were deliberately targeted and blocked, so they wouldn't be able to warn us of what was about to happen. So we wouldn't be able to stop it. The one thing we are sure of is that the long night has broken out beyond its normal boundaries, into the unsuspecting everyday world, and taken part of it for its own."

"But where did this happen?" said Molly.

"The Wulfshead Club is gone," said the Matriarch.

Eddie and Molly looked at each other, shaken and shocked. The Wulfshead Club was one of the most popular watering holes and neutral grounds for the supernatural and super-science community. Good and bad people lined up beside each other at the long bar, and even bought each other drinks. Unlikely friendships were made, unusual alliances formed, and as a result a lot of really bad stuff never happened. Everyone approved of the Wulfshead. Eddie and Molly had spent a lot of time there, with friends good and bad.

"How can it be gone?" Molly said angrily. "The Wulfshead is famous for its protections! Really serious protections!"

"But apparently not strong enough to keep out the long night when it wanted in," said the Sarjeant-at-Arms.

"So what has it become?" said Eddie. "Just another club in the Nightside?"

"No," said the Matriarch. "It's gone, Eddie."

"As far as anyone can tell, the Wulfshead doesn't exist any more," said the Sarjeant. "Which means everyone inside the Club at the time is almost certainly dead."

Eddie reached out for Molly's hand, and she squeezed it tightly. Both of them wondering what friends they might have lost.

"What do we know for sure?" said Molly.

The Matriarch concentrated on Eddie. "Technically, you are still our field agent in London. But after we thought Dr DOA had killed you, I made the decision to appoint a new London agent. A very bright and determined young lady called Nina. You wouldn't know her. I sent her to check out the situation, given that the Wulfshead main entrance point has always been somewhere in Soho."

"You sent Nina because she's new, and therefore expendable if something went wrong," said Eddie.

"Of course," said the Sarjeant. "She knew that. A teleport bracelet took her straight to the Club's door. She says the door is still there, but it doesn't open onto the Club any more. Just a street in the Nightside. She had a good look but didn't go through, mindful of the long-standing Pacts and Agreements that keep the family out of the long night."

Eddie nodded stiffly. "She did the right thing. Was she able to identify which street it was?"

"Blaiston Street," said the Matriarch.

Molly pulled a face. "Yeah, I know it. One of the scummiest, nastiest, and most desperate places in the Nightside."

"No wonder you know it," said the Sarjeant.

Molly fixed him with a look. "Don't push your luck, Cedric."

Everyone else stirred uneasily because you just didn't talk to the Sarjeant-at-Arms like that. The Matriarch looked like she was about to say something. Molly looked at her, and the Matriarch thought better of it.

"Could the Wulfshead be hidden away somewhere on Blaiston Street?" said Eddie, steering them back on track.

"Unknown," said the Matriarch. "We've been unable to make contact with the Club, or anyone in it."

"Has anything like this ever happened before?" said Eddie.

"No. Never," William said immediately. "The Nightside's boundaries were laid down and guaranteed at the time of its creation, back before history began. Contained forever within the spiritual heart of London."

"Then why is this happening now?" said Eddie.

"I don't know," said William unhappily. "My assistant is currently searching through the stacks in the Old Library, looking for everything we have on the background and nature of the long night. Unfortunately, that covers a lot of territory and a lot of books, and much of what's in them is blatantly contradictory. Of course, that's the Nightside for you, right there . . ."

"Do we have any idea who might have been inside the Club when it vanished?" said Molly.

"No," said the Sarjeant.

"Then talk to the Management!" said Eddie. "They run the place, they must have means of communication that we don't have access to. All right, we don't know who they are, no one does, but we must be able to talk to them . . ."

"The time for secrecy is past," said the Matriarch. "We are the Management."

Eddie rocked in his chair, as though he'd been hit. Molly's mouth flattened into an angry straight line. One of the great secrets of the hidden world had just been revealed, right in front of them.

"*What?*" said Molly, dangerously.

"The most secretive group of all, with business connections all through the hidden world, is really us?" said Eddie. "Of course. I should have known."

Molly turned in her chair to glare at him. "How could you not know this? You ran the family for a while!"

"They didn't tell me everything," said Eddie.

"Clearly," said Molly.

"It was decided long ago that we should have an entirely separate group to deal with practical matters," said the Matriarch. "So the rest of us could concentrate on our main mission. Down the centuries, the Management became a family within the family, and finally moved outside it, so they could deal with the rest of the hidden world without anyone knowing their connection to the Droods. We put them in charge of the Wulfshead Club so we could keep an eye on things there."

"And why did we feel the need to do that?" said Eddie.

"Because you always know where you are with your enemies," said the Sarjeant-at-Arms. "But you never know when a trusted friend or ally might decide to stab you in the back."

"Are the Management real Droods or not?" Molly asked. "And would they be more likely than you to know what's really going on in the Nightside?"

"We have reached out to them through the usual channels," the Matriarch said steadily. "But they haven't replied. They haven't been based in Drood Hall for centuries. They are separate from us. Droods with no torcs and no armour."

"How can you be a Drood without a torc?" said Molly.

"It's complicated," said the Sarjeant.

"You mean, like the Grey Bastards?" said Eddie.

"Exactly," said the Matriarch. "Your late uncle James' illegitimate brood. Many of them have joined the Management down the years, as a way of doing service to the family and proving themselves worthy to join us. But the Management also contains people not even distantly related to the family. The Management has become a business concern."

"They must know about the Wulfshead by now," said Eddie. "Why haven't they contacted you?"

"We don't know," said the Sarjeant.

Molly turned suddenly to glare at Ammonia Vom Acht. "Why are you here, in person? You never leave your coastal bolt-hole unless you have to."

"The Matriarch convinced me I was needed here, to protect the family," said Ammonia. "If there is someone or something behind this change in the Nightside, they'll be anticipating a reaction from the Droods. The Hall could be their next target."

"Ethel?" said Eddie. "I thought protecting the family was your job?"

"I'm your guardian angel, not your nanny," said Ethel. "I provide you with armour so you can look after yourselves, as well as the world."

"Speaking of protecting the family," said the Sarjeant, "show Eddie what you have for him, Armourer."

Maxwell and Victoria quickly produced something very like a crown: a silver circlet studded with chunky, glowing crystals. Maxwell handed it to Eddie, who turned it dubiously back and forth. He'd seen something like it before, constructed to protect Ammonia from the invading thoughts of others. A crown to make the wearer psychically invisible. He looked at the Sarjeant.

"Why would I need something like this?"

"Because I'm sending you into the Nightside to find out what's going on there," said the Matriarch.

"Normally your torc would be enough to keep you from being noticed," said Max.

"But this is the Nightside, where things are never normal," said Vicky.

"So we made this for you," said Max.

"So no one will know that a Drood has entered the long night," said Vicky.

"As long as you don't do anything to draw attention to yourself."

"Well obviously, Max."

"I was just saying, Vicky."

"Of course you were, dear."

Molly raised a hand. "Why don't I get one?"

"You don't need one," said the Sarjeant. "No one in the Nightside would be surprised to see you there."

"Do I have to wear this?" said Eddie, just a bit plaintively. "I'll look like an idiot . . ."

"No one will be able to see it," Max said reassuringly.

"I can see it!" Molly said immediately.

"It'll be invisible once it's activated," said Vicky.

"Just put it on," said Max.

"Think I'll wait till I have to," said Eddie.

"Try not to break it," said Max.

"It's a prototype," said Vicky.

"Aren't they all?" said Eddie. He put the crown in his lap. "What else have you got for me? Any useful guns or gadgets?"

"Just this," said Maxwell.

Victoria handed Eddie the Merlin Glass, and he accepted it with a sense of resignation. No matter what he did with it, or who he gave it to, the Glass always seemed to find its way back to him. An old-fashioned hand-mirror, its silver back was covered with intricate chased scroll-work of a vaguely Celtic nature. The lines always looked to Eddie as though they might start moving if he looked at them long enough, so he took care not to.

"We haven't had time to do any real work on it," said Vicky.

"But as far as we can tell, it is functioning as it should," said Max.

"Though it is hard to tell."

"At least the Glass doesn't have Morgana La Fae hiding inside it any more," said Max, beaming happily.

"I don't know how we missed that, Max," said Vicky.

"Well, it wasn't like we were looking for her, was it, darling?"

"Of course, dear. You're quite right, as always."

"Hush, sweetie, you'll embarrass me."

They turned to Eddie and smiled tentatively at him in unison, and he sighed inwardly. He knew that smile. It meant they were about to hit him with the bad news.

"By your own account," Max said carefully, "a lot happened to the Merlin Glass during the Moonbreaker mission."

"So there is always the chance the Glass could prove to be just a tad . . . unreliable," said Vicky.

"But if you have any problems at all, just bring it straight back to the Armoury," said Max.

"Assuming it doesn't get me killed," said Eddie.

"Well, yes, obviously," said Vicky. She looked at Max. "What an odd thing to say."

"Field agents . . ." said Max.

"You are to go to Blaiston Street immediately, Eddie," said the Matriarch, wrenching back control of the conversation. "And once there discern exactly what has become of the Wulfshead Club and all the people who were in it at the time."

"Why me?" said Eddie. "I was on leave. I'd earned it. You said so."

Again, the Matriarch looked to the Sarjeant-at-Arms.

"You are going," said the Sarjeant, "because you are the best investigatory field agent we have. And because you've visited the Nightside before. Molly will accompany you because she knows the Nightside better than any of us. And because we couldn't stop her going with you if we tried."

"Damn right," said Molly. And then stopped to carefully consider the last few remarks, to see if she'd been played.

"Let me be very clear, Eddie," said the Matriarch, leaning forward across her desk. "This is to be an information-gathering mission only. You are not authorised to take any direct action or to put on your armour for any reason. The Nightside Authorities must not know a Drood has entered the long night, in violation of the Pacts and Agreements. We don't want any direct conflict with them at the moment. Just find out what you can and report back."

"I can do that," said Eddie.

"Me too," said Molly.

"We know how to follow orders," said Eddie.

"It's just that usually we can't be bothered," said Molly.

"Oh, this can only go well," said William.

Ammonia surprised everyone then with a brief bark of laughter.

"Go now," the Matriarch said to Eddie and Molly. "The Council will remain. We still have much to discuss."

The Sarjeant looked at Eddie, and Eddie knew this was his cue to raise the matter they'd discussed earlier, as to whether the Drood family should consider going to war. But he didn't say anything. He didn't know nearly enough about what was really going on to feel like committing himself to anything. And the only place he could hope to find that kind of information was on Blaiston Street. So he thought he'd keep his thoughts to himself until he got back.

He rose to his feet and bowed to the Matriarch, perhaps just a little ironically. Molly rose to her feet, looked down her nose at the Matriarch, and blatantly ignored the Sarjeant-at-Arms. They strode out of the Sanctity, side by side, and didn't look back once.

They walked back through the Hall, where people were still running around like someone would shoot them somewhere painful if they didn't. Eddie wondered vaguely why they weren't all out of breath by now, leaning against a wall with swimming heads and trying not to throw up. If there was one thing he'd learned as a field agent, it was the importance of pacing yourself, so you still had something left when you needed it.

"She didn't actually tell us much, did she?" Molly said finally.

"Apart from that bomb-shell about the Management, no," said Eddie. "I don't think any of them know much, for certain. That's why they're all so upset. Droods aren't used to being in the dark. Which is why the Matriarch was so ready to send a field agent into the Nightside and risk defying the Pacts and Agreements."

"She's up to something," said Molly.

"Of course," said Eddie. "My family is always up to something. But this strikes me as a particularly bad idea."

"You have been to the Nightside before," said Molly.

"It's one thing for an agent to sneak in and out, as part of an on-going mission," said Eddie. "It's quite another for us to be sent in by the Matriarch on official business. If we screw this up and get noticed . . ."

"You really think anyone will give a damn?" said Molly. "What do a few ancient Pacts and Agreements matter?"

"They're the only thing that keeps the Droods from going to war with the Nightside," Eddie said steadily.

Molly looked at him. "Really?"

"Really."

"Let's not screw up then. Hell, let's not go."

"We have to," said Eddie. "And not just because of what might have happened to the people in the Wulfshead. This is important, Molly. It matters. The Nightside isn't supposed to change. Ever."

"Neither is the Wulfshead," said Molly. "It was supposed to be a safe place, where people from all sides of the moral divide could find refuge from the storm. Neutral ground that you can depend on is hard to find. I hate to think how many friends we might have lost . . ."

"The sooner we find out the truth, the better," said Eddie. "If only so we can set about avenging those we've lost."

Molly looked at him seriously. "Who do you think is behind this?"

Eddie shrugged. "It's not like there's any shortage of suspects. The long night is full of bad people, powerful people, and really bad really powerful people. One of the reasons why I've always said the whole place should be shut down, by force if necessary. It's a haven and a breeding-ground for half the evils we end up having to do something about."

"Just like the rest of your family," said Molly. "You only see what you want to see. There are just as many good people as bad in the Nightside. And all the shades of grey. And anyway, you're missing my point. Who is there left who's powerful enough to do something like this and not give a damn about the Droods' response? Down the last few years we've wiped out everyone big enough to pose a real threat. Or even an unreal threat. There's nobody left!"

"No one we know of," said Eddie. "The most dangerous enemy is always going to be the one you don't know is out there."

"Oh, very profound," said Molly.

"I thought so," said Eddie.

"Enough talking," said Molly. "Cram the crown on your head and fire up the Merlin Glass so we can get going. I need to be doing something."

"I think we'd better wait till we're out in the grounds," said Eddie. "You saw how touchy the defences were when we arrived. If I activate the Merlin Glass inside the Hall, odds are the alarm systems will go into meltdown, and my entire family will come running with every weapon they can lay their hands on."

"We could handle it," said Molly.

"Well, yes, probably, but I don't want to see anyone hurt."

Molly beamed at him. "You can be very thoughtful sometimes, Eddie."

"One of us has to be," said Eddie.

Once they'd left the Hall and moved off into the grounds, Eddie stopped and looked around him. It all seemed very quiet and peaceful. No one else was around, and even the gryphons and peacocks had wandered off some-where else. Eddie thought he could sense the underground defences stir-ring in their bunkers, but they had enough sense not to bother him twice. As he looked around the calm and settled scene, it was hard to believe that one of the great fundamentals of the hidden world had changed, and changed the rest of the world with it.

"Your family won't be the only ones who are upset," said Molly, reading his mind with the ease of long familiarity. "You can bet it's kicking off all over the Nightside by now, with everyone blaming everyone else, and all the lower orders looking for some way to make a quick profit."

"We need to step on this hard," said Eddie. "Get things back to normal as quickly as possible, before things get out of hand."

"Probably a bit late for that," said Molly.

"Let us hope not," said Eddie. "Or the Matriarch will have her war af-ter all."

Molly looked at him. "She'd start something like that, without even be-ing sure who's behind this?"

"She doesn't need to know that," said Eddie. "She could decide the only sure way to stop the Nightside expanding, and protect the rest of the world, is to take control of the Nightside. By force. Put an end to the long night once and for all."

"You really think she'd do that?" said Molly.

"She's getting there," said Eddie.

"Would the rest of the family go along? Would you?"

"Of course," said Eddie. "She's the Matriarch."

"But the Sarjeant was saying . . ."

"He might say a lot of things, right up to the point where the Matriarch makes her decision. But after that, it's always going to be *Anything, for the family.*"

"You honestly think you'd win?" said Molly.

"Don't you?" said Eddie.

Molly looked away. Eddie looked at the silver crown in his hands, pulled a face, and settled it on his head. It was so light he couldn't even feel it was there.

"How does it look?" he said, trying to sound cheerful.

Molly turned back to look at him. "How does what look?"

"The crown! I've got it on!"

"I can't see it," said Molly. She frowned, concentrating. "And I should be able to, with my witch's Sight."

"Good to know the Armourer are still on top of things," said Eddie.

"Hold it, why can I still see you?"

"Because I'm only psychically invisible," Eddie said patiently, "not physically invisible."

"Is there a switch that makes you less insufferable, as well?" said Molly.

Eddie shook the Merlin Glass out until it was the size of a door, hanging on the air in front of him, then ordered it to show him the entrance to the Wulfshead Club. His reflection immediately disappeared, replaced by a view of a familiar dark alley-way. A hot, damp wind blew through the door towards him, reeking of filth and decay. He stepped through the door, with Molly following right after him, and just like that, they were somewhere else.

Eddie shut down the Glass and put the hand-mirror away in the pocket dimension he kept in his trousers. It occurred to him it was well past time he had a good turn-out just to check what was in there. He'd picked up all kinds of useful things on field missions, just on the grounds they might come in handy someday. He pushed the thought aside as it occurred to him that something about the alley didn't look right. Something was off. He looked quickly around him. Molly picked up on his mood and did the same.

"The traffic noises at the end of the alley sound wrong," Eddie said finally. "They're too loud. Usually they sound dim and distant, because this alley-way is only loosely connected to the everyday world. This is one of the in-between places, which is why they put the door to the Wulfshead here."

"It smells like something died in here. Recently," said Molly. "So no change there."

"The graffiti's disappeared," said Eddie.

"What?" said Molly.

"The walls used to be covered with graffiti," said Eddie. "You know, *Cthulhu Does It in His Sleep*, that sort of thing. And it's all gone."

The bare, brick walls were dark and grimy and running with condensation, without a mark on them.

"It's not like anyone would have stolen the graffiti," said Molly. "Maybe someone finally got around to cleaning up the place."

"You couldn't shift that unnatural graffiti with a flame-thrower and a bucket of holy water," said Eddie.

And then he stopped and silently pointed at a cat that had just strolled into the alley. A scruffy thing with matted fur, it gave every impression of being entirely at ease with its surroundings.

"Now that's just wrong," said Molly. "You'd never find a cat in this alley-way before."

"Of course not," said Eddie. "The things would eat it."

Molly looked at him. "What things?"

"I never felt inclined to find out," said Eddie. "Did you never wonder why there aren't any rats here?"

"I thought that was them moving in the garbage."

"No, that's the garbage."

Molly fixed the cat with a cold glare. "You. Leave. Now."

The cat stopped and regarded Molly thoughtfully. It then performed a dignified about-turn and left the alley, as though that was what it had meant to do all along.

"Okay," said Eddie. "I'm impressed."

"We should have brought Scraps.2," said Molly.

"He'd only have shot it."

"Exactly." Molly pointed to one section of the wall, near the end of the alley. "At least the door to the Wulfshead is still where it should be."

They approached the door cautiously. Set flush with the brickwork, the solid silver slab was deeply engraved with threats and warnings in angelic and demonic script, but Eddie only had to look at them for a moment to see they were blurred and distorted, like a bad copy. There was no door-handle, but that was normal. The Wulfshead wasn't supposed to be easy to get into. The dully gleaming metal surface was running with condensation like the rest of the alley-way. Eddie frowned. It wasn't that hot. He reached out a hand to test how warm the door was but stopped immediately when Molly dropped a hand on his arm.

"Don't," she said quietly. "That's not condensation. It's sweat."

Eddie looked at her. "Are you sure?"

"Smell it."

Eddie leaned in close, took a deep breath, and quickly retreated. "Oh, that's rank. Almost . . . animal. That door is sweating."

"Why would it do that?" said Molly.

"I don't know," said Eddie. "Maybe it's nervous."

"What has a door got to be nervous about?"

"We're here."

"There is that," said Molly.

"The door is a fake," said Eddie. "Like the writings. It's alive."

"Try it with your name," said Molly. "If the door is still connected to the Club, the entrance protocols should be enough to get us in."

Eddie pronounced his name carefully, but there was no response from the door. He subvocalised his activating Words, and the golden armour surged out of his torc and surrounded him in a moment. His face mask was entirely blank, without gaps for mouth or eyes, though he could see perfectly clearly. Because experience had taught the Droods that this particular look was very good for making enemies wet themselves. Eddie stretched slowly. Putting on his armour was like waking from a long doze into full wakefulness. He felt like he could take on the entire world and everything in it. He placed one golden hand on the sweating door, and it flinched away from his touch. Eddie made a fist and grew thick metal spikes out of his knuckles. The door trembled in its frame. Eddie grinned behind his featureless mask and addressed the door.

"I am Eddie Drood, and this is Molly Metcalf. You really want us mad at you?"

"Eddie," said Molly. "You're threatening a door . . ."

"A living door," said Eddie. "Though that might not be the case for very much longer."

"Okay," said Molly. "I just heard that thing whimper. It's scared of you."

"Good," said Eddie. "Everything sensible is scared of a Drood in his armour."

"But I can't help noticing the door still hasn't opened," said Molly.

Eddie grew a long, golden blade out of his right glove. He showed it to the door.

"Co-operate, or it's can-opening time."

The door disappeared, leaving just a dark gap in the wall.

"What a sensible door," said Molly.

"I thought so," said Eddie.

He drew the golden sword back into his hand, then studied the new opening with all the sensors built into his mask. That included infra-red and ultraviolet, but he still couldn't see an inch beyond the opening.

"The dark is keeping me out," he said finally. "If the Wulfshead is still there, I should be picking up something."

"The field agent said she could see Blaiston Street," said Molly.

"Maybe she stuck her head in," said Eddie.

"I wouldn't," said Molly.

"Only one way to be certain," said Eddie. "Step through and see for ourselves."

"You do that," said Molly. "I'll be right behind you."

"Why am I going first?"

"Because you're the one wearing armour."

"Good point."

Eddie stepped into the darkness, and Molly followed him.

They stood side by side on a filthy, lonely street, lit only by a night sky full of stars and a freakishly oversized moon. There was no sign anywhere of the Wulfshead Club. Eddie looked quickly up and down the street, but there was no one else about.

"We're in the Nightside," said Molly.

"I had noticed," said Eddie. "Even though that wasn't one of the recognised ways in. Is this Blaiston Street?"

"Yes," said Molly. "I've been here before."

"What were you doing in a neighbourhood like this?"

"Business," said Molly.

Eddie nodded. He knew better than to ask for details. He looked behind him. The doorway was still there, just a dark gap in a grimy brick wall. Eddie armoured down, leaving him just another visitor to a street where no one belonged. He smiled briefly at Molly.

"I don't want to attract any attention."

"Then you've come to the right place," said Molly. "No one cares who you are in this place because if you're on Blaiston Street, you've fallen off the bottom of the world."

Eddie looked around some more and shook his head disgustedly. "You were right. This is a shit-hole."

"Even the worst-off people need somewhere to go," said Molly.

Blaiston Street looked like what it was: the back-end of nowhere. Shabby dwellings on a shabby street, for people who'd run out of future. Slum terraces lined both sides of the street, long rows of human misery with broken and boarded-up windows. Everything looked foul and diseased, falling apart and falling down. The street-lamps had all been smashed, possibly because the locals felt more at home in the shadows.

Rubbish had been dumped in festering piles all along the street, and the grimy brick walls were covered with obscene graffiti in a mixture of languages. Half the houses looked like they'd collapse if they weren't holding each other up. Steam rose from sewer gratings, drifting like disease on the wind. Homeless people lay curled up inside ragged blankets in the back alleys. The whole street stank of decay, physical and spiritual.

"This is the real face of the Nightside," said Eddie.

"No," said Molly. "It's just one face."

"Let's get this done," said Eddie. "And hope my psychic crown is working, in case I have to raise my armour to take care of business . . ."

"We're only supposed to gather information," Molly said carefully.

Eddie snorted loudly. "That's never been what we do. We're hands-on people. We get answers by beating them out of the case."

"I don't think you can beat up a street," said Molly. "Even with Drood armour."

Eddie looked up and down Blaiston Street. "The Wulfshead has to be here somewhere. The door brought us here."

Molly frowned. "If someone in the Nightside is planning to extend its territory, why start with Blaiston Street?"

"Because it's expendable?" said Eddie. "I'm more interested in how something like this was able to overwhelm the Wulfshead, with all its protections. Maybe it's trapped here, inside one of these buildings. People could still be alive, inside the Club."

"Let's hope it's not too late to rescue them," said Molly. "Come on; the sooner we get this done, the better. It's only a matter of time before the Authorities pick up on us."

"Let them," Eddie said immediately. "We are here for as long as it takes to get answers. This street has attacked my world and abducted my friends. Someone's got to pay for that."

"Information gathering only, remember?"

"Since when do you care what the Matriarch wants?"

"Since it involves the Nightside," Molly said steadily. "You don't want to start something you might not be able to finish."

"Remember who you're talking to," said Eddie. "I'm a Drood."

"Remember where you are," said Molly. "Normal rules do not apply in the long night. Including the one you're most used to: that Droods always win."

Eddie strode off down the street, and after a moment, Molly followed on behind.

Although Eddie wasn't prepared to admit it, Blaiston Street was creeping the hell out of him. He could feel the pressure of unseen watching eyes, heavy with malice. His footsteps sounded loudly on the quiet, as though warning he was coming. Molly moved at his side, barely making a sound.

"I'm remembering a story I once heard in Strangefellows," she said quietly. "Of a house on this street that wasn't a house but rather some kind of creature: a predator from outside our reality. It only pretended to be a house so it could lure people in and eat them."

"That sounds like the Nightside," said Eddie. "What happened to this hungry house?"

"John Taylor destroyed it, years ago. Leaving only an empty lot and some rubble. But if I'm remembering the address correctly, and I'm pretty sure I am because things like that have a tendency to stick in your mind, there's a house standing where the empty lot should be . . ."

She pointed it out, half-way down the left-hand terrace. It didn't appear to be any different from all the other houses in the row. Just crumbling bricks and mortar, smeared windows, and no lights showing anywhere. They walked over to it, as though they just happened to be strolling in that direction. Dirty stone steps led up to a paint-peeling front door. Eddie considered the closed door thoughtfully.

"It feels like the house is looking at me," he said. "And not in a good way. I can almost hear it breathing. What are your magics telling you, Molly?"

"Nothing. I'm getting absolutely nothing." Molly frowned fiercely. "And that's wrong. If this were just another house, I should be picking up ghost images from the past, emotional undercurrents, psychic imprintings . . . all the usual stuff. But instead it feels like nothing's there. Which has to mean the house, or someone inside it, is blocking me. And there aren't many who can do that."

They looked at the door, and it looked calmly back, inviting them to enter.

"Are you going to armour up now?" said Molly.

"Not just yet," said Eddie. "I don't want to frighten off whoever's in there or give them any warning of what I can do. In your story, the house was alive."

"And sentient," said Molly. "A predator from Outside."

Eddie shrugged. "This is the closest thing to a clue we've found. I say we go in and kick the crap out of it till it tells us everything we need to know. I'm really in the mood to beat up something evil."

"Never knew you when you weren't," said Molly. She grinned back at him. "Let's do it."

They strode up the stone steps to the door. Up close, Eddie thought the house looked . . . off. As though the details didn't quite add up. The texture of the wall wasn't right, and the dimensions of the door and the windows were subtly wrong. As though someone had built a house without ever having seen one, only heard a description from someone else. Eddie stood before the closed front door and looked it over, careful not to touch it. He couldn't see any obvious booby-traps. Molly reached out and grabbed hold of the door-handle, then snatched her hand back, grimacing.

"It felt like a slug!"

"Don't even think of wiping your hand on my sleeve," Eddie said sternly.

Molly scowled at the door and gestured sharply with her left hand. The door slammed back against the inside wall, with a crash loud enough to wake the living and the dead. There was no reaction from anywhere inside the house. The hallway appeared entirely ordinary, and completely empty, but so dimly lit it was barely brighter than the street.

Eddie looked at Molly. "I could have done that."

"You were taking too long." Molly wrinkled her nose. "What is that smell?"

"Damp, nasty, and decidedly organic," said Eddie. "Much like the door in the alley-way . . ."

"Well spotted."

"I thought so."

Eddie strode into the house like he'd come to condemn it, tear it down, then piss on the rubble. Molly hurried to catch up with him. The bare floor-boards gave queasily under their feet. They didn't feel like wood; they felt soft, almost spongy. The plaster walls were cracked, and heavily spotted with damp and mould. Eddie glanced behind him. The front door had already closed itself. The only other door was at the far end of the hallway, ensuring they would have to go deeper into the house. Into the belly of the beast. Eddie headed straight for the door, not even looking around. Nothing here mattered, it was all just part of the illusion, the come-on. The real house was waiting for him inside. He stopped before the door and reached out for the handle. He braced himself, anticipating the same bad reaction as Molly, but the handle felt perfectly normal. As though the house didn't need tricks any more. Not now it had its prey right where it wanted. Eddie opened the door and stepped quickly through, before the house could change its mind, and Molly was right there with him.

It didn't look like the inside of a house any more. It looked like the interior of the Wulfshead Club, but again the details were all wrong . . . twisted and distorted. The Club stretched away before them, like one of those dark corridors that seem to go on forever in nightmares. The floor was sticky, dragging at their feet and making every step an effort. The air was close and hot, thick with the stench of blood and death and decay. Instead of the Club's usual bright fluorescent lights, a dim blood-red glow seemed to issue from everywhere at once. As though they were walking through something's guts.

The plasma screens covering the walls, which should have been showing private indiscretions of the rich and powerful for the amusement of the patrons, were all blank. The walls bowed in, and the ceiling slumped down. The long high-tech bar appeared half-melted, as though the solid steel had run like candlewax. The bloody light seemed to thicken and congeal up ahead, as though hiding secrets yet to be revealed.

It was like being inside a bad fever-dream of the Wulfshead.

"This is why the Nightside was able to take the Club, despite its protections," Molly said quietly. "When the long night expanded, this predator from another reality just swallowed up the Club with everyone in it. I can't see far in this light. Can you?"

"Not without putting on my armour," said Eddie. "And I don't think I want this place to know about that just yet. I can feel it watching me. It can tell there's something different about me, that's why it's holding off for the moment. It's curious. Stick close."

"Damn right," said Molly.

They moved slowly forward, and the floor groaned with anticipation at every step. Eddie could feel a pressure on the air, a sense of resistance, as though he were underwater. The walls bulged slowly in and out, and he could hear a heavy susurration, like breathing. The air was uncomfortably warm and sweaty, like the inside of a hothouse. The smell of death and decay was almost overwhelming. And then Eddie stopped, and Molly stopped with him, as the blood-red light cleared a little to show them what lay sprawled on the floor ahead.

Bodies lay scattered the whole length of the Club, or the thing that looked like the Club. Dozens of dead men and women in ungainly poses, left to lie where they had fallen. Eddie couldn't see any obvious signs of violence. They looked like they'd died because they couldn't survive in the new environment the house had made when it engulfed the Wulfshead and changed it. The bodies had sunk part-way into the floor, as though it was slowly sucking them down. Their flesh looked withered, drained, used up from where the house was feeding on them.

"I know these people," said Molly. Her voice was sharp and clear in the quiet, and very dangerous. "Allies and enemies, and everything in between. People I laughed and drank with, and occasionally tried to kill, for money or a cause. And now they're so disfigured, I can't even tell which of them were important to me."

"It doesn't matter," said Eddie. "We'll avenge them all."

Not far away lay Monkton Farley, the consulting detective. In his smart Nineteen Twenties suit, complete with snap-brimmed fedora hat. Only his head and one shoulder still protruded above the floor. The house had eaten the rest of him. His face was so shrivelled and sunken it was easier for Eddie to recognise the outfit. He knelt beside what was left of the body, and the floor gave under his knee, just to remind him the house was watching.

"I can't say I ever really liked him," said Eddie. He might almost have been talking to himself. "I admired him, sometimes. He was very good at what he did, when he wasn't standing around letting his fans tell him how great he was. And he was half Drood, after all. One of the family."

He patted Farley on the shoulder, as though apologising, and rose to his feet. His face was set in harsh lines, and his eyes were cold.

"Tell me, Molly. How do you kill a predator the size of a house?"

"John Taylor did it," said Molly. "But how wasn't part of the story."

"Of course not. That would be too easy."

The floor rose and fell suddenly, as though something below had taken a deep breath. Eddie and Molly staggered back and forth, clinging to each other for support and to avoid tripping over the half-sunken bodies. The walls bowed heavily inwards, while a thick liquid dripped down from the bulging ceiling.

"What is this stuff?" said Molly.

"Smell that sharp acidic tang?" said Eddie. "Digestive fluids. I think the house has run out of patience."

A large mirror on the wall behind Eddie slumped forward and fell on him. It snapped around him like a cloak, then contracted with vicious strength. Eddie lurched back and forth on the bucking floor, tearing at the mirror with his hands, unable to throw the thing off. Molly fought her way forward to help him, against everything the floor could do to stop her.

"Don't touch the thing with your bare hands!" Eddie yelled to her. He had to stop and gasp for breath, as the mirror contracted again. "All right! I've had enough!"

He armoured up, and the golden strange matter swept over him in a moment. The living mirror flinched away from his armour, as though disgusted or afraid. Eddie used his armoured strength to break the mirror's hold, then tore the thing off him and threw it away. The mirror oozed across the heaving floor.

Molly blasted the mirror with fire from her hands. It scorched and blackened, heaving and convulsing, but wouldn't die. Until Eddie picked it up and tore it apart with his golden hands. The pieces collapsed into rot and slime.

Molly turned her fires on the nearest wall. The heaving surface darkened like burned meat, but the flames didn't catch and couldn't spread. The floor bucked, as though in pain, throwing Eddie and Molly this way and that. He grabbed onto the high-tech bar to support him, and his hands tore through the steel, as though it had gone soft. Across the walls, thick purple traceries of throbbing veins spread like vines. A slow, heavy thudding sounded on the air, like a giant heart-beat.

Eddie grew sharp spikes from the soles of his golden feet, to help him keep his balance. The floor shuddered. Eddie laughed briefly.

"Apparently I'm not to its taste. Are you all right, Molly?"

"Fine!" she said loudly. "Just fine!"

She drew up both her feet and folded her legs under her, so that she was hovering in mid air. Thick digestive fluids rained down on Molly, burning her bare flesh. She cried out, as much in disgust as pain, and surrounded herself with a field of shimmering protective energies. Eddie knew how much that took out of her. And, that she couldn't keep it going for long. The digestive fluids trickled slowly down his armour, unable to make any impression.

A huge, inhuman eye opened in the wall next to Eddie and studied him with godlike scorn. Eddie punched it with his golden fist. His arm plunged on into the eye, right up to the elbow, and the eye snapped shut and disappeared. Leaving nothing behind but a wall with Eddie's arm trapped inside it. He planted one foot against the wall to brace himself and heaved back with all his armoured strength. The wall clamped down and wouldn't release him. Digestive fluids splashed over him in a shower, only to run harmlessly down the golden armour. Eddie pulled back, and the wall stretched out . . . until finally it was forced to release him, with a wet, sucking sound. Eddie staggered backwards. Steam rose up from the open wound in the wall where his arm had been, as though just the touch of his armour had hurt it.

Long, fleshy tentacles snapped down from the ceiling to wrap themselves around Molly as she hovered in mid air. They closed around her protective field, applying a crushing pressure from all sides, trying to force their way in, to get to her. Molly tried to expand her field, to force them back, but already she was getting tired. More and more tentacles dropped down from the lowering ceiling. A glowing witch knife appeared in Molly's hand, and she thrust it through the shimmering energies to saw doggedly at one jerking tentacle after another.

Eddie looked around him. The floor had swallowed up most of the bodies. The blood-red light was thicker and darker, and the interior of the Wulfshead Club looked more than ever like something's guts. Digestive fluids rained down. The house was hungry . . . and the door through which Eddie and Molly had entered was gone, long gone.

"Molly!" Eddie yelled. "Teleport yourself out of here!"

She stopped sawing at a tentacle to glare at him. "I'm not going anywhere without you!"

"I'm safe, inside my armour! You're not, because that field isn't going to last. Go! I'll join you in a few moments."

"How are you going to get out?"

"I have a plan!"

"Oh well," said Molly. "If you've got a plan . . . Because that's always worked out so well in the past."

She snapped her fingers and disappeared. The tentacles tangled together in the place where she'd been. And then they reached out to Eddie, standing alone. The digestive fluids were coming down in torrents now, and the light was going out. Eddie could just see the last of Monkton Farley sinking into the floor. Eddie moved quickly over, took a firm grip on what was left of the body, and ripped it out of the floor. He threw it aside and peered into the dark gap left behind. A great breach in the flesh of the house, leading down to its stomach. Eddie could see massive teeth grinding together and horrible things moving. He laughed behind his featureless mask and jumped down into the hole.

Out on Blaiston Street, Molly stood in the middle of the road, staring at the house. It still looked deceitfully ordinary from the outside. Not even a hint of blood-red light at any of the windows. It had been some time since Molly teleported out, and there was still no sign of Eddie. Her hands clenched into fists at her sides. She should never have left him. He thought nothing could touch him while he was in his armour; but this was the Nightside. She drew her glowing witch knife again and started determinedly toward the front door. If the house wouldn't open up, she'd cut her way in.

And then the whole house shook and shuddered. The road trembled under Molly's feet, as though in sympathy. The house screamed, an awful, inhuman sound wracked with pain and horror . . . and collapsed suddenly, falling in upon itself, as though everything that had held it together had just been torn away. The house that was not a house, and never had been, rotted and fell apart until there was nothing left but pieces of disturbingly organic rubble on an empty lot.

And there was no sign of Eddie anywhere.

Molly ran forward, calling his name, ready to blast the whole tenement apart and everything underneath it. Only to stop short when the empty lot erupted as a golden fist punched up through the ground. Eddie dug his way out and stood swaying for a moment while he got his breath back. He saw Molly, armoured down, and strode off the lot to join her, grinning broadly.

"Hi, Molly. Miss me?"

She made her witch knife disappear, then threw her arms around Eddie and hugged him fiercely. Finally she stepped back and punched him hard on the shoulder.

"Ow!" said Eddie. "What was that for?"

"For worrying me!" said Molly. "What did you just do?"

"I let the house try to eat me," he said. "Jumped right down into its stomach. The teeth broke against my armour, and when the house tried to digest me anyway . . . the golden strange matter poisoned it. I thought it might. Remember how the floor flinched away from my feet, and just the touch of my hand burned the wall?"

"You took one hell of a risk," said Molly.

He smiled easily. "That's the job, when you're a Drood."

Eddie and Molly stood together, looking at the empty lot. The house was gone now, and so was what little had remained of the Wulfshead Club. Along with all the people who'd been inside it when the Nightside broke its barriers. Blaiston Street was completely still and utterly silent. Even after everything that had happened, no one had come out to see what was going on. Because this was a street where people only survived by minding their own business.

"So many dead . . ." said Eddie. "And I couldn't even save the bodies, for their families."

"They wouldn't have wanted to see what was left," said Molly.

"We lost a lot of good people," said Eddie.

"Good and bad and in between," said Molly. "The Wulfshead always was that kind of Club."

"So it was," said Eddie.

They managed a small smile for each other.

"We'd better go," said Eddie. "Once I called on my armour, the crown stopped hiding me. You can bet people are already hurrying here to ask a whole bunch of questions I have no intention of answering, then shout at me a lot."

"Better use the Merlin Glass," said Molly. "Get us out of here fast. So we're done?"

"No," said Eddie. "The house wasn't responsible for the Nightside's expanding; it just took advantage of it. Someone's behind all of this. They have to be found and stopped. Whatever it takes. Because if the Nightside keeps spreading, keeps pushing its way into our world . . . This is what's coming for all Humanity."

He made a door with the Merlin Glass, and he and Molly stepped through. The door disappeared after them, and only the long night remained: cold and quiet and empty.

CHAPTER THREE

Heads of State

Howard stood in the centre of the Ops Room, watching the screens. Usually that helped him feel like Head of Operations: the man in charge, protector of his family, and master of all he surveyed. But not today. His family, his world, and everything he believed in were under threat and under siege. He could feel it, even if there was nothing to see on any of his screens. The Nightside crashing out beyond its boundaries had changed everything. And something that ground-breaking didn't just happen; someone had to be behind it. An unknown enemy was out there somewhere, planning and plotting, and Howard was watching for him.

He was deathly tired. He'd been on his feet for fourteen hours now without a break, and no end of his shift in sight. He was here for the duration. His head ached, his back was killing him, and his feet weren't talking to him. He realised he still had a cup of tea in his hand. He sipped at it and pulled a face. His mind had been busy with so many other things, he'd let the tea get cold. He put the cup down on the nearest workstation and stretched his back slowly. It didn't help.

He couldn't complain; he was still better off than his operators, sitting endlessly at their workstations studying the screens before them. Frowning with concentration for fear they'd miss something important. At least he could move around the room, change what he was looking at, close his aching eyes for a moment without worrying he'd let the family down. Howard sighed quietly and glanced at the big clock on the wall.

"Listen up, people," he said, quietly and calmly. "It's time to run our regular hourly scan. Standard procedure, concentrate on what you're doing, get it right. Start at the outside and work your way in."

No one actually said anything, but Howard could feel a mood of resigned irritation in the Operations Room. They'd been running the scans every hour on the hour ever since they came on duty, and no one had turned up a trace of anything even slightly out of the ordinary. But it had to be done. The automatic systems were supposed to alert the Room to any significant change the moment it happened, but Howard couldn't trust the systems any more. They hadn't warned him about the Nightside. So he would see the scans were run, every hour on the hour, until the Matriarch personally assured him the crisis was at an end.

"Start with the really long-range sensors," he said, soothing his people with calm, familiar words. "Fire up the existential engines and the maybe machines, and let's see what's stirring in the Darque Latitudes."

His people went to work without a murmur, searching for any signs of trouble in the supernatural realms, that uncertain area between death and life. First up on the floating holographic displays were the usual shifting views of poltergeists. Dark, raging shapes like living thunder-storms, beating endlessly against the barriers that kept them out of the material world, searching for a weak spot so they could force their way in. Not for the first time, their behaviour reminded Howard of a spoilt child throwing a tantrum.

Next, the Ops Room looked for ghosts. An endless sea of faces filled the display screens. Overlapping and superimposing, silently shouting faces wracked with loss and horror flickered on and off like interrupted signals. Howard never let it get to him. The chances of seeing someone he knew were vanishingly small. What mattered was that none of them were manifesting anywhere near Drood Hall. Some were just images caught in Time, trapped in repeating loops; others, the last fading vestiges of a personality, as its psychic fingers were prised off the edges of the waking world by the relentless pull of the hereafter. Real ghosts, the spirits of the dead returned to haunt the living, were fortunately very rare. When they did occasionally turn up at the Hall, the family wasted no time in sending them on to their reward. Because otherwise they could be a real pain in the arse. No one can hold a grudge like a ghost.

Next, the operators checked for the possessed, the undead, and all the other things that tried to insist they were alive when they clearly weren't. No trace anywhere in the Hall grounds, or the surrounding country-side. Checking for such things was just a formality; Howard could trust the automatic systems to catch them because their physical presence alone should trigger any number of really loud warnings. And if any did manage to get into the grounds, the weapons systems would blast them into confetti before they could stagger two steps towards the Hall.

The holographic displays changed yet again as the operators checked for signs of attack from other dimensions, adjoining realities, even other timetracks. Again, any such incursion should trip all the major alarms, but Howard had reached the point where he didn't trust anyone but his own people, and even then only when he was standing over them. One by one the operators signed off, confirming what Howard was seeing on the displays. Everything was quiet, nothing out of the usual. Nothing to worry about.

Till the next scan.

The displays cleared, to show shifting scenes of the Hall grounds. Nothing was moving apart from a few grounds staff here and there, tending to the lawns and fighting the flower-beds. The gryphons and the peacocks were patrolling their usual areas, ostentatiously ignoring each other. Howard watched the precog gryphons carefully, but they didn't seem bothered by anything. And the peacocks were blessedly quiet, for the moment. The damned things were so over-sensitive they'd been known to sound off if the wind changed direction. But they did make excellent living alarms.

Howard murmured in one operator's ear, and the young woman's fingers darted across her keyboard. The scenes changed again. Swans drifted majestically on the artificial lake, with no sign of the undine. The hedge maze was quiet, and the standing stones watched the boundaries. The disguised entrance was shut down, and Drood Hall stood firm and strong against the world. As it should. All protections and defences were in place, the seen and the unseen and the really nasty hidden surprises. The only excitement was up on the roof, where all manner of magnificent flying machines were still busy landing and taking off. Howard smiled slightly as he watched the landing-pad crews running back and forth, frantically waving their little flags and shouting themselves blue in the face at anything that tried to jump the queue. They'd never been worked so hard before and were loving every minute of it. Let them have their moment. It wasn't often they got to feel important.

The last of the operators finished their scans, and the Operations Room fell silent. Everyone looked to Howard, and he nodded briefly.

"Well done, people. Scan complete. There shall be Earl Grey and chocolate hob-nobs for all."

A single alarm sounded, harsh and strident. Everyone's head snapped around as they turned to look. Howard stared. It wasn't one of the regular alarms. He moved over to stand behind the operator as she stared in horror at the flashing light on her workstation. Howard leaned in beside her, steadying her with his presence. She shut down the alarm and concentrated on her screen.

"What is it, Angela?" Howard said quietly.

"Something is heading straight for us," she said. Her voice was calm, but she had to work for it. "Something that doesn't fit any of our usual criteria, and it's coming from a direction I can't even identify."

"Any idea what it might be?"

"No! I don't know . . . I can't get a fix on it, or track it."

Howard straightened up and looked around the Ops Room. "Everyone link their stations to Angela's. This has top priority till I tell you otherwise."

He went back to stand in the centre of the room, so he could watch everything at once. The holographic displays weren't showing anything. Whatever was on its way, it wasn't coming from any of the usual trouble spots. A quiet murmur of troubled voices ran through the Ops Room as the operators conferred, trying to work out what it was by ruling out what it wasn't.

It's not heavenly or infernal.

It's not coming from the higher or lower dimensions, the shimmering plains or the broken lands.

Could it be interplanetary, some new form of warp drive?

Someone's been watching too much television. The early-warning systems would pick up anything like that the moment it entered our solar system.

I can't get my head around how it's moving. Like it's travelling sideways across Time and Space.

Hold it; has anyone thought to check whether someone's signed out the old Armourer's Bentley?

First thing I thought of; it's in the garage, being searched for hitch-hikers after its last other-dimensional trip.

Whatever this is, it's coming right for us. Like a bullet from a gun.

Howard picked up the red phone and was put straight through to the Matriarch. That was what it was for. She answered immediately.

"Yes?"

"This is Howard in Ops. Someone or something will be arriving here at any moment. We have been unable to identify it."

"You don't think the Hall's protections will keep it out?" said the Matriarch. Her voice was as calm as his. They might have been discussing the weather.

"We can't be sure," said Howard. "This is so different, it might slip past our defences because they won't see it as a threat. Whatever it is, it's travelling fast, and it's coming at us like the wrath of God. I strongly recommend you send armoured Droods out into the grounds to meet it."

"I'll inform the Sarjeant-at-Arms," said the Matriarch. The line went dead.

Howard put the phone down. He felt a little easier, now he knew the Sarjeant-at-Arms was on the job. He looked around the Ops Room and was pleased to see everyone steadily watching their screens. It was one of the strengths of the Droods that when emergencies occurred, everyone could be relied on to do what was necessary, quickly and efficiently, just as they'd been trained. Howard moved unhurriedly among his people, leaning over shoulders to peer at their screens and murmur the occasional encouragement. They were all doing everything they could, even though it wasn't getting them anywhere. All they could be sure of was that something was getting steadily closer.

"Has anyone thought to check for an energy signature?" said Howard. "You know Molly Metcalf likes to change the signature on her teleport, just to mess with us."

"It's not her," said a young man, scowling at his screen. Howard had to concentrate for a moment to remember the man's name.

"How can you be so sure, David?" said Howard.

"Because I've got every signature she ever used on record, and this is nothing like them."

"It's almost here!" said another voice, and everyone stopped what they were doing to look at the displays.

Out in the grounds, nothing was moving anywhere . . . apart from the company of armoured Droods streaming out the front door, led by the Sarjeant-at-Arms.

"Excuse me, sir," said David. "Why hasn't the Sarjeant armoured up?"

"Cedric always likes to leave it to the last moment," said Howard. "He says, because it makes the enemy under-estimate him. More likely because he's a show-off."

There was a brief murmur of laughter, quickly cut off as Angela raised her voice.

"It's here! It's right on top of us! There. Screen Three!"

Everyone turned to look. Some actually rose to their feet to get a better view. There was no opening of a dimensional door, no prising apart of Space and Time by unnatural energies, not even a bright flash of light. Just a single figure, suddenly standing on the grassy lawns, staring calmly at Drood Hall.

"Oh hell," said Howard. "It's John Taylor."

A babble of voices broke out. No wonder they hadn't been able to identify the unexpected visitor; Walker of the Nightside had never come to Drood Hall before, in the whole history of the long night and the Drood family.

"Quiet please, people," said Howard, and his barely raised voice cut across the uproar. The operators who'd stood up quickly sat down again. Howard addressed the room without once taking his eyes off Screen Three. "Keep scanning, people. I want to know how John Taylor got into the grounds, past all our protections and defences."

"On it," said Angela, her voice calm and composed again. "Our scanners aren't picking up anything. As far as they're concerned, he isn't even there. How is that possible?"

"It's John Taylor," said Howard.

"Is he really a threat?" said David. "I mean, he's just one man. How dangerous can he be?"

"As dangerous as he wants to be," said Howard.

*   *   *

Standing in the middle of the wide, rolling lawns, John Taylor looked interestedly around him. He'd heard about the magnificent Drood grounds all
his life, but he'd never expected to see them. They spread away like a great
green sea, under cloudless blue-grey skies that made a pleasant contrast to
his world of endless night and neon-lit streets. And the Hall itself was quite
staggeringly huge. For the first time, John understood how big the Drood
family was. They weren't just a clan; they were an army. An advance guard
of armoured Droods was already heading straight for him, plunging across
the lawns like so many animated golden statues. With a very familiar figure
at their head. John looked back at the Hall. People in the long night would
never believe he'd actually been here. He wondered if there was a gift shop;
perhaps he could pick up some postcards and a few T-shirts.

The armoured Droods were moving inhumanly quickly. John considered them thoughtfully, wondered if he should be impressed or intimidated that such a show of force had been turned out in his honour, and
opted for neither. He was Walker of the Nightside; it was up to them to be
impressed. He looked casually at the gold pocket-watch in his hand, as
though he was just checking the time of his arrival, then put it away. No
point in letting the Droods know it contained a portable Timeslip. They'd
only try to take it away from him. He struck a casual pose and waited
calmly for the Sarjeant-at-Arms to reach him.

A robot gun rose up from its underground bunker and targeted him
with its long barrels. John looked at the gun thoughtfully, and it hesitated.
John could almost hear the Hall's security people screaming at the gun to
stand down. *Don't shoot! That's John Taylor! God knows what he might do!* He
didn't smile. A calm exterior under extreme provocation just added to the
mystique.

The robot gun sank sullenly back into the ground, and the grass
closed over it. John looked around unhurriedly as a pair of gryphons came
lurching across the lawns. Seriously ugly creatures, with a definite air of
hunger about them. John reached into his jacket pocket and brought out
the bag of special treats he'd brought with him. Martian meat balls, left
over from the last time Martians from an alternative timeline had invaded
the Nightside. For months afterwards, Martian meat had been top choice
in all the best Nightside restaurants. These particular morsels had been

wrapped in smoked red weed and soaked in the juices of human adrenal glands. Quite possibly the least requested bar-snack in Strangefellows' history. John had made a point of collecting some from Alex before he left. Alex had been glad to get rid of them. He claimed some of them had started moving around when he wasn't looking. John had heard of the Droods' gryphons and thought Martian meat balls might be one of the few snacks no one had tried bribing them with.

And sure enough, the gryphons loved them, nuzzling at his hands with their soft mouths every time he stopped to see if they'd had enough. When the bag was finally empty, John put it away and scratched the gryphons cautiously between the ears. They seemed to like it. They sank down on either side of him and leaned heavily against his legs, just to make it clear he wasn't going anywhere. Apparently even bribery had its limits. John didn't mind waiting.

The armoured Droods finally arrived, spreading out to surround the infamous John Taylor. The Sarjeant-at-Arms looked him over carefully. He still hadn't put on his armour. The two men nodded to each other. Two very dangerous men, who both knew better than to start something they didn't have to.

"Hello, John," said the Sarjeant.

"Hello, Cedric," John said cheerfully. "Haven't seen you in Strangefellows for a while."

"I've been busy. You know how it is."

"Unfortunately, yes."

"To what do we owe the honour of this entirely unexpected visit, John?"

"I'm here to speak with the Matriarch."

The Sarjeant looked at him carefully. "And why would you want to do that?"

John looked back at him calmly. "You know why."

The Sarjeant-at-Arms shook his head slowly. "You should have informed us you were coming. There are proper channels, and procedures."

"You should have told us you were entering the Nightside," said John.

"You'd better talk to the Matriarch," said the Sarjeant.

John smiled brightly. "That's what I thought."

The Sarjeant glared at the gryphons. "Get out of here, traitors. Undone by simple bribery. Anyone would think we didn't feed you at all."

The gryphons lurched away, entirely unembarrassed by his tone. The Sarjeant indicated the way to Drood Hall with a sweep of his arm, waited for John to set off, and strode along beside him. The armoured Droods went with them, still surrounding John at what they hoped was a safe distance. Because this was Walker of the Nightside, after all.

John strolled along, taking his time and refusing to be hurried. Apparently completely at his ease, he studied his surroundings with happy curiosity, as though he were at the head of a parade, or a state head on a diplomatic visit. The Sarjeant strode along, looking straight ahead and saying nothing. After a while, John looked at him.

"Is it true? You can summon any weapon you want out of nowhere?"

A large gun appeared in the Sarjeant's right hand, pointed unwaveringly at John. "Not from nowhere. From the Drood Armoury. Where we keep the most powerful weapons known to Man."

"Nice gun," said John.

"Don't try to take the bullets out of it," said the Sarjeant. "It doesn't use bullets."

"You'd better have this," said John.

He handed the Sarjeant-at-Arms the trigger for his gun. The Sarjeant looked at it, then at his gun. He sighed quietly, accepted the trigger from John, and made both it and the gun disappear. They walked on together in silence. When they finally reached the front door, the Sarjeant turned to address the accompanying armoured Droods.

"I can take it from here. You spread out across the grounds. Watch for other intrusions. If Walker can get past all our defences and protections, others may be able to as well."

"What are our orders of engagement?" said the nearest Drood.

"Anyone appears in our grounds, I want them taken down. Alive, if possible. I am prepared to accept damaged."

The Droods moved quickly away. John watched them go, then looked at the Sarjeant.

"You're mellowing, Cedric."

"Don't you believe it, John. Shall we go in?"

They went inside, and the front door closed firmly behind them.

John Taylor looked interestedly around the Hall as they walked through it. Openly fascinated, though careful not to appear in any way impressed. The weird and the unusual came as standard in the Nightside, but he wasn't used to this scale of luxury. He chatted easily with the Sarjeant as they walked. Away from the others, the two men were able to relax a little.

"Nice place you have here," said John.

"We think so," said the Sarjeant. "Is it everything you thought it would be?"

"Pretty much. I have seen bigger and better, mostly on the Street of the Gods, but you've got style. They mostly go for gaudy."

"Why are you here, John? Really?"

"Did you honestly think we wouldn't notice an armoured Drood operating inside the Nightside?"

"He's hardly the first Drood to enter the long night," said the Sarjeant. "You and I have spent many an evening drinking together in Strangefellows. Usually with the old Armourer."

"I miss Jack," said John.

"We all do," said the Sarjeant.

"Let's be real about this," said John. "Everyone knows Droods occasionally come to the Nightside to let their hair down, just like everyone else, and as long as they do it incognito, no one gives a damn. Everyone's welcome in the long night, that's the point. But this was different. This was a Drood throwing his weight around, in his armour, in public."

"Blaiston Street is public?" said the Sarjeant. "That shit-hole?"

"When Eddie put on his armour, it was like a beacon in the dark," said John. "Everyone noticed. What was the Matriarch thinking?"

"You've heard about what happened to the Wulfshead Club," said the Sarjeant.

"Of course," said John. "Have you heard about what happened on the Street of the Gods?"

The Sarjeant-at-Arms looked at him. "No."

John brought him up to date. The Sarjeant's scowl deepened.

"I don't like the implications of that," he said finally.

"The gods were convinced something really bad is coming," said John. "Bad enough to frighten even them."

"Are they really gods?" said the Sarjeant.

"Real enough to kick an atheist's arse," said John. "Are you sure you haven't heard of any possible threat or danger heading our way?"

"No," said the Sarjeant. "Nothing. And we should have; that's part of our job. To anticipate trouble, so we can step in and put a stop to it before it gets out of hand. Everything seemed quiet . . . till the Nightside broke its boundaries. You had no warning of that?"

"No," said John. "First I knew was when the Authorities called me in to give me the bad news. I've never seen them in such a state."

"They were shocked?" said the Sarjeant.

"They were scared," said John. "Nothing is supposed to happen in the Nightside, or to the Nightside, that they don't know about."

"But such things do happen," said the Sarjeant.

"Well, yes," said John. "But not like this!"

"Can the Authorities pull the Nightside back inside its old boundaries?" asked the Sarjeant.

"No one I've talked to has any idea of how that could be done," said John. "Because no one has a clue as to what caused it."

"Or who," said the Sarjeant.

"There is always that, yes," said John.

"Just when you think the day can't get any worse," said the Sarjeant.

"It's not the day you have to worry about," said John. "It's the night."

The Sarjeant-at-Arms took John Taylor to the Sanctity. All the way through the Hall, hurrying Droods stopped dead in their tracks to stare openly at John. The Sarjeant wouldn't allow him to stop and talk with anyone, so John smiled and waved in all directions, like visiting royalty who just happened to be passing through. The Sarjeant glared at the Droods until they started moving again. Meanwhile, John was quietly memorising as much of the Hall's lay-out as he could, without being obvious about it. He'd probably never get such a chance again, and information like this could prove valuable.

When they finally reached the long corridor that led to the Sanctity, John took in the two armoured Droods standing guard at the closed doors and smiled easily at the Sarjeant-at-Arms.

"Bet you I can steal their torcs without them even noticing."

"Please don't," said the Sarjeant.

The guards opened the double doors long before John and the Sarjeant arrived, and stood well back to let them enter. And then closed the doors very firmly behind them.

John didn't even glance back. He was too busy looking around the secret heart of Drood Hall, which as far as he knew no outsider had ever seen before. It occurred to him that he was standing right in the middle of Drood Hall, surrounded by an armoured army who probably wouldn't be that keen on letting him leave. Not after all the things he'd seen. John decided he wasn't going to think about that and looked calmly at the Matriarch. She was sitting behind a simple table, ignoring the various communication devices arrayed before her. There was no one else in the Sanctity. The Matriarch nodded coolly to John, and he nodded easily in return.

"Hello, Maggie. I bring salutations from the Nightside. I would have brought you a gift, but everyone knows the Droods already have everything worth having."

"You can wait outside, Sarjeant," said the Matriarch, not taking her eyes off John.

"Are you sure?" said the Sarjeant. "It's not proper procedure for a Matriarch to be left alone with a dangerous enemy."

She gave him a hard look. "I am a Drood. I can take care of myself."

"Of course you can," said the Sarjeant-at-Arms. "I'll be right outside. If you need me."

He left the Sanctity, carefully closing the doors behind him. John looked thoughtfully at the Matriarch.

"No Sarjeant-at-Arms, no advisory Council . . . just the two of us? How cosy. I am honoured."

"No witnesses," said the Matriarch. "Just in case you and I come to terms no one else needs to know about."

"You mean, agreements the family wouldn't approve of," said John.

"Exactly," said the Matriarch. "And, of course, so that if I do find it necessary to do something extreme to you, no one else will ever know."

"Spoken like a true Drood," said John.

The Matriarch gestured for John to sit on the chair facing her. He dropped onto it and lounged bonelessly, almost defiantly at his ease. And then they both stared at each other for a while. Two powerful leaders who'd heard so much about each other but never thought they'd ever meet. John smiled suddenly.

"I know; you thought I'd be taller."

"And you thought I'd be older," said the Matriarch. "Were you really a private eye, originally?"

"Yes," said John. "Did you really start out as a gardener?"

"Yes," said the Matriarch. "How far we've come . . ."

"We have a lot in common," said John, sitting forward to show the straight-talking had started. "Both of us doing a job we never wanted because we weren't given any choice in the matter. You look out for your people, and I look out for mine. Which means we're both expected to make whatever decisions we find necessary, for the good of all. So let's talk."

"Let's," said the Matriarch. "What the hell did you think you were doing, arriving in our grounds without any advance warning? That is not acceptable!"

"A Drood entered the Nightside," said John. "Not in any way incognito, and enforced his will through his armour. That is not acceptable, and you must have known it. Do I really need to remind you of the rules and obligations laid down by the Pacts and Agreements specifically designed to keep us from each other's throats? The Droods stay out of the long night, and in return no one in the Nightside interferes in Drood business."

"Like you could," said the Matriarch.

"Oh, some of us could," said John. "You'd be surprised. You have no idea what powers lie sleeping in the darkest parts of the long night."

"All the more reason to worry about what they might do if they ever got out," said the Matriarch.

"The strength of the long night is that whatever happens in the Nightside, stays in the Nightside," John said easily. "Everyone is far too busy doing things to one another to give a damn about what happens in the outside world. Sin is a very tiring business. It takes a lot out of people. All we have ever asked is to be left alone, to concentrate on our own damnations and salvations."

"But that isn't true any longer, is it?" said the Matriarch. "The long night has reached out and engulfed part of our world. The Wulfshead Club is gone, and all the people inside it are dead."

"I know," said John. "Some of them were friends of mine."

"Something had to be done about that," said the Matriarch.

"But you chose to do the one thing you must have known would only make things worse," said John.

"It was supposed to be just an information-gathering mission," the Matriarch said carefully. "Eddie was not authorised to take any action."

"But you sent Eddie!" said John. "The one field agent famous for never following orders!"

"Are you saying he should have left that creature where it was, to eat more people?" said the Matriarch, her voice cold and implacable.

"He should have left it to me," said John. "The Nightside deals with its own problems." He sat back in his chair and changed tack. "Discreet visits by Droods are one thing, but after what Eddie did, people were bound to notice. Voices are being raised all over the Nightside. Old powers are stirring, feeling threatened, things that should never have been disturbed. There's already a lot of talk about retribution. Doing something dramatic to restore the Nightside's honour by evening the score. Something bad enough to make sure no Drood ever dares intrude on the Nightside again."

"Are you threatening me, Walker?"

"I'm going out of my way not to. For the moment, the Authorities are still on top of things. But only as long as you don't do anything to escalate matters. I was sent here to lay down the law, the Pacts and Agreements that have maintained the balance between us for so long."

"Say what you have to say," said the Matriarch. "I'm listening."

"No more Droods in the Nightside, for any reason," John said flatly. "If any further problems should arise, contact the Authorities through the proper channels, and I will deal with them."

The Matriarch sat very still, staring at him. She didn't say yes or no. John stared calmly back, hiding his racing thoughts behind an unreadable face. This wasn't going the way he'd thought it would. He'd expected a clash of attitudes, of established power bases butting heads over territory, but nothing that couldn't be sorted out with some hard words and harder bargaining. But the Matriarch didn't seem interested in that.

"What do the Authorities know, about the way the Nightside expanded itself?" the Matriarch said finally.

"Nothing," said John.

"I find that hard to believe."

"Well, that's your problem, isn't it?"

"Listen to me, Walker," said the Matriarch. "The Droods only put up with the Nightside's existence because it's always been confined within London's limits. Now that's changed . . ."

"The Authorities don't know any more about what's happening than you do," said John. He was careful to keep his voice calm, even though he felt like shouting. Why wasn't she listening to him? "We already have people investigating the situation. I will find out what's going on. That's what I do. But this, all of this, is Nightside business. Not yours."

"It was," said the Matriarch. "But now, things have changed. Everything has changed. Understand me, Walker; we are the Droods. We protect this world by destroying anything that poses a threat to Humanity."

"We are the Nightside," said John. "And we don't care."

"Don't care was made to care."

"Not on the best day you ever had."

He rose to his feet. The Matriarch rose quickly to hers. She started to summon her armour, and John fixed her with a look.

"Don't. Really."

The Matriarch hesitated. Because he might be bluffing, or he might not. Even the Droods couldn't be sure when it came to John Taylor.

He didn't wait to see what would happen next. Without quite understanding why, it was obvious the talks had broken down. He activated the pocket-watch he'd sneaked into his hand, and the portable Timeslip took him away. The doors to the Sanctity slammed open, and the Sarjeant-at-Arms came storming in, an energy gun in each hand. He saw that John was gone and stopped. The Matriarch glared at him.

"You're too late!"

The Sarjeant dismissed his guns. "Ethel said the talks were deteriorating. What happened?"

"He wouldn't listen to me," said the Matriarch. "I tried to warn him . . ." She raised her voice. "Ethel! How was Walker able to leave like that, despite all the Sanctity's protections? You assured me that was impossible. That's why I met him here!"

"Beats me," said Ethel. "It's all very odd. But he is John Taylor, after all. A man of many mysteries."

"And a real pain in the arse," said the Sarjeant. "Matriarch, I need to know: Why weren't you able to reach an agreement?"

The Matriarch sat down behind her table again and composed herself. "Because neither of us could afford to give an inch. Have Eddie and Molly returned from the Nightside yet?"

"They just appeared in the grounds," said the Sarjeant. "Eddie ripped a robot gun out of the ground and crushed it into a ball because it dared to check him out. And Molly blew up a tree because she didn't like the way it was looking at her. I think we can safely assume they are not in the best of moods."

"How was John Taylor able to hear about Eddie's destroying the house, confer with the Authorities, and get here . . . before Eddie and Molly could return?" said the Matriarch.

The Sarjeant shrugged. "It's the Nightside. They do things differently there."

"Send Eddie and Molly in to see me," said the Matriarch. "And tell the Council to attend as well. We have important matters to discuss. And Sarjeant, start putting things in order."

The Sarjeant-at-Arms looked at her for a long moment, as though giving her time to withdraw her order. When she didn't, he nodded slowly. "Has it really come to that?"

"Not yet," said the Matriarch. "But we are one step closer."

CHAPTER FOUR

What Do You Do When No One Knows Anything?

Eddie and Molly walked back through the Drood grounds. Behind them a tree burned quietly, as though not wanting to draw attention to itself. The grounds stretched away in every direction, very still and very quiet. After a while, Molly shot Eddie a sideways look.

"Why are you in such a bad mood, Eddie?"

"I'm not in a bad mood," he said, staring straight ahead. "You're the one who just incinerated a perfectly innocent tree."

"I'm used to acting out," said Molly. "You're the one who keeps it all bottled up inside. So you'll pardon me if I was just a little surprised to see you compress an entire robot gun into something the size of a Christmas-tree ornament, then call it a bastard. That has to mean something. So, what's wrong?"

"We screwed up the mission," said Eddie. He still wasn't looking at her.

"How can you say that?" said Molly. She had to increase her pace to keep up with Eddie as he strode along, almost as though he was trying to leave her and her questions behind. "We found the Wulfshead Club, and the poor bastards trapped inside, and we destroyed the thing that killed them. Which is a lot more than we were sent there to do."

"But that's the point!" said Eddie. "We did too much and got ourselves noticed. I got us noticed. A Drood operating in his armour stands out in the long night like a leper in a whore-house. There will be repercussions."

"You mean the Authorities?" Molly shrugged. "They'll get over it. The

Nightside is used to people breaking the rules. I often think the only reason the long night has any rules is so people can have fun ignoring them."

"More importantly," said Eddie, as though he hadn't heard a word she'd said, and quite possibly he hadn't, "we didn't do what we were supposed to do. We didn't discover why the Nightside was able to break its boundaries. Let alone who might be behind it."

"We were busy," said Molly. "We had to deal with what was in front of us . . . Look, Eddie, it's up to you; either you stop walking faster and faster till I have to run to keep up with you, or I will trip you up and sit on you till you calm down."

Eddie slowed down because he knew she wasn't joking. He still didn't look at her. "Once I'd used my armour against the house, we had to leave the Nightside. The mission was compromised."

"That wasn't your fault!" said Molly.

"I never said it was."

"Then why are you brooding? If you frown any harder, your eyebrows will join up."

Eddie sighed heavily. "Because we've only just started this case, and already everything is slipping out of our control."

"We'll get it back," said Molly. "We always do."

Eddie finally looked at her. "As you already pointed out, in the Nightside, the rule that Droods always win doesn't apply."

"Then we'll make it apply," said Molly.

They walked for a while in silence. Molly kept a careful eye on Eddie. He seemed strangely tired and worn-down. It wasn't like him to take a setback so hard.

"You need a nice lie-down in a darkened room," she announced. "With some soft music, a damp cloth on your forehead, and my hand down the front of your trousers."

Eddie laughed briefly, but she could hear the effort in it. "You really think we're going to be allowed to take a rest?"

Molly snorted loudly. She felt one of them should sound convincing. "Like to see anyone stop us. Anybody gives me a hard time, I'll just point them in the direction of the burning tree."

"It's probably gone out by now," said Eddie.

"Then I'll set it alight again!"

Molly broke off and looked around sharply as she caught a movement on the edge of her vision. She slapped Eddie on the arm.

"What are armoured Droods doing, out in the grounds?" she said. "And look, there are more of them."

"Droods in full armour?" said Eddie. He stopped to get a better look, and Molly stopped with him. "I wouldn't normally expect to see something like that for anything less than an imminent invasion."

"Could be manoeuvres . . ." said Molly.

"Nothing's scheduled," said Eddie. "Something must have happened while we were away."

"Get that guilty tone out of your voice right now," Molly said firmly. "Not everything is about you."

"That's not how it feels," said Eddie.

They strode through the front door into the entrance-hall, and once again the Sarjeant-at-Arms was there waiting for them. He looked as coldly impassive as ever, but Eddie saw something in the man's stance that he didn't like. The Sarjeant looked worried. And given that the Sarjeant never worried, about anything . . . Eddie gave the Sarjeant-at-Arms his best hard look.

"All right. What happened?"

"The Matriarch wants you in the Sanctity," said the Sarjeant. "Immediately. Come with me."

Molly placed herself bodily between Eddie and the Sarjeant, stuck her fists on her hips, and glared right into his face.

"No. Eddie is tired, and you can't have him. He's worn himself out on family business, been very nearly eaten by a house, and he isn't going anywhere except to his room for a long lie-down. Feel free to argue with me, and I will feel free to fill your underwear with mutant rabid scorpions."

The Sarjeant didn't flinch. Eddie had to admire the man's poise, since they all knew she meant every word she said.

"It's all right, Molly," said Eddie. "I can rest later."

"No, it isn't all right!" Molly said fiercely. She turned to face him, and Eddie was shocked to see tears in her eyes. They might just have been tears of anger and frustration, but he didn't think so. Molly spoke directly to him, ignoring the Sarjeant, her words tumbling over each other in their hurry to get out. "How many times have your family nearly killed you in the past, working you to the bone and sending you straight back into danger when you were clearly exhausted? They ask too much of you, Eddie, and you always do it. I nearly lost you to Dr DOA and his poison! I won't lose you to your family! Whatever this is, it can wait."

"I'm sorry, Molly," said the Sarjeant, astonishing Eddie again, because the Sarjeant-at-Arms wasn't a man given to apologies. "This really can't wait. While you were gone, we had a visit from John Taylor. He insisted on speaking to the Matriarch."

Eddie and Molly looked at each other, then back at the Sarjeant.

"Walker was here?" said Eddie. "Inside the Hall?"

"Why?" said Molly.

"To complain about your actions," said the Sarjeant. "He spent some time talking privately with the Matriarch, negotiating over future Drood involvement with the Nightside. I'm told it did not go well."

Eddie sighed heavily. "Take me to the Matriarch." He turned to Molly. "I have to do this."

"Not on your own you don't," said Molly, glowering dangerously at the Sarjeant. "I'm going with you. No one gets to push you around except me."

"Your presence has also been requested," said the Sarjeant. "The Matriarch believes we're going to need your help."

Eddie looked to Molly. "Did we take a side turn on our way back and end up in some other reality?"

The Sarjeant led Eddie and Molly through the Hall to the Sanctity. The previous busy clamour, of Droods rushing back and forth on urgent missions, had descended into loud and fractious chaos. Everyone was standing around in small groups, talking animatedly about John Taylor's visit. Droods weren't used to dealing with outside interference in their own home. There was much in the way of raised voices, and even more waving of arms, as they argued over what it all meant. Some seemed shocked, some angry, and a few looked actually scared.

Having Walker show up in person was like having one of the Four Horsemen of the Apocalypse riding up to your door to ask for directions.

The Sarjeant-at-Arms did his best to follow his orders and get Eddie and Molly to the Sanctity as quickly as possible, but in the end he just couldn't stand it any longer. He slammed to a halt and raised his voice, demanding everyone's attention. That broke across even the loudest conversations, stopping them all dead. Because when the Sarjeant raised his voice, everyone listened. He was responsible for internal discipline in the family, and everyone knew he wasn't afraid to get his hands bloody doing it.

"You all have duties and responsibilities," the Sarjeant said coldly. "Get back to work. We are Droods; we don't do impressed. Go!"

The groups broke up as everyone ran for their lives. They didn't look any happier, or even particularly reassured, but they had been reminded of the importance of their tasks. And the even greater importance of not upsetting the Sarjeant-at-Arms. He waited a moment, to be sure everyone was moving, then set off for the Sanctity again. Eddie and Molly followed on behind. Eddie was frowning. He wasn't used to seeing Drood discipline break down so completely. But that was the Nightside for you. Everything about the long night undermined the way things were supposed to be.

And then the three of them stopped again, as a messenger from the Armoury appeared out of nowhere to plant himself right in front of the Sarjeant and block his way. For a moment Eddie thought the Sarjeant would just keep going and walk right over the man. The messenger was clearly one of the Armourer's lab assistants, in the usual burned and stained lab coat, with a long tear down one sleeve where something had got really annoyed with him. Tall and dark-skinned, his name turned out to be Romesh. Like all lab assistants, he was young, eager, cocky, and completely lacking in any self-preservation instincts. Or he wouldn't have got in the Sarjeant's way. Romesh smiled vaguely at the Sarjeant-at-Arms, then fixed his gaze on Eddie.

"The Armourer's compliments, and can they please have their psychic crown back."

"What, now?" said Eddie. "I'm on my way to see the Matriarch. I'll drop it off at the Armoury later."

Romesh shook his head quickly. "Maxwell and Victoria were most emphatic. They said they needed to examine the crown the moment you returned, to see what exposure to the long night had done to it."

There was never any point in arguing with a lab assistant; it genuinely never occurred to them that anything outside the Armoury mattered. Eddie reached up, found the crown on his head by touch, and took it off. The silver circlet appeared in his hands, and Eddie was surprised to discover several of the embedded crystals were seriously scorched and blackened.

"You see?" said Romesh, all but snatching the crown out of Eddie's hands. "Someone in the Nightside was doing their best to shut the crown down from the moment you arrived."

"How did anyone know to look for it?" said Molly, but Romesh was already hurrying off with his prize.

"That's a good question," said Eddie. "Any ideas, Cedric?"

"No," said the Sarjeant.

He set off for the Sanctity again, not even glancing back to check that Eddie and Molly were following him. Because it never occurred to him that they wouldn't be.

"Do you know why the Matriarch wants to see me?" Eddie asked after a while. "It can't be just to make my report; I already told her the basics the moment we were back in the grounds."

"The Matriarch has need of you," said the Sarjeant, staring straight ahead.

"What does she want me to do now?" said Eddie. "Given that my last mission went so well."

"You'll have to hear that from her," said the Sarjeant.

"She'd better not shout at Eddie," Molly said darkly. "Or I will rip out her vocal cords and tie them in knots."

"This isn't about what just happened in the Nightside," said the Sarjeant. "Not everything is about you. The Matriarch has an important decision to make, and she values your opinion. Both of you."

Eddie and Molly looked at each other.

"Well," said Molly, "that's a first. Things must really be bad."

"They are," said the Sarjeant.

"Are we back to what you were talking about earlier?" Eddie said carefully. "The decision you weren't sure she should make?"

"You had your chance to stop her," said the Sarjeant. "That time is past. She has already made the decision, for good or ill. All that remains now is how best to carry it out."

"What are you two talking about?" said Molly.

"War," said Eddie. "The Matriarch is going to declare war on the Nightside."

"What?" Molly glared at both of them. "Why the hell would she want to do that?"

"To stop the long night before it overruns us all," said the Sarjeant.

"But that's not going to happen!" said Molly. "We'll find a way to stop it."

"This is one way to stop it," said the Sarjeant. "And to make sure it can never happen again."

"This is crazy!" said Molly. "Tell him, Eddie!"

"Does the Matriarch have a plan?" Eddie asked the Sarjeant.

"The Matriarch always has a plan," said the Sarjeant.

"You say that like it's a good thing," said Molly.

"The family needs more information on exactly what is going on in the Nightside," said the Sarjeant. "We also need to know what the world's other secret organisations know about that. I think she plans to contact them and demand some answers."

"Oh, that can only go well," said Eddie.

"Eddie . . ." said Molly. "War? Really?"

"It's what the family is for," said the Sarjeant. "When all else fails."

The three of them strode back into the Sanctity, and it was as though they'd never been away. The full Council was there again, attending the Matriarch. William the Librarian and his wife, the telepath Ammonia Vom Acht, sitting side by side and holding hands. Though given the deeply worried looks on their faces, Eddie had to wonder which of them was supporting the other. The Librarian looked rather more ruffled and out of sorts than the last time, no doubt the result of being dragged back from the Library without enough time to prepare his public face. Ammonia looked ready to bite someone's head off, but then, she usually did. The fact that she was holding her peace for the moment was a good sign; it showed she was making an effort, for her husband's sake. Ammonia could get very protective when she thought her husband's mental stability was being threatened. Particularly by his own family.

The Armourer Maxwell and Victoria were also sitting together, holding hands so tightly their knuckles had gone white. Eddie's first thought was to wonder who was looking at his psychic crown if they were here, then he frowned as he took in the fresh chemical stains and burns on the front of Maxwell's lab coat, and the way someone else's blood was dripping off Victoria's sleeve. Neither event was particularly unusual where the Armoury was concerned, but Eddie was surprised to see such obvious evidence of Maxwell and Victoria being hands-on. They usually had enough sense to delegate the rough stuff.

All four members of the advisory Council avoided Eddie's and Molly's eyes as they sat down facing the Matriarch again. Eddie sat stiffly, arms folded, studying the Matriarch thoughtfully. Molly sat down hard and glared at everyone. The Sarjeant-at-Arms took up his usual position, standing at the Matriarch's shoulder. Ready to do whatever was required of him.

Eddie looked at the empty table-top in front of the Matriarch and raised an eyebrow.

"What happened to all the comm gear, Maggie?"

"I didn't want to be disturbed during these discussions," said the Matriarch.

Her voice was calm and composed, her gaze cold and focused. And from the way she carefully didn't rise to Eddie's bait of using her name, he thought he'd better stick his oar in first, before she started ordering him to do things he just knew he wasn't going to approve of.

"I know you said not to use my armour in the Nightside, but I didn't have any choice."

"I don't care about that," said the Matriarch.

"You don't?" said Eddie.

"I approve and validate all your actions in the long night," said the Matriarch, almost in passing. "Other, and far more important, matters concern us now."

"Are we talking about John Taylor's visit?" said Eddie. "I can't believe he actually came all the way here just to complain about me."

"And me!" said Molly, determined not to be left out of anything.

"That was just one of the things we talked about," said the Matriarch. "We were more concerned with the on-going relationship between the Droods and the Nightside. And which of us has responsibility for enforcing the long night's boundaries. Unfortunately, a compromise turned out not to be possible. Walker has ordered the family to stay out of the Nightside, under any circumstances, on threat of dire penalties."

"He threatened the family," said the Sarjeant.

"He wouldn't do that!" said Molly.

"Wouldn't he?" said Eddie.

Molly stopped to think about it, then scowled reluctantly. "Well . . . he might. If he was ordered to by the Authorities. He's not the free agent I used to know, ready to defy anyone to look after people who couldn't protect themselves. He's Walker now, and that comes with duties and responsibilities as well as power. I told him not to take the job."

"A Walker, inside Drood Hall," said the Sarjeant. "Such a thing has never happened before, in all the family's history."

Eddie didn't say anything, but he remembered meeting the previous Walker in the Winter Hall, that strange version of his home he'd briefly been trapped in, during his time in Limbo. That Walker was supposed to have been the elf Puck, under a glamour, but it had never been confirmed. Eddie decided not to raise the point. The situation was complicated enough as it was.

"Eddie!" the Matriarch said sharply. "Are you still with us?"

"Just considering the implications," Eddie said smoothly.

"You worked with Walker during the Great Spy Game, to take down the Independent Agent . . ."

Eddie was shaking his head before she'd finished. "That was the previous Walker. He's been dead for some time now. I barely know John Taylor."

Molly looked at him. "You once told me you worked with him on a few cases, back in the day."

"That was when he was just a private eye," said Eddie. "And not in the Nightside. You know the man better than I do."

Everyone looked to Molly, and she shrugged uncomfortably. "I know John . . . but we were never close. We just had a lot of enemies in common."

"Did you work with him?" said the Sarjeant.

"Sometimes," said Molly. "Other times, we were on opposite sides. This was back before I got involved with Eddie and calmed down a lot." She glared around the room, daring anyone to comment. No one said anything, and she continued, "John's a good man, in his own way. All right, his mother was a Biblical Myth, and he has been known to work both sides of the street to get the job done, and he is married to a psychopathic bounty-hunter . . . but he's an honourable man. Mostly. He's done a lot to protect the whole of Humanity, not just the Nightside."

"Really?" said the Matriarch. "My understanding was that he spent most of his life as a down-at-heel private eye, taking charity cases from the previous Walker."

"Then you heard wrong," said Molly.

"John Taylor was never just a private investigator," said the Sarjeant. "He had a destiny. Everyone in the Nightside knew that even if they didn't know what. There were some rumours that he would bring about the end of everything. How do you think he acquired such a worrying reputation?"

The Matriarch fixed him with a cold glare. "You never told me any of this before."

"It wasn't relevant before," said the Sarjeant.

"Amazing what you can pick up, drinking in Strangefellows," murmured Eddie.

The Matriarch looked at the Sarjeant, to see if he had anything more to say, and when he didn't, she made an impatient noise.

"We will talk more about this later, Sarjeant."

"Of course," said the Sarjeant. He turned his full attention on Molly. "Is there anything else you can tell us about John Taylor?"

"You really don't want to cross him," said Molly. "He's like the Droods. He always wins."

"We need to talk about the Wulfshead," said the Matriarch. "I'm still not clear as to why the Club was targeted during the Nightside's expansion. Given that it was known to be a haven for some very significant people, whoever is behind the expansion must have known attacking the Club would attract attention. Was there perhaps someone in the Club who might have known something?"

"We found a lot of dead people inside the Wulfshead," said Eddie. "But the bodies were hard to identify. The house had been feeding on them . . ." He paused as he remembered, then made himself continue. He was a field agent. He'd seen worse. "We did find Monkton Farley, the consulting detective. Or what was left of him. Maybe he discovered something, on one of his cases."

"He never reached out to us, through any of his usual contacts," said the Matriarch.

Eddie looked at her. "I didn't know he had any contacts with the family."

"Monkton Farley was one of our secret informants," said the Sarjeant. "Keeping us up to date on what was happening in the murkier quarters of the hidden world. His way of doing service, to earn himself a place in the family."

"Of course; he was one of James' sons," said William. "One of the Grey Bastards."

"He was family," said the Matriarch. "That makes this personal. He will be avenged."

"Have you heard anything from the Management yet?" Molly said pointedly. "The Wulfshead was their Club."

"Not a word," said the Sarjeant. "Their continued silence is worrying. We have to consider the possibility that whoever is behind all of this may have targeted the Management and silenced them, before the Club was attacked."

"Why would they do that?" said Eddie.

"Perhaps the Management knew something," said the Sarjeant, "that we couldn't be allowed to find out."

"There's no doubt everything that's happened was carefully planned," said the Matriarch. "All we've been doing is reacting to things as they happen. That has to stop. We need to take the advantage, regain control of events."

"But we can't be sure which actions would be most useful till we have a better idea of what's really going on in the Nightside," said the Sarjeant.

"That's why we need you, Eddie," said the Matriarch. "And you, Molly. To go back into the Nightside, under-cover, and find out as much as you can."

Eddie and Molly looked at each other, then around the room. Everyone else looked steadily back at them. Eddie stared steadily at the Sarjeant-at-Arms.

"You really think this is a good idea? Going back in, after Walker told us to stay out?"

"They won't be expecting that," said the Sarjeant.

"Sneaking in for a quick look around is one thing," said Eddie. "Operating as a Drood agent would mean breaking the Pacts and Agreements. Do we really want to do that, after all these years?"

"The Pacts may have served a purpose once," said the Matriarch, "but I'm not sure that's true any longer. Walker is only concerned with the security of the Nightside; I have a larger responsibility."

"It's still a hell of a risk," said Eddie. "Do we have the right to break the ancient Agreements?"

"We exist to defend Humanity," said the Sarjeant. "All of it, not just the rights and privileges of one small group. Yes, it is a risk. But, *Anything, for the family.*"

There was a long pause as everyone thought about that.

"Who set up these Pacts and Agreements, originally?" Molly asked.

"It was a very long time ago," said the Matriarch. "Back at the founding of the family, in the time of the Druids. No records survive from that time."

"Actually . . ." said William, clearing his throat carefully, "that may not be entirely accurate, Matriarch."

The whole room was staring at him now. The Matriarch fixed the Librarian with a stern commanding gaze.

"I was told there were no such records."

"That was always my understanding too," said the Sarjeant-at-Arms, adding his cold stare. "I should have been informed, for security reasons."

"What would you have done?" said William. "Put an armed guard on them? You know as well as I do, Cedric, most of the really old books in the Old Library are perfectly capable of looking after themselves. These particular records were lost to the family for centuries, till Eddie found the Old Library and returned it to us. The book in question is so ancient its words are etched on bronze sheets, in an odd mixture of Latin, Greek, and eccentric Coptic."

"All dead languages," said the Sarjeant.

"Well, quite," said William. "It's our original copy of the Pacts and Agreements, setting out all the details and obligations on both sides. I found it quite by accident while looking for something else. Isn't that always the way? The book was locked inside a chest wrapped in glowing chains and protected by a quite spectacularly nasty curse."

"A chest you just happened to open?" said Molly.

William grinned suddenly. "No one keeps secrets from me in my Library. I never said anything about the book before because its existence was supposed to remain secret."

"You should have told someone!" said the Sarjeant. "What if something had happened to you?"

"I did tell someone," said William. "I told my old assistant, Raphael. Not what was in the book, just where it was. Of course he turned out to be an Immortal spy . . . So after he was killed, I told my new assistant, Ioreth.

And Ammonia, of course, after we were married. Because a man shouldn't try to keep secrets from his wife. Especially if she's a telepath. Am I wandering? It feels like I'm wandering . . ."

"You're doing very well, dear," said Ammonia. And then she glowered around the room, daring anyone to contradict her.

"But why did this book have to be kept so secret?" said Eddie. "Something so important to the whole family?"

"Because the personage who first dictated the Pacts and Agreements wanted it that way," said William.

"Who?" Molly said loudly. "Who are we talking about, so important and powerful in their own right, that they could lay down the law to the Droods and the Nightside?"

"Gaea, of course," said William. "Mother Earth. The living embodiment of the entire world just appeared in the Old Library one day, not long after I discovered the book. I almost had a coronary. Though she turned out to be very nice. Quite charming and delightful, in fact . . ." He realised Ammonia was looking at him coldly, and hurried on. "Gaea told me she put the original deal together to keep the Droods and the Nightside apart. The Droods hadn't been around long at that point, but they had already made it clear they were determined to impose order and security on the hidden world. Gaea said it was important that the Nightside should exist and remain separate. And that she didn't so much arrange a deal as bang heads together on both sides till everyone agreed to play nicely."

"Do we know who agreed to this deal?" said Molly. "Which people, in the Droods and the Nightside?"

"No names are recorded anywhere," said William. "I'm guessing no one wanted to take the blame." He paused, then smiled apologetically. "Gaea spent some time talking with me, about a great many things . . . but I really don't remember most of them. I wasn't at my best, back then. Not long out of the asylum, still getting used to being around sane people . . . It had been a long time since I was part of the family . . ."

He stopped, pressing his lips together to keep his mouth from quivering. Ammonia took hold of both his hands and held them firmly.

"You'd been through a lot," said Eddie. "You hardly talked to anyone, back then."

"I always got on better with books, than people," said William. He smiled at Ammonia. "Till I met you, of course. So, I don't remember most of what Gaea had to say. Which is a pity because I'm sure it was all very interesting and probably important. But I do remember her being very firm, that the Nightside had a purpose as well as a function. She also told me to keep the book's existence a secret, so I did." He sighed briefly. "I suppose it's time to get the book out again and work on a translation. So we can all be sure exactly what it says."

"Gaea doesn't do personal appearances any more," Molly said thoughtfully. "She retired from her office and lives a simple human life far away from everyone. No one bothers her. I mean, would you?"

Eddie remembered talking to Gaea not that long ago, inside the Castle Inconnu of the London Knights. She was their oracle, the Lady of the Lake. Along with her visit to William, that suggested Gaea still took some interest in worldly matters. Eddie decided not to say anything about that, for the moment.

"What matters now is that Gaea must have given up much of her power when she gave up her office," said the Matriarch. "So she's no longer in a position to object to anything we decide to do."

"And what have you decided to do?" said Eddie.

"I'm still working on it," the Matriarch said steadily. "I need to be sure the family is ready and prepared to do whatever may prove necessary. The long night cannot be allowed to continue to expand, till it covers the entire world; and we can't allow anything or anyone to stop us doing whatever is necessary to prevent that. The Pacts and Agreements were set in place to enforce a status quo that no longer exists."

It won't, if we go to war, thought Eddie, but he didn't say it.

The Matriarch turned to the Armourer. "Maxwell, Victoria, I need you and your people working full out to equip every member of this family with all the weapons and devices you have."

Maxwell and Victoria looked at each other. Eddie knew that look. It was the *Who's going to tell her she can't have what she wants* look. In the end, Maxwell bit the bullet.

"Mass production is not something we do, Matriarch. Like all the Armourers before us, we mostly produce prototypes."

"Which we then give to field agents, to test under practical conditions," said Vicky.

"Till they break or stop working."

"Which is, unfortunately, often the case."

"We're always working to improve things," said Max, defensively.

"Of course we are," said Vicky. "You tell her, dear."

"I am telling her, dear. You must understand, Matriarch, a lot of good ideas turn out to be merely good ideas."

"Suddenly, much becomes clear," said Eddie. "I always wondered why I had to return all my weapons and gadgets to the Armoury every time I returned from a mission. Why I had to write all those long reports on how everything worked in the field. And why I kept being given new toys for every new mission."

"Like all secret organisations, we are part of an arms race," said Max.

"With our enemies and with each other," said Vicky.

"We always have to be seen to be at the very top of our game," said Max.

"We have to be cutting edge, to maintain our profile," said Vicky.

"The rest of the time, we put all our effort into maintaining and upgrading the things that do work," said Max.

"Like the computers, the scanners, the defences and protections," said Vicky.

"So everything I was ever given . . . was never really reliable?" said Eddie.

"You had your armour," said Max.

"That's all a Drood ever really needs," said Vicky.

The Matriarch looked speechlessly at the Armourer, then turned to glare at the Sarjeant-at-Arms.

"Did you know about this?"

"Of course," said the Sarjeant. "The Armourer reports directly to me, as head of security."

"Why was I never told?" said the Matriarch.

"Most Matriarchs work it out for themselves," said the Sarjeant. "And then keep it to themselves, for the good of the family. Which is what I assumed you were doing."

"You can rely on us to ensure everything that comes out of the Armoury is the very latest thing," said Max.

"And that no one else will have anything quite like it," said Vicky.

"Keeping the enemy off balance and on their toes is part of the job," said Max.

"And we're very good at that," said Vicky.

"Everything we produce works, for a while."

"And when they stop working, there's always something new and different waiting to replace it."

"Have you ever come up with anything that worked and kept working?" said Eddie.

"Of course!" said Max. "Some things become standard items, like the Colt Repeater."

"Or the medical-repair blobs, or the portable doors," said Vicky.

"And some Armourers produce genuine wild cards," said Max. "Like Jack's racing Bentley that can go sideways through Space and Time, or the dimensional engine Alpha Red Alpha."

"Things we're still trying to understand and replicate, years later," said Vicky.

"So the Armoury doesn't really have an armoury of weapons?" said Molly.

"It's all the Matriarchs' fault!" Max said loudly. "Always demanding new and better toys!"

"There's never enough time to spend working on any one idea, for all the years of careful development it would take to perfect it," said Vicky.

"We don't have years!" said the Matriarch.

"We know!" said Max.

"That's why we keep producing prototypes," said Vicky.

"You can have everything we've got," said Max.

"Because we never throw anything away," said Vicky.

"And they'll work, for as long as they work."

"But you're still better off relying on the armour."

"Because the armour always works," said Max.

"Hold it," said Molly. "We need to talk about the world-sized elephant in the Sanctity. What if Gaea decides she's not happy to see her personal Pacts and Agreements being broken? What if she decides to come out of retirement and stop you? By force, if necessary? You can't fight Mother Nature."

"She's been away too long," said the Sarjeant. "The better part of her has been asleep for millennia."

"And if she does come back," said the Matriarch, "we have the forbidden weapons of the Armageddon Codex."

"You can't use those!" said William, sitting bolt upright for the first time. "They're only for when reality itself is under threat!"

"Isn't it?" said the Matriarch. "What else would you call the rise of the long night?"

There was a long pause, as everyone thought about that. Molly elbowed Eddie sharply in the ribs and glared at him. He knew she wanted him to challenge the Matriarch over what she intended to do, like the Sarjeant wanted, but Eddie still wasn't sure. The Matriarch was right, in that the Nightside couldn't be allowed to extend its boundaries indefinitely. That had to be stopped. By going to war, if necessary. But the forbidden weapons? He once persuaded the old Armourer to open up the Armageddon Codex for him, and the terrible things he saw in there still haunted him.

The Sarjeant-at-Arms cleared his throat, and everyone turned to look at him.

"Gaea is not who or what she was," he said carefully. "We only have to look at the state of the world today to see that."

"You ready to bet the farm?" said Molly.

"Yes," said the Matriarch. "Anything, for the family. For Humanity. Gaea may have been our Mother Earth once, but we've grown up since then."

"Given the state of the world today, I'm not so sure that's a good thing," said Molly.

"The point is," the Matriarch said heavily, "we will do whatever we have to, and use whatever weapons we have to, in order to put the world right again. To protect it from the threat of the long night. That is why the family Armourers created the forbidden weapons . . ."

She broke off as the Sarjeant cleared his throat again.

"Actually, Matriarch . . . Nothing in the Armageddon Codex was created by us. We . . . acquired the forbidden weapons down the centuries, picking them up here and there."

"And where, exactly, did we acquire these weapons?" said Eddie. "Or should that be, who did we steal them from?"

"This seems to be a day for questions no one ever thought to ask before," said the Matriarch. "Well, Sarjeant? Armourer? Librarian?"

There was a long pause.

"That information was suppressed long ago," William said finally. "Of course, there are still a great many books in the Old Library still waiting to be catalogued, never mind read. It's always possible the knowledge is there. Somewhere."

"It doesn't matter," said the Sarjeant. "They're ours now."

"But are we really ready to use them?" said Eddie.

"Only in self-defence," said the Matriarch.

"Where have I heard that before?" said Eddie.

"Are you questioning my authority?" said the Matriarch.

"Of course," said Eddie. "That's what I do. That's why you wanted me here."

The Matriarch surprised everyone then with a brief smile. "Exactly. I can always rely on you to tell me what I need to hear, whether I want to hear it or not. You are the sounding-board I test my ideas against, to see if they have value. But at the end of the day, Eddie . . . I make the decisions for this family. Not you. Cross that line, and I will have the Sarjeant-at-Arms arrest you."

Eddie looked thoughtfully at the Sarjeant. "Like to see you try that, Cedric."

"Right," said Molly, grinning unpleasantly.

"I lead this family," said the Matriarch.

"Of course you do," said Eddie. And then he thought, but didn't say, *Right up to the point where I decide to take it away from you.*

The Matriarch accepted his words at face-value and smiled around the room, in a good mood again. "Now, you're probably wondering why I summoned you all here. I have decided to call a Summit Meeting, for all the more important secret organisations. So we can discuss possible combined actions against this mutual threat."

"That's your big plan?" said Molly. "To gang up on the Nightside?"

"The sooner we put an end to this situation, the less damage and loss of life there will be, on both sides." The Matriarch looked challengingly around the room. "No one wants a long war."

War, thought Eddie. *She finally used the word* war. He caught the Sarjeant-at-Arms looking at him, but he still didn't know what to say for the best. So he said nothing.

"We don't have time for the usual formalities," said the Matriarch. "All the diplomatic courtesies and endless arguments over acceptable neutral ground. And there's always the possibility of a breach in security. We can't have anyone else knowing about this."

"Because we don't want people knowing we couldn't do this on our own and had to beg for help?" said Eddie. "Or because we don't want certain groups to know the kind of sneaky deals we make behind their backs?"

"It's not about help, or deals," said the Matriarch. "We just need to do this as quickly and efficiently as possible."

"Right," said Molly. Packing a world of sarcasm into one drawn-out word.

The Matriarch turned to Ammonia Vom Acht. "I need you to make telepathic contact with the proper representatives of each group, so we can talk."

"They're not going to like that," said Ammonia. "It'll mean breaking through their protections. And I'm not comfortable with their knowing I can do that."

"Needs must when the devil drives, my dear," said William. "Even if she is just an ex-gardener with a power complex. Do it, Ammonia. We need to know where we stand with the other organisations before we start anything."

"For you, William," said Ammonia.

Both of them glowered at the Matriarch, but she just stared impassively back. Ammonia frowned, concentrating. A strange new tension filled the air, an almost overwhelming sense of Ammonia's presence. As though she were growing, looming over them, filling the chamber . . . and then suddenly it was gone. Ammonia scowled and shook her head slowly.

"They've been upgrading their defences again. I could break through, but there's no telling how much time that would take." She turned to Eddie. "I'm going to need the Merlin Glass, to use as a focusing agent."

Eddie reluctantly took out the hand-mirror and passed it to Ammonia. She accepted it, then pulled a face.

"If you could only feel the sticky psychic imprints from all the people who've used this thing in the past, you'd never touch it again. I'm going to have to scrub my psyche down with wire wool afterwards."

She shook the Glass out to door size, and it leapt from her hand to hang on the air before her. Instead of showing her reflection, the Glass was full of buzzing static. Ammonia scowled at it, and the Glass slowly cleared to reveal an interior view of Castle Inconnu, home to the London Knights. It looked like a fairy-tale castle, with walls of warm yellow stone, bubbling fountains in huge galleries, and great, sweeping stairways. And then that view was suddenly swept aside, replaced by a full-bodied woman in a long gown of shimmering white samite. Her face was handsome rather than pretty, topped with golden hair tied in old-fashioned braids. She glared out of the Glass at Ammonia.

"I should have known. Only you would have the brass balls to punch right through our defences. What do you want, Ammonia?"

"Allow me to present the London Knights' foremost telepath, witch, and on-going mystery," said Ammonia. "Vivienne de Tourney. Also and more properly known as Vivienne La Fae."

Eddie looked sharply at Ammonia. "Hold it. Any relation to Morgana La Fae, the ancient sorceress who was, till very recently, imprisoned in the Merlin Glass?"

"Depends on who you talk to," said Ammonia. "Some say this is Morgana's sister. Some say she's just a distant descendant, and others say she only uses the name to mess with people's heads. Other people say other things. No one knows the truth except Vivienne; and she's not telling."

"Because it's no one else's business," said Vivienne. "What do you want, Ammonia? I'm right in the middle of breaking a young Knight's spirit, and he's loving every moment of it."

The Matriarch launched into a terse explanation of the Droods' position over the expanded Nightside. Vivienne raised a hand before the Matriarch was even half-way through.

"We already know about that. And take it from me, the London Knights will not become involved in any action that includes the Droods."

"Perhaps I should speak to Grand Master Kae," said the Matriarch.

"I'm here to protect Kae from people like you," said Vivienne. "The London Knights may be on speaking terms with the Droods these days, but some of us still remember when we were at war. We will never turn our backs on you again."

"But the Nightside . . ." said the Matriarch.

"We already have people investigating what's going on in the long night," said Vivienne. "And we'll make our own decisions about what needs doing." She deliberately turned away from the Matriarch to scowl at Ammonia. "This conversation is at an end. Don't ever disturb me like this again, or I will fill your subconscious with psychic tapeworms."

Vivienne de Tourney disappeared from the Merlin Glass, and the buzzing static returned. Almost with a sense of relief. Ammonia looked at the Matriarch.

"On the whole, that went as well as could be expected. Do you want me to carry on? It's not going to get any better."

"Continue," the Matriarch said steadily. "I need to talk to the Soul-hunters."

"Them?" said Molly. "Why the hell would you want to talk to them? They're crazy! You have to be crazy to get into the Soulhunters. In fact, you'd have to be crazy to want to get in."

"But they know things no one else knows," said the Matriarch. "Do it, Ammonia."

The telepath shrugged and concentrated on the Merlin Glass again. The static swayed this way and that, as though meeting resistance, before clearing to reveal a tall and unhealthily slender individual in a pale laven-der suit with padded shoulders. He turned unhurriedly to study the Drood Council, then struck a studiedly louche pose. The front of his jacket hung open to reveal he wasn't wearing a shirt, just a black string tie. His skin was grey and looked like it could use a good scrub down with a wire brush. His face was sunken and hollowed, as though consumed by spiritual fires, and his eyes were disturbingly knowing. His smile didn't fool anyone. He knew that and didn't give a damn.

"Well, well, how nice. Good to see you . . . good to see anyone, really. It's not often we have visitors. I do love to tell people things they need to know, but they never thank me afterwards. Of course, when you've stared reality in the face and French kissed her like your favourite sister, it's bound to change the way you see things."

"Oh hell," said Molly. "We've got Demonbane."

The Soulhunter turned his disquieting gaze on her. "Hello, Molly! How nice to see you again, sweetie."

"I was never your sweetie!" Molly said loudly.

Demonbane pouted, an expression no more real than his smile. "That's not what you said in the sewers under Paris."

"Talk to me, Soulhunter," said the Matriarch.

Demonbane favoured her with his meaningless smile and a patently insincere bow. "Mother Drood! Well, well, I am honoured! What can I do for the illustrious Drood family? Do you want to know the true meaning of life and death, or what goes walking between the stars we can't see and lusts after human souls? Or would you like me to tell you the real reason why you should be afraid of the dark?"

The Matriarch started her speech again, but the Soulhunter interrupted her before she was even well underway.

"We know about that, and we don't care. We have more important things to worry about. And I think it's only fair to say, we'd rather bite our own heads off than play nicely with the Droods. We do have standards. Bye-bye, everybody."

"No!" said the Matriarch. "You need to listen to me!"

"Kiss my stigmata," said Demonbane.

And just like that, he was gone. The buzzing static returned, with a palpable sense of wishing it had never gone away. Ammonia shook her head hard, as though trying to dislodge something.

"Sometimes I wonder if they're even human any more, after everything they've seen . . . Who do you want me to try next?"

Before the Matriarch could say anything, the static was blasted out of the Merlin Glass and replaced by Old Father Time, in all his terrible authority. The Matriarch looked quickly at Ammonia.

"Why is he here? I didn't tell you to contact him!"

"That is the personification of Time itself, a living legend of Shadows Fall," said Ammonia. "He can do whatever he feels like doing, and I'm not going to be the one to tell him he can't. That isn't even what he really looks like. It's just a human shape he puts on to interact with us, like a hand inside a glove puppet. Because the human mind couldn't cope with any more than that. You talk to him. Just looking at him makes my mind hurt."

Old Father Time appeared to be an old man with shoulder-length white hair, a haughty face, and penetrating eyes. Dressed to the height of Victorian fashion, he gripped the lapels of his jacket with both hands and started talking before the Matriarch could even open her mouth.

"Of course you weren't going to summon me," he said testily. "I come when I'm needed, not where I'm wanted. It simplifies things. And I would think even the Droods would have more sense than to bother Shadows

Fall. But I know about the Nightside, and I know what you're planning. I see everything. The whole of the chronoflow is my domain."

Molly looked at Eddie, and he gave her a *Don't ask me* look. He studied Old Father Time with great interest, fascinated to see one of the great powers and enigmas of Shadows Fall. The town where legends went to die when the world stopped believing in them. Only sometimes, they didn't die . . .

"I know what's going to happen," said Old Father Time. "And no, you can't stop it. Because you're part of it. No one in Shadows Fall will help or hinder you because this is your fate, your destiny." He shook his leonine head sadly. "So arrogant, so sure of yourselves, so ready to impose your authority on others . . . You will be the horror in the long night, the nightmare in the Nightside. You will come right to the edge of a terrible abyss, and jump anyway. Because you are . . . what you are. But in the end, there is still a faint chance, still a slender hope . . . If one good man can do the right thing."

He disappeared from the Merlin Glass, and the return of the buzzing static came as a relief. It was like being lectured by God's stand-in.

"So," said the Matriarch. "It would appear we can forget about any assistance from Shadows Fall."

"Really?" said Eddie. "That's what you got, from what he just said? Didn't you listen? We are going to be the terrible thing that everyone in the Nightside is so afraid of!"

"Which is as it should be," said the Sarjeant-at-Arms. "It's always been part of our job description, to be scarier than the threats we face."

"Exactly," said the Matriarch.

Eddie looked to Molly. "You talk to her. She's not listening to me."

"If you can't get through to her, I don't know what you expect me to do," said Molly. "I could knock her down, sit on her, and scream in her ear; and she still wouldn't listen to me."

"Hush, Molly," said the Matriarch.

"See?" said Molly.

"Ammonia," said the Matriarch. "I want to talk to the Carnacki Institute."

"The Ghost Finders?" said Eddie. "What can they do to help?"

"They have sources in realms even we can't reach," said the Matriarch. "And unlike the Soulhunters, it hasn't driven them crazy."

The Merlin Glass cleared abruptly, to show the new head of the Carnacki Institute sitting at his desk, looking straight at the Matriarch. JC Chance looked perfectly splendid in his expertly cut ice-cream-white suit, with his handsome face, rock-star mane of long black hair, and very dark sun-glasses. He looked at the Matriarch as though he could see right through her and shook his head firmly.

"No."

"You don't even know what I was about to ask," said the Matriarch.

"It doesn't matter," said JC. "Word has got around as to what you're intending to do, and you are not dragging us in with you."

"You're very well informed, for a company of ghost chasers," said the Sarjeant.

"We have more sense than to get involved with the Nightside's problems," said JC, still giving his whole attention to the Matriarch. "The long night goes its own way and always has, right back to its creation. Some say that's the whole point. Nothing any of us can do will make any difference."

"Speak for yourself," said the Sarjeant.

"I just did," said JC.

"Who have you been talking to about this?" said the Matriarch.

"The dead," said JC, quite calmly. "We talk to them all the time, in our line of work. Of course, you can't trust a lot of what they have to say. The dead always have their own agenda." He paused, to study the Matriarch thoughtfully through his very dark sun-glasses. "How desperate must you be, that you had to come to us for help?"

"You can't sit this out," the Matriarchy said forcefully. "If we don't stop the Nightside from expanding, the long night will come for you too."

"Operating in the dark on a regular basis teaches you one thing above all others," said JC. "You have to have a little faith."

"What if I ordered you to help us?" said the Matriarch. "Do you really think you can defy Drood authority?"

JC took off his sun-glasses. His golden eyes burned with a fierce unearthly light.

"Don't contact us again," said JC Chance.

He disappeared from the Glass. The Matriarch turned to Ammonia.

"Bring him back! I wasn't finished!"

"I didn't break contact," said Ammonia. "He did. Which is . . . interesting. Because a simple Ghost Finder shouldn't be able to do that."

Molly looked at Eddie. "What was wrong with his eyes?"

"I don't know," said Eddie. "But I think I'd pay good money not to have to see them again."

"Get me the Department of Uncanny," the Matriarch said to Ammonia. "As the Government's office for dealing with the weird and unnatural, they won't be allowed to hide under the bed."

But when Ammonia concentrated on the Merlin Glass, nothing happened. She couldn't get through. It was no different when she tried to contact the Spawn of Frankenstein.

"Word has got around," Ammonia said flatly. "They've reinforced their barriers and battened down the hatches. It'll be the same with everyone now. I can't break through without endangering them and myself. Which I'm not going to risk just for a conversation we can all predict anyway. We're on our own."

"They may be a bunch of wimps," said Molly. "But they're not stupid."

Ammonia shut down the Merlin Glass and gave the hand-mirror back to Eddie. He slipped it into his pocket dimension without saying anything, but he was thinking hard. He hadn't known the Glass could be used to break through other people's protections.

"Traitors! Cowards!" The Matriarch looked like she was going to explode. Her face had gone a dangerous shade of purple, and she slammed her fists down on the table as she glared at everyone. "Those damned fools would let the world be destroyed rather than give up their own petty territories! Because some ideas are just too big for them. This . . . This is why the Droods exist! To do the big necessary things that no one else has the guts to do!"

No one said anything. The Matriarch took a deep breath, unclenched her fists, and sat back in her chair. When she spoke again, she sounded her usual cool and composed self.

"We'll deal with them later. For now . . . we need more information. Eddie, Molly: I'm sorry, but I don't see any other way. Before I can make a final decision on the best course to take, I must know more about what's happening inside the Nightside. You have to go back."

"Why does it have to be us?" said Molly, before Eddie could say anything. She glared defiantly at the Matriarch. "Eddie's in no fit state to do this, and you know it! He nearly died because of Dr DOA. You promised him a long break."

"Yes," said the Matriarch. "I did. I'm sorry, Molly, but I can't trust anyone else with this mission."

"Even though my last little trip didn't exactly go to plan?" said Eddie. "I'm the reason Walker paid his first-ever visit to Drood Hall."

"You are the only agents I can send who stand a good chance of going unrecognised," said the Matriarch. "Because you both have well-established cover identities that the Nightside will accept. Shaman Bond and Roxie Hazzard."

Eddie and Molly looked at each other.

"She may be a pain, but she has a point," said Eddie. "Shaman has a reputation for turning up anywhere, and you've spent a lot of time in the Nightside as Roxie."

"You honestly think this is a good idea?" said Molly.

"We need more information," said Eddie.

"That's not what I asked," said Molly.

"I know," said Eddie.

And he thought, but didn't say: *As long as it's us getting the information, we can decide how much of it to share with the Matriarch.*

"Walker will have alerted his people to watch for any evidence of Drood actions," said the Sarjeant. "So you really can't use your armour this time, Eddie. Under any circumstances. Walker must not know you're there."

Eddie looked at the Armourer. "Any new toys on offer, to help us?"

"Against the kind of things you'll be facing in the Nightside?" said Max.

"We provide guns and gadgets, not miracles," said Vicky.

"Probably not a good idea to carry anything into the Nightside that could identify you as Drood agents," said the Sarjeant.

"What about his torc?" said Molly. "You already said it wouldn't be enough on its own; that's why you gave him the psychic crown."

Eddie sat up straight. "I am not going into the Nightside without my torc. I don't do suicide missions."

"No one is asking you to," said the Matriarch. "The crown was just insurance. I have faith in the torc to keep your true identity obscured, and so should you."

"Ethel?" said Eddie.

Her calm and reassuring voice issued from the air right in front of him. "I designed the torcs to hide this family from all prying eyes, as requested. It's strange matter, like your armour; weird stuff I brought with me from my own dimension. I'd back it against anything in this world. But, this is the Nightside we're talking about, which is very definitely not of this world . . . So, basically, all bets are off."

"Terrific," said Eddie.

"You can't expect us to fool John Taylor," said Molly. "He's sneaky."

"We're sneakier," the Sarjeant-at-Arms said calmly. "And we've been at this a lot longer than he has. I'll have half-a-dozen field agents do loud and threatening things right on the borders of the Nightside. That should hold his attention long enough for you to get in without being noticed. After that, you're on your own."

"No change there," said Molly. She looked steadily at Eddie. "You don't have to do this if you don't want to."

"I have to," said Eddie.

"I swear, if you say *Anything, for the family*, I will punch you out, and everyone else in this room." Molly sighed heavily and scowled at the Matriarch. "What are we supposed to be looking for, exactly?"

"Somebody must know something," the Matriarch said steadily. "I need to know why the Nightside has broken its borders and who is behind it. You are authorised to buy this information, make any deal necessary; or beat it out of people. I don't care. But I have to know."

"You'd feel right at home in the Nightside," said Molly.

The Matriarch turned her attention to the Armourer. "While Eddie and Molly are gone, I want everyone in the Armoury focused on coming up with something that will stop the Nightside from expanding any farther."

"That could take years!" said Max.

"Decades!" said Vicky.

"The Nightside was created by Lilith!" said Max. "A being so old and so powerful, her very existence can only be described in terms of parables."

"No one knows how or why she did it," said Vicky.

"No one even knows for sure where or when the Nightside really is."

"We don't know how the boundaries were put in place or what maintains them."

"And Lilith . . . is John Taylor's mother," said Max.

"We don't do miracles," said Vicky. "But she did."

The Armourer stared jointly at the Matriarch with the closest Eddie had ever seen to open mutiny.

"We don't know anything that matters about the Nightside," said Max.

"Nobody does," said Vicky.

"Then you'd better start working on it, hadn't you?" said the Matriarch.

"I think that's our cue to leave," Eddie said quietly to Molly.

"Just when it was getting interesting . . ." said Molly.

They got to their feet.

"We'll report back when we know something," Eddie said to the Matriarch.

"Try not to get noticed this time," said the Sarjeant-at-Arms.

Eddie and Molly walked back through the Hall, taking their time, not going anywhere in particular, just walking. Eddie was glad to get away from the Matriarch and her Council, so he could think more clearly, without interruptions. He had a lot to think about. Molly strode along at his side and said nothing. She could see Eddie was thinking hard and waited patiently for him to share his thoughts with her. After they'd been walking for some time, and he still hadn't, Molly thought she'd better prompt him.

"So," she said. "We're going back into the Nightside. I can show you some of my favourite drinking haunts." When that didn't get a reaction, she tried again. "Do you have a plan? Please tell me you have a plan, because I've never been any good at those. Unless they involve hitting people, setting fire to things, or blowing up whole neighbourhoods." Still no response. "All right, how are we going to get into the Nightside? We can't use the Merlin Glass. Walker will have people looking for that."

"We'll have to use one of the more traditional routes," said Eddie. "Something Shaman and Roxie would know about."

"Good thinking," said Molly, relieved he was speaking again. "Which one do you fancy? I know several."

Eddie smiled at her. "Of course you do. The Nightside's always been a home away from home for you, hasn't it?"

"Can I help it if I feel more comfortable there than in this control-freak establishment? No wonder you left home the first chance you got."

"And yet, I keep coming back," said Eddie. "What does that say about me?"

"That you need me around, to remind you there are other options," Molly said cheerfully. "What are we going to do, once we get to the Night-side?"

"Ask questions and see where the answers lead us," said Eddie. "Like the Matriarch said, someone must know something."

"In other words, you don't have a plan. We're just going to make it up as we go along."

"Yes," said Eddie.

"So we do know what we're doing," said Molly. "Good. I was worried there, for a moment."

They left Drood Hall through a side-door, without being noticed. Everyone else was too busy running their very important errands, looking out for the Sarjeant-at-Arms, and excitedly discussing Walker's visit, all without slowing down. Eddie and Molly were old news now, and therefore invisible. Eddie was quite pleased about that. Molly wasn't. She didn't like being taken for granted.

"Maybe I should give all the statues Tourette's," she said grimly.

"What? Again?" said Eddie.

"All right, you think of something!"

"Later," said Eddie.

Out in the grounds, Eddie had the Merlin Glass open a door onto a grimy back alley off Oxford Street. No one noticed their arrival, one of the Glass' more useful side-effects. After the pleasant quiet of the Drood grounds, the roar of London traffic and the constant babble of raised voices was almost deafening. Eddie shook the Glass down and put it away, while Molly took the opportunity to work a quick transformation on herself.

Roxie Hazzard was a tall, muscular redhead in a black leather jacket, a T-shirt bearing the legend DIE SCUM DIE, battered old jeans, scuffed cowboy boots . . . and a length of steel chain wrapped loosely around her waist. A well-known adventurer and trouble-maker in her own right, Roxie was almost as well-known in the hidden world as Molly Metcalf. Originally created as an alternative persona for when Molly wanted to party in the Nightside without dragging her reputation along with her, Roxie Hazzard soon developed her own history and legend. Which did come in handy when Molly felt the need to do things she didn't want Eddie to know about.

He liked to think he'd reformed her.

She struck a pose for Eddie, in the stained light of the alley-way, and grinned invitingly. "So, what do you think?" she said, in a low, sultry voice. "Am I as good-looking as Molly?"

"You're always Molly to me," said Eddie, diplomatically. "You know, I'm never sure . . . Is that just a glamour, or is there an actual physical transformation?"

"Get close enough and find out," said Roxie.

"Later," said Eddie.

Roxie strode out of the alley-way, taking the lead, and Eddie let her. Of such small compromises are relationships made. They emerged into the bright lights and packed pavements of Oxford Circus, and headed for the tube station. People gave Roxie Hazzard lots of room, almost without thinking about it, but scarcely noticed Eddie. Which was just the way he liked it. Back when he'd been the Droods' main field agent in London, streets like this had been his domain. To protect and police. Eddie missed the simple anonymity of those days, before he became . . . whatever he was now. A legend, perhaps? He hoped not. He didn't want to end up in Shadows Fall.

He used his torc to raise his Sight, to show him all the secret inhabitants of the hidden world. And there they were, walking unseen and unsuspected right in the middle of a modern metropolis. Alien Greys in smart suits and sun-glasses, because they thought it helped them blend in. Light Beings, shimmering and scintillating as they danced through the crowds on their unknowable missions. And all the other kinds of abhumans and semi-humans, just getting on with their lives. You don't have to visit the Nightside to mix with the unreal and the uncanny; you just need to open your eyes.

If Humanity knew who and what they shared their world with every day, they'd go out of their minds. Which is why the Droods go to such trouble to ensure most people never know just what it is they're being protected from.

Eddie and Roxie descended into the Underground, and Eddie started to search his pockets for his Oyster Card, to work the ticket barriers. Roxie just sniffed and snapped her fingers, and the barriers sprang open obligingly. Eddie and Roxie went down into the depths for as far as they could go, then looked around until Roxie pointed out a small sign over a carefully unobtrusive door. The words were in Enochian, that artificial language created back in Elizabethan times specifically so men could talk with angels. Basically it read THIS WAY. It didn't say, *Abandon all hope*; that was understood.

The door opened to reveal an elevator with featureless brass walls and no control panel. Once Eddie and Roxie were inside, the door slammed shut, and the elevator went sideways, at some speed. The door finally opened again, onto a long, white-tiled passageway, curving steeply downwards. Heavy claw-marks had been gouged into the wall ahead of them, cutting through a thick display of arterial spatter that was still dripping. More fresh blood was scuffed along the floor, from where something heavy had been dragged away.

"It's way past time for another culling of the trolls," said Roxie.

Eddie shrugged. "Budget cutbacks . . ."

They followed the passageway down, being careful where they put their feet, until a sudden sharp turning shepherded them onto a brightly lit platform that looked much like any other. Except that the destinations board said: SHADOWS FALL, HACELDAMA, ARCADIA, and NIGHTSIDE. Spread along the length of the platform, waiting for the next train to arrive, were a shaggy werewolf in a Hawaiian T-shirt, a group of headless monks and their seeing-eye velociraptors, half-a-dozen old-school punks with tall Mohicans and satanic circuitry implanted in their flesh instead of tattoos. And one tall, powerful, and extremely naked warrior woman covered from brow to toe in blue woad markings, reading the *Financial Times* with great concentration. The battle-axe on her hip was singing something wistful in old Gaelic.

A busker with multiple personality disorder was singing a cappella versions of West End show tunes, in close harmonies with himself. The cap at his feet held spare change from places that didn't even exist any longer. Eddie contributed a few coins because karma can be a pain. Two white-faced mimes were beating the crap out of a recalcitrant vending machine with invisible hammers, sending cans of soft drink flying in all directions.

No one paid Eddie and Roxie any attention after the first quick glance. Most people in the hidden world knew Eddie as Shaman Bond: a familiar face on the scene, a con man and a chancer, always on the look-out for some profitable trouble to get into. Eddie had put a lot of effort into establishing that affable and acceptable persona, to the point where he often felt more comfortable being Shaman Bond. If only because Shaman didn't have to carry around Eddie's family history. And no one gave Roxie Hazzard a second look in case she took offence and kicked the crap out of them. Eddie and Roxie found a quiet space for themselves and stood together, waiting for the next train.

It wasn't long before a blast of uncomfortably hot compressed air slammed past the platform, ruffling clothes and scorching faces, running ahead of an approaching train. It blasted out of the tunnel-mouth and stormed into the station, screeching like a demon let out of Hell on day release. A long, shining, silver bullet with no windows anywhere.

The train screeched to a halt, rocking slightly. Just one extremely long carriage whose heavily reinforced doors hissed open to reveal pleasantly illuminated and surprisingly comfortable compartments. Eddie and Roxie stepped aboard through the nearest door, while everyone else went out of their way to choose other doors. Eddie said nothing. Roxie took it as her right.

Once they were inside, and the door had hissed shut, Eddie looked carefully up and down the compartment. All the seats were empty apart from one young woman with a shaved head and a third eye tattooed on her forehead. She was wearing nothing but thin black leather straps with chunky silver spikes that stood out starkly against skin with the dead white pallor of someone who hadn't seen the sun for a long time. She was reading a large leather-bound volume with completely blank pages. Except Eddie knew they weren't blank, to her. The unblinking white-on-white eyes marked her as a graduate of the Deep School, the Dark Academie. The one place you can go when even the Nightside can't deliver the kind of forbidden knowledge you're looking for.

Eddie and Roxie sat down facing the young woman, in the middle of the compartment. So they could keep a watchful eye on her and anyone entering the compartment from either direction. The price of safety is eternal vigilance, and a constant readiness to kick off big time. The train pulled out of the station with a resigned sigh, and the carriage rocked from side to side in a not-unpleasant way as it picked up speed. There were no windows because the train had to pass through the kind of places you really wouldn't want to see. The steel walls had been specially reinforced to keep things out. The train would get them where they were going, but no one ever said it was the safest way to travel. The Nightside isn't supposed to be easy to get to.

After they'd been travelling for a while, Roxie leaned forward to address the young woman sitting opposite, but she started talking before Roxie even opened her mouth.

"Eddie Drood: field agent, torc bearer, a legend in his own lunch-time. And Molly Metcalf, the wickedest witch that ever was, and a spanner in the works of the world machine. Also known as Shaman Bond and Roxie Hazzard. What do you want? I'm busy."

"I just wanted to ask about your fellow Dark Academie graduate Hadleigh Oblivion," said Roxie. "I've a feeling we might be bumping into him in the Nightside."

"What do you want to know?" said the young woman, still not looking up from the blank pages of her book.

"What does his title mean?" said Roxie. "Detective Inspectre?"

"It's his responsibility to investigate crimes against reality itself."

"Okay," said Roxie. "But what does that mean?"

"Hadleigh Oblivion knows what's real and what isn't," said the young woman. "Everyone else only thinks they do. Even Walker and the Authorities bow down to the Detective Inspectre when they must. Just as you will if you go up against him."

"You think we're going to?" said Eddie.

"You want to know who's behind the changes in the Nightside," said the young woman.

"And Hadleigh knows?" said Roxie.

"The Detective Inspectre knows everything."

"What if we don't want to meet him?" said Eddie. "Our last encounter didn't go at all well. He wanted to drag me down to the Dark Academie, so they could take my armour away."

"And you stopped him," said the young woman. "A lot of people are still talking about that."

"But what is it that makes him so special?" said Roxie.

The young woman smiled for the first time. "Some say . . . he's realer than we are."

Eddie and Roxie looked at each other.

"Why do you have white-on-white eyes?" said Eddie.

"To see more clearly."

"Why doesn't Hadleigh Oblivion have eyes like yours?" said Roxie.

"Because he's not just a graduate of the Dark Academie; he's an instructor."

Eddie and Roxie decided they'd asked enough questions.

The journey after that was reasonably uneventful. Nothing out of the usual. Something large and heavy tried to smash its way through the carriage wall, but the solid steel held firm, and the dents flattened themselves out again. Whatever was outside howled with rage, a vicious, inhuman sound, then dropped away and was quickly left behind. For a while, something ran back and forth on the carriage roof with soft pitter-patter feet, laughing breathlessly. It stopped abruptly, and its voice sounded inside the carriage, sweet and seductive, like a porn star choking on honey.

"Let me in, let me in. I want to stir my sticky fingers in your flesh and make you over into new and exciting things."

The young woman finally raised her eyes from her book and addressed the ceiling. "Knock it off. Or I'll tell Hadleigh about you."

There was a pause, then the soft footsteps pitter-pattered off in search of easier prey. The young woman went back to her reading. Eddie and Roxie sat back in their seats, feeling just a little outclassed.

The train finally slammed to a halt, and the door hissed open onto a platform in the Nightside. Eddie and Roxie disembarked, leaving the young woman on the train with her book. Crowds of people, and some things that were only trying to look like people, and some things that were just things, surged along the platform and shouldered each other aside in their eagerness to get to the escalators first. All kinds came to the Nightside, for all kinds of reasons; and none of them could wait to get started. Eddie and Roxie allowed themselves to be carried along with the tide, up the escalators and out into the long night. And then Eddie stood his ground, ignoring the crush, to get a good look at where he'd come to. There had never been time for sight-seeing on any of his previous brief visits to the Nightside, but given the current circumstances, he felt a definite need to better understand just what he was going to be dealing with. Roxie stood quietly at his side, letting him take all the time he needed.

Wherever Eddie looked, it was all hot neon and cold-eyed predators. Packed crowds hurried up and down the pavements, in desperate pursuit of pleasures that might not have a name but certainly had a price. The street was full of fever-bright colours and impenetrable shadows; shop-windows full of dreams, only a little used; and any number of people more than ready to sell their souls. Or someone else's.

Phosphorescent fairies went tumbling across the night sky, darting and wheeling and throwing off multi-coloured sparks like living Catherine wheels. Something impossibly huge with wide membranous wings moved slowly across the huge moon, actually blotting it out for a while. And here and there the Awful Folk, vast and misty, went walking through buildings as though they weren't even there.

Roxie finally took Eddie by the arm and moved him off down the street because she knew that if she didn't, he'd just keep standing there, finding new things to look at. Eddie let her do it, studying everything with keen fascination while trying not to look like a tourist. He didn't want to stand out.

All kinds of vehicles surged up and down the road because in the Nightside, the traffic never stops. Everything from sedan chairs carried by indentured poltergeists, to taxis that ran on debased holy water, and ambulances that ran on distilled suffering. Motor-cycle messengers who snorted powdered virgin's blood to keep them going, and some things that only looked like cars so they could sneak up on slower-moving traffic and eat them. Insanely long, articulated vehicles thundered along, carrying all kinds of goods to all kinds of places. There were no traffic lights and no pedestrian crossings. None of this was news to Eddie; he'd read all the reports, but it was something else entirely to see it with his own eyes. To feel the terrible, relentless vitality of the long night, the desperate needs and ruthless ambitions, the sense that anything was possible here, anything at all. If you had the money to buy it or the guts to go after it.

Eddie peered into shop-windows full of everything that was bad for you: you or someone else. Books full of forbidden knowledge, remaindered and second hand. Drugs and potions so you could play Russian Roulette with your brain chemistry; waters from the spring of eternal youth, still and sparkling; and assorted bottles full of untamed moods and wild imaginations. Everything you ever dreamed of or were afraid to admit you wanted, all of it at unbeatable prices.

Night-clubs that catered to every taste, their doors left open so heavy bass beats or mournful jazz could spill out into the street. Languorous women smiled on every street-corner, while discreet establishments offered sin and temptation and every variation on a good time you could think of. Barkers and shills loudly proclaimed the glories within, promising everything that ever woke you from your sleep in a hot sweat and did everything short of grabbing hold of passers-by and throwing them inside.

So they could be cheated, abused, even killed. There were no protections here, apart from *Buyer very much beware.*

Eddie ended up striding quickly down the street, staring straight ahead.

"I don't think I approve of a lot of this," he said finally.

"This is the Nightside, and no one cares what you think," Roxie said cheerfully. "Anything goes; and your conscience is your problem."

"There is no right or wrong here," said Eddie. "No morality, only endless shades of grey."

"Now you're getting it," said Roxie. "Freedom, real freedom, has to include the right to try anything, even if it's bad for you. Perhaps particularly then. There are no laws in the long night, no restraints, and no safety nets. Which is why everyone here has never felt so alive. No one runs faster or more happily than the dog who's finally been let off his leash."

"People could get hurt," said Eddie. "People could die."

"Oh, they do," said Roxie. "All the time. That's part of the thrill."

"We're never going to agree on this," said Eddie.

"No reason why we should," said Roxie. "Oh hell, look who it isn't."

Because it was the Nightside, one of the first people they bumped into was someone they already knew. Dead Boy came sauntering down the street towards them, hands stuffed deep in the pockets of his greatcoat, smiling easily. He planted himself right in front of them and fixed them with his dark, feverish eyes.

"The name is Shaman Bond," Eddie said quickly.

"Of course it is!" said Dead Boy, dropping Eddie a roguish wink. "Hello, Roxie! Killed anyone interesting recently? What are you two doing in the Nightside? Is this something to do with the Drood in his armour I heard about earlier? I did wonder if that might be Eddie Drood. No one else would dare. Don't worry; I won't tell anyone."

"Of course you will," said Roxie. "You can't help yourself. Just try not to do it till we're gone."

"Oh sure," said Dead Boy, entirely unoffended. "I know who you are too. Nothing like being dead to help you see the world more clearly. The dead have no illusions. How's your sister Isabella?"

Roxie glared at him. "Keep your voice down! She's fine. And she told me to tell you, she only goes out with things that have a pulse."

"Doesn't know what she's missing," sniggered Dead Boy. "But I was just being polite. I'm in a relationship these days. Have you met my car?"

He gestured expansively at the gleaming, futuristic vehicle hovering next to the pavement because it didn't have any wheels. The silver sheen was almost painfully bright, and the sleek lines were so fiercely aerodynamic, the car looked like it could drive between raindrops without getting wet.

"I thought the traffic here never stopped?" said Eddie.

"The rules of the road don't apply to my girl-friend," Dead Boy said proudly. "She wanted to say hello to you."

The car shuddered and stretched, the long lines flexing and flowing as the car stood up and took on a human form. She draped an arm across Dead Boy's shoulders and beamed happily at Eddie. He nodded resignedly as he recognised the tall and buxom sex droid from the Twenty-Third Century. It took more than one orgy to change her name to Silicon Lily. She was smartly turned-out in a classic little black dress, cut just high enough at the back to show off the bar-code and copyright notice on her magnificent left buttock. Her frizzy steel hair sparked with static, her eyes were silver, and she smelled of pure musk. Silicon Lily was a luxury model and wanted everyone to know it.

"Hello, lover," she said to Eddie in a rich sultry voice. "Been awhile, hasn't it?"

"*Lover?*" said Roxie, dangerously.

"Aren't you glad to see me, darling?" Lily said to Eddie, not even glancing at Roxie.

"Well, *darling?*" said Roxie. "Are you glad to see her? And aren't you going to introduce us?"

Eddie thought seriously about running but was pretty sure either of them could tackle him and bring him down before he got half-way down the street. So he sighed inwardly and did the honours. Remembering at the last moment to remind Lily that he was currently Shaman Bond.

"I didn't know you were a transforming droid, Lily?" he said finally.

"A girl doesn't tell all her secrets on a first date," said Lily.

"So there was a date?" said Roxie.

"I'm with Dead Boy now," said Silicon Lily. "Isn't he cute?"

"Not the word I would have used," said Eddie.

"You two have a history?" said Roxie, fixing Eddie with a disturbingly cold gaze.

"Only in the sense that history is a thing of the past," said Eddie.

Roxie put her arm through his and grinned cheerfully. "You're so easy to tease. Relax, lover. We've all got at least one dubious ex in our past."

"What are you doing in the Nightside, Shaman?" said Lily. "You do know Walker has put out the hard word on Eddie Drood?"

"Hell of a price on your head," Dead Boy said cheerfully. "Not necessarily attached to your body. I might be tempted to go after it myself if I cared about money, which mostly I don't. Once you're dead, you don't feel the need for all the usual necessities. It's very liberating."

"What about me, lover?" said Silicon Lily. "Aren't I a necessity?"

"You are a luxury," said Dead Boy, hugging her to him with a grip that would have damaged anyone normal. "But I couldn't exist without you."

"Do you know what's happened at the Wulfshead?" said Roxie.

"Yes," said Dead Boy. "Good thing I prefer to drink at Strangefellows."

He wasn't really being hard-hearted. It was just that, being dead, he didn't take death as seriously as everyone else.

"We're here looking for information on why the Nightside's boundaries have changed," said Eddie.

Dead Boy shrugged. "I don't think anyone knows what's going on there. Came as a complete surprise to everyone I know. But then, I don't move in the best-informed circles. Your best bet would be to ask at Strangefellows. They always have the best gossip. People there often know things that haven't even happened yet. Though to be fair, that's mostly because they're the ones planning it. Come with us, we'll take you."

"Right!" said Lily. "I feel like stretching my legs."

She turned back into a car, a process that wasn't any less disturbing for being seen in reverse. Dead Boy got into the driving seat but didn't even try to touch the steering wheel. Lily always insisted on driving herself. Dead Boy rooted around inside the glove compartment and came up with a half-full bottle of vodka and a packet of chocolate hob-nobs, and cheerfully indulged himself while Eddie and Roxie got into the back seat. Roxie shot Eddie a sideways glance.

"How does it feel, to be back inside your old girl-friend again?"

Eddie pretended he hadn't heard.

Lily steered her way expertly through the packed traffic, thanks to a carefully calculated mixture of inhumanly fast reflexes and open intimidation. Eddie leaned back in his seat and watched the streets flow by in a smear of multi-coloured neon. So many people, bustling up and down the narrow pavements, so full of life and energy. It had honestly never occurred to Eddie before, that so many people would want to come to the Nightside. Knowing it was dangerous, knowing the odds were stacked against them, but still chasing their dreams. Eddie might not approve of the nature of some of those dreams, but he had to admire the courage it took to pursue them.

A white truck suddenly pulled out in front of the futuristic car and slammed on its brakes, forcing Lily to slow down too. The back of the truck burst open, and long leprous tentacles shot out. Lined with vicious, toothed suckers, the tentacles stretched out to engulf the car and drag her into the crimson maw inside the truck. Eddie sat up straight, but before he could do anything Lily opened up with her dual flame-throwers. Bright yellow flames scorched and blackened the writhing tentacles, which snapped back into the truck's interior. Lily then opened fire with her front-mounted machine-guns, and the heavy bullets chewed up the crimson insides of the truck. Black blood spurted, and the truck veered back and forth across the road before finally mounting the pavement and ploughing into the front of a night-club that proudly promised zombie strippers: THEY'RE DEAD AND THEY DANCE! The truck had barely come to a halt before scavengers were all over it, intent on reducing it to its most basic components before anyone else could get there. Lily blasted her horn several times in savage satisfaction and drove on.

"My girl-friend is badass!" Dead Boy said proudly.

Roxie leaned in close to Eddie. "If Lily is the car, where do the bullets for the guns come from?"

"Best not to ask," said Eddie.

When the four of them finally descended the metal stairs into Strangefellows, the place was packed and the joint was jumping. Eddie looked around warily as he and Roxie followed Dead Boy and Silicon Lily towards the bar. No one seemed to be paying him or Roxie any particular attention. The bar looked much as he remembered it from the few times he'd been there before: loud and extravagant and clearly not giving a damn for any number of proprieties. The music was deafening, the floor was sticky with things best not thought about, and the air was thick with several kinds of illegal smoke. It smelled like breathing someone's underwear. And the crowd . . . was a typical Nightside crowd.

Several large and burly men in battered chain-mail sat around a table, drinking hot mead spiked with hemlock. Their grubby white tabards had a red cross on the front, painted in fresh blood. They were St Catherine's Crusaders, vowed to indulge in every sin and vice, the better to understand and fight them. No wonder they ended up in the Nightside. A number of ghosts had bellied up to the bar, their arms leaving smoky blue trails of ectoplasm on the air every time they lifted a glass to where their mouths used to be. They were drinking the memories of forgotten wines from empty bottles. The bar's speakers pumped out *The Silver Beatles' Greatest*

Hits, and the Tribe of the Gay Barbarians was line dancing on the bartop. And Harry Fabulous, your Go To Guy for everything no one else could get you, lurked quietly in a shadowed corner, dealing bootleg experiences, enchanted switch-blades, and exorcism patches for possessed computer software.

Just another night at Strangefellows.

People greeted Dead Boy and Silicon Lily happily enough as they passed. A bit warily in Dead Boy's case because he had a tendency to get into trouble wherever he went. Mostly because if there wasn't any, he'd start some. A few faces here and there nodded easily as they recognised Shaman Bond. No one was ever surprised to see Shaman anywhere.

Rather more people appeared to know Roxie Hazzard. There were any number of raised voices, cheerful salutations, and offers to buy her drinks. Just as many people glowered at her or kept their heads down, hoping not to be noticed. Roxie grinned easily about her and kept going. A warrior woman in a blood-spattered military uniform that smelled strongly of smoke and brimstone reminded Roxie that her dues for the Mercenaries Guild were late again.

Not for the first time, it occurred to Eddie that Molly had a life of her own, away from him.

They reached the bar, and Dead Boy set about getting the drinks in. Brandy for Roxie, a Beck's for Shaman, a Blue Nun for Lily, and an Angel's Ruin with a formaldehyde chaser for Dead Boy. A normal enough round of drinks, for Strangefellows. Dead Boy was happy to stand his round, for a change. Apparently he was flush after a recent job, body-guarding a Four Horsemen of the Apocalypse tribute act on their tour of the Nightside.

Alex nodded easily to Roxie as he sorted out the drinks but had to be introduced to Shaman. Alex admitted grudgingly to knowing the name, by reputation. Roxie leaned in close to Eddie.

"You worked with John Taylor on a few cases; as Eddie or Shaman?"

"Only as a Drood," said Eddie, quietly. "He doesn't know Eddie and Shaman are the same man."

"But if he's seen your face . . ."

"I wore my mask," said Eddie.

"You worked cases with someone and never even showed them your face?" said Roxie. "Droods . . ."

"Haven't seen you in here for a while, Roxie," said Alex, placing a large brandy in front of her.

"I've been busy," said Roxie. "Interdimensional hell-wars won't fight themselves, you know."

"And someone hired me to find the Maltese Falcon," Eddie said smoothly. "The hardest part was finding a cage strong enough to hold it."

Alex just nodded. He'd heard stranger things. "Didn't know you two were an item . . ."

"We're not," Eddie said quickly. "We were both hired by the same patron, to find out what the hell's going on with the Nightside's boundaries."

"That's all anyone wants to talk about," said Alex, "but nobody knows anything. There's some serious betting going on as to who's behind it. First choice was the Droods because they're behind most things, but that idea went belly-up after one of them appeared on Blaiston Street looking for answers."

"I thought Droods came here to drink all the time?" said Eddie, carefully casual.

"Oh sure," said Alex. "The old Armourer, and the current Sarjeant-at-Arms, and a few others. As long as they're discreet, and keep their armour to themselves, no one gives a damn. We'll let anyone in here. Worse things than Droods drink here every night." He glared down the bar at the Tribe of the Gay Barbarians. "Get off my bar! Those boots are ruining the finish!"

And that was when a half-breed succubus wearing a communion dress spotted with unspeakable stains, and gnarled horns curling up from her forehead, appeared suddenly out of the crowd to grab Roxie by the shoulder and spin her around. She pushed her face right into Roxie's, took a good look, and stepped back grinning triumphantly.

"This is Molly Metcalf!" she said loudly. "I can See right through her glamour. And if she's here, Eddie Drood can't be far away! Who wants to split the reward money with me? All we have to do is make the witch talk, and we'll all be rich!"

Roxie punched the succubus out, and she crashed to the floor. A Neanderthal in a biker's jacket went to grab Roxie, and Eddie kicked him square in the nuts. The Neanderthal folded up with a low, anguished moan.

"Fight!" Dead Boy said happily. He picked up a table and broke it over the Neanderthal's back. Silicon Lily zapped an approaching ghoul with the Taser built into her left hand; and just like that, everyone was hitting everyone else. In a bar like Strangefellows, old grudges and long-time feuds were never far from the surface, and everyone was always ready to seize the opportunity to get their retaliation in first. Fists flew, heads butted, and every bit of furniture that wasn't nailed down was put to good use in hand-to-hand combat.

Eddie turned to Roxie. "Time we were leaving."

"Well past time," said Roxie, knocking back what remained of her drink.

"Can you use your magics to get us out of here?"

"The bar has anti-magic protections," said Roxie. "Which is the only reason it's still standing. We'll have to get out of here the hard way."

"Suits me," said Eddie.

He concentrated, and thin tendrils of strange matter shot down his arms from his torc, to form golden knuckle-dusters on his fists. He set off towards the exit, knocking down anyone who tried to stop him or even looked as though they might be about to. Roxie protected his rear with the occasional vicious back-elbow or savage kick.

Alex yelled for his muscular bouncers to restore order. Betty and Lucy Coltrane immediately waded in, smashing through the heaving crowd with practiced brutality. Bodies went flying in all directions. Alex produced a glowing baseball bat, vaulted over the bartop, and set about him with grim impartiality. He didn't mind the occasional brawl, it helped to clear the air, but he did object to the cost of replacing all the broken furniture.

Eddie had almost reached the metal stairs when Roxie called out sharply. He looked back to see a were-bear squeezing Roxie in a bear-hug, pinning her arms to her sides. She struggled frantically but couldn't break the hold. The bear laughed.

"Die, witch!"

"Really shouldn't have said that," said Eddie.

He drew his Colt Repeater from his pocket dimension, called for a silver bullet, and shot the bear through his left eye. The bear's head snapped back, his arms relaxed their hold, and the bear's body was human again by the time it hit the floor. Over by the bar, Dead Boy stopped strangling a really big snake just long enough to punch the air with one fist.

"Hardcore, Shaman!"

Roxie glared at Eddie. "I do not need saving!"

"Of course not," said Eddie. "It's just that we're in a bit of a hurry. You can save me next time."

"Damn right," said Roxie.

They headed up the stairs, side by side.

CHAPTER FIVE

Much Ado About Droods

There is only one church in the Nightside, and you won't find it any-where near the Street of the Gods. St Jude's is tucked away in a quiet corner of the long night, shadowed and obscured, no part of the Nightside's usual gaudy riot. It doesn't advertise, it doesn't reach out, and it doesn't care if you pass by on the other side. The church is old, older even than Christianity itself. It has had many names down the centuries and is currently dedicated to the patron saint of lost causes. The bare stone walls are grey and featureless, with only narrow slits for windows, and the slanting roof has never even heard of gargoyles. Or guttering. Inside, a slab of ancient stone serves as an altar, facing rows of blocky, wooden pews. There are no services, no regular meetings, and no clergy. St Jude's isn't there for comfort or contemplation; it's just your final chance for sanctu-ary, salvation, and one last desperate word with your God.

It's not a church to enter lightly. Prayers are heard in St Jude's, and sometimes answered.

John Taylor went walking through the Nightside, taking his time because he wasn't in any hurry to get where he was going. He passed by store win-dows full of wonders, night-clubs full of temptations, and women on street-corners with hungry eyes . . . and had no interest in any of them. John was thinking about what good, if any, his visit to Drood Hall had actually ac-complished. He hadn't expected much, so he couldn't say he was disappointed, but even so . . . He only went because the Authorities told him to, and he always did what they said. Except for when he didn't. He might be Walker now, but he was still his own man. Or so he liked to think.

He'd been sent because with the Nightside's boundaries apparently out-of-control, the Authorities were worried they might be seen as weak. And the Drood throwing his weight around in his armour had been a definite provocation. John had to make his report to the Authorities now, and he really wasn't looking forward to it. Despite everything he and the Matriarch had said, or possibly even because of it, the Droods and the Nightside were currently on a collision course. When the unstoppable force meets the immovable object, someone's going to get hurt. John couldn't help feeling the whole thing had been a waste of time that could have been more profitably spent trying to identify whoever was behind whatever was going on.

He also didn't like the fact that he'd been summoned to meet the Authorities at St Jude's, instead of their usual luxurious headquarters in Uptown. The ancient church was not the kind of place anyone went by choice. Of course, it was famously neutral ground . . . or perhaps the Authorities just didn't want to be interrupted until they'd finished deciding what the hell they were going to do.

John slowed his pace as he approached the low, squat building. It stood alone, as though too good or too scary to mix with its neighbours, and dirty yellow candlelight seeped out the slit windows like warning lights on a ship carrying dangerous cargo. John's business had brought him to St Jude's on several occasions before, and it had always led to a major change in his life. The last time had been when he married Suzie Shooter. He headed resignedly for the only door, a heavy slab of stained oak with absolutely nothing inviting about it; and at the last moment it swung open to reveal the Lord of Thorns, standing stiff and stern in the doorway to block his way.

Unnaturally bright light surrounded the Lord of Thorns, not in any way like a halo. Tall and imposing, he had a face as solid and weathered as a block of granite, and with his grey hair, beard, and robes he looked like some Old Testament prophet who'd just come down from the mountain with some really bad news about the real relationship between God and Man. Originally set in place to be the Nightside's Overseer and Judge of Last Resort, he'd served his office faithfully for centuries before being sabotaged by the previous Walker. Undermined and side-lined, he was now largely forgotten and irrelevant. He spent all his time in St Jude's, looking after the place; as a form of penance for what he saw as his failings.

Once the most powerful force in the Nightside, he now kept himself busy sweeping out an old church and keeping the candles lit. Those figures in the long night with a working memory and a sense of history were all waiting for the other shoe to drop. The Lord of Thorns stood before John Taylor, and John had to admit the old man still looked pretty damned scary. So, of course, he just nodded casually and smiled easily.

"Hello, Thorns. Still working as the janitor? I keep hoping you'll do something about the ambience. Maybe put down some traps."

"Something bad is coming to the Nightside," said the Lord of Thorns, in his harsh gravelly voice.

"So people keep telling me," said John. "I don't suppose you'd know who, or what?"

"I don't get involved any more," said the Lord of Thorns. "I remain separate, like St Jude's. This is a matter for men."

"I suppose I'm glad you're still here," said John. "I half expected to find you'd run for the hills, along with everyone on the Street of the Gods."

The Lord of Thorns showed his grey teeth in something that might have been meant as a smile. "I am not a god. I have a greater purpose. And, I still have my chores to perform." He turned his head briefly, to look back into the church. "They're waiting for you."

"The Authorities?" said John.

"If they weren't, I'd have kicked them out long ago," said the Lord of Thorns. "They don't have the right attitude."

"Of course not," said John. "This is the Nightside. We don't really do the respect thing."

The Lord of Thorns stepped out into the night, to allow John to enter the church. "Tell them to put something in the poor-box before they leave. Or I'll turn them upside down and shake them till their pockets are empty."

He might have been joking or he might not. John nodded politely and went inside.

The interior of St Jude's was brightly illuminated by row upon row of candles, set in niches along the inside of the walls. The candle-flames never wavered, and the light never faltered, as though determined to push the shadows back into the corners and keep them there. The Authorities were gathered together down at the far end, before the stone altar, talking animatedly while still keeping their voices low. Not out of respect, but because St Jude's had the power to intimidate even the greatest movers and shakers in the long night.

St Jude's was not a place for loose talk or loose thoughts. Because this was a place where everything you said and thought mattered.

The Authorities broke off from their discussions and looked around sharply as John strolled down the narrow central aisle to join them. His footsteps sounded loudly on the bare flagstones, as though announcing him. None of the Authorities looked particularly pleased to see him, but then, they never did. So he gave them all his best casual smile and nod, just to show he didn't give a damn. And to remind them he only served the Authorities because he'd chosen to do so, and that could change at any time.

Julien Advent, the legendary Victorian Adventurer, managed a brief smile in return. He was the only one John had any time for. Julien had created his own version of the Hyde formula, back in the Eighteen Eighties, designed to release men's better angels instead of their worst. He took the potion himself and became the greatest hero of his age. Until he fell (or more properly was pushed) through a Timeslip and ended up in the Nightside in the Nineteen Sixties. Talk about culture shock. But Julien quickly decided he'd found a new world in even more need of someone like him and set about the impossible task of raising the tone of the place. He did this by setting a good example, protecting those in need, and beating the crap out of anyone who made the mistake of not taking him seriously. Julien Advent was an old-school hero and adventurer, and therefore dealt with the long night's many moral ambiguities in the same way Alexander the Great dealt with the Gordian knot.

He still dressed in the old Victorian fashion, a stark black and white style that echoed his values, complete with a sweeping crimson-lined opera-cloak. Tall, dark, and handsome, he hadn't aged a day since he first appeared in the Nightside. As editor of the long night's very own crusading newspaper, the *Night Times*, he fought for truth and justice in a new way. John often wondered why Julien stayed in the Nightside, and the only time he asked, the answer was simply: *Because they need me.*

Julien Advent led the Authorities, inasmuch as anyone did, or could.

On the other hand, the woman standing beside him was one of the most frightening things in the Nightside. Jessica Sorrow the Unbeliever could look at anyone or anything and make them disappear forever, through the sheer force of her unbelief. Which meant everyone and everything around her only continued to exist for as long as she believed in them.

Jessica wore a grubby white shift and nothing else. Unhealthily pale and slender, she burned with a terrible energy that would have consumed anyone else. Long dirty hair fell around her bony face in ragged strands, and her wide, staring eyes were yellow as urine and feral as a cat's. She clutched a battered old teddy bear to her, as though it were the most precious thing in the world. John had found that old childhood friend for her, and it helped ground her in reality. John always thought of Jessica as a defused bomb that might not stay defused. She stared at him unblinkingly and seemed to recognise him, which was as much as he could hope for. Because for Jessica Sorrow, sanity was always going to be a sometime thing.

She held the power that backed up the Authorities' decisions.

Annie Abattoir was six-foot-two, muscular, and attractive in an exotic sort of way. She struck a grand pose and looked challengingly at John, as though daring him to justify taking up her time. John wasn't impressed. She did that with everyone. Annie was a fabled assassin and seductress, secret agent and confidence trickster, feared and respected in a dozen countries. She'd never explained why she'd found it necessary to retreat to the Nightside; she might be looking for someone, or hiding out . . . or she might be playing a really long game. Annie wasn't the kind to answer questions. Wise men treated her politely and watched their backs at all times. She was invited to join the Authorities only because that made it easier for them to keep an eye on her. And she did come in handy when someone needed intimidating. For everything else, they had Jessica Sorrow.

Annie was wearing a long crimson evening dress, with matching elbow-length gloves, and John didn't need to see the dress' cut-away back to know she had protective mystical sigils carved into the flesh between her shoulder-blades. Annie had always been very hard to kill, but that hadn't stopped an awful lot of people from trying.

She gave the Authorities style.

Larry Oblivion just nodded curtly to John. They'd worked a few cases together, but they'd never been friends. Even before Larry was killed. One of the famous Oblivion Brothers, Larry had been murdered, then brought back from the dead. Now known as the dead detective, the post-mortem private eye, he was pale of skin, hard of face, uncompromising in his beliefs, and not noted for his sense of humour. Larry didn't eat or drink or sleep because he didn't need to. And because he saw no point in pretending to be something he wasn't.

Always sharp and slick, with never a hair out of place, Larry wore his Gucci suit with impeccable style. Just because he was a zombie, he didn't see any reason to let himself go. Not many people suspected it, but John knew for a fact that Larry packed a wand. Given to him by Queen Mab of the Fae, Larry could use it to stop Time for a while. Just enough to give him the advantage.

He was the cutting edge of the Authorities.

The newest addition to the group leaned casually against the stone altar and looked down his nose at John. Brilliant Chang started out as an enforcer for the Dragon Clan, and one side of his face was still covered with the tattoo that marked him as a combat sorcerer. He stayed with the Dragons just long enough to pay off his family's debts, then killed every member of the Clan in one bloody evening. He never did explain why, and no one had ever felt like pressing him.

These days Brilliant was an investigative reporter for the *Night Times*, which was probably an even more dangerous occupation. He specialised in uncovering truths that the wealthy and powerful would much rather remain hidden, and made a point of pursuing the really nasty people no one else could touch. He collected death threats the way other people collected compliments, and for much the same reason. Large and blocky in his white linen suit, Brilliant was always calm and collected, even when he was killing people. Perhaps especially then.

He was the Authorities' enforcer. Even if no one ever admitted it.

John waited patiently as they all looked at each other, none of them wanting to be the first to speak. In the end, Julien Advent cleared his throat politely.

"Good to see you, John. Might I enquire where Suzie is?"

"Hunting down some outstanding bounties," said John. "She'll be back as soon as she's made arrangements for transporting the bodies."

Julien stirred uncomfortably. "Should she be doing that? I mean, in her current condition?"

"Don't be so Victorian, Julien," said Annie. "She's pregnant, not incapacitated. And even if she were, I'd still back Shotgun Suzie against anyone dumb enough to give her a hard time."

"Suzie can look after herself," said John. "That's one of the few things in this world you can always depend on."

"But it seems there are some things you can't," Brilliant said heavily. "So let's get down to business."

"My thoughts exactly," said John. "As long as the Nightside's boundaries remain uncertain, we're going to have problems with the Droods. Isn't there anything that can be done to pull back the boundaries, or at least hold them where they are?"

"We have people working on that," Larry said coldly. "But since we have no idea what's behind this sudden change . . ."

"Can I just ask, why are we meeting here, of all places?" asked John.

"Because this is the one place we can be sure the Droods can't listen in," said Julien.

John nodded reluctantly, acknowledging the point, and started his report on what had happened at Drood Hall. He hadn't got far before Annie interrupted him.

"We don't need the details. Just the high points."

John looked at each of the Authorities in turn, to make sure they were all of the same mind. Brilliant and Larry nodded, while Julien looked troubled but went along. Jessica already looked like she was thinking about something else.

"The Matriarch and I could not agree on a compromise," said John. "But then, that was never really in the cards. I told her that from this point on, no Drood would be allowed to enter the Nightside, under any conditions."

"And how did she take that?" said Julien.

"How do you think?" said John.

Brilliant scowled. "So we're back to relying on the Pacts and Agreements?"

"No," said John. "Now we're enforcing them. Droods have been visiting Strangefellows incognito for ages, and no one ever said anything . . . because as long as they were careful to stay under the radar, it wasn't worth making a fuss over. And, occasionally, they'd tell us things we'd never have found out on our own. But now . . ."

"How, exactly, are we supposed to enforce this ban?" said Annie. "They're Droods! There are things in the Nightside that might be capable of taking down a Drood in their armour, but do we really want to risk letting them off the leash?"

"Are we ready for a war?" said Jessica.

Everyone jumped, just a little, then looked at her carefully to see if she had anything more to say. When she didn't, they all breathed a little more easily and pressed on.

"No one wants a war," said Julien.

"That's never stopped one breaking out in the past," said John.

"It all comes down to these changes in the boundaries," said Larry. "So far, no one I've talked to has been able to explain them. They just keep saying it's impossible. Like that's ever been a problem for the Nightside."

"Have you come up with anything yet, John?" said Julien.

"I'd only just started my investigation when you hauled me away to go talk to the Droods," said John. "It's always possible people will talk to me, where they wouldn't to your people, but as far as I can tell, no one's heard anything. None of the usual Major Players are involved, and no one new of any stature has entered the long night recently. I haven't a clue who's behind this or what they might want."

"They want a war," said Jessica.

They all jumped again. Brilliant scowled at Jessica, who was already looking somewhere else.

"Maybe we should have her ring a little bell before she says anything. Just to give us some warning."

"Good luck with that," said John.

Jessica turned her head suddenly to look at Brilliant. "You're not wearing a tie."

Brilliant's tie disappeared. Everyone stood very still. John could feel his hackles rising, along with a strong desire to be absolutely anywhere else. Because once Jessica Sorrow started not believing in things, there was no telling where it would end. Jessica turned away to study something only she could see, and everyone relaxed a little.

"It could be said that Eddie Drood did us a favour by disposing of the predator house," John said carefully. "I know from personal experience how hard they are to kill. Does anyone know how the damned things keep getting in?"

"A question for another time," said Annie. "The point is, Eddie shouldn't have put on his armour. He should have let us deal with it."

"Friends of his died in the Wulfshead," said Julien.

"We all lost someone we knew," said Larry.

"A Drood would only put on his armour in the Nightside if he was ordered to, by his Matriarch," said Brilliant. "This had to be a deliberate provocation. To prove he could do something we couldn't, then see what we would do in response."

"That's a bit of a jump, isn't it?" said John.

"Is it?" said Annie. "We all know the Droods have never approved of the Nightside. We offend their old-fashioned sensibilities. And after everything we've been through in the last ten years, from the angel war to the Lilith War to the civil war, they could see us as weakened. Vulnerable."

"Eddie's actions must mean a change in Drood policy," said Brilliant. "That they're ready to enter the Nightside and impose their authority on us. We can't let them do that."

"John has ordered them to stay out," said Julien.

"And you think they'll listen?" said Brilliant. "They're Droods! We have to put plans in place to stop them."

"No one has ever kept the Droods out of anywhere when they wanted in," said Larry. "So we do this the Nightside way. Hard, unyielding, and underhanded."

"You really think the Droods are ready to take on the whole Nightside?" said John. "Word is they've had their own problems and reverses in the last ten years. And anyway, all kinds of organisations have tried to take over the Nightside, for all kinds of reasons . . . and every single one of them has had their heads handed to them."

"But this is the Droods we're talking about," said Larry. "They honestly think they can't be beaten. And history tends to support that."

"If we could prove to them that we're dealing with the problem of the boundaries . . ." said John.

"But we aren't," said Brilliant.

"They'd find some excuse anyway," said Annie. "Tell everyone that if we can't enforce our own boundaries, they'll do it for us. For everyone's good. And then they'll start sending in field agents, to sort out this problem or that, taking over more and more of our responsibilities, till they're ready to shoulder us aside and lay down the law. Drood law."

"And that would be the end of the Nightside as we know it," said Larry.

"No more party time," said Jessica.

It was a measure of how disturbed everyone was that they hardly reacted at all.

"The Droods must know we'd never accept that," said John. "And not just us . . . no one in the Nightside would stand for having all their fun taken away. They'd rise."

"But the Droods are an army," said Larry. "We're not. And they have that armour."

"They're testing us," said Annie. "Deciding whether we're prepared to fight back. If we don't make a stand right now, that's all it will take to convince them they can do this."

"But any over-the-top reaction from us could start the war anyway," said John.

"We have to send them a message," said Larry. "No Droods in the Nightside. For any reason."

"I already told them that," said John.

"And you think they'll listen?" said Annie. "They're Droods!"

"We can't risk antagonising them!" said Julien.

"They only respect force," said Brilliant.

"We have to send them a message they can't ignore," said Larry.

"The next Drood who comes here . . ." said Annie. "Make an example of them."

The Authorities looked at each other, but none of them said anything. The silence dragged on.

"You need to be very specific here," John said finally. "What exactly do you want me to do, as Walker?"

"It doesn't have to be you personally," said Annie.

"It probably shouldn't be you," said Larry. "Plausible deniability, and all that. It'll be enough that the Droods know even if they can't prove it."

"But it has to be done," said Brilliant.

"If a Drood enters the Nightside, despite everything you've told them, that's an open act of defiance," said Larry. "And that has to mean . . . the Drood doesn't get to go home again."

"Kill him," said Brilliant. "It's the only action they'll pay any attention to."

"I can't condone murder," Julien said flatly.

The others looked at Julien Advent for a long moment, and he stared unflinchingly back.

"It isn't murder if we authorise it," said Brilliant. "It's an execution."

"One life," said Annie. "To save many. On both sides."

"I could do it," said Jessica.

Everyone turned to look at her. She was such a small thing, to be so powerful and so terrible.

"I could decide I didn't believe in him," said Jessica Sorrow. "That way there wouldn't be any body or any evidence."

"You haven't disbelieved a living person in some time," said Julien.

"I know," said Jessica. "You've been helping me. You're very kind."

"Because every time you disbelieve anything," said Julien, "you believe in your own reality a little less. You could just disappear. You mustn't do this, Jessica."

"That's why I found you that teddy bear," John said carefully. "To remind you that you're real. So you wouldn't need to do this any more."

"I believe in the world," said Jessica. "Enough to fight for it."

"Please don't," said Julien.

"You don't have to do this, Jessica," said John. "It's not like there's any shortage of killers here. If this has to be done . . ."

"You know it does," said Larry.

"That's easy for you to say," said John. "What do you care about who'll die in the war? You're dead."

"I still care," said Larry. "That's why the Drood has to die."

John looked at Jessica. Now she'd decided she wasn't needed after all, her eyes were already far away. John looked steadily at the other Authorities.

"How do you kill a Drood?"

"Before he puts his armour on," said Brilliant.

"We can't depend on catching a Drood field agent off guard," said Larry.

"I still have contacts, among my old professional killing fraternity," said Annie. "I'll ask around. Discreetly."

Julien Advent shook his head. "How have we come to this?"

"We didn't start it," said Annie.

"We're just doing what's necessary," said Brilliant.

"You knew this was a dirty job when you took it," said Larry.

"I thought I could make a difference," said Julien. "It seems I was wrong. I'm sorry. I can't be a part of this. I'm sure you'll have no trouble finding a replacement for me."

He walked out of the church and didn't look back once. Larry started to go after Julien, but Annie stopped him.

"It's better that he's not involved. We can live with this; he couldn't."

"And you know Julien," said Brilliant. "Once he's made up his mind . . ."

"We need him!" said Larry. "He's our moral compass. I mean, look at us . . . An ex-enforcer, an ex-assassin, a dead man, and a crazy woman." He stopped and looked at Jessica. "No offence."

Jessica looked at him. "What?"

"We don't need a moral compass," said Brilliant. "Not for this. All we need is the guts to see it through. Julian can rejoin us afterwards. Without a stain on his character."

"It has to be me," said John. "It's my responsibility as Walker."

The Authorities didn't say anything, but he knew they'd all been waiting for him to say that.

"What am I supposed to do in the meantime?" said John. "While I wait for a Drood to show up to be executed?"

"Reach out to everyone you know," said Brilliant. "Somebody must know something about what's happening."

"We'll do the same with our people," said Larry.

"You don't suppose . . . this could be some natural occurrence?" said Annie. "The Nightside feeling its age and the need to stretch out a little?"

"No," said John. "The boundaries of the long night haven't changed by so much as an inch since they were first laid down by my mother, at the Nightside's creation."

Annie looked at him sharply. "Could this be a sign she's returning? You promised us she was gone forever!"

"She's gone," said John.

"This is Lilith we're talking about," said Larry.

"If she were back, I'd know," said John. "Trust me; everyone would know."

"But who is there, powerful enough to undo something Lilith created?" said Larry. "That has to be a pretty short list."

"It isn't going to be anyone obvious," said John. "Because whoever it is would know that's the first thing we'd think of. No . . . this has to be someone new. Someone or something we've never faced before."

"Who would want to bring down the Nightside?" said Annie.

"Someone who disapproves of our very existence," said Larry. "Like the Droods."

"Someone who's afraid of us," said Brilliant. "Or of something we might do . . ."

"Unless this is someone's idea of helping us?" said Annie. "Making the Nightside bigger, to make us more powerful?"

"We can't hope to understand any of this till we know who's behind it," said John. "Put out a reward for information. A really big one. Because people in the Nightside will do anything for money. Let them do all the hard work and bring the answer to us."

"Good idea," said Larry. "We'll do that while you think about the best way to kill a Drood."

A look passed between the Authorities.

"You can go now," said Brilliant.

"We need to discuss the situation further," said Annie.

"In private," said Brilliant.

"We'll call you back when we need you," said Larry.

"And, John . . ." said Annie. "This would never have happened under the old Walker."

John turned his back on them and walked out of the church.

Outside St Jude's, John found the Lord of Thorns looking up at the night sky and frowning. Which was never a good sign. John went over to stand beside him. He studied the flaring stars and the oversized moon but couldn't see anything out of the ordinary.

"What are you looking at, Thorns?" he asked finally.

"Does the moon seem bigger to you than normal?" said the Lord of Thorns.

John considered it carefully. "No." He looked thoughtfully at the Lord of Thorns. He was pretty sure he already knew the answer to the question he was about to ask, but he had to try. "You were put here to be Overseer to the Nightside. Isn't there anything you can do, about the changing borders? If you could just put them back where they were, you could prevent a war."

"Everything has a beginning and an end," said the Lord of Thorns, still staring at the night sky. "No one ever said the long night was forever."

"You'd like that, wouldn't you?" said John. "The end of the Nightside. Because then your position as Overseer would finally be over."

"No," said the Lord of Thorns. "I need the Nightside to continue, so I can continue my penance." He turned suddenly to look at John with his fierce, cold eyes. "You're asking the wrong questions. The change isn't what matters; it's who stands to gain. Ask yourself: Who do you know, who would be pleased to see the Nightside destroyed?"

"You mean the Droods?" said John.

But the Lord of Thorns had already gone back to scowling at the night sky.

John Taylor walked away from St Jude's, thinking hard. The only thing he was sure of was that he couldn't let a Drood be killed in the Nightside. The whole Drood family would rise up to avenge one of their own. There would be war. But given that open war between the Droods and the Nightside wouldn't be in either side's best interests, whose interest would it be in? Who was there who'd go to these lengths to see the Droods and the Nightside humbled and possibly even destroyed? Who would want that?

John's head hurt. He growled under his breath, and people on the street fell back to give him even more room. John decided he didn't understand the situation because he didn't know enough about it. Therefore, he needed more information on the subject. He took out his gold pocket-watch and opened it, and the Timeslip swept him away to where he needed to be.

There are a great many repositories of rare and arcane knowledge in the long night. The Prospero and Michael Scott Memorial Library, the Museum of Unnatural History, Savage Hettie's Lost and Found, the Linda Lovecraft Library of Spiritual Erotica, and the H P Lovecraft Memorial Library. Those last two were really just different versions of the same thing, from two very different dimensions. Both buildings had been squabbling over the same location in the Nightside for some time, popping in and out and shouldering each other aside, replacing each other over and over again . . . Until John negotiated a truce, by threatening to blow both of them through a hole in reality if they didn't stop messing him about. Now the two buildings settled for standing side by side, engaged in a silent battle to see which could attract the most patrons. John had already decided on the H P Lovecraft Memorial Library, for its Really Restricted Section.

He stood before the huge building, studying the impressive frontage, the ever-open front door, and the barred windows to keep books from escaping. A steady series of determined if somewhat furtive-looking scholars plunged in and out of the front door, avoiding one another's eyes. Because no one ever came to the H P Lovecraft Memorial Library looking for the kind of information anyone else would want them to have.

It was strictly for the most discerning and the bravest of scholars, interested in forbidden knowledge, suppressed secrets, and incredibly dangerous books. The kind that would read the scholars if they weren't careful. A Library for the most hardened of researchers, who wouldn't be put off in their pursuit of awful truths by such little things as real and present dangers to their sanity and their souls.

John considered the front door and decided against it. If people saw Walker entering such a place, word would get around. John didn't want anyone knowing he was looking for the kind of answers you could only find in the H P Lovecraft Memorial Library. In particular, he didn't want his mysterious adversary to know. Fortunately, John knew of a secret side-entrance, shown to him by the last Head Librarian, who'd owed John a really substantial favour.

He drifted casually over to an unobtrusive side-alley and darted into it when he was reasonably sure no one was looking. He hurried down the side of the Library, into the darkening shadows of the unlit passageway. Anywhere else he might have worried about encountering mutant killer rats, or undead muggers, or any of the other regular hazards to be found in a Nightside alley-way, but the H P Lovecraft Memorial Library had its own defences. And they ate anything they considered a threat. They wouldn't bother John because he wasn't a threat to the Library and because he was Walker.

He found the side-door easily enough, by the light of a flickering will-o'-the-wisp hovering above it, which was only ever visible to the Right Sort of Person. The sign on the door said HERE BE KNOWLEDGE in much the same way old maps used to say *Here Be Monsters*. He used his special key, courtesy of the previous Head Librarian, rest in peace wherever he was, and let himself in.

The place hadn't changed at all since John was last there. It never changed because it was what it was. Endless shelves packed full of enlightenment, ancient and modern, embracing science and sorcery and everything in between or beyond . . . stretching away for just that little bit farther than the human mind could comfortably tolerate. Waiting for someone brave enough to come along and test themselves against the kind of books that saw each new reader as a challenge. There were rows of reading-desks, because this was very definitely not a lending library. All of them occupied, with a clock ticking down the time left to each student because there was always a queue. Scholars from everywhere and everywhen sat in silent contemplation over the book of their choice, concentrating fiercely as they struggled to work out which of them was in charge.

They were all so taken up with their studies, they didn't even notice the infamous John Taylor as he passed them by, heading for the Really Restricted Section. Where the Library kept the kind of books most people didn't even know existed. Books that shouldn't exist in any sane and rational world. It took John some time to make his way there, following the colour-coded lines on the floor that only the most privileged visitors were allowed to see, until finally he stood before a heavily reinforced door crawling with unpleasant protections. John carefully pronounced the proper passWords, and the door opened. To reveal the ghost of the current Head Librarian, deliberately blocking the doorway so he could glare disapprovingly at John Taylor.

The Ghost Librarian had been eaten by a book when he let his defences slip for a moment, then brought back by the other books because they missed him. He was now a thin, dusty presence in a faded suit, with dark hollows for eyes and no patience at all for anyone who made his job more difficult than it needed to be. John sighed inwardly. He couldn't help feeling it would be nice if he could just bump into someone, now and again, who was actually pleased to see him.

"What are you doing here, Taylor?" said the Ghost Librarian, in his dusty voice. "I thought I made it very clear on your last visit that I never wanted to see you in here again."

"I need to consult the books in this Section," John said patiently. "I do still have my special clearance."

The Ghost Librarian smiled nastily. "It's been revoked. You are not welcome here. You upset the books."

"I'm Walker," said John. "Which means I can have *you* revoked."

The Ghost Librarian looked like he was about to weep dusty tears of pure frustration. "It's not fair," he said bitterly. "The barbarians have taken over the cathedral. Go on, then! Run amok in the stacks! See if I care . . ."

He flickered out like a faulty light bulb. John entered the Really Restricted Section, and the door closed itself firmly behind him. He could hear any number of locks closing, with malicious intent. He allowed himself a small smile. Like that would make any difference. He set off confidently through the endless rows, stuffed full of books on all kinds of subjects. Including some that would make a sewer-rat puke with existential disgust. There wasn't much light; the Section was kept deliberately gloomy in the hope it would encourage some of the more dangerous editions to continue sleeping. The reading-desks had their own specially shielded lamps, but all of them were empty.

As far as John could tell, he had the whole place to himself. Which was a good thing but just a bit worrying. There was usually someone around, researching something they shouldn't. Perhaps the Really Restricted Section had known he was coming and tidied up the place, just for him. John moved deeper into the stacks.

There were books bound in human skin, elven skin, and dragon skin. Books written in blood and bile and brimstone. Some actually glowed in the dark because they were radioactive. Books in every language under the sun and the moon, from every culture and country, some of which didn't exist any more, and some that never had. Because they had been made to have never existed. But then, that's critics for you. There were books that spoke directly to the reader's mind, and some that, given half a chance, would replace the reader's mind and go walking out of the Library in the reader's body. Books from before history began and from alternative futures of varying unlikelihood.

Or so it was said. No one knew for sure, not least because most of the people who went into the Really Restricted Section never talked about what they found there.

Some of the books stirred on the shelves as John passed, muttering querulously to each other. Some were singing. A few were growling. John kept going until he came to the Index, hanging on a side-wall. It was actually a repurposed Speaking Mirror, programmed with all available information on what could be found in the Really Restricted Section. If you searched hard enough, and something didn't sneak up on you in the gloom while you were distracted. John planted himself before the Index, which immediately showed him a reflection of the back of his head, just to be awkward. John identified himself, and the Index groaned loudly.

"I knew it was going to be one of those days. All right, tell me what you want, so I can tell you why you can't have it."

"I'm Walker. I get to see everything."

"Well dip me in chocolate and throw me to the ladyboys. Colour me impressed. What do you want? I'm busy!"

John paused. "What with?"

The Mirror sniggered. "If you don't know, I'd be a damned fool to tell you."

"I need to see the Nightside copy of the Pacts and Agreements between the long night and the Drood family," said John.

"Why on earth would you want to see them?" said the Index. "It hasn't got any pictures, you know. Wouldn't you rather look at something spicy? We've got all kinds of filth in here."

"I need the original Pacts and Agreements," John said firmly. "Because it occurred to me that I haven't got a clue what's in them. I want to know all the details, all the limitations and obligations. Just in case there's something I can use . . ."

"Well, you're no fun," said the Index. "Are you sure I can't tempt you with some nice hot, sweaty elf porn? *Fifty Shades of Fae?*"

The Index sniggered loudly. John fixed the Mirror with a long, thoughtful stare.

"How would you like me to smear your surface with soap?"

"You wouldn't dare!"

"Try me."

"Bully!" hissed the Index. "All right, let me see, let me see . . . where are the Pacts and Agreements filed . . . Ah. Now that is odd."

"What is?" said John.

"They're not where they're supposed to be," said the Index. "As in, they're gone. Someone has checked them out."

"Who?" said John, just a bit loudly.

"I don't know! Don't shout at me; it's not my fault! Whoever took them didn't leave a name. Which is also odd because they shouldn't have been able to remove them at all. Not without tripping all kinds of alarms. Which they didn't. And why didn't any of this bother me till now? I'm going to have to think about this."

"Hold it!" said John. "I'm not finished."

"Oh, what now? Are you still here? I can feel one of my heads coming on."

"You haven't got a head."

"I might have. Somewhere. You don't know."

John thought quickly. "Where can I find books on the Droods?"

The Index snorted loudly. "All over the place. In every section, under every subject. Try being more specific. It might get you somewhere, you never know."

John thought some more. "Their history. In particular, I want to know about all the times the Droods have gone to war."

"Then you're going to be here awhile. Follow the golden arrow. And don't dog-ear any of the pages if you like having fingers!"

The arrow appeared, floating in mid air. John followed it off into the stacks. The arrow kept darting on ahead, then waiting impatiently for him to catch up, like an over-eager dog. It finally stopped before one particular shelf and snapped off. John leaned in close, to study some of the titles. There were hundreds of books, about hundreds of Drood wars, in different places, different times, and even different dimensions. John picked out half-a-dozen, pretty much at random, and carried them over to the nearest reading-desk.

He read carefully at first but was quickly reduced to skipping, in self-defence. It was as though the Droods had never met a war they didn't like. They'd fought everyone, often more than once, and never lost. They'd come close on occasion, been badly hurt and terribly reduced in numbers, but they always came through in the end. And then rebuilt themselves into an even stronger force. Because all Droods were trained to be fighters from early childhood. It wasn't just their armour that made them unbeatable.

John sat back in his chair and thought some more. He couldn't let a Drood be killed in the Nightside. The one thing all the books agreed on was that the Droods would follow a family vendetta to the last drop of their enemy's blood. The Droods might not have faced an enemy like the Nightside before, but John wasn't sure that would be enough to stop them. He'd seen the long night take on angered angels and insane gods and more than hold its own . . . but this was the Droods. Even if the Nightside could hold them off, it could end up destroyed in the process.

So he'd better figure out a way to take down the first Drood to enter the Nightside that didn't involve killing him. Preferably something so humiliating that no Drood would ever want to risk its happening again. That should be enough to buy both sides some time . . .

And he had to figure out who the hell had stolen the Nightside's copy of the Pacts and Agreements. More than ever it seemed there was something in them he needed to know.

John looked at the shelf full of books. There had to be something he could use. If only he could find it.

CHAPTER SIX

Deciding Who Dies

The alley outside Strangefellows seemed particularly quiet and deserted as Eddie and Molly hurried away from the bar, as though the alley were holding its breath to see what would happen next. The shadows were very still and very dark. Molly stopped abruptly and looked back the way they'd come, so Eddie had to stop with her. He recognised the look on Molly's face. It meant she was looking for someone to start something, so she could finish it.

"We're not running away," he said quickly.

"Are you sure?" said Molly. "Because it really does feel like that."

"There was no point in staying once your cover had been blown."

"That wasn't my fault!"

"I never said it was," said Eddie. "So please put down those loaded fists. No one is going to be in any hurry to pursue the infamously bad-tempered wild witch. Who is looking even more wild than usual."

"Compliments? Really?" said Molly, looking at him for the first time. "That's what you're going with?"

"I was just making the point that we have as much time as we need to think about what we're going to do next," Eddie said patiently.

"You do the thinking," said Molly. "I'm going to be busy for a while, laying down some really nasty booby-traps."

"Not necessarily a good idea," Eddie said carefully. "You are going to want to come back here someday."

"Oh, all right," said Molly. "Just a few unpleasant surprises, then. They'll expect that. A girl has to think of her reputation."

"This mission is effectively over," said Eddie. "Now everyone knows who Roxie Hazzard really is, no one will want to talk about anything else."

"You could stay," said Molly. "People expect Shaman Bond to keep bad company."

"I don't like how quickly it all went pear-shaped," said Eddie. "What were the odds of someone's just happening to turn up at Strangefellows who could see through Roxie to recognise you?"

Molly nodded slowly. "You think someone sent her?"

"Don't you?" said Eddie.

"But that would have to mean someone knew we were going to be at Strangefellows, as Roxie Hazzard and Shaman Bond."

"Exactly," said Eddie. "That's why I got us out of there so quickly. In case there was a part two to the plan. I always thought coming back here so soon was a bad idea, but now I'm starting to wonder if Blaiston Street was a trap too. Designed to put me in my armour. I need to get back to Drood Hall and talk to the Matriarch. About a lot of things."

He shook the Merlin Glass out to door size. Cheerful light from the grounds outside Drood Hall spilled through into the dark alley-way, and Eddie was convinced some of the nearer shadows flinched. Molly scowled at the great rolling lawns on the other side of the door, then turned her glare back in the direction of Strangefellows. She looked very much like she wanted to argue some more, so Eddie pushed her through the open doorway and hurried after her. The Merlin Glass disappeared, taking its light with it, and shadows filled the alley-way again.

Molly turned on Eddie, to demand what the hell he thought he was doing pushing her around, and he was just getting ready to defend himself, by armouring up if need be . . . when they both realised they weren't where they should have been. Instead of the wide-open grounds, they were inside the Hall, in the Sanctity. Facing the Matriarch, the Sarjeant-at-Arms, and the Council. Again.

The Merlin Glass shrank back into a hand-mirror and forced itself into Eddie's hand, as though it were frightened. Eddie put the Glass away, without taking his eyes off all the people staring at him. Molly was so startled she actually forgot about being angry. She grabbed hold of Eddie's arm and murmured urgently in his ear.

"What the hell just happened? How is this even possible?"

"The very first thing I intend to ask," said Eddie. "Once you've stopped cutting off the circulation in my arm."

"Want me to get us out of here?" said Molly. "I've got a new teleport spell that will blast us right through whatever shields they think they've got."

"Tempting," said Eddie. "But save it for later. I want to know what's going on here. Watch my back while I hit them with some pointed questions. But please don't turn anyone into a frog without checking with me first."

"I don't always turn people into frogs!" said Molly. "Though having said that, haven't you ever wondered what a frog in golden armour would look like?"

"Talk first, threaten later," said Eddie.

"You're getting old," said Molly. "You'll be acting reasonably next."

"Let's not get carried away," said Eddie.

"If you two have quite finished muttering to each other . . ." said the Sarjeant-at-Arms.

Eddie ignored him and the coldly staring Matriarch and looked around at the assembled Council. He needed time to think. His first thought was that the Librarian appeared to be in even worse shape than last time. William's clothes were a mess, his hair was all over the place, and his gaze was worryingly distant. As though he couldn't be expected to maintain the appearance of normality, or even something resembling sanity, under so much pressure. Ammonia was sitting very close to her husband and glaring daggers at the Matriarch and the Sarjeant, who were both carefully avoiding her gaze. Presumably on the grounds that if they recognised how upset she was, they might have to do something about it. Anyone else would have had enough sense to be quite seriously worried at the thought of upsetting the world's most powerful telepath, but the Matriarch was too busy being in charge, and the Sarjeant didn't do worried. So Ammonia settled for holding William's hand in both of hers and glowering in a way that strongly suggested she was planning future vengeances.

The Armourer Maxwell and Victoria were also sitting close together, in battered lab coats that looked like something really nasty had happened worryingly close, not that long ago. More than ever they looked like schoolchildren who'd been summoned before their Headmistress and were anticipating harsh words. Given the way they'd let their side down at the last Council meeting, by not being able to give the Matriarch what she wanted, they were clearly hoping for a way to ingratiate themselves and get back in her good books. Eddie didn't like the thought of that. The Armourer was never more dangerous than when they were feeling personally threatened.

"I didn't expect to see you again so soon, Eddie," the Matriarch said loudly. "What happened? Why have you returned?"

Eddie fixed the Matriarch with his best cold stare.

"Never mind that! How were you able to take control of the Merlin Glass in mid-flight? The only person who could do that was the old Armourer, and Uncle Jack swore to me he was the only one who knew how!"

Eddie turned his glare on Maxwell and Victoria, but before he could accuse them of anything, Ethel's voice rang out on the air.

"I did it."

There was no trace of the rose-red glow that usually marked her presence, just a calm voice that seemed to come from everywhere at once.

"Why?" said Eddie, cramming a whole world of questions and emotions into just the one word.

"Because the Matriarch asked me to," said Ethel.

"You're being very obliging to her, all of a sudden," said Eddie. "It wasn't that long ago the two of you weren't even talking to each other. So what brought this on?"

"Events are escalating," said Ethel.

Eddie waited for her to expand on that . . . and when she didn't, he had no choice but to turn back to the Matriarch. "All right, why are you still talking with the Council, Maggie?"

"Yeah," said Molly. "What he said, only with much more of an implied threat and an added air of sudden and unrestrained violence."

"We have to stay on top of things," said the Matriarch, carefully keeping her gaze fixed on Eddie. "To make sure they don't get out-of-control. Make your report, Eddie. What happened in the Nightside, that you had to come home in such a hurry?"

"No one in Strangefellows knows anything about the boundary changes," said Eddie. "Which effectively means no one in the long night knows. And we had to leave in a hurry because someone blew Molly's cover."

"They knew me," said Molly. "Both of me."

"Did you know them?" said the Sarjeant.

"No," said Molly. "So somebody must have told her, then aimed her at me."

"Are you implying someone knew you were going to be in the bar, as Roxie?" the Sarjeant asked.

"I'm not implying anything," said Molly. "I'm stating it as a fact."

"And the only people who knew where we were going, and when we'd be there, are in this room," said Eddie.

There was a stir among the Council, but the Matriarch was already shaking her head.

"No one here betrayed you, Eddie. Ammonia would know. Ethel would know."

"Then how the hell did this happen?" said Eddie.

"There's a lot going on that we don't understand right now," said the Sarjeant. "But my people are working on it."

"I feel so much more secure for knowing that," said Eddie.

"You should," the Sarjeant-at-Arms replied.

"I'm going to miss Roxie," said Molly. "It was always so much fun, being her."

Eddie turned to look at her. "You've always enjoyed being Molly. Even when it was wholly inappropriate and downright dangerous to everyone around you."

"Well, yes," said Molly. "But as Roxie I was free to do all the things that Molly couldn't."

"I won't ask," said Eddie.

"Best not to," said Molly.

"If we could get back to discussing why this mission was as big a failure as your last one," said the Sarjeant.

"None of what happened was Molly's fault!" said Eddie. "We had no way of knowing someone was going to sabotage us."

"Bad things happen in Strangefellows," said Molly. "It's that kind of bar."

"There is that," said the Sarjeant.

The Matriarch turned her cold glare on him. "You told me you'd stopped drinking there."

"I have," said the Sarjeant. "I stopped when Jack died. It wasn't as much fun without him. But it was the spontaneity of the place that made it so interesting. Anything could happen."

"Why are all of you still here, still talking?" Eddie said loudly. "I thought it was agreed you weren't going to make any decisions till Molly and I had returned with more up-to-date information?"

"We received new information, not long after you left," said the Matriarch. "One of our agents in the Nightside informed us that the Authorities are planning some kind of pre-emptive strike against us."

"What kind of strike?" said Eddie.

"Never mind that," said Molly. "Since when have the Droods had agents inside the Nightside?"

"Since always," said the Sarjeant. "We have agents everywhere."

"Why was I never told about this before?" said Molly.

"Because you didn't need to know," said the Sarjeant.

Molly turned to Eddie. "Did you know?"

"No," said Eddie, looking thoughtfully at the Sarjeant. "This is news to me too."

"I didn't just go drinking in Strangefellows for my own pleasure," the Sarjeant explained. "It was a good way to make contacts with useful people. So we'd always have some idea of what was going on in the long night."

"I summoned the Council to discuss this new threat," said the Matriarch. "Because if the Authorities are behind it, we could all be in danger."

"You can't keep calling William back here just because you need your hand held!" said Ammonia. "It's not good for him."

The Matriarch nodded, accepting the point, and nodded reassuringly to William. "If you need to be excused from future meetings, Librarian . . ."

"No, I do not," William said stiffly. He met the Matriarch's gaze firmly. "If the family is in danger, I need to know what's going on. Don't fuss, Ammonia. I can cope."

Ammonia didn't look even a little bit convinced of that, but she didn't say anything.

"What kind of pre-emptive strike are we talking about?" Eddie asked, determined not to be side-tracked. "An open assault, on Drood Hall?"

"Possibly," said the Sarjeant. "If John Taylor can appear in our grounds out of nowhere, despite all the shields and protections we put in place just to keep people like him out, what's to stop him coming back at the head of an armed force?"

"You assured me such an invasion was impossible, after all the very expensive upgrades I authorised," said the Matriarch.

"This is John Taylor we're talking about," said the Sarjeant. "A man with an extensive history of doing things everyone else believed impossible."

"Do these local agents of yours know anything about what the Authorities might be planning?" said Eddie.

"Not so far," said the Sarjeant. "Did you hear anything at Strangefellows?"

"No," said Eddie. "But then, we didn't know to ask."

"And the Authorities have a lot of experience when it comes to holding their cards close to their chest," said Molly.

"Whatever the Authorities are planning, they've made their intentions clear," said the Matriarch. "So, we have decided the only way to stop the expansion of the Nightside, and put an end to the Authorities' plans, is to bring the whole of the long night under Drood control."

"And to hell with the Pacts and Agreements," said the Sarjeant-at-Arms. "They no longer serve any useful purpose."

"It's long past time we put a stop to the Nightside," said the Matriarch. "Pretty much every evil we face has its roots there."

"It's always been a safe haven, for all kinds of villains and dubious characters," said the Sarjeant.

Eddie looked at the Sarjeant, surprised he wasn't defending some of the more appealing aspects of the Nightside. Like drinking in Strangefellows. Something had changed in the Sarjeant, and Eddie wanted very much to know what.

"The only way to seize control of the Nightside, and hold it," Eddie said carefully, "would involve a full-on invasion. You'd have to commit all of the Droods, the entire family, in their armour."

"Yes," said the Matriarch. "No holding back and no quarter; surrender or die. We have to do this, Eddie. It's necessary."

"But it's not practical!" said Eddie. "It would take months of preparation, just to organise such an invasion!"

"We can be ready to go in a few hours," said the Sarjeant. "The family has long-standing contingency plans in place, with everything we need to know already worked out."

"You have plans to attack the Nightside?" said Molly.

"We have detailed plans on how to take down all our enemies," said the Sarjeant. "And all of our friends and allies."

"Just how long-standing are these plans of yours?" said Molly.

"Most of them go back centuries," said the Sarjeant. "Constantly updated, of course. Because we always knew a day like this would come, when we had to be prepared to fight for our survival, and the world's."

"Do your friends and allies know you've always been ready to attack them, as well as your enemies?" Molly asked.

"Our duty is to protect Humanity from all threats," said the Matriarch. "Wherever they come from. Today's friend could be tomorrow's enemy."

"It can happen," Eddie said to Molly. "Remember, you used to think Manifest Destiny were good guys. Till you saw what they had in their cellars."

Molly didn't say anything. She just glared dangerously at the Matriarch and the Sarjeant-at-Arms.

"We all hoped these plans would never have to be used," said the Matriarch, staring unflinchingly back at Molly. "But we had to have them. Just in case."

Molly turned her glare on Eddie. "Did you know about this when you were running the family?"

"I knew there were plans," Eddie said steadily. "I never looked at any of them because I never needed to. But that could have changed. Remember when we discovered the family had been infiltrated by the Loathly Ones? What if they'd got into any of the other secret organisations, ones we currently think of as friends and allies? We'd have had to take them down, to save the Earth from being destroyed by the Hungry Gods. It has always been our job to be prepared for any emergency. And . . . to do whatever is necessary."

Molly turned away from him, to stand on her own. Her back was stiff, and her arms were tightly folded, as though to hold in her churning emotions. She said nothing, thinking her own fierce thoughts. Which worried Eddie. Molly Metcalf was never more dangerous than when she was thinking. But there was nothing he could do about that now. All he could do was concentrate on what was in front of him. He turned reluctantly to face the

Matriarch and the Sarjeant-at-Arms. He chose his words carefully before he spoke and addressed them mostly to the Sarjeant, the only other man in the room with the experience of leading Droods into battle.

"How are we supposed to get into the Nightside? There are no roads for us to drive down, no territory we can fly over or land on. No practical approaches at all, in the real world. We'd have to use the traditional ways: the hidden doors and the shadow roads. And you can be sure the Authorities will have all of them sealed off or barricaded by now. Because they're bound to have long-standing contingency plans of their own. They'll defend the entrances they can't block with all kinds of forces, turn the approaches into bottlenecks and killing grounds, and make us pay in blood and slaughter for every foot of ground we seize. The Authorities are dangerous because they think like us. With the right tactics, they could keep us out forever!" He stopped as a thought occurred to him. "I suppose . . . I could use the Merlin Glass, but you know the size of door it makes. We'd have to file the family through two by two! How big an attack force do you think we'd get in before an army arrived to stop us?"

His voice had become so loud he was almost shouting at the Matriarch. The Sarjeant-at-Arms was looking at him threateningly because no one was ever supposed to shout at the Matriarch. But she seemed perfectly unruffled by Eddie's manner or the point he was making. She didn't even glance at the Sarjeant for support. A cold hand closed around Eddie's heart as he realised they already had an answer. And from the look on their faces, one they knew he wasn't going to like.

"There is a way into the Nightside that they won't be expecting," said the Matriarch. "Armourer, if you please."

Maxwell and Victoria sat up straight in their chairs. This was their area, and their chance to shine.

"We can use Alpha Red Alpha," said Max. "The whole point of the dimensional engine is to translate Drood Hall out of this world when it's under threat and put it somewhere secure till it's safe for the Hall to return."

"We can use the machine to transfer the Hall right into the middle of the Nightside," said Vicky. "And the whole family with it."

"Alpha Red Alpha is powerful enough to smash through any shields the Authorities could put in place," said Max.

"They'll never see it coming!" said Vicky.

"And with Drood Hall inside the Nightside, we'll have an impregnable base right in the heart of the Authorities' territory," said Max.

"Giving us supply lines they won't be able to interrupt," said Vicky.

"Yes, dear, I was just getting to that," said Max.

"From such a central point, we could spread out and occupy all the important areas in a matter of hours," said Vicky. "And take down all the Major Players along the way."

"I was just about to say that!" said Max.

"Oh, I'm so sorry, dear," said Vicky. "You go right ahead."

"I'm going to, dear," said Max. He gave the Matriarch his most confident look. "If we hit the Nightside hard enough and fast enough, we should be able to bring the invasion to a successful conclusion with minimal damage and loss of life."

"On either side," said Vicky.

Molly spun around suddenly to face them, and the Armourer actually flinched back in their chairs. Eddie didn't think he'd ever seen Molly so angry.

"And what if you can't do it quickly, or cleanly? What if it all goes wrong? What if the Authorities dig in, and the fighting goes on and on, and the bodies start piling up?"

The Armourer huddled together like frightened children, in the face of such a fierce attack, and looked to the Matriarch for support.

"We're Droods," said the Matriarch. "We do what's necessary and count the costs afterwards. We're doing this to save the whole world from being overrun by the long night."

Molly looked like she was about to erupt. Eddie cleared his throat, and her gaze snapped to him. He met her anger calmly and shook his head slightly, meaning: *We'll talk more about this when we're alone.* Molly scowled and subsided reluctantly. Eddie nodded thankfully to her. He wasn't sure which side of the argument he was on, but he could tell there was no point in arguing with people when they'd already made up their minds.

"Thank you, Molly," said the Matriarch, her voice carefully calm and reasonable. "We will take your opinions under consideration."

Eddie winced. Molly had never responded well to people who tried being reasonable. Particularly if she decided they were just being patronising. Eddie let his hand drift down to the trouser-pocket where he kept his pocket dimension. If necessary, if someone pushed Molly too far and it looked like she was about to lose it, he was pretty sure he could whip out the Merlin Glass, slam it down over Molly, and send her somewhere else before she could do something everyone but her would regret. And then hope he could make it up to her later. He couldn't allow Molly to attack his family, not when they might be needed to save the world.

"You possess the most up-to-date knowledge on the Nightside, Molly," said the Matriarch, graciously. "It would be very helpful if you could find the time to sit down with some of our people and tell them everything you know. About the place, the people, all the secrets they think no one else knows. Such information could prove invaluable in the war that's coming."

"You really think I'd help you plan the deaths of my friends?" said Molly. Her voice was a very cold and very hard thing. "I'd rather die. I'd rather all of you died . . ."

The Council stirred uncomfortably. Ammonia let go of William, so she could concentrate on the threat before her. William didn't notice, his thoughts somewhere else. Maxwell and Victoria thrust their hands into their coat pockets, in search of something they could use to protect themselves. The tension in the room ratcheted up a whole other notch as the Sarjeant-at-Arms took a step forward. Eddie stuck his hand in his pocket dimension and grabbed hold of the Merlin Glass, ready to put himself between Molly and his family. Even if he wasn't sure which of them he was protecting. But the Matriarch just spoke calmly and rationally to Molly, choosing her words carefully so as not to sound too much like an adult lecturing a wilful child.

"A bloodless coup is in everyone's best interests, Molly. The lives you help to save could include your friends'."

Molly stood very still, her hands clenched into fists. She said nothing, her face unreadable, then she turned her back on everyone again. Everyone relaxed, just a little, and various hands emerged empty from various pockets. The Matriarch ignored Molly's behaviour and turned her attention to William.

"Librarian, I . . . William!"

His head came up, and Eddie could almost hear William's attention snap back into focus.

"Yes, Maggie? Did you want something?"

"We're going to need the most detailed maps of the Nightside you can provide," said the Matriarch. "I need to be sure of what we're getting into."

The Librarian was already shaking his head. "Oh, I have maps, lots of maps, ancient and modern, but none of them are worth a damn. The problem is, you see, that the geography of the Nightside is always changing. Growing and shrinking and transforming itself . . . Perhaps because that's the only way it can accommodate all the sinning that goes on there."

"How is that possible?" said the Matriarch. Making it clear this was a practical and not a philosophical question. She really wanted to know.

William looked at her pityingly. "It's the Nightside."

The Matriarch turned to address Molly's stubbornly turned back. "Is this why you were so sure an invasion wouldn't work? I need you to help me understand, Molly."

Molly thought about it, and turned back to face the Matriarch and her Council. She still looked angry, but at least she seemed ready to talk. Perhaps because she felt on safer ground discussing things that were common knowledge in her part of the hidden world.

"Some parts of the long night are as old as civilisation, while others can appear spontaneously as you watch. Some institutions have survived for centuries, while others come and go in the blink of an eye. It's the nature of the Nightside, that the only constant is change. An area dedicated to freedom of choice has to be free to be what it wants to be. Or needs to be. Most of the central locations are fixed and certain, because people want them to be, but how you get to them can change without warning.

"Popular establishments get physically bigger as they become more successful, while less popular places shrink and fade away. As one club or business stumbles, it is immediately forced aside and replaced by another. Darwinism in action. The Nightside can give a whole new meaning to the phrase *hostile takeover.* And even beyond all the mechanisms of sin and temptation, there are levels to the Nightside. What you see is never going to be all of what you get. Whole worlds can hide within innocent-looking buildings, and ordinary-seeming doors can lead to dimensions of pleasure or traps for the unwary. There are things underground that have been sleeping for centuries, that only a fool would waken . . . And do I really need to remind you about the Street of the Gods?"

"At least we don't need to worry about that," said the Sarjeant. "It's empty."

"What?" said Eddie.

"According to the latest reports, the gods have run away," the Sarjeant explained. "Apparently they looked into the future and saw us looking back at them. They couldn't hit the road fast enough."

"And you think that's a good thing?" said Eddie. He could tell his voice was rising again and didn't give a damn. "Old Father Time was right! We are the terrible thing that's coming! How destructive, how deadly, are we going to be that even the beings on the Street of the Gods don't want to be around when we turn up? How much more evidence do you need that this invasion is a really bad idea? For everyone!"

The Matriarch looked back at him, entirely unmoved. "Are you going to calm down, Eddie, or do I need to get you a paper bag to breathe into? The gods have good reason to fear us. They know we couldn't afford to go easy on beings as powerful as them. But I am only interested in taking control of the Nightside; if I can find a way to do that without spilling a drop of blood, I will happily accept it. The reason for all this discussion and planning is to find a way to do that as painlessly as possible. Go on, Molly; what else do we need to know about the geography of the Nightside?"

Molly looked at her for a long moment, disturbed that her words weren't having the desired effect on the Matriarch. She took a deep breath and tried again.

"You have no idea of what you're getting into. How can you invade a place where the streets come and go, and reality itself can be rewritten while you wait? By strength of will, by unknown forces, or just the whim of the moment? Street signs offer opinions as much as directions, and the last time I consulted a Nightside A–Z, the details on the pages changed before my eyes."

She looked challengingly at the Matriarch, who stared calmly back.

"We'll just have to conquer everything as we come to it," said the Matriarch. "Take control of strategic locations and hold them."

"How can you hold something that can change shape in your grasp to bite you?" said Molly.

The Sarjeant-at-Arms cleared his throat, and everyone turned to look at him. Because when he had something to say, you'd better listen.

"I'm afraid it's even more complicated than that, Matriarch. We'll have to block off all the entrances and exits to the long night, once we're inside. Including all the Timeslips. Not just to prevent people from leaving but to keep the Authorities from summoning reinforcements. There are quite a few who'd come running to defend the Nightside, either because they have a vested interest in seeing it continue or because they believe in what they think it represents. And there are others who'd join in the fighting, just for a chance to strike at the Droods in someone else's territory. We can't risk this conflict spreading, or we could end up embroiled in even more wars outside the long night."

The Matriarch looked to Molly, who shrugged quickly.

"I don't know where all the exits are. I don't think anyone does. And the Timeslips come and go according to rules and notions only they understand. Some think they might be sentient, while others think they're like the weather. And you can bet the Authorities have any number of secret exits, so important people can escape the Nightside in times of trouble."

"Don't forget the Nightside has its own House of Doors," said Eddie. "Where the Doormouse builds and sells dimensional Doors. The last time Molly and I were in the showroom, there were Doors to places I wasn't even sure existed. The Doormouse has sold Doors to us in the past, which means he'll sell to anyone. And these are just the ways in and out that we've heard of. There's no way we can seal the Nightside off completely."

"We need a blanket cover, for everything," said the Matriarch. "Armourer?"

Maxwell and Victoria looked at each other. They seemed a little surprised, and even put-out, as though they thought they'd already done everything that could reasonably be asked of them. This was their moment to shine, to prove their worth, but it was obvious to Eddie it had never occurred to them they would have to come up with an answer to this particular problem. But you don't say no to the Matriarch, particularly when the Sarjeant-at-Arms is standing scowling beside her. So the two of them put their heads together and murmured urgently. Eddie watched ideas come and go in their faces, possible solutions raised and shot down over and over, until finally they found something they could both agree on. They sat back and did their best to smile confidently at the Matriarch.

"We don't have anything specifically designed to do what you want," said Max.

"But we do have Alpha Red Alpha," said Vicky.

"The most powerful dimensional engine ever created," said Max. "We've spent a lot of time investigating its potential capabilities."

"On our own time, of course," said Vicky.

"Well, obviously, dear," said Max.

"Tell the Matriarch what it can do, dear. You're so good at putting things into words."

"But you did a lot of the basic research, dear."

"But it was your idea originally! You tell them! And don't be so modest, sweetie. This is no time to be putting yourself down. Their trouble is, they don't appreciate you."

"Oh, hush, dear." Max smiled tentatively at the Matriarch. "It is our opinion that Alpha Red Alpha could be made to broadcast a signal powerful enough to block any dimensional changes."

"To lock on to one set of Space/Time coordinates, and impose them on everything surrounding the machine," said Vicky.

"Powerful enough to cover the whole of the Nightside?" said the Sarjeant.

"Oh, certainly," said Max.

"Theoretically," said Vicky.

"The mathematics are perfectly sound," said Max.

"We just haven't had a chance to try it," said Vicky.

"So there's no telling what the side-effects might be."

"Or how much energy it would use up."

"The dimensional engine could burn itself out," said Max.

"Or it could drain all of the Hall's power and its reserves," said Vicky.

"We just don't know."

"But it should work."

"Oh yes, it should work."

"But we can't tell you for how long."

"Find out," said the Matriarch.

Maxwell and Victoria bobbed their heads eagerly, already looking forward to some properly authorised experimenting.

"Whether this works or not, you still haven't addressed the real problem," Eddie said doggedly. He glared at the Matriarch. "You're arguing over the details and missing the point! You're still clinging to the old idea, that the Droods always win. Which is understandable. It's practically part of our job description. But we've never taken on anything like the Nightside before! All our plans and aims are worthless when set against an enemy we don't understand and can't predict!"

"Damn right!" Molly said loudly. "You have no idea what's waiting for you! There are things in the long night no one should disturb, things even Walker and the Authorities couldn't hope to control. And these are people who've won victories against angels from Above and Below, and Lilith herself!"

The Matriarch nodded, to show she was listening, but remained unmoved. "You were there when we defeated the Angelic and Demonic Droods, Molly. You helped us destroy the Hungry Gods. This family has never been afraid to take on agents of Light or Darkness, or anything in between. We do what needs doing. Nothing else matters."

"You're not doing this because it's necessary!" Molly's voice was rising again. "You're doing it because you want to! Because this situation has finally given you the perfect excuse to do what you've always dreamed of doing. To stamp out the one place in the world where the Droods have never been able to enforce their inflexible, puritanical, cold-hearted authority! You won't be happy till the whole world bends its knee and bows its head to you and does what it's told!"

"You're right," said the Matriarch. "I do dream about that, sometimes."

Molly stormed out of the Sanctity. The Matriarch turned to Eddie.

"Go after her. Stop her. Calm her down and bring her to her senses. Or we'll do it for you."

"Don't push your luck, Maggie," Eddie retorted.

The Sarjeant-at-Arms looked like he was about to say something. Eddie shot him a challenging look, and the Sarjeant thought better of it. Eddie looked coldly around the Council.

"You're supposed to be her advisors. So talk her out of this. For all our sakes."

He turned his back on them all and left the Sanctity.

*   *   *

Out in the corridor, Molly hadn't got far. She was surrounded by half-a-dozen Droods in full armour. They were maintaining a respectful distance, for the moment, but they weren't letting her go. Eddie strolled over to join them, working hard to look calm and composed, and not at all like he was about to kick all their arses. One of the Droods turned his featureless golden mask to face him.

"Hello, Eddie. Good of you to join us, but we don't need any help. We have the situation under control."

"No, you haven't," said Eddie. "You only think you have. Because Molly is being uncharacteristically patient with you, for my sake. You can tell that because, otherwise, she'd have done something quite appallingly unpleasant to you by now. She only held off because she knew I was coming. Would I be correct in assuming that the Sarjeant-at-Arms called for you to be here? Before Molly and I even appeared inside the Sanctity? Yes, I thought so. And no, I can't read your face through that mask, but your body language is a dead give-away. What are your orders exactly?"

"First and foremost, to maintain order in the Hall," said the faceless Drood. "To contain the wild witch Molly Metcalf, and prevent her from causing any trouble. To remove her to a safe and secure location that has already been prepared for her. Somewhere she can be kept safely, and comfortably, till the present problem with the Nightside has been dealt with. These are long-standing orders, Eddie. And we will carry them out."

"Not on the best day you ever had," said Eddie. He nodded apologetically to Molly. "My family does like to have plans in place for every eventuality. Try not to take it personally. I'm sure there are standing orders where I'm concerned."

"Yes," said the faceless Drood. "There are."

Eddie smiled at him. "Okay, you're annoying me now. Get lost, and take your little bully-boy buddies with you."

The circle of armoured Droods stirred uneasily but held their ground.

"The witch's room is waiting for her," said the faceless Drood. "We can open a secure room for you too if you like."

"You really fancy your chances?" said Eddie.

"We can handle the witch."

"But can you handle her and me?" said Eddie.

The Drood looked at him for a long moment, then turned and strode away. The other Droods hurried after him. Their armoured feet made a low thunder on the bare floor-boards, to disguise the fact that they were running away. Eddie looked thoughtfully at their departing backs.

"I must be losing my touch. He actually stopped to think about it. I can see I'm going to have to do something more than usually destructive while I'm here, just to restore my reputation."

"I'll help," said Molly. She looked at him for a long moment. "Are you really ready to take on your entire family just for me?"

"I'd take on the whole world for you," said Eddie.

Molly smiled. "Of course you would."

"They didn't try to hurt you, did they?" said Eddie.

"They knew better than that," said Molly. "Eddie, what are we going to do?"

"I don't know," said Eddie. He stood and thought for a while, and Molly waited patiently, never doubting he would come up with an answer. Finally Eddie nodded firmly. "We need to visit the Old Library. Take a look at the original Pacts and Agreements. William should have arranged for a translation by now. Maybe there's something in the original copy we can use to make both sides behave."

"You mean like a sinner reading the Bible, looking for loopholes?" said Molly.

"Exactly," said Eddie.

They'd barely got half-way down the long corridor when Eddie came to a sudden halt as a Drood with a familiar but very unexpected face came walking down the corridor towards them. Molly stopped beside Eddie.

"What's wrong, Eddie? Who is that?"

"That . . . is Luther Drood. Field agent for Los Angeles. We worked together on a case once when I had to go to LA. What the hell is Luther doing here? He never comes home."

They waited for Luther to join them. He took his own sweet time doing it, just to show he was his own man, but finally stopped before them and nodded politely. A tall, heavy-built man in his fifties, he had a bronzed and heavily lined face, close-cut grey hair, and a bushy grey moustache, and was wearing an offensively gaudy T-shirt over blindingly white shorts, with designer flip-flops. Like most of the people in his adopted city, Luther went to some effort to appear calm and laid-back.

"Eddie," said Luther.

"Luther," said Eddie.

"Molly!" said Molly, not to be left out.

The two men met each other's gaze steadily, neither giving an inch. Molly could sense a history between them, and not a good one.

"So, what did the two of you get up to in LA?" she said, after the silence had dragged on just a little too long.

"I turned a dragon inside out," said Eddie.

"And you destroyed a landmark hotel," said Luther.

"You get to have all the fun, Eddie," said Molly.

"The next hotel is all yours," said Eddie, not taking his eyes off the other field agent. "What are you doing here, Luther?"

"I was summoned, by the Matriarch," said Luther. "Is it true, what I've been hearing about the Nightside?"

"Probably," said Eddie.

"Damn," said Luther. "The only place I know of that's actually worse than Los Angeles. The long night . . . where the sinning is easy, and the bill will take your breath away."

"What are you doing here, Luther?" said Eddie, refusing to be sidetracked.

"You'll have to excuse me," said Luther. "The Matriarch is waiting to talk to me."

He strode past them, heading for the Sanctity doors. The two guards were already holding them open for him. Eddie and Molly watched Luther go.

"That man needs more fibre in his diet," said Eddie.

"Why would the Matriarch send for him in particular?" said Molly.

"Good question," said Eddie.

He broke off, as the entire Council came hurrying out of the open Sanctity doors. William and Ammonia bustled down the corridor and straight past Eddie and Molly, not even glancing at them. In times of trouble, William always headed for the Old Library. The only place he really thought of as home.

Maxwell and Victoria took advantage of Eddie's and Molly's distraction to nip smartly past them on the other side. By the time Eddie turned to look, they were just two lab coats heading for the Armoury at speed. Presumably because they were looking forward to playing with Alpha Red Alpha and seeing if they could teach it some new tricks, but also because they really didn't want to speak to Eddie and Molly.

The Sarjeant-at-Arms was the last to leave the Sanctity, and the two guards moved quickly to close the doors behind him. The Sarjeant headed straight for Eddie and Molly and planted himself in front of them.

"We need to talk," he said bluntly.

Eddie was immediately suspicious. Normally he was only able to prise information out of the Sarjeant through threats, intimidation, or blackmail. So he decided he wasn't going to be rushed into anything and merely raised an inquisitive eyebrow.

"The Matriarch dismissed her entire Council the moment Luther walked in," said the Sarjeant.

"You didn't know she'd sent for him?" said Eddie.

"No," said the Sarjeant. "And I'm supposed to know things like that. She threw us all out the moment he appeared, even though we hadn't finished explaining the realities of the situation to her. All because she was so keen to talk to Luther in private."

"Do you know him?" said Molly.

"Only by reputation," said the Sarjeant. "First-class field agent, still running Los Angeles long after he should have been retired and brought home."

"You don't know why that is either," said Eddie. "Even though you should."

"And now he has the Matriarch's private ear," said the Sarjeant. "Even though he shouldn't."

"She's planning something," said Molly.

"Of course she is," said the Sarjeant. "She's the Matriarch; she's always planning something. But usually she has the good sense to discuss things with me first. An audience as private as this can only mean she wants Luther to do something she knows I won't approve of. Something she is determined not to be talked out of."

"What could be so bad, that you wouldn't approve of it?" said Eddie.

"I don't know," said the Sarjeant. "But it can't be anything good."

Luther looked at the Matriarch, sitting easily behind her desk, then deliberately looked away to take in the huge, empty chamber.

"I'd forgotten how big the Sanctity is, but then, it's been such a long time since I was last here . . . Just the two of us, is it?"

"Yes," said the Matriarch. "Ethel has assured me that she won't be listening in."

"And you believe her?" said Luther.

"I have to," said the Matriarch.

"Why all this solitude and secrecy for our little chat?" said Luther.

"Sit down," said the Matriarch. "And I'll tell you."

Luther looked at all the empty chairs, picked one up, and set it down directly opposite the Matriarch. He sat down, took a moment to arrange himself comfortably, and only then gave the Matriarch his full attention.

"The last time I was allowed to come home, Martha was still Matriarch. Eddie was merely the secondary field agent for London, and our armour came from the Heart, not Ethel. So much has changed, but not the job we do. Or the kind of things I'm asked to do."

"Some things never change," said the Matriarch.

"Why am I here?" said Luther. "Why bring me back, after so many years?"

The Matriarch took a moment to shake her head slowly at his outfit. "Please tell me you haven't gone native."

"It's just protective colouration, to help me fit in," said Luther. "So people will think I'm one of them and talk openly. I'm still a Drood. The only moral man in that cesspit of a city."

"And that is why you're here now," said the Matriarch. "I've given orders for all field agents to return to the Hall, but I wanted to talk to you first."

Luther frowned. "All of them? Won't that leave us dangerously vulnerable, out in the world? While the cats are otherwise occupied, the mice will think they can get away with things."

"We can always put down some poison," said the Matriarch. "I needed to see you first because I have a special assignment for you."

Luther sat back in his chair, careful to keep the smile off his face. He knew where he was now. The Matriarch wanted something from him, and since she wasn't just giving him orders, that suggested she needed his co-operation. Luther wondered what he could get in return for that.

"I need you to go into the Nightside," the Matriarch said levelly. "And kill John Taylor."

She looked at him, waiting for a response. Luther sat quietly, his face impassive, thinking hard.

"I'm not saying no," he said finally. "But I have to ask why?"

"Because as the current Walker, and a living legend in his own right, John Taylor is the nearest thing the Nightside has to a leader. Kill him, and we cut off the head of any resistance before it even starts."

Luther thought about it some more. "You want me to go in under my cover identity, Philip Harlowe?"

"No," said the Matriarch. "I need you to do this in your armour. I want it done hard and brutal and bloody. Make an example of him, Luther. I need to send a message to the whole Nightside: *If we can kill John Taylor, none of you are safe.* That should demoralise them, make them less inclined to fight our invasion when it happens."

Luther nodded slowly. "Getting in shouldn't be too difficult, but getting out afterwards . . ."

"I've made arrangements," said the Matriarch.

"Why me?" said Luther.

"You mean, why not Eddie?"

"He is the best field agent we've got," said Luther. "Though I'd never admit that to his face. And John Taylor won't die easily. Maybe you should send the best, to be sure of having a real chance."

"Eddie is an excellent agent," said the Matriarch. "But he's not an assassin. He'll kill when he has to, to do his duty; but something this . . ."

"Cold-blooded?" said Luther.

"Yes," said the Matriarch. "Something as cold-blooded as this might be beyond him. Whereas you have always done good work for the family, quietly disposing of people who might otherwise have caused us a lot of trouble."

"Martha was supposed to be the only one who knew that," said Luther. "I did hope that after she died, my sins might be buried along with her. I should have known better."

"Yes, you should," said the Matriarch. "All Matriarchs keep private records, to be passed down to our successors. And your file made for particularly interesting reading. I had a feeling you'd come in handy someday."

"If you and Martha valued my work so highly, why was I never allowed to come home?" said Luther. "No matter how many times I asked."

"You're here now," said the Matriarch. "Do this one job for me, for the family, and I will make you a permanent member of my advisory Council. You'll never have to leave the Hall again. If that's what you want."

"Yes," said Luther. "That is what I want."

"Won't you miss Los Angeles?"

"Only in the way you miss the shit you scrape off the bottom of your shoe."

"And that, right there, is why I need you," said the Matriarch. "My cold-blooded, incorruptible agent. So you'll do it? Remove this obstacle from our path?"

"Of course I'll kill him," said Luther. "Anything, for the family. But you must know . . . When Eddie finds out, and you can be sure he will, he's not going to like this. It won't fit his idealistic view of what he thinks the family is. What he believes we should be. We're not supposed to kill good men."

"After this is done, Eddie will understand the necessity, or he won't. But either way, it'll be too late for him to do anything. He'll have no choice but to go along."

Luther chose his words carefully. "The last time a Matriarch disappointed him, Eddie kicked her out of office and took control of the family himself."

"He only got away with that because no one believed it could be done," said the Matriarch. "Now we know better, measures have been put in place."

"You'd have to kill him to stop him," said Luther.

"Yes," said the Matriarch.

"And then you'd have to kill Molly Metcalf, to keep her from avenging him."

"Yes," said the Matriarch.

Luther looked at her. "And you really think you can do that . . . What do you know that I don't?"

"More than you could possibly imagine," said the Matriarch. "All that matters is that Eddie and Molly serve the family and not the other way around. I would hate to lose them. They're two of the best weapons at my command. But needs must . . ."

"When the Matriarch drives," said Luther.

"Precisely."

"I'll kill John Taylor for you," said Luther. "Because that's what I do. When do you want it done?"

"Now," said the Matriarch.

She opened a drawer in her desk and brought out a thick silver bracelet studded with brightly coloured crystals. She put it down on the desk before her and pushed it toward Luther. He reached out and picked it up carefully.

"A teleport bracelet," he said. "The last time I was here, the old Armourer was still trying to get the bugs out of it. I watched one of the prototypes being tested, down in the Armoury. It worked perfectly fine as it teleported the upper half of the wearer away and left the lower half still standing there. It took the lab assistants hours to clean up all the blood."

"Maxwell and Victoria have assured me that all of the problems have been worked out."

Luther sniffed loudly. "Yes, well, they would say that, wouldn't they?"

"You can be sure this one has been very thoroughly tested," the Matriarch said patiently. "It's the one the Sarjeant-at-Arms uses to take him to Strangefellows."

"Ah, well," said Luther. "If Cedric trusts it . . ."

He slipped the bracelet over his hand, and it immediately clamped down around his wrist. Luther studied the colour-coded crystals, while being very careful not to touch any of them.

"I assume it's still green for go and red for return?"

"Of course."

"What do the other colours do?"

"They complicate things," said the Matriarch. "So leave them alone. The bracelet is preprogrammed to take you straight to Strangefellows at a time when we have reason to believe John Taylor will be there."

Luther raised an eyebrow at that, but the Matriarch said nothing. He nodded, acknowledging that he didn't need to be told everything, and she continued, "I don't want any challenges or speeches; just kill him. In your armour, so everyone knows who and why. Then hit red, and the bracelet will bring you home."

"John Taylor is supposed to have all kinds of special protections and defences," Luther said carefully. "Does the family have any idea what they might be?"

"No," said the Matriarch. "No one does. That's why they work."

"How am I supposed to get past them when I don't even know what they are?"

"Don't give him time to use them," said the Matriarch. She smiled briefly. "If this were easy, I wouldn't need you."

Luther nodded. He got to his feet, touched the green crystal, and disappeared. The Matriarch looked at the space where he'd been for a long moment. There was no way in hell she could have a man like that on her advisory Council, but she'd think of something. Perhaps he'd die during the Nightside invasion. Stranger things had happened. She raised her voice.

"Ethel!"

The voice appeared out of the air right in front of her.

"All right, I can hear you. No need to shout."

"Have you been listening?" said the Matriarch.

"No," said Ethel. "You told me not to, so I didn't. One of these days I'll get my head around this whole privacy thing. As if you humans weren't alone enough, trapped inside your heads . . ."

"Ethel!"

"Yes! I'm here! What do you want?"

"I need to know: Can I rely on your assistance once I lead the family into the Nightside?"

"No," said Ethel.

The Matriarch waited, well past the point where it became obvious that the voice had nothing more to say. "That's it? You're not even prepared to discuss it?"

"No," said Ethel.

"Get out," said the Matriarch.

"I'm gone," said Ethel.

The Matriarch sighed tiredly. Just because she'd expected the answer didn't make it any easier to take. She looked around the huge, empty chamber of the Sanctity. The heart of the Hall, and the family. She supposed she shouldn't be surprised to find how hollow it was. She sat and thought for a long time, about all the awful things she was going to have to do to win this war. Perhaps, when it was all over, they'd allow her to retire, put someone else in charge, so she could go back to her gardens. And only have to make the kind of decisions where no one got hurt. Or maybe she'd die during the Nightside invasion. Stranger things had happened.

She'd never wanted to be Matriarch; they'd had to bully her into taking the position. But as long as she had the job, she would do what needed doing. And try to live with it afterwards.

Anything, for the family. For Humanity.

Luther appeared in the shadows at the back of Strangefellows. He tensed, waiting to see if he'd triggered any kind of alarm, then relaxed when nothing happened. No one was paying him any attention, and there was no reason why they should. The torc was hiding that he was a Drood, and since he'd spent his entire career in Los Angeles, it wasn't likely anyone here would recognise him. Luther strolled out of the shadows, doing his best to appear calm and confident, just someone who'd dropped in for a drink.

Strangefellows was packed from wall-to-wall with all kinds of people, and some things that wouldn't pass for people even if you put a gun to their heads.

The weird stuff didn't bother Luther. He'd seen enough of that in LA. He quickly spotted John Taylor standing at the bar, talking to the grim-faced bartender, looking entirely at his ease and not at all dangerous. But Luther knew better. Luther made his way unhurriedly through the packed crowd, moving with quiet confidence and casual arrogance, because anything else would have got him noticed. He got to the bar, waited for just the right moment, then eased in behind John Taylor and armoured up. The golden strange matter swept over him in a moment, and immediately the cry went up.

"A Drood! There's a Drood in the bar!"

John spun around impossibly quickly. As though he just knew there was only one place a Drood could be, and only one person a Drood would have come for. The Matriarch had strongly implied she wanted John beaten to death with golden fists, but Luther had no intention of getting that close to the legendary John Taylor. A long golden sword shot out from his glove, and Luther raised it on high.

The bartender produced a glowing baseball bat from behind the bar and threw it to John, who snatched it out of the air even as Luther brought the golden sword swinging down. John shielded himself with the bat, and to Luther's astonishment, his strange-matter blade rebounded from the glowing wood. The impossibly sharp strange-matter edge hadn't even made a dent. The bartender laughed triumphantly.

"Merlin gave me that bat!"

Everyone in the bar opened up on the Drood. Normally they wouldn't get involved in a private fight, but this was a Drood. They shot at Luther with all kinds of guns, threw glowing knives, and hit him with any number of spells and curses, a fusillade of fear and hate that would have wiped out anyone else in a second. But the strange-matter armour just soaked it all up, while Luther didn't even feel the impacts. He scowled behind his mask. He'd only just started his attack, and already it felt like everything was going wrong. He couldn't help feeling that the smart option would be to give it up as a bad job and teleport out. But if he did, the Nightside would be able to say they frightened off a Drood . . . and John Taylor would know he'd been marked for death by the family. They'd never be able to sneak up on him again. Besides, Luther had given his word to the Matriarch that he would get the job done. He wanted so much to be able to go home again.

He could still do this. He was a trained swordsman, while all John Taylor had was a baseball bat. If he pressed the attack hard, and didn't give John a chance to use any of his tricks . . . Luther cut at him again, putting all his armoured strength into the blow, and though the glowing bat absorbed most of the impact, there was still enough there to drive John back a step. Luther hacked and cut viciously, trying to force the bat aside so he could get at John. But though he was forced to retreat step by step, John somehow continued to hold his attacker off. He stared calmly into the featureless golden mask, refusing even to look scared, or worried. Luther fought on, forcing John to stay on the defensive. He didn't know what a baseball bat magicked by Merlin Satanspawn could do to his armour, and he didn't want to find out.

The attacks from the rest of the bar had stopped. Luther and John were too close now, and moving too quickly. Luther piled on the attack, and because he had golden armour, and John was only human, Luther finally beat the bat aside, leaving John momentarily defenceless. Luther drew back his blade for the killing thrust.

There was a sound like thunder, and something hit him hard in the back. The impact threw Luther away from John, slamming him up against the bar. The pain was so bad it knocked all the breath out of him, and he had to lean against the bar while he waited for his legs to steady themselves. He'd never felt pain like it. The armour had always protected him before. He could feel blood streaming down his back, inside the armour. Lots of it.

Luther gasped for breath and fought back the pain so he could concentrate on killing John Taylor. The man was still standing there, watching him carefully to see what he would do. Luther straightened his back and raised his sword again. He grinned fiercely behind his face mask, and blood spilled down his chin. He was hurt, but he could still do the job. He drew back his sword, to thrust it through John Taylor's gut, and the shotgun roared a second time.

The impact slammed him into the bar again, but this time Luther didn't feel it. He couldn't feel anything. His legs gave out, and he sat down hard on the floor. He didn't feel that either. It was starting to worry him. He couldn't seem to get his breath. He could see the golden sword retreating back into his hand because he couldn't concentrate enough to maintain it. He wondered how he was going to complete his mission now. And then he stopped worrying about anything, and his head dropped forward.

His last thought was *It's the Nightside.*

Most of the bar's patrons were already running for the exit. They'd just seen a Drood killed, and they really didn't want to be around if more of the family turned up. The few that remained stayed well back, fascinated but wary, knowing they were seeing history in the making. A live Drood in his armour was rare enough; to see one killed was almost unheard of. John

Taylor nodded to Suzie Shooter, standing at the foot of the metal stairs, still training her double-barrelled pump-action shotgun on the Drood. Tall and sturdy, cold and collected, with a grimly handsome face and long blonde hair, Shotgun Suzie was a Valkyrie in black motor-cycle leathers, with bandoliers of bullets crossing her chest.

She was due to give birth in about five weeks. She'd had to have her leather jacket specially tailored to accommodate the bump. She walked slowly forward, still covering the unmoving Drood with her shotgun, and the few people remaining fell back even farther to give her plenty of room. More of them decided it was well past time they were somewhere else. The rest were wondering how much the *Night Times* would pay for photos. Or the *Unnatural Inquirer.* Suzie reached the bar and ignored the Drood body as she looked John over carefully, assuring herself he was unharmed.

"No one messes with my man," she said in her cold voice.

"Hello, Suzie," said John. "Great timing."

"You never could resist making an entrance," said Alex. He leaned over the bar to peer at the Drood. "Look at all that blood. I've only just had the place cleaned up after your last visit."

"I'm a professional," said Suzie. "Blood comes with the job." She looked steadily at John. "You probably could have beaten him, but I didn't feel like risking it."

John passed the glowing baseball bat back to Alex. They exchanged a quiet nod because that was as far as either of them would go to acknowledging how close it had been. Suzie studied the dead Drood, and John moved in beside her. The Drood's golden head hung down, and his back was bent right over, revealing jagged rents in the armour. Blood dripped steadily out of the holes and onto the floor. John looked at Suzie.

"How did you do that?"

"I picked up some strange-matter ammunition from the Gun Shoppes of Usher," said Suzie. "I'd heard about the Drood operating on Blaiston Street, and I wanted to be prepared. I could only afford a dozen shells. Apparently strange matter is really hard to get hold of."

John knelt beside the Drood, studying the holes in the armoured back.

"He is dead," said Suzie. For her, that was always going to be a statement, not a question.

"Oh, he's very dead," said John. "That's the problem. You just killed a Drood."

"You're welcome," said Suzie.

"No, you don't get it," said John, as he straightened up again. "This means war, between the Nightside and the entire Drood family."

"Not necessarily," said Alex. "We just dispose of the body and swear blind he was never here. Wouldn't be the first time. Someone will pay good money for a chance to examine that armour. We could make a lot of money here. I don't suppose either of you have contact details for the Dark Academie?"

"The Authorities instructed me to make an example of the next Drood to show up in the Nightside," said John. "They wanted this. They'll make sure word gets back to Drood Hall, so they can take responsibility."

"They wanted you to kill someone, just to make a point?" said Suzie.

"Yes," said John.

"Were you going to do it?" said Alex.

"I was thinking about it," said John.

"They should have asked me," said Suzie, staring coldly at the dead body. "Damned fools. Did they think this would impress the Droods and keep them out? They always avenge their own."

"You knew that, and you still killed him," said John. "You were ready to piss off the whole Drood family, to save me."

"No one messes with my man," Suzie said again.

"You've done enough work for the Authorities that they can still claim the kill as their own," said John. "Alex, give me one of those cheap and dirty teleport spells you keep behind the bar, to get drunks home safely."

"Oh, come on, John!" said Alex. "Don't do this! There's serious money to be made out of a dead Drood!"

"No," said John. "He goes home. A sign of respect might help to cool the Droods' anger."

"You really think that?" said Suzie.

"No," said John. "But I have to try."

Alex handed him a purple patch that wriggled and squirmed eagerly. John slapped it onto the Drood's bent back, just above the jagged holes, and the body disappeared before John could even tell the patch where to take it.

"Must have had a teleport built into his armour," said John. "With return coordinates programmed in."

"I can see hope running for the horizon," Alex said gloomily.

"God help us all," said John.

"Praise the Lord and pass the special ammunition," said Suzie.

CHAPTER SEVEN

The Road Paved with Good Intentions

N o one knows how old the Old Library really is. Some say the oldest parts of the collection reach back to the very first Drood Hall and that the Library has transferred itself from Hall to Hall down the centuries. Always growing, always expanding, accumulating ancient texts and secret histories and forbidden knowledge that no one else could be trusted with.

The Old Library was lost to the family for many years until Eddie found it and brought it back. William has been in charge for some time now because he's the only one who isn't scared of it. Possibly because he's still a little bit crazy. There are books in the Old Library that know more than is good for them, along with others that know things that used to be true but aren't any longer, and some things that shouldn't be true but unfortunately are. William has put a lot of work into cataloguing the contents of the Old Library and will happily tell you all about it until you beg him not to.

Eddie and Molly entered the Old Library, and the doorway closed silently behind them. It had been awhile since they'd last been there, but nothing had changed. The vast, cavernous space was filled with rows upon rows of shelves that stretched off into the distance for as far as the eye could follow, and quite a lot beyond that. The Librarian kept promising to produce a map, right after he finished the Index. He didn't seem to have any trouble finding his way around, but everyone else stuck to the coloured guide-lines on the floor if they knew what was good for them. Eddie and Molly looked around them, and stacks of books looked back, on every subject you could think of, and quite a few things best not thought on too much if you liked sleeping at night.

Eddie and Molly followed the blue line on the floor, which usually led straight to the Librarian. Unless he didn't want to be found, in which case you could follow any colour you liked for as long as you liked, until it led you back to the exit. William's way of hinting that he didn't want to be bothered. Eddie scowled about him suspiciously. It always felt to him like there were monsters lying in wait, watching from the shadows. Or the shelves. The butter-yellow light was soothing enough, until you realised it came from everywhere at once, and the air was thick with drifting dust motes and the heavy scents of old paper and leather bindings. Eddie sometimes wondered what would happen in the event of a fire, but he was pretty sure the books would never allow that to happen.

Eddie and Molly stopped abruptly as they heard footsteps approaching, then relaxed as Ioreth emerged from the stacks to greet them. The Assistant Librarian was a cheery, scholarly type, wearing a faded brown monk's habit. He had a pleasant face, a shaved head, and one gold earring. He also had the disposition of a saint, or he'd never put up with William.

"Hello, Ioreth," said Eddie. "Are you any closer to deciding on how you want your name spelt? We can't keep changing it . . ."

Molly frowned. "And why are you still dressed as a monk?"

"William says he finds it soothing," said Ioreth, just a bit long-sufferingly. "You wouldn't believe the outfits we had to go through to find something we could both live with. So! Here you are again! The Matriarch has ordered me to provide you with every assistance possible, right up to the point where she changes her mind and tells me not to. I am, of course, happy to help you with whatever you need unless it involves the Nightside, in which case I don't want to know. Awful place."

"Tough," said Molly. "We want to see whatever books you've got on the long night."

"Trust me," said Ioreth. "You really don't."

"There must be something here we can use!" said Molly. "You've got lots of books here!"

"Yes, we have, and please don't touch any of them! The kind of histo-ries you're talking about are stored among the really dangerous books, the volumes of mass destruction. Literary predators, just waiting for a chance to prey on an unwary mind. This is not a petting zoo! Even I have to wear special gloves when I handle some of the books in the Restricted section. They're knitted for me specially, by cloistered nuns of the Salvation Army Sisterhood. It's come to something when my gloves are holier than I'll ever be."

"The Nightside can wait," said Eddie. "I need to talk to William about the Pacts and Agreements."

Ioreth winced. "Do you have to? He's not really himself at the moment, whoever that might be. He always goes into a bit of a decline when Ammo-nia has to leave."

"She's gone?" said Eddie. "I was hoping she'd stick around, to help out with the invasion."

"That was never going to happen," said Molly. "A mind as receptive as hers in the midst of so much blood and slaughter? It would destroy her."

"She wanted William to go with her," said Ioreth. "Asked him to leave Drood Hall and go stay with her. But he couldn't do that. Not even for her. Of course, he won't be going in with the invasion. He'll stay behind and help guard the Hall, in the family's absence."

He glanced back into the stacks, just a bit nervously. "He's just got out the Drood copy of the Pacts and Agreements. He knew you'd want to see them. I'll take you to him, but I have to warn you: What you see is all you're going to get. I can't tell whether he's less focused than usual, or more. Don't blame me if he thinks you're pixies."

Ioreth led Eddie and Molly off the main route and into the less-travelled areas of the Old Library. He was careful to maintain a respectful distance from the books on the shelves, and Eddie and Molly followed his example. Eddie wasn't sure he'd ever ventured this deep before. It was hard to be sure, given that there weren't any landmarks: just row after row of tightly packed book-shelves staring ominously back at him. He had a strong suspicion the Old Library liked to change its lay-out when it thought no one was looking. Expanding quietly, to accommodate its ever-growing number of books. Many of which seemed to find their way to the Old Li-brary under their own power.

If all you wanted was to do research, or borrow the odd book, there was the regular Drood Library. Full of interesting and highly useful materials. The Old Library existed to store the kind of knowledge you only went looking for in emergencies.

Ioreth, Eddie, and Molly finally found the Librarian sitting at a reading-desk, with a huge leather-bound volume set out before him. William wasn't reading it; he hadn't even opened the book yet. The front cover was so faded as to be almost colourless and had no title or any other markings. William didn't look up as the others approached, giving all his attention to the book like a fighter sizing up a worthy opponent.

"Hello, Eddie and Molly. And Ioreth, of course," said William, not lifting his eyes from the book. "Took you long enough to get here. This is it. The family's original copy of the Pacts and Agreements existing between the Droods and the Nightside. As laid down by Gaea herself, some fifteen hundred years ago. Or thereabouts."

"It's worn it well," said Eddie, just to be saying something.

William smiled briefly. "Because it's been so rarely consulted, I should imagine. The book has all kinds of protections in place to keep its contents safe from unauthorised eyes."

"What kind of protections?" Molly asked, taking a professional interest.

"Basically, no one gets to open the book unless it thinks Gaea would want them to," said William. "That's why I've been waiting for you. I didn't want to even try opening it till everyone was here who needed to be here."

They all moved behind him, so they could look over his shoulders. William took a firm hold on the front cover and opened the book. There was a sudden new tension on the air, as though William had just opened the door to a lion's cage. He laid the front cover down carefully and gave his full attention to the gleaming metal pages that made up the book.

"Why aren't you wearing gloves?" Molly said abruptly. "Ioreth said he had to wear special gloves before he could handle the really dangerous books."

"I'm the Librarian," William said patiently. "The books respect me. Ioreth is still earning their trust. They haven't forgotten how my last assistant turned out to be a traitor. One of the reasons why I've got him wearing that monk's robe; it helps the books tell him apart."

Ioreth leaned in close to Eddie and Molly. "It probably also helps that the books are just a little bit frightened of William. I don't think they've ever encountered a mind like his before."

"The leather used to make the book's covers came from human skin," said Molly.

Eddie raised an eyebrow. "You can tell that, just by looking?"

"Yes," said Molly.

"I won't ask," said Eddie.

"Best not to," said Molly.

"Supposedly, the leather was made from the skin of one particular Drood who objected a little too loudly about the nature of the Agreements," said Ioreth. "Gaea could be really hardcore, back in those days."

They all examined the pages carefully as the Librarian turned them. The lines of text etched into the metal were elegantly inscribed and just went on and on, without punctuation or break or ending.

Molly shook her head. "Some of this was supposed to be written in Latin, but I don't recognise anything here."

"The book can only be read by members of the Drood family," said William. "It doesn't recognise you as part of the blood line."

Molly glared at the book. "Snob. Bet you I could make it recognise me."

"Possibly," Eddie said quickly. "But we really don't want to upset it, do we? William, how is the translation process going?"

"Sorry," said William. "I forget not everyone has my background."

He produced a long, slender wand carved from somebody's arm-bone, etched from one end to the other with ancient elven script. William swept the wand across the page like a scanner, and just like that the words made sense. Eddie and Ioreth made low, satisfied sounds. Molly's frown deepened.

"Still doesn't make any sense to me. So someone had better start reading aloud before I decide to get cranky."

"What exactly are you looking for, Eddie?" said William.

"A way out of this mess," said Eddie. "Something to convince the Matriarch that open conflict won't get the family anywhere. But from what I'm seeing . . . It's all just quid pro quo stuff. You don't do this, and we won't do that, backed up by dire warnings of what Gaea will do if either side does anything to defy her. And Ioreth was right; some of these threats are pretty hardcore. She starts with promises of earthquakes and plagues, then escalates. But it's clear no one ever expected Mother Earth to retire. Least of all her. Without her authority to back them up, these agreements are worthless. Because there's no other mechanism in place to enforce them."

"So basically, we need someone as ancient and powerful as Gaea to come in and make both sides behave," said Molly.

They all raised their heads from the book to look at each other, then peered cautiously off into the shadows.

"William," said Eddie, "have you thought about asking the Pook what it feels about all of this?"

"I've thought about it," said William.

They were all uneasy now, as though just saying the Pook's name might be enough to summon the creature. It claimed to be one of the wild things of Creation, already old when the world was young. A crafty, mischievous, mercurial spirit that appeared to this one and to that one, as the mood moved it. A mostly invisible giant white humanoid rabbit, the Pook had followed William home from the Happy Daze Asylum for the Criminally Insane because it had taken a fancy to him. It came and went as it pleased, occasionally dispensing words of warning or wisdom, and on rare occasions protected the Librarian from harm in terrifyingly whimsical ways.

Just its presence in the Old Library worried the Droods greatly, but none of them had any idea how to get rid of it.

"I think it's probably wisest not to disturb the Pook unless we absolutely have to," William said carefully. "It doesn't like being bothered. And, it keeps stealing my socks."

Eddie and Molly turned to Ioreth, who shrugged. "Well, somebody is, and it's not me."

Molly turned back to William. "You don't think the whole family's going to war qualifies as an emergency?"

William gestured for all of them to lean in close, so he could lower his voice. "How could we be sure which side the Pook would choose?"

They all straightened up, thought about that, then looked around the Library again. The endless rows of books stared silently back, and nothing moved in the shadows between them. As far as they could tell. Molly gestured vaguely at the shelves.

"Are you sure there isn't a book here somewhere that could tell us how to stop the Nightside expanding?"

William nodded judiciously, acknowledging the point. "There are indeed any number of books about the Nightside. Its nature, its history, and everything and everyone who's ever been connected with it. But most of what's in those works is blatantly contradictory and no use whatsoever when it comes to trying to understand what makes the long night work. We have no idea how it maintains itself or what its capabilities or restrictions might be. There are lots of theories, and even more guesses, but nothing in the way of hard evidence. The long night is big enough and dark enough to conceal a great many mysteries. We only recently discovered that Lilith was responsible for its creation."

"So that there would always be one place on Earth free from the tyranny of Good and Evil," said Molly.

"Why would God allow that?" said Eddie.

"Mysterious ways, remember?" said Molly.

"Gaea has gone on record, more than once," Ioreth said diffidently, "insisting that the Nightside serves a necessary purpose." He looked quickly around him. "I keep worrying she'll turn up suddenly and tell us to knock it off or else. And given that this is Mother Earth we're talking about, the *or else* could cover a lot of really unpleasant ground."

William shook his head firmly. "No. Gaea has made it extremely clear she has no intention of being Mother Earth again."

"Do you know why?" said Molly.

The Librarian was suddenly evasive. "There are a great many books on the subject, but since none of the authors have ever spoken to Gaea herself, I don't think we can accept any of them as definitive. The consensus seems to be she just got really fed up one day, threw her hands in the air, and said *All right then, have it your own way!* And walked off the job forever." William stopped for a moment, to think about it. "There have been a great many suggestions as to what the last straw might have been. I tend to favour the fall of Camelot, but that could just be me being romantic."

"How could she walk out on us?" said Eddie.

The Librarian raised an eyebrow. "It's not as though there was anyone around powerful enough to tell her not to."

"Why didn't she go to Shadows Fall?" said Molly.

"Because that's where you go when the world stops believing in you," said William. "And lots of people still believe in Gaea. Much to her annoyance."

"Have you talked to her recently?" said Eddie.

William became even more evasive, avoiding everyone's eye. "I may have. My memory isn't what it was. If it ever was."

"She lives in that small country town these days," said Molly. "Would it do any good to send her a message?"

"I've no doubt she already knows," said William. "She knows everything. She just doesn't care any more."

Eddie wasn't so sure about that. The Gaea he'd met at Castle Inconnu hadn't acted as though she'd given up on Humanity. He suddenly realised he'd been quiet for so long, the others were staring at him.

"Sorry. Just thinking. Go on."

"Go on with what?" said William.

"Nothing good will come of this invasion into the Nightside," said Ioreth. "Even if Gaea doesn't punish us, there are any number of powers and forces in the long night who'd be only too willing to take up the slack."

"Does that mean you won't go?" Molly enquired.

"Of course I'm going," said Ioreth. "I'm a Drood."

William nodded slowly. "Anything, for the family."

"Even when it's madness?" said Molly.

William smiled sadly. "Perhaps especially then. And who knows madness better than me?"

"It's still not too late to find a way to stop this," said Eddie.

They all looked around sharply as a bell started tolling. A slow, implacable, foreboding sound, full of terrible significance. Like an iron bell in a cemetery at midnight. Eddie and Ioreth looked at each other, and Molly couldn't read the expressions on their faces. William slammed the book shut and rose to his feet, all the usual vagueness gone from his face. Something was happening, but Molly didn't know what.

"Eddie?" she said.

"We have to go," he said flatly, not looking at her.

Molly grabbed hold of his arm. "What is it, Eddie? Some kind of warning? I've never heard anything like that before. What does it mean?"

"The cloister bell isn't there to warn us of bad things coming," said William. "It tells us that the worst has already happened."

"It means a Drood has been murdered," said Eddie. "And that the whole family is under threat." He turned to William. "You stay here. Ioreth, look after him."

"No," William said flatly. "This could be connected with what's happening in the Nightside. You and Molly go on ahead. Ioreth and I will catch up."

Eddie didn't even pause to nod in agreement; he was already off and running. Plunging back through the stacks, heading for the painting and the exit, with Molly right behind him.

They raced through the Hall, and everywhere they went, more Droods came running. Men and women with fear and panic in their faces, and a grim determination. No one seemed to know who it was that had been murdered, but apparently a body had turned up in the entrance-hall. So that was where everyone was going.

"Does this mean there's a killer inside the Hall?" said Molly, already fighting for breath but refusing to be left behind.

"No," said Eddie. "There's a different alarm for that."

They ran through the corridors and down the long stairways, until finally they reached the entrance-hall and had to force their way through the packed crowd that had already gathered. Raised voices filled the air, some of them almost hysterical. Eddie took the lead, shouldering people aside when they didn't move fast enough, and Molly stuck close behind him. When Eddie finally reached the front of the crowd, the Matriarch and the Sarjeant-at-Arms were kneeling beside the unmoving body of a Drood in his armour, with as much anger as sorrow in their faces. Eddie knelt beside them. Molly hung back. This was a family thing, and she could tell her presence would be an intrusion. Eddie stared at the dead Drood, lying face-down with jagged holes in his armoured back.

"What happened?" said Eddie.

"He just appeared here," the Sarjeant said heavily. "Teleported in. There was a transfer parasite on his back. I crushed it."

Eddie looked at him sharply. "Why did you do that? It could have told us something."

"It was a Nightside thing," said the Sarjeant.

Eddie looked back at the body. "Is that where he died? What was he doing there?"

"Someone in the long night has murdered one of us," said the Matriarch.

"Do we at least know who this is?" said Eddie.

"We can't know that till we lower his armour," said the Sarjeant. He indicated the ragged holes with an entirely steady hand. "They shot him in the back. Typical Nightside tactics. The only way they could bring down a Drood."

The Matriarch raised her voice. "Ethel!"

"I'm here," said Ethel, her disembodied voice calm and comforting. "It's all right. I know what needs doing."

The golden armour streamed back into the torc around the dead man's neck. The Sarjeant took hold of the body and turned it over, revealing Luther's face. There was blood all over his mouth and chin, and his eyes stared blankly, as though he couldn't understand how such a thing could have happened to him. The Matriarch made a low, pained sound.

"But . . . I was only just talking to him, earlier!" said Eddie. "How is this possible?"

"It's my fault," said the Matriarch. "I sent him to the Nightside. To talk to the Authorities. And this is what they did!"

She broke off and looked away. Eddie thought he understood. The Matriarch believed she'd sent Luther to his death.

"It's not your fault," said Eddie. "You couldn't have known this would happen."

"I should have known," said the Matriarch. "It's the Nightside. This is what they do."

She rose to her feet. Her face was cold and set, masking the conflicting emotions raging within her. The crowd watched and said nothing. Waiting to be told what to do. The Sarjeant and Eddie got to their feet. They looked at each other, then the Sarjeant moved over to stand with the Matriarch.

"What are your orders?" he said quietly. "You are the Matriarch; you must decide what is to be done about this."

While the two of them were talking, Molly seized the opportunity to move in beside Eddie and talk quietly to him.

"Eddie, you must know this isn't right! The Authorities wouldn't just murder a Drood in cold blood, then dump his body here. They'd have to know an insult like this would mean war!"

"Not now, Molly," said Eddie, still looking at Luther.

"Yes, now!" Molly positioned herself between Eddie and the dead body, forcing him to look at her. "We have to talk about this, before hysteria sets in and no one wants to talk sense. Before this all gets out of hand!"

"Too late," said Eddie. "We're at war now. We always avenge our fallen dead." His gaze as he looked at Molly was cold and inflexible. "Sending his body back to us like this was an act of contempt. Saying to the Matriarch, to the family, *Look what we can do. We can kill a Drood, in his armour.* The Authorities will pay for this; and God help anyone who gets in our way."

"We don't know the Authorities are responsible for this!" said Molly.

"Who else could it be?"

Molly looked away. She didn't have an answer.

The Sarjeant called for someone to take the body to the hospital Wards. Two Droods armoured up and carried Luther away with as much dignity as possible. The Sarjeant yelled after them.

"Tell them I want a full autopsy! I want to know everything about how Luther died. And especially how the bastards were able to get through his armour."

Eddie watched the body disappear into the crowd. No one said anything. At some point, the cloister bell had stopped tolling. Molly watched Eddie carefully and stayed close to him, trying to be supportive.

"I think what makes it worse," said Eddie, "is that I never really liked the man. He was a pain in the arse to work with, in LA. A real holier-than-thou type. He made no secret of the fact that he didn't approve of me. Luther was old-school Drood, unflinching in his morality. Saw any form of compromise as weakness. And yet he had contacts everywhere in Los Angeles; they said no one could work a crowd like Luther. I never liked him, but to see him like that, shot in the back just for doing his duty . . . He was our last chance to stop this war, Molly, and the Authorities threw it back in our faces."

"You have to get to the bottom of this, Eddie," said Molly. "Find out what really happened . . ."

"Too late," said Eddie. "All that matters now . . . is revenge."

The Matriarch raised her voice so everyone could hear her. "Sarjeant-at-Arms, prepare the family for war. We will begin our invasion of the Nightside in one hour."

No one in the crowd said anything. They just quickly moved away, heading for their designated posts. The Matriarch and the Sarjeant went to leave, but Eddie put himself in their way. He addressed the Matriarch in his most reasonable tone, ignoring the Sarjeant.

"We can't be ready in one hour. We just can't. I know you're upset about Luther, but we can't afford to rush things. We have to plan this properly."

"The standing arrangements have already been distributed to the Heads of all Departments," the Matriarch said tonelessly. "I did that before I sent Luther into the Nightside. There's no point in holding back any longer. We have nothing more to say to the Authorities except *Surrender or die*. Everyone in the family knows what they have to do. And we have to go now, before the Authorities can properly prepare their defences." She smiled humourlessly. "They may think they can intimidate us into backing down, but they should have remembered, we're Droods. We don't get scared; we scare everyone else."

Eddie started to answer her, but the Sarjeant cut bluntly across him. "Either you're with us, or you're not. Which is it, Eddie?"

"I know my duty," said Eddie. "Anything, for the family."

The Matriarch turned away from him to face the Sarjeant. "Do whatever you have to, but I want the whole family mobilised and ready to leave in one hour. No excuses. Anyone gives you any trouble, tell them you speak in my name. If they still give you trouble, you are authorised to strike them down and put someone else in their place. And I want a report from the Armourer, right now, as to whether they're ready with Alpha Red Alpha, and God help them if they're not. Go!"

The Sarjeant nodded quickly and hurried away. The entrance-hall was suddenly very empty and very quiet. Eddie looked at the Matriarch, and she stared steadily back at him. Molly stayed back, not wanting to distract

Eddie from saying what he needed to. The Matriarch looked at Eddie, almost pityingly.

"I know you didn't want this. Do you think I did?"

"I don't know what to think," said Eddie.

"You still have doubts."

"I worked with Luther," said Eddie. "He was an experienced field agent. He would never have allowed anyone to sneak up behind him."

"Unless he was distracted," said the Matriarch. "He must have been talking to the Authorities, and they held his attention while John Taylor got into position. And shot Luther in the back."

"You think Taylor did this?" said Eddie.

"Who else would the Authorities trust with something this important?" said the Matriarch.

That was too much for Molly. She came striding forward, raising her voice, even though she knew she shouldn't.

"There's no way John would do something like this!"

Eddie tensed, expecting the Matriarch to order Molly to be silent or even banish her from the Hall. He was ready to defend Molly, and to hell with the consequences, when the Matriarch surprised him by answering Molly quietly and calmly.

"Taylor has no choice but to do what he's told, now he's Walker. If it makes any difference, I doubt he shot Luther himself. Guns have never been Taylor's style. More likely, he had his woman do it. The bounty-hunter. Or are you saying Shotgun Suzie would never shoot a man in the back?"

Molly didn't say that. She couldn't. The Matriarch nodded understandingly.

"This is all part of the Authorities' plan. To make clear their defiance. Do you really believe the Nightside could enlarge its territory without the Authorities knowing? They wanted this war, for their own reasons. We'll ask them why when we have them kneeling and beaten before us. Eddie, Molly, prepare yourselves for the invasion."

She walked away, her back straight and her head held high. Leaving Eddie and Molly standing alone in the middle of an empty hall. Molly turned desperately to Eddie.

"This doesn't make any sense! Why would the Authorities do this?"

"It's the Nightside," said Eddie. "They must see a profit in it somewhere."

"I could go to the Nightside, alone," said Molly. "Separate from the Droods. I could talk to John privately, find out exactly how Luther died."

"You don't have enough time to get there by any of the traditional routes," said Eddie. "And you can be sure they've got shields in place to stop anyone teleporting in."

"Then give me the Merlin Glass!"

"The Authorities will be looking for that," said Eddie. "They'll have people waiting for you the moment you step through."

"I can take anything they can throw at me!"

"Probably," said Eddie. "But what if you can't? If the Authorities take you prisoner, they won't hesitate to threaten you, to pressure me."

"Are you saying you won't give me the Glass?"

"I'm saying I can't!"

Molly shook her head, scowling hard. Not angry at him but at the situation. She could feel the walls closing in around her and all the ways out disappearing. "There must be something we can do to stop this madness before it starts."

"It's too late," said Eddie. "It was too late the moment a Drood was murdered. Nothing can stop the war now." He looked carefully at Molly. "I don't have any choice in this, but you do. I have to go, but you don't. If you have any doubts as to where your sympathies lie, go to your wood between the worlds, lock all the doors, and stay there. I'll send word once it's over, and it's safe for you to come out again."

Molly shook her head stubbornly. "I can't do that. My place is at your side, wherever you are and whatever you're doing. You're going to need me."

"But in your heart," said Eddie. "Whose side are you on?"

"Yours," said Molly.

He put his arms around her, and they held each other tightly, like two children lost and abandoned in a dark wood, with no way home. In the end, Eddie let go first. He had to be strong, for both of them.

"At least if I'm there, I can be their conscience," said Eddie. "Help keep them focused. Keep the collateral damage to a minimum. But a lot of what we do will depend on what the Authorities have waiting for us. You saw what happened at the Wulfshead Club. If the Matriarch is right, and the

Authorities are behind the Nightside's expansion, that means everyone inside the Club was sacrificed in order to bring this situation about. Someone condemned all our friends to death. And that means something has gone very wrong with the Authorities. That has to be put right, or no one inside or outside the long night will ever be safe again."

"You must be feeling better," said Molly. "You've started making speeches again."

"You have to admit, the world will be a much safer place once the Nightside comes under Drood control."

"I don't have to admit any such thing!" said Molly. "The one truly free place on Earth is the last place Droods should be. They might discover that all they need to do is cut their apron strings, and they could live their own lives."

"After all this time, you still don't understand my family," said Eddie. "Our duty has never been to the family but to Humanity. We serve because we choose to, because it's the right thing to do."

"Then why did you have to run away from home to live your own life?" said Molly.

"You'd think I would have learned not to argue with you by now," said Eddie.

"Damn right," said Molly, but her heart wasn't in it.

"Once we're inside the long night, stick close to me," said Eddie. "And I'll stick close to the Matriarch and the Sarjeant. Make sure they don't deviate from this swift, decisive strike they're supposed to be so keen on. Maybe we can bring about a bloodless coup after all and save lives on both sides."

"You really believe that?" said Molly.

"I have to believe that," said Eddie.

Sometime later, Eddie and Molly sat side by side in his room at the top of the Hall. Staying out of everyone's way, lost in their own thoughts. Eddie sat on the edge of his bed, leaning forward over his clasped hands, staring at the floor. Molly sat beside him, saying nothing because she didn't know what to say. Eddie had decided he didn't want to be any part of the Matriarch's planning process. That was as far as he could go, to distance himself from what was happening. He would be a soldier in this war but not a general. As though that way he could avoid taking any responsibility for what happened.

Molly had to wonder how long that decision would last once the fighting started and the killing began. She'd already drawn her own line in the sand, in her mind. She would go so far and no further, and if the family crossed that line, if they tried to make her or Eddie cross it . . . she would do something. She hadn't decided what, yet. She felt trapped, like Eddie. He felt bound by his duties, to his family and to Humanity, while she was torn between her need to stand by her man and protect him and her obligations to all her friends and allies in the Nightside.

Whatever happened, someone was going to get hurt.

Ethel's voice sounded suddenly in the room. "Eddie, Molly . . . The Matriarch is assembling the family out in the grounds. It's time."

"Can't you stop this, Ethel?" said Molly.

"No," said Ethel.

"Where do you stand on this?" said Eddie, raising his head at last.

"I don't," said Ethel. "I'm not involved. This is a human thing, done for human reasons. I can't make this decision for you or I'd be running the family. I would be your ruler, not your friend. And you really wouldn't want that."

"Will you be with us, in the Nightside?" said Eddie.

"No," said Ethel.

They waited, but she had nothing more to say. Eddie got to his feet, and so did Molly. They looked around the room, taking in its familiar details, wondering if they would ever see it again. Wondering if they would ever see the Hall again. Or if they'd be able to see it in the same way, after everything they'd done. Because they both knew that war changes everything, whether you win or lose.

They left the room, and Eddie closed the door quietly and turned his back on it.

They walked down through a quiet, echoing Hall. No one else was about, and nothing was moving anywhere. It reminded Eddie eerily of the Other Drood Hall, that he and Molly had discovered in a different dimension. Where all the Droods were dead because they'd fought a war they couldn't win.

"Are we the last people here?" said Molly.

"No," said Eddie. "We'll be leaving a skeleton staff behind, to oversee the Hall's defences. So it can't be taken away from us while we're gone. Most of the defences and protections are computer-controlled, but my family hasn't survived this long by relying on the efficiency of machines. Everyone who can fight is going, but not the old and the young, the sick and people like William . . . Who wouldn't be any help anyway. Don't worry about the Hall. It'll be fine."

"Trust me," said Molly. "That isn't what I'm worrying about."

They managed a small smile for each other, then hurried on through the heavy silence of the deserted Hall. Finally they strode out of the front door, to find the Drood family assembled on the lawns. Standing proudly in their golden armour, gleaming brightly under the grey sky, in endless ranks and rows. It occurred to Eddie that the last time he'd seen so many Droods together, it had been for the late Armourer's funeral. Not a good omen.

All the Droods looked different. They'd moulded their armour into new shapes, to fit their individual needs. Some of the changes were subtle, while others were downright grotesque. Everything from stylised knights in medieval armour, to technological battle suits bristling with weapons, to demonic gargoyles with fangs and claws. The armour's strange matter could be reshaped by an effort of will, but it took a lot of concentration to maintain the new form. So the Droods' chosen shapes were mostly for psychological effect, to strike fear and horror into the hearts of the enemy when they first met. Once the fighting began, the armour would quickly revert to its standard form.

"Damn . . ." said Molly. "You really are an army."

"When Droods go to war, let the world beware," said Eddie.

The Matriarch and the Sarjeant-at-Arms were standing together by the front door, facing the massed ranks of the armoured Droods. They hadn't put on their armour yet, so everyone could see their faces. They looked out of place: the Matriarch in her smart suit and the Sarjeant in his butler's outfit. Eddie and Molly strode past them and took up positions beside the front row. Eddie armoured up, and Molly looked at him as if she'd lost him. The man she loved had become just another faceless Drood. The Matriarch started talking, and everyone paid attention.

"You all have your orders, and your objectives. You know what this is about. Don't let anything stop you. Make the family proud."

The Droods all spoke at once. *"Anything, for the family!"*

Eddie added his voice. Molly didn't.

The Matriarch and the Sarjeant armoured up, and he gave the nod to the Armourer. Maxwell and Victoria were standing off to one side, backed up by their own armoured ranks, in stylised golden lab coats. The lab assistants were going to war.

A control column appeared in front of Maxwell and Victoria, all shining steel and blinking lights, and they bent over it to work the controls. That great dimensional engine, Alpha Red Alpha, stirred to life deep beneath Drood Hall. A strange juddering vibration ran through the armoured ranks, building steadily in their bodies and in their souls; and then, just like that, Drood Hall and all the Droods disappeared from the world. And reappeared in the Nightside.

CHAPTER EIGHT

First Blood

t quickly became clear that Drood Hall wasn't where it was supposed to be. Instead of materialising in the heart of the long night, surrounded by important people and vulnerable targets, the Hall was standing among grimy terraced houses on a deserted street.

"Where the hell are we?" said the Matriarch.

"We're on Blaiston Street," said Eddie. "Where the predatory house used to be before I killed it. You remember, the house that ate the Wulfs-head Club."

"This is not where we were supposed to arrive!" said the Matriarch.

"Yeah, well, that's the Nightside for you," Molly said sweetly. "Always full of surprises."

Drood Hall stood tall and imposing and very out of place under a star-speckled sky, looming over the mean and stunted buildings surrounding it, bathed in the shimmering light of the oversized full moon. The two long rows of shabby terraces that Eddie remembered from his last visit had been warped and twisted into a great circle surrounding the Hall. As though they'd been pulled in by the fierce gravity of the Hall's impor-tance. The Matriarch turned to the Sarjeant-at-Arms to demand answers, but it was obvious he was just as thrown as she was.

"Something would appear to have gone wrong with Alpha Red Alpha," offered Eddie. Doing his best not to sound pleased, amused, or even a little bit *I told you so.*

The Sarjeant looked around for the Armourer, but it was hard to identify anyone in the golden crowd milling confusedly around in the street.

"Maxwell, Victoria!" he said loudly. "Get your arses over here, right now! I want to know what's happened, and why, and you had better have an answer I can understand!"

"I wouldn't bet on it," said Eddie. Molly nodded solemnly.

The Matriarch turned on them angrily. "If I thought you had anything to do with this . . ."

"Grow up, Maggie," said Eddie. "It's not us; it's the Nightside."

What had been an impressive army of armoured Droods was now scattered the whole length of Blaiston Street. Most of them were stumbling around, staring numbly this way and that, as they tried to orientate themselves in their new setting. They'd prepared themselves for the strange new sights and neon-lit temptations detailed in their briefings, braced themselves for resistance and even open violence, but this ratty neighbourhood in the middle of nowhere had thrown them completely. A lot of them looked as though they were afraid to touch anything in case they caught something. Their carefully sculpted battle suits collapsed as their concentration shattered, reverting to the basic golden form. Which would still have been pretty impressive if they hadn't all looked so obviously lost. A few had grown weapons from their hands and were looking around hopefully for someone to use them on, but the street remained completely silent and utterly deserted.

Maxwell and Victoria hurried forward to present themselves to the Matriarch and the Sarjeant-at-Arms, and all four of them armoured down so they could see one another's faces clearly. This was not a moment for misunderstandings.

"We don't know why we're here," Max said quickly, before the Matriarch could say anything.

"And we don't know what went wrong," said Vicky. "But this is, after all, the Nightside. Where standard science and basic logic famously don't apply all of the time. Or even if they just don't feel like it."

"But look on the bright side!" said Max. "We have quite definitely arrived inside the long night!"

"Yes!" said Vicky. "Look at that moon!"

"It shouldn't be that size, should it, dear?"

"Much bigger than it should be, dear."

"We really must look into that while we're here."

"When we get the time."

The Sarjeant made an impatient sound, and Maxwell and Victoria quickly looked back at him.

"We have most definitely made it past any and all defences the Authorities might have put in place to stop us," said Max, smiling weakly at the Matriarch.

"And they certainly won't expect us to be here," said Vicky. "So we still have the advantage of surprise!"

The Armourer kept talking, piling on the information and the theories, at least partly because as long as they were talking, the Matriarch and the Sarjeant couldn't shout at them. Eddie and Molly moved off a little way, to have a quiet discussion of their own.

"This *is* Blaiston Street, isn't it?" Eddie asked. He armoured down, because wearing his armour in an empty street felt like an over-reaction. "I mean . . . it's changed a lot since we were last here. It looks so much older . . ."

"I had noticed," said Molly. "The houses aren't just dirty and shabby; a lot of the brickwork is actually crumbling and falling apart. The whole street looks . . . decayed. Decades older, maybe more . . ."

"And no sign of life anywhere," said Eddie. "Have we arrived at the right time? Could Alpha Red Alpha have sent us into the future? Could that have been the Authority's defence, to deflect our transition so we passed through Time as well as Space on our way here?"

"If they had anything powerful enough to interfere with Alpha Red Alpha, I think I'd have heard about it," Molly said doubtfully.

Eddie looked up at the night sky. "The moon is still the same. Far too big and far too close, like a giant eye watching everything. But the stars . . . I don't recognise any of those constellations . . ."

"You wouldn't," said Molly. She looked up at the flaring stars, which burned fiercely in huge clusters, shot this way and that in vivid displays, and occasionally just blinked out, as though they'd simply got bored with the whole thing. "This is normal for the Nightside. The stars are always changing, reassembling themselves into new patterns. Just another hint that you've left the everyday world behind. Trust me, we haven't moved in Time. This is still the same day as when we left."

Eddie looked at her. "How can you be sure?"

"All part of a witch's Sight," Molly said airily. "To See the world as it really is and to know exactly where and when we are."

"So what happened to the buildings?" said Eddie.

"Well," said Molly. "If you want a wild stab in the dark, which is rather appropriate considering where we are, maybe Alpha Red Alpha's energies did something . . ."

"No," said Eddie. "If the dimensional energies were that out-of-control, we would have been affected."

Molly looked at him sharply. "Hold everything, go previous, throw it into reverse. You mean that machine could have aged us too?"

"Or delivered us here in any number of little pieces," said Eddie. "Uncle Jack and I used to have long and quite disturbing conversations about Alpha Red Alpha, back when he was Armourer. About all the things that could go wrong and why using it was such a bad idea except in the gravest of emergencies. We don't understand that machine nearly as well as the Matriarch thinks Maxwell and Victoria do."

"Why didn't you say any of this before?" said Molly.

"I did," said Eddie. "Loudly and repeatedly. But the Matriarch didn't want to hear it, and the Sarjeant didn't give a damn. They couldn't have their precious invasion without the dimensional engine, so they just closed their eyes and hoped for the best." He looked around him, worrying his lower lip between his teeth. "I think . . . what's happened here is nothing to do with us. It's the result of the boundaries changing. The Nightside was never supposed to be any larger than it was originally created to be."

Molly looked around her and nodded slowly. "So the territory itself has become strained, and weakened . . . Could this change spread, do you think? To the rest of the long night?"

"If the Nightside itself has become unstable . . . Who knows?" said Eddie. "More than ever, we need to find out who was responsible for the change and make them put things back the way they were. Before it's too late."

The Droods clustered unhappily together before Drood Hall. If only because there was some feeling of security in numbers. They milled around aimlessly, talking loudly over each other. They weren't used to being caught so completely wrong-footed. All their careful planning and detailed briefings had come to nothing, and their usual Drood confidence was off in a corner crying its eyes out. They weren't scared, as such, but they were shaken. They looked to the Matriarch and the Sarjeant-at-Arms for answers, but they were too busy arguing with the Armourer, so the Droods argued with each other, just for the comfort of hearing their own voices in the eerie hush of the deserted street.

Eddie watched their discipline deteriorate and thought he understood. They'd never encountered anything like the long night before. This wasn't just another place, or even another world; the Nightside had a spiritual ambience all its own. The usual certainties were gone, and what remained felt more like a dream. The kind you were grateful to wake up from. There was an especially oppressive feeling to Blaiston Street that was affecting the Droods despite the protections built into their armour. They were in the night that never ends, where it's always three o'clock in the morning, that time when you lie awake in your bed and wonder what happened to the life you meant to have. If anything you'd achieved meant anything, and if what lay ahead was worth the struggle of getting there.

If there was any point at all in going on . . .

More and more Droods were asking urgent questions of the Matriarch and the Sarjeant, and raising their voices angrily when they didn't get an answer, which was almost unheard of among the heavily disciplined Droods. But the Matriarch and the Sarjeant were still intent on getting useful information out of the Armourer and becoming increasingly angry over the evasive answers they were getting. The lab assistants moved in behind Maxwell and Victoria, to provide support. They'd armoured down as well, to show off their lab coats because they usually impressed people.

Eddie and Molly looked at each other, nodded resignedly, and shouldered their way through the Droods to confront the Matriarch and the Sarjeant. No one gave them any trouble. The Droods might be feeling a bit shaken by their current circumstances, but they hadn't lost their minds. Eddie waited until he was right in front of the Matriarch, then raised his voice.

"Everybody shut the hell up!" And everybody did, including the Matriarch, the Sarjeant, and the Armourer. Just a bit shocked that anyone would talk to them like that. Eddie smiled. "That's better. We have to ask the right questions, or we're never going to get anywhere. So, Armourer: Could something or someone in the Nightside have drawn us off course? Interfered with Alpha Red Alpha's trajectory, the way Ethel intercepted the Merlin Glass, so Molly and I appeared inside the Sanctity instead of the grounds?"

Maxwell and Victoria put their heads together for some urgent murmuring, then turned to their lab assistants. Voices began to rise as they discussed all kinds of theories and got nowhere fast.

"Shut up!" said Eddie, again, and silence reluctantly fell, along with a certain amount of sulky annoyance. "If you don't know, just say so."

"We don't know," said Max.

"And if we don't, no one does," said Vicky.

"However . . . given that we don't know how Ethel interfered with the Merlin Glass . . ." said Max.

"And to be fair, there is an awful lot we don't know about Ethel . . ." said Vicky.

"Then let's ask her," said the Matriarch. She raised her voice. "Ethel! Speak to me!"

They waited, but there was no response. The silence dragged on uncomfortably, until Eddie cleared his throat. Everyone turned to look at him.

"You know something," said the Matriarch. "What do you know, Eddie?"

"Ethel spoke with me in my room, before I left," said Eddie. "She made it very clear she had no intention of getting involved with the invasion. We're on our own."

"Why didn't she tell the rest of the family that?" asked the Sarjeant.

"Why did she tell me and not the Matriarch?" said Eddie.

"She did tell me," said the Matriarch. "I just couldn't believe she'd abandon us . . ."

Mutterings rose up among the gathered Droods before the Sarjeant glared them back into silence.

"Why would Ethel turn her back on us?" said the Sarjeant. It wasn't clear whether he was addressing the Matriarch or Eddie.

"She disapproved of the war," said Eddie. "And given some of the things we've done that she has approved of . . . Still, look on the bright side. At least she didn't take back her torcs and her armour."

The Matriarch turned her attention to Molly. "You know this area. Where is Blaiston Street in relation to the rest of the Nightside?"

"Right out on the edge," said Molly, with a certain sense of satisfaction. "This is where the boundary changed, remember? We're about as far as we could be from the centre of things."

The Sarjeant glared at the Armourer. "Fire up the dimensional engine again. Have Alpha Red Alpha put us where we should have been, right in the heart of the Nightside. We can't launch an invasion from here!"

"We've been trying to summon the remote-control column," said Max.

"But it isn't answering," said Vicky.

"We'll have to go back inside the Hall and run a whole series of diagnostics on the machine," said Max.

"Before we dare try using it again," said Vicky.

"And that could take some time," said Max.

"Quite a lot of time," said Vicky. "Given that we don't have a clue what's gone wrong."

"We can't hang around here any longer," the Matriarch decided. "The Authorities must know we've arrived. I don't want to give them time to organise their defences. Split the family into the agreed groups and start the attack, Sarjeant."

"You can't just march into the Nightside!" said Molly.

"What if the Authorities already have people in place, waiting to meet you?" said Eddie.

"Then we walk right over them," said the Sarjeant. "We're Droods. That's what we do."

Eddie gestured angrily at the watching Droods. "Are you kidding me? Look at the state of them, huddled together like sheep in a thunder-storm! If someone were to jump out of one of these houses and shout *Boo!* they'd run a mile!"

"They're soldiers," said the Sarjeant. "They'll remember that when the fighting starts."

"I thought you wanted a bloodless coup," said Molly.

"That's up to the Authorities," said the Matriarch.

"Come on, think about this!" said Eddie. "We've only just got here, and already the plan's gone wrong. This is no way to fight a war."

He sounded angry because he was. He didn't like to see his family looking this thrown, this lost. Even in the Nightside.

"You people should be frightened," Molly said darkly. "The Nightside is going to eat you alive."

"Not another word, Molly," said the Matriarch. "We all know where your loyalties lie."

Molly was ready to take that as a challenge, but Eddie put a hand on her arm. She looked at him angrily, and he met her gaze steadily. Molly shrugged quickly, turned away, and didn't say any more. The Matriarch raised her voice to address the Droods, but they were too busy arguing among themselves to listen. The Sarjeant-at-Arms summoned a gun into his hand and fired it into the sky. The sound was deafening in the narrow street, and everyone snapped around to look at him. The Sarjeant addressed the suddenly silent crowd in a cold, firm voice.

"Let me remind you of the unofficial Drood motto: *Shut the hell up and soldier.* You have your armour and your training, and you can rely on both of them to get you through this. You are Droods. You have a job to do, so get on with it. You can start by searching the houses on this street. Tear them apart if you have to but find me someone I can question. And put up a perimeter! I don't want anyone coming or going without us knowing about it. Why are you still standing there? Move!"

The Droods quickly broke up into small groups and went charging up and down Blaiston Street, kicking in one door after another. No one was in the mood to knock. They slammed into the silent houses, yelling for someone to show themselves, feeling better now they had something to do. Using their armour made them feel strong and in control again, just as the Sarjeant had known it would. They stormed through house after house, searching every room and smashing anything that got in their way. Because brick and wood and stone were no match for their armour. They raged up and down the long, circular street, calling out to each other in increasingly confident voices . . . But they didn't find anyone. All the houses were empty, the occupants long gone.

While all this was going on, the Matriarch turned her fiercest stare on the Armourer. "Take your people back into the Hall. Go down to the Armoury and do whatever it takes, but get Alpha Red Alpha working again!

I want to know why it dumped us here. Did someone else take control, and if so, who? Tear that machine apart if you have to, but get me some answers. Go! Now!"

Maxwell and Victoria nodded quickly, rounded up their assistants, and hurried back inside the Hall. Eager to get to work and even more eager to get away from the Matriarch. Eddie looked thoughtfully up and down the deserted street, then moved in beside Molly, who was scowling out into the dark.

"Have you noticed?" Eddie said quietly. "Even the homeless people are gone. There's no one in the alley-ways."

"Of course they're gone," said Molly, not looking at him. "People in places like this can always tell when something bad is coming. That's how they stay alive."

"Are you mad at me?" said Eddie.

"I'm mad at your whole damned family," said Molly.

"Well," said Eddie. "No change there, then."

She looked at him and managed a small smile. "They shouldn't be here, Eddie. We shouldn't be here. It's all going to go horribly wrong . . ."

By now the Droods were returning. Between them they'd searched the entire circular terrace, house by house and room by room, and hadn't found a single person to interrogate. The Matriarch just nodded, as though she hadn't expected anything else.

"Sarjeant, move the family out. I want all the designated target areas under our control as quickly as possible, so we can start laying down some law."

"You heard the Matriarch!" the Sarjeant said loudly to the assembled Droods. "Follow your standing orders, and don't take any shit from anyone."

"Is that really how you want to do this?" Eddie said to the Matriarch.

She looked steadily back at him. "I will see the Nightside razed to the ground from boundary to boundary if that's what it takes. So I can be sure the long night will never threaten the world again."

"You'd have to kill everyone here to be sure of that," said Molly.

"Let's hope that won't be necessary," said the Matriarch. She turned back to the Sarjeant. "Find the Authorities and make them surrender. From fear of what we've done and what we might do. After that, all the other power groups in the Nightside will go along."

Molly started to say something, but once again Eddie put a hand on her arm.

"Sarjeant-at-Arms!" said the Matriarch. "Move the family out!"

"And remember," Eddie said quickly, "you can't use your phones to communicate; they won't work in the Nightside."

"Everyone, stick to torc-to-torc communication," said the Sarjeant. "More secure, anyway. Let's go, people! You've all got your special compasses from the Armourer. They'll guide you to where you need to be."

"Let's just hope they work better than Alpha Red Alpha," said Eddie.

The armoured Droods marched out of Blaiston Street and into the long night, and the thunder of their golden feet was like the threat of a coming storm. They held their heads high, their usual Drood confidence restored. Smashing up a whole street of houses had put them in a good mood. A Drood in his armour could smash a hole through the world. They'd just needed to be reminded of that. Eddie watched them go and wished he felt that confident. He was worried about what would happen once they left the relative sanity of Blaiston Street and encountered the more-extreme dangers of the Nightside. Where the threat was as often to the soul as to the body. But they were Droods. Trained to fight and win under any and all conditions. Whatever they met, they should be strong enough to break it, tear it down, and set it on fire, as long as they remembered they were Droods. Eddie turned to the Matriarch.

"What do you want Molly and me to do?"

The Matriarch looked to the Sarjeant, and he spoke for her.

"We have a special mission for you. Go to Strangefellows and kick everyone out. Do as much damage as you feel necessary, but we need that bar under Drood control. The knowledge that we hold Strangefellows will help to undermine local resistance. It's a symbol of the Nightside. We need it broken."

Eddie nodded. That made sense. However . . .

"John Taylor and Suzie Shooter have been known to drink there," he said carefully. "What are our orders, if we run into them?"

"If they put up a fight," said the Matriarch, "or if it looks like they might escape, you are authorised to kill either or both of them. For Luther."

Eddie nodded but didn't say anything. Molly didn't even nod. The Matriarch sighed quietly.

"I know; you'll both make up your own minds, as always. But if you can't hold on to them, I'll have no choice but to order them killed on sight. I'm sending you two to Strangefellows because you're the only ones with a real chance of taking them alive."

Eddie and Molly left Blaiston Street and set off into the long night. Molly seemed to know where she was going, so Eddie let her take the lead. He was concerned with his own thoughts. In their own way, and for their own reasons, the Matriarch and the Sarjeant were being kind. They knew he had no stomach for the kind of open street fighting the Droods would inevitably get caught up in. Strangefellows was a simple task, and there was always the chance he wouldn't even get to meet John Taylor and Shotgun Suzie. He wondered what he would say to them if he did.

To his surprise, after only a few streets, the badlands disappeared, and they entered a more civilised part of the Nightside. Familiar hot neon burned on every side, colourful shops and restaurants and clubs lined the streets, and the pavements were packed with people hurrying back and forth. Traffic roared endlessly along the wide-open road, as though it had never been away. Molly noticed Eddie's surprise and smiled.

"You're never far from anything, in the Nightside. The best and the worst of things are always lying in wait, just around the next corner."

"How far is it to Strangefellows?" said Eddie.

"Not far."

"What do you think of our mission?" Eddie said bluntly.

Molly scowled, and people on the pavement moved quickly to give her even more room. "I had no idea your family had such detailed plans for the overthrow of the Nightside."

"Neither did I," said Eddie.

"But you used to run the family!" said Molly. "How can there be so many things about them that you don't know?"

"It's a big family, and I wasn't in charge for long," Eddie said steadily. "They didn't tell me everything."

"Clearly," said Molly. "You should have asked a lot more questions, while you had the chance."

"I was busy!" said Eddie. "Trying to keep the Hungry Gods from destroying the world."

"Excuses, excuses," said Molly.

They walked for a while in silence, and when Molly spoke again, she carefully didn't look at him.

"Do you really think your family can win this war, Eddie?"

"Of course," he said, just as carefully not looking at her. "It's what we do. We've fought a lot of wars in our time. We prefer to prevent them where possible, that's what field agents are for . . . But we're always training for the next one. We've fought secret wars all across the world. All right, the Nightside threw some of the younger ones for a while, but it didn't last. They were expecting an easy start; they know better now. We've fought every kind of enemy you can think of, Molly, and some beyond your wildest nightmares."

"The Nightside is different," said Molly.

"It's not like we're going to be facing an army," said Eddie, looking at her for the first time. "Or even a properly trained resistance. Most people here will take one look at armoured Droods marching down their streets and quite sensibly run for their lives."

"Only till they realise your family mean to put a stop to their fun," said Molly. "You have no idea what most of these people went through just to get here, for a chance to find what they need. Or what they'll do to hang on to it once they've found it. People here will fight for any number of reasons. And you have to remember, there's a lot more to the Nightside than just people. There are Forces and Powers here that have nothing in common with the Street of the Gods. Ancient creatures and presences from before and outside of history, who won't stand for being crossed."

"Hopefully, they'll have enough sense to stay out of a fight they can't win," said Eddie. "Or, what could still be a mostly peaceful occupation will deteriorate into blood and slaughter on a grand scale. Droods are trained to fight to win, whatever it takes."

"And if it does come down to fighting in the streets, to bodies piling up and blood running in the gutters?" said Molly.

"I'll deal with that when I have to," said Eddie.

Molly didn't say anything more. She knew she'd pushed him as far as she could.

They walked on through the Nightside, and people surged past them, laughing and talking loudly, enjoying themselves as they searched for their own particular pleasures and damnations. Or planned the best way to profit from someone else's. Hot music blasted out the open doors of nightclubs that never closed, while predators and prey circled each other in a dance that both sides relished. And everywhere people rushed to buy the things they weren't supposed to want but always had and always would. Dreams by the pound and hope in pretty colours, men and women chasing fulfilment and heart's ease in small, easy-to-manage doses. Love for sale, on every street-corner. Love, or something like it. The streets were alive with possibilities for good and bad and everything in between.

Eddie looked at the people passing by, with their laughter and chatter, their desperate needs and overwhelming longings, as though it were just another night in the Nightside. How could they not know that everything had changed? Couldn't they feel it, on the air? That life as they knew it was effectively over? Eddie wondered what would happen if these happy, driven creatures did dare to defy the Droods. How far would his family go against unarmed civilians, to stamp out all forms of resistance? Eddie didn't like where his thoughts were taking him, but he couldn't stop thinking about it.

"How, exactly, are we supposed to take control of Strangefellows?" Molly said finally. "Alex can't do that some nights, and he runs the place."

"I'll armour up and tell everyone to leave," said Eddie.

"What about the ones who won't?" said Molly.

"Those are the ones I'll make an example of," said Eddie.

Molly made a brief noise, indicating that she wasn't at all convinced. "Given some of the things that come to Strangefellows for a boisterous night out . . ."

"They've never met anyone like me," Eddie said calmly.

"And then there's Alex."

Eddie looked at her. "That long streak of misery? What's he going to do? Scowl me to death?"

"Don't under-estimate him," said Molly. "Alex is descended from Merlin Satanspawn."

"Really?" said Eddie. "I didn't know that."

"There's a lot about Alex Morrisey that most people don't know," said Molly. "You can't run a bar like Strangefellows for as long as he has without acquiring some really nasty ways of restoring order. There's a lot more to him than meets the eye."

"There would have to be," said Eddie. "Don't worry. I can handle Alex."

"Without killing him?"

"I don't want to kill anyone," said Eddie.

"What if John Taylor and Shotgun Suzie are there?" said Molly.

"I hope they are," said Eddie. "I want to talk to them. I need to know what happened to Luther. There has to be more to his death than just the obvious. If we could only get to the bottom of that, I'm convinced we could still stop this madness before it gets really out of hand."

"How are you going to stop your family," said Molly, "when they've already gone to war?"

"By negotiating some kind of compromise with the Authorities," said Eddie.

Molly pulled a face. "They're not known for being big on compromise."

"They'll see reason," said Eddie. "Even if I have to make them. Of course, that will depend on how complicit they were in Luther's murder."

"They might not have had anything to do with it," Molly said carefully. "This is the Nightside. People die here all the time."

"Do you honestly believe an experienced Drood field agent, in his armour, could be taken down without someone's having carefully planned it in advance?"

Molly didn't answer him. She couldn't. After a while, she tried again.

"If nothing else, Strangefellows always has the best gossip. If you'll just take the time to talk to some people before you boot everyone out the door, you'll almost certainly find someone who can tell you what happened. And even make a really good guess as to who was behind it. Of course, getting them to talk . . ."

"I am fully prepared to offer major bribes with one hand and extreme violence with the other," said Eddie.

"Well, yes," said Molly. "That is the Nightside way. You'll fit right in at Strangefellows."

"Now you're just being nasty," said Eddie. He thought about it. "I let the crowd drive us out last time rather than put on my armour and blow my cover. But I can't take it easy now, no matter what. Are you sure you want to come along? You might not be comfortable with some of the things I'll have to do."

"That's what I usually say to you," Molly said briskly. "This is my world you're walking through now, Eddie. I was widely versed in being violent and unreasonable long before I met you."

"You're not telling me anything I don't know," said Eddie.

"And anyway," said Molly, "you're going to need me to watch your back. Strangefellows can be a pretty rough bar even at the best of times."

There is an old military adage, that no plan survives contact with the enemy. The Droods hadn't been in the more-populated areas of the Nightside long before all their carefully worked out designs and intentions went to hell in a hand-cart.

The Sarjeant-at-Arms led his column of armoured Droods down one of the main streets in the financial district, and was quietly satisfied with the way people gave them plenty of room. A few tourists came rushing up, wanting to take selfies with him, but he quickly sent them on their way. He'd been assured this was one of the main routes for Nightside traffic, and he was there to shut it down. To bring all of it to a screeching halt. Because if the Droods could stop the traffic that famously never stopped, that proved they could do anything. Wars were won in the minds and souls of the enemy as well as on the battle-field.

People crowded together to point and comment and try to film the golden-armoured Droods with their phones. The Sarjeant smiled behind his featureless mask. Let them waste their time. Nothing artificial could see or record a Drood in his armour unless the wearer allowed it. How else could the field agents do their work unnoticed in this surveillance-heavy age? People were chattering excitedly on their phones, describing what they were seeing, but the Sarjeant didn't care about that. Let the word go out that the Droods had finally come to the Nightside and that the old ways of decadence and tolerance were coming to an end. Some of the tourists applauded the Droods as they passed, thinking it was all a parade laid on for their benefit.

The Sarjeant chose his moment carefully, then strode out into the middle of the road. He turned to face the on-coming vehicles and raised one hand with quiet authority, to bring the traffic to a halt. And every single vehicle on the road ignored him, merely swerving aside at the last moment. Anyone else they would have just run over for being dumb enough to get in their way, but the golden armour made them wary, at least enough to give it the benefit of the doubt. The Sarjeant stood there for a while, with traffic speeding by on either side of him, some so close he could have reached out and touched them . . . and then he picked one particularly large articulated vehicle and walked straight at it. The truck sounded its horn, and when the Sarjeant just kept coming, the truck swerved to avoid him. The Sarjeant moved quickly to block its way again, and the articulated vehicle decided enough was enough. It aimed itself right at the Sarjeant and put the hammer down.

The Sarjeant-at-Arms waited until the truck was almost upon him, lowered one golden shoulder, and braced himself. The truck hit him square on, and the whole front of the cab concertinaed as the golden shoulder sank deep into the radiator. The whole front of the cab collapsed in on itself, and the Sarjeant was forced back several feet by the impact. Sparks rose up from his golden feet as they skidded along the road, until the Sarjeant dug his heels in and forced the truck to a halt. It rocked back and forth, compacted to half its previous length. Dark smoke rose up from half-melted tyres. The Sarjeant tore himself free from the front of the cab, rending the solid steel with only the barest effort, and stepped away from the wrecked truck, entirely unaffected by the impact. Drood armour doesn't take any nonsense from the physical world.

But still the rest of the traffic continued to shoot past, not even slowing as it avoided the Sarjeant and the wrecked truck. He gestured for the rest of his Droods, and they marched out into the road to take up positions blocking the way. People watching pointed and chattered excitedly. There's nothing the Nightside likes more than a spot of free entertainment.

The traffic slowed down a little, but only to make it easier for them to dodge and dart around the standing Droods. The vehicles ignored all raised hands, waving of arms, or shouted commands to stop. The traffic had places to be and business to be about, and just kept going. The Droods looked to the Sarjeant for orders, and he gestured brusquely for them to leave the road and return to the pavement. He'd tried it the easy way; so now it was time for the hard and unpleasant alternative.

The Drood way.

He arranged his people in front of one of the biggest financial buildings. The uniformed flunkey at the door didn't even deign to glance at them. The Sarjeant looked up at the building, then out across the open road. It would do.

"Bring it down," said the Sarjeant.

The Droods went to work with a will, smashing through the outer walls of the ground floor. Bricks shattered under golden fists, steel buckled, and windows blew apart, as the Droods destroyed everything that held the building up. The uniformed doorman looked on in horror, then ran over to grab at the nearest Droods to stop them. The armoured figures just ignored him, dragging him around like a doll. The doorman gave up and ran inside the building, to sound the alarm. The Droods tore through the outer wall as though it were made of paper, and jagged cracks raced up the face of the building. Windows blew out in their dozens, and glass shrapnel rained down. People who'd drawn closer to enjoy the destruction ran for their lives.

The Droods worked on, taking their time. Partly because they were enjoying themselves and partly to give the people working inside the building time to escape. The Droods weren't trying to kill everyone. Not yet. The building lurched forward, leaning out over the road as its supports were eroded. People poured out of the main door, shouting and screaming and pushing at each other in their eagerness to escape the toppling building. Some of the staff realised they'd never get to the ground floor in time and threw themselves out of windows. Many landed badly, breaking bones and splashing blood across the pavements. One woman jumped from a top-floor window, even though it was obvious she would never survive the fall. One Drood stopped what he was doing just long enough to catch her and put her safely to one side before returning to his work. Some of the tourists applauded. One of the building's owners identified the Sarjeant-at-Arms as the man in charge because he was watching while the others worked, and ran over to remonstrate with him, almost jumping up and down on the spot with incandescent rage.

"Stop this! You can't just destroy my building!"

"I think you'll find I can," the Sarjeant said calmly.

"You have no right!"

"Of course I do. I'm a Drood."

The owner put a hand on the Sarjeant's shoulder, and tried to force the Sarjeant to face him. The Sarjeant clubbed him down with a single blow. Because people should know their place. The owner lay in the gutter, bleeding out from his crushed skull, staring unseeingly at what used to be his building as it leaned even farther out across the road.

The frontage was cracking and falling apart now, raining down bricks like jagged hailstones. This didn't bother the Droods, safe inside their armour, but people watching drew even farther back. Most were leaving the area. The building let out a deep groan, as though it had suffered some mortal wound, and toppled slowly and remorselessly out across the road, slamming down like the fist of God. The impact sent people staggering back and forth, as though they'd been caught in an earthquake. The smoke slowly cleared, and the golden-armoured Droods turned to admire their work.

Rubble and wreckage blocked most of the road, but there was still a gap left through which traffic could pass. Drivers had to slow down to navigate the gap, but they kept going. Because nothing stopped the traffic in the Nightside. The Sarjeant shrugged. He'd tried being reasonable, but if the world wasn't going to cooperate . . . He nodded to the waiting Droods.

"Go out into the road and stop the traffic. Whatever it takes."

The Droods spilled out onto the road, and went eagerly to meet the roaring traffic. Now the vehicles didn't have the speed or the space to avoid them, the Droods just grabbed hold of things with their golden hands and forced the traffic to stop. Sometimes the vehicles would accelerate, trying to break free or run the Droods over, and then golden hands would punch through bonnets to smash engines, or sink fingers into a steel door to flip the vehicle over onto its side.

The remaining traffic didn't like that at all. Every single one of them poured on the speed and went to meet the waiting Droods, to knock them aside or plough them under. Their attitude was clear: *Get out of the way or die.* The first car to reach a Drood sounded its horn continuously, like a challenge. The Drood ran straight at it and punched the car in its radiator. The car slammed to a halt, flipped up into the air, and somersaulted over the Drood's head, before crashing upside down beyond him.

A stretch limousine aimed itself squarely at another Drood, trusting to its extra weight to do the job. The Drood stood his ground, and the limousine driver lost his nerve at the last moment. He slammed on the brakes, and the limousine screeched to a halt a foot or so short of the waiting Drood. Who then strode calmly forward and tore his way through the car, ripping it apart as he went. He walked through the stretch limousine from end to end, crashing through it as if it were made of paper. The car fell apart into two halves, collapsing onto its sides. They rocked back and forth, slowly settling, while a group of shaken party girls emerged from the wreckage and staggered away. The uniformed chauffeur fought his way out from behind the air-bag and lurched over to confront the Drood.

"How the hell am I supposed to explain this to the insurance company?"

"Easy," said the armoured figure. "Act of Drood."

Some of the heavier trucks still hadn't given up on the idea that they could run over a Drood if they just built up enough speed. They hit their accelerators for all they were worth and bore down on the waiting Droods. Who took that as an insult. They were only supposed to stop the traffic, but if people were going to try to kill them . . . They ran at the approaching trucks, their armour driving them on at inhuman speed, and hit the trucks like living battering-rams. Cabs broke apart, and drivers exploded out through their windscreens, to lie broken and bleeding on the road.

Other Droods picked up handfuls of rubble from the fallen building and threw them at the trucks with terrible strength. Just for the fun of it. Bricks and stones punched through windscreens, to behead drivers in their seats. Some Droods ripped up street-lights, tearing them out of their concrete settings, and threw them like javelins, spearing drivers behind their steering wheels. Some trucks still kept coming, so the Droods picked up whatever cars were nearest and threw them at the approaching vehicles. Trucks burst into flames, skidded off the road, and mounted the pavement. They smashed through watching crowds, sending bodies flying in flurries of blood, then buried themselves in shop-fronts.

The street was full of smoke and fire, the sound of crashing vehicles and the screams of the wounded and the dying. Golden figures sent cars flying sideways with sweeps of their arms, then high-fived each other. As far as the Droods were concerned, the Nightside had started it and so deserved everything it got.

Everyone who wasn't hurt or dying went running for their lives. The remaining traffic slowed to a halt, on both sides of the toppled building.

The Sarjeant-at-Arms moved unhurriedly among his people, praising them for their efforts and calming them down. Although all Droods were trained in how to use their armour from an early age, unless the call to war came, most would never get the chance to leave the Hall and prove what they could do. The Hall had come under attack several times in recent years, and some Droods had gone out into the grounds to defend it, but this was the first time the whole family had been allowed out into the world to face an enemy. Many of them had dreamed about what their armour could do, and what they could do in their armour, and now they had been set free . . . they loved it. It helped that they had been told everyone they were likely to meet in the Nightside was a designated target, villains of the first order, worthy only of Drood contempt, so it never even occurred to them to feel bad about what they'd done. They laughed happily and cheered each other, boasting of what they'd accomplished, and in the end the Sarjeant just stood back and let them get it out of their system.

They'd been blooded, and that would help them when it came time to face the real horrors.

Everyone looked around sharply as a single massive truck came storming down the road towards them, weaving in and out of the parked traffic with deadly purpose. It was big and brutal, with no markings on its dully gleaming metal sides. Even the windscreen had been darkly tinted, to hide the driver from view. The truck drew steadily closer, building its speed, the roar of its engine openly menacing. The Droods quickly broke off from their celebrations and turned to face the new threat. One of them marched up the road to face it, a short, stocky woman with blood already dripping from one spiked golden fist, courtesy of the driver in a stopped car who'd been stupid enough to point a gun at her. She went to meet the truck, and it changed direction to head straight for her.

The Drood stood her ground and waited for the truck to come within reach. At the last moment the whole front of the truck opened up to reveal a great crimson maw, lined with rows of rotating teeth like a living meat-grinder. The mouth engulfed the startled Drood in a moment and sucked her in. She didn't even have time to scream.

The other Droods cried out in shock and horror and raced toward the truck, which had slammed to a halt and was now backing quickly away, content with its prize. The Droods grew long swords and heavy battle-axes from their golden hands and surged forward, driven on by the inhuman speed of their armour. They were already overtaking the truck when it suddenly slowed, and stopped. The Droods hit it from all sides, their impossibly sharp blades slicing through the dull metal, and the front exploded outwards, as the female Drood cut her way out. The truck might have been a living thing, but its insides were no match for Drood armour. She emerged clutching a massive heart in one golden hand and held it above her head as a trophy. She crushed the heart, and thick, dark blood rained down like a waterfall, sliding frictionlessly over her golden armour. The truck screamed once and died.

And that was it. The rest of the traffic had come to a complete halt, and there were no more acts of defiance. No more vehicles came down the road from either direction; word had got out, and everywhere else, the traffic was choosing other routes. But for the first time ever in the Nightside, the road here was still and silent. The Sarjeant sent his people to move among the stopped vehicles and persuade the drivers to show themselves.

But somewhat to the Droods' surprise, many of the vehicles turned out not to have drivers, as such. Some taxis had cyborged drivers, permanently plugged into the machinery that ran the cars, while others were manned by more than usually focused poltergeists. Some vehicles had corpses tied to their steering wheels, to disguise their true nature as CARnivores, predators of the road. There was a possessed ambulance that ran on the existential despair of its passengers and was quite snooty about it, and a driverless hearse stuffed full of more bodies than it could adequately explain.

And that was when the television news crew turned up. Roving reporter Charlotte ap Owen and her cameraman Dave. They came jogging down the street, darting in and out of the parked cars, the wreckage, and the bodies, ignoring it all as they headed straight for the man in charge. Charlotte slammed to a halt in front of the Sarjeant, took a moment to get her breath back, then smiled determinedly into his blank face mask. Anyone else would have been intimidated; she just took it as a challenge. Charlotte was short, blonde, and busty, wearing a skin-tight leopard-skin bodysuit, for that all-important audience identification. She had a face so surgically perfect as to be almost characterless, and a smile so full of teeth most people couldn't help thinking of sharks. If only because they knew a predator when they saw one.

Dave the cameraman came puffing up to join them, burdened as he was by the heavy camera perched on his shoulder. Anonymously dressed, he practised being unnoticeable so as not to distract people's attention from Charlotte, and so they wouldn't notice what he was doing with his camera. He did everything Charlotte told him to and made her pay through her perfect teeth for the privilege.

Charlotte pointed her microphone at the Sarjeant like a weapon. "Hi! I'm Charlotte ap Owen, reporting for Nightside Television News. Can you please identify yourself, sir, and tell our viewers what it is you're doing here?"

The Sarjeant just nodded. He'd been hoping a television crew would turn up, so he could intimidate a greater number of people.

"I am the Drood Sarjeant-at-Arms."

"Wonderful! This is news!" Charlotte said breathily. "And what brings the Droods to the Nightside, Sarjeant? Do the Authorities know you're here? What about the ancient Pacts and Agreements? And now you've stopped all this traffic, what are you going to do with it?"

The Sarjeant looked at her. "You're not bothered about all the bodies?"

"This is the Nightside, Sarjeant. We have a special clean-up crew who do nothing but sweep up bodies at regular intervals, to stop them mounting up."

"The Nightside is now under Drood control," the Sarjeant said heavily. "Drood law. We will make the long night a much safer place, for everyone. In the meantime, don't get in our way."

"But what gives you the right to impose your concerns on the Nightside?" Charlotte asked winningly.

"We're Droods," said the Sarjeant.

Charlotte turned away and made a swift throat-cutting gesture to Dave. He immediately lowered his camera so it was pointing at the ground, and Charlotte turned back to the Sarjeant. She wasn't smiling any more, and as a result looked rather more human.

"We're off the air now, so there's absolutely no point in trying to intimidate me. You can speak freely. I'll almost definitely quote you later, but I won't name you as a source. You've made a hell of a mess here, Sarjeant.

What's going on? Is this something to do with the Nightside's changing boundaries?"

The Sarjeant looked past her, at the cameraman. "She does like to ask questions, doesn't she?"

"Like you wouldn't believe," said Dave. "Say something, or she'll never shut up."

"We're here to make you people behave," said the Sarjeant. "Whatever it takes. Your life as you knew it is over. If you were sane, you'd be grateful, but if you were sane, you wouldn't be here. So you can surrender, or we can stamp every single one of you into the ground. Your choice. Where is your Headquarters? I'll put one of my people in charge of it, for future propaganda."

Charlotte and Dave looked at each other.

"We don't have a Headquarters, as such," Charlotte said carefully. "We are the Television News. Just Dave and me, and a roomful of tech."

"We cover what goes on inside the Nightside," said Dave. "Everything else comes in from outside stations, other countries, sometimes even other dimensions. The long night is a cosmopolitan audience."

"People don't come to the Nightside to watch television," said Charlotte. "We provide local news for local people, and there aren't many of them. Certainly not enough to justify more than just the two of us."

"So your report isn't going to reach that big an audience," said the Sarjeant. "Which means . . . we'll just have to carry on doing this the hard way. Hit the Nightside, and keep on hitting it and hurting it, till the news gets around. Or till there isn't a soul left living in the long night to oppose us."

He turned his back on the news crew and walked away, gathering up his Droods and leading them off into the waiting night. He didn't care whether the traffic started up again. He'd proved he could stop it, and that was all that mattered. Charlotte and Dave watched him go until they were sure he was a safe distance away, then Charlotte turned to Dave and gestured at his camera.

"Tell me you got all of that."

"Of course," said the cameraman. "They never realise: just because the camera is pointing at the ground doesn't mean the sound isn't still recording. I got every word he said. You want me to broadcast it?"

"Not just yet," said Charlotte. "First, we'll see how much the Authorities will pay to hear it before everyone else."

John Taylor was one of the locals watching when the Sarjeant made his debut on local television. He sat slumped in his chair on what he'd expected to be his time off and thought furiously.

The Nightside didn't have suburbs, as such, just a few areas that were more secure than others. Mostly because of the kind of people who lived there. John and Suzie lived in a detached, three-up three-down two-sideways desirable residence out on the fringes of the long night in between a Time-travelling Eternal called Garth and an alien hunter from the future called Sarah Kingdom. They were good neighbours. They kept to themselves.

Suzie Shooter stood beside John's chair. She'd kept her own name after she married because no one felt like telling her she couldn't. She was still wearing her leathers, with the jacket hanging open to give her bump room to breathe. And so she could balance her drink on it when she was sitting down.

"So," said John. "We are now at war with the Droods."

"You say that like it's a bad thing," said Suzie. "Don't frown like that; none of this is your fault. It's mine."

"No, it isn't," said John.

"I killed the Drood in Strangefellows," said Suzie. "I don't regret it. He should never have tried to kill you. But that's why his family is here." She looked at John thoughtfully. "You could always hand me over to them. As a peace-offering."

"No, I couldn't," said John. "Maybe if I told them the truth about what happened . . ."

"They already know," said Suzie. "He had to have been following orders. Which means they wanted this."

"So all that's left to us now," said John, "is to win the war. Even though the Droods never lose."

"They've never gone to war with the Nightside before," said Suzie. "And they've never fought anyone like us. Should we contact the Authorities?"

"They must know by now," said John. "And they'll have enough on their hands trying to put together a credible resistance. No, I'm Walker, so it's down to me to do something to stop the Droods in their tracks . . . We need more information on what they're up to. They must have spread themselves pretty thin, to cover the whole of the long night, so maybe there's a weak spot in that we can take advantage of. I think we need to go talk with Argus."

Suzie looked at him. "You never mentioned that name before. Have you been keeping secrets from me?"

"Of course," said John. "I'm Walker."

The gold pocket-watch transported both of them to a grubby little back street in one of the less-well-travelled areas of the Nightside. They appeared outside a shabby storefront, whose starkly lettered sign above the single whitewashed window said WELCOME TO THE NIGHTSIDE TOURIST IN-FORMATION CENTRE! None of the few people on the street showed any interest in the place. Suzie studied the sign suspiciously.

"I didn't even know we had one of these."

"Not many do," said John. "Most people research what they're looking for on the UnderNet, before they come anywhere near the Nightside. And even the most gullible of tourists would know better than to venture inside a place like this."

"Then why do we have a Tourist Information Centre?" said Suzie.

"We don't," said John. "It's camouflage."

A small bell over the door tinkled sadly as John led Suzie into a small and gloomy office. Flapping posters on the walls showed gaudy images of places of interest. VISIT THE STREET OF THE GODS, WHERE MIRACLES HAP-PEN EVERY HOUR ON THE HOUR! VISIT THE MAMMON EMPORIUM, HOME TO RETAIL CHAINS FROM A DOZEN DIFFERENT DIMENSIONS, FOR AN OUT-OF-THIS-WORLD SHOPPING EXPERIENCE! VISIT FREAK FAIRE, FOR THE DISCERN-ING EROTICIST ONLY! There was dust all over the place, more than a suspicion of cobwebs, and a general feeling of quiet despair. A single dark figure lurked behind a desk at the back of the office, peering out from behind piles of information leaflets that hadn't been disturbed in ages. John crooked a finger at him.

"Mr Carter . . . Get out from behind there and make yourself useful for once."

Carter emerged reluctantly from behind his desk and slouched forward to scowl unhappily at John and Suzie. A sullen figure in a grubby undershirt and jeans, he looked furtive, unhealthy, and sleazy to the core.

"At your service, sir and madam. What do you want?"

"This appalling specimen is Basil Carter," John said to Suzie. "Not his real name, to keep the locals from bursting in and lynching him. He serves here as an alternative to a lifetime sentence in the Nightside's very worst dungeons, down in Shadow Deep. He was given this opportunity by my predecessor, in a rare moment of mercy, on the grounds that Carter's very existence would help discourage people from coming in. He also looks after Argus."

"Who is this Argus?" Suzie asked, looking thoughtfully at Carter in a way that made the man very nervous.

"Walker's window on the world," John said grandly. "He sees and hears everything that happens in the Nightside. How is he doing, Basil?"

Carter shrugged. "Much as usual. He doesn't change. I should know— I'm the one who has to change him, and may I remind you we're running out of nappies again? I hate this job! I suppose you want to see him . . . This way."

He led them through a concealed door at the rear of the office and into the much larger room beyond. All four of its walls were covered from floor to ceiling with hundreds of flickering viewscreens. Images came and went, faster than the human eye could follow, displaying visions of every location in the Nightside. Constantly changing and updating themselves, they showed everything that was happening in the long night at that moment. Miles of cables connected the screens to a series of lumpy machines clustered together at the back, criss-crossing the open room like a spider's web produced by something out of its head on weapons-grade crystal meth.

Sitting in the middle of all this was a gaunt and silent figure, naked apart from an adult nappy. He sat bolt upright, held in place in his chair by a series of tight leather straps. His skin was grubby, his face was blank, and he stared at nothing with dull, unblinking eyes. Wires sprouted from his shaved head, where holes had been drilled to admit them and give direct access to his brain. He didn't react to having company because he didn't know they were there. He smelled bad.

John glared at Carter. "You need to take better care of him, Basil."

"Or what?" said Carter. "You'll find someone to replace me? Go ahead! There are days when even Shadow Deep looks good compared to this!"

"You take better care of Argus or you can take his place in the chair," said John.

Carter looked at the floor and didn't say anything. Suzie looked at John.

"This is Argus," said John. "Not so much a name, more a job description. The god with a thousand eyes. His brain's higher functions have been surgically removed, so they won't interfere with his connection to the computers. Argus sees everything that happens in the Nightside and reports on anything red-flagged by his programming."

"It never ends, does it?" said Suzie. "He never leaves that chair."

"Don't feel sorry for him," said John. "He's not a volunteer. Only the very worst and foulest of criminals undergo this process. If you knew what he did before he was Argus, you'd think this was a mercy."

"Of course your predecessor did this," said Suzie. "It's the kind of thing Henry would do."

"Argus makes Walker's job possible," said John. "How else could I always know what's going on, in an area the size of the Nightside? But don't put all the blame on Henry. There's no telling how long this, or something like it, has been going on."

"How does it work?" said Suzie.

"Damned if I know," said John. "But because Argus sees and hears everything, I can step in and put a stop to things before they get out-of-control. Usually." He moved forward, slipping carefully past the hanging cables, until he was standing next to Argus. Suzie followed him. Carter didn't. "And, occasionally, I can use Argus to reach outside the Nightside and call for assistance. On those rare occasions when we need specialist help with special problems. People like the Carnacki Institute, or the Soulhunters. But I can't see either of them agreeing to go to war with the Droods, over us."

"Why didn't Argus tell you Droods had entered the Nightside?" said Suzie.

"I don't know," said John. "He should have." He leaned forward and addressed the thing in the chair. "Argus, show me the Droods in the Nightside right now. What are they doing?"

The viewscreens immediately showed armoured Droods marching

through different parts of the Nightside. Heading for the offices of the *Night Times*, the Uptown Clubs, the Hawk's Wind Bar & Grill, and many other places of interest. The Droods had already penetrated deep into the long night, in their separate groups. One screen showed Molly Metcalf walking down a street with an unidentified figure at her side. Presumably a Drood out of his armour.

"Those two are heading for Strangefellows," said John. "I'd better warn Alex."

"We're going to need bigger guns," said Suzie. "I'll go visit the Gun Shoppes of Usher, see what they have on offer for truly apocalyptic occasions."

"You do that," said John. "I'll intercept Molly Metcalf and the man with her, who just might be Eddie Drood."

Suzie looked sharply at John. "You're going to need me with you if you plan on taking them down. They're dangerous."

"All I have in mind is a little civilised conversation," John said easily. "It may not be too late to put an end to this madness."

"And if it is?" said Suzie.

"Then I'll have to speak very harshly to Eddie and Molly," said John. "In my capacity as Walker."

"Give them hell," said Suzie.

They both looked around sharply as all the viewscreens snapped off. Carter made a loud, whining noise. Eddie looked sharply at the thing in the chair.

"Argus! What's happening?"

"Telepathic interference, from a source outside the Nightside," said Argus, in a cold, dead voice. "We are under attack by the telepath Ammonia Vom Acht, wife to a Drood. She is shutting us down. I know this because she wants you to know this. And to know there is nothing you can do to stop her."

"We'll see about that," said John. "Carter, mind the store."

He produced his gold pocket-watch, and the portable Timeslip whisked John and Suzie away to Strangefellows.

They appeared in front of Alex Morrisey as he tried to force some more than usually recalcitrant bar-snacks back into their cage. He didn't jump.

He was used to stranger things than them appearing out of nowhere. As long as he didn't have to immediately reach for a weapon, he considered himself ahead. John looked around, but Strangefellows was unusually empty, for once.

"Where is everyone?" said Suzie.

"They all went running off to see what was happening for themselves, the fools," said Alex. "I told them, stay here where it's safe, watch it all on television, but no . . . I think some of them fancied their chances against a Drood. Idiots. What are you doing here?"

"Argus is under attack by Ammonia Vom Acht," said John.

"Hold it," said Suzie. "You told him about Argus, and you didn't tell me?"

"I already knew," said Alex. "I am wise and wonderful and know many things."

"We will talk about this later," Suzie said to John.

"Looking forward to it immensely," said John. "Anyway, Ammonia is interfering with Argus, and I need some help to ward her off. Are you still on good terms with Vivienne de Tourney, Alex?"

"Name-dropper," said Alex. "I can talk to her, but . . ."

"Try," said John.

Alex produced a phone from beneath the bar and punched in a really long number.

"Who is Vivienne de Tourney?" said Suzie.

"Major-league telepath, or witch, depending on how you look at these things," said John. "Currently affiliated with the London Knights. She hasn't any love for the Nightside, but she really doesn't like Droods. And she has a connection with Alex. Not a particularly nice one, but . . ."

"Story of my life . . ." said Alex. "Viv, it's Alex! I need a favour."

An image suddenly appeared, standing before them: Vivienne de Tourney, dressed in a black leather dominatrix outfit, complete with domino mask. She was carrying a cat-o'-nine-tails and glared at all three of them impartially.

"What is it? I'm busy!"

"So I see," said Alex.

He quickly explained the situation, and Vivienne swore harshly. "The Droods have entered the Nightside? After we told them not to? They've got some nerve. And putting Ammonia Vom Acht onto the front line; that's really pushing your luck. She never was that stable. I mean, have you seen who she married? Still, give me one good reason why I should get involved and risk dragging the London Knights into this mess?"

"Because your real name is Vivienne La Fae, sister to Morgana," said Alex. "Both of you were very close to Merlin Satanspawn, my ancestor. Which means we're family, in a weird and probably highly unnatural way. Also you do this for me, and I will owe you a favour."

"A big one," said Vivienne.

"Aren't they all?" said Alex.

"Oh, all right," Vivienne said ungraciously. "I just know I'm going to regret this . . . But it would be a pleasure to stick a spoke in Ammonia's work. Just to put her in her place . . . There. Done. I've kicked her back inside her own head, and locked her out of the Nightside. But I can only keep this up till the London Knights find out. At which point they'll probably order me to stop, to avoid bringing them into open conflict with the Droods. The last war between them didn't go too well for either side." She broke off and looked away. "Don't be so impatient, Gawaine darling; I'll be with you in a moment." She looked back at Alex. "You do know Molly Metcalf and Eddie Drood are on their way to Strangefellows?"

"I'm on top of that," said John.

"Best place to be," said Vivienne, and vanished. Alex gave John a hard look.

"Eddie Drood and Molly Metcalf are coming here, and you didn't think to tell me?"

"I was going to," said John. "I didn't want you distracted."

"You know they're going to want to question me about what happened to that Drood," said Alex.

"The one I killed," said Suzie.

"What do you want me to do?" said Alex.

"Tell them the truth," said John.

"Are you kidding me?" said Alex. "That has never worked out for me before, and I'm not about to start now."

"Tell them," said Suzie. "And then tell them to come and find me."

John's pocket-watch dropped Suzie off outside the nearest branch of the Gun Shoppes of Usher. Foremost supplier of weapons, explosives, and all the more exotic means of sudden fatalities in the Nightside. The Gun Shoppes knew Suzie of old, but when she tried the door, it was locked. Which was unheard of. The Gun Shoppes never closed. They were famous, or more properly infamous, for supplying twenty-four-hour access to death and destruction to whoever wanted it. Suzie drew her pump-action double-barrelled shotgun from the holster on her back and pointed the gun meaningfully at the closed door. She didn't need to say anything; the Gun Shoppes knew Suzie of old. After only the slightest of pauses, the door unlocked itself and swung open before her. Suzie holstered her shotgun with a flourish and strode in.

Mr Usher was already standing behind the counter, waiting for her. He was always behind the counter, no matter which branch you visited. The Shoppe's owner, manager, and high priest. There was a lot of discussion as to who and what he really was, and so far no one had come up with an answer that anyone could live with.

A respectable-looking middle-aged man in a smart if unremarkable suit, Mr Usher always manifested an air of cultivated politeness. He had a square face, a receding hairline, and rimless eyeglasses perched half-way down his nose. A look that hadn't changed in centuries. He seemed more like an undertaker than anything else, presumably because he was in a similar line of business. His constant professional smile didn't even come close to touching his eyes. He was a businessman, everything for sale and nothing on credit. When he spoke, he sounded like every salesman you had ever heard, except he didn't have to try too hard. Because everyone wanted what he had to sell.

Anyone else would have been intimidated by his presence, but Suzie honestly didn't give a damn. Mr Usher nodded calmly.

"Hello again, Suzie. I had a feeling you might be coming to see me."

"Is that why you locked the door?" said Suzie.

"There are Droods about," said Mr Usher.

Suzie looked around her. As usual, there wasn't much to look at. There were no weapons on display, no posters, and no advertising. You didn't come to the Gun Shoppes of Usher to browse; you already had something in mind, something no one else could supply, or you wouldn't be there. You ask Mr Usher for what you want, and he goes out back and gets it for you. No one knows what there is out back of every Shoppe, or even exactly where this "back" might be; but it must be really big to contain all the things Mr Usher has been known to return with.

He didn't care whether you wanted the thigh-bone Cain used to smash in Abel's skull or the assassin's pistol that started World War I; anything was yours for the asking. Though the price was always just that little bit more than you wanted to pay.

"I need more of those strange-matter bullets," said Suzie. "Lots more. I'll take all you've got."

"Unfortunately, we're out," Mr Usher said smoothly. "The supply has dried up. Apparently the source discovered what you used them for."

Suzie frowned. "What source?"

"You don't need to know," Mr Usher said firmly. "The point is, we no longer stock them."

"All right," said Suzie. "Give me the Speaking Gun."

The atmosphere suddenly seemed distinctly chillier. The Speaking Gun was not a thing to speak of lightly. It could detect the echoes of the Word God spoke when creating the universe, which still resonated in all things. The Gun could detect the specific echoes in absolutely anything, then speak them backwards, effectively de-creating the object in question. A weapon originally designed to destroy angels and demons, the Speaking Gun took a toll on all who used it. But there was nothing like it for getting the job done.

"I'm afraid I can't help you with that," said Mr Usher.

"Why not?" said Suzie. "I've used it before and survived. Can you think of anything more likely to take down a Drood?"

"Unfortunately," said Mr Usher, "John Taylor has given me strict instructions where the Speaking Gun is concerned. That I was not to supply it to you, or to him, or to anybody else. On the grounds that it is simply too dangerous to be allowed out in the world."

Suzie looked at him for a long moment. She honestly hadn't expected that.

"John isn't here," she said finally. "And I am."

She didn't reach for her shotgun. She didn't need to. Just by being who she was, the threat was implicit. And very real.

"Mr Taylor was most emphatic," Mr Usher said carefully. "He said he would use his authority as Walker to have all branches of my Shoppe banned from the Nightside. And since the long night is one of my very best markets . . . I regret I am unable to assist you in this matter."

Suzie nodded. Her threat to Mr Usher was nothing, compared to John's threat to close him down. Particularly when she didn't really want to kill Mr Usher. Not when there were a great many useful things he could still supply her with. She decided to change tactics.

"What have you got in stock that I can use against the Droods?"

"I've got a white flag you can wave," said Mr Usher.

Suzie's frown deepened. She wasn't known for her sense of humour. Mr Usher looked at her thoughtfully.

"I do have something . . . Though I'm not sure whether you'll want it."

"Is it a weapon?" said Suzie.

"Yes."

"Then I want it."

"The Droods' strange-matter armour is as strong as it is because it comes from another dimension," said Mr Usher. "So to break it, you need something stronger and stranger, from a different reality."

He reached beneath the counter and brought out a pair of heavy chain-mail gloves. Suzie was about to ask what use they would be when Mr Usher slipped them on and reached beneath the counter again to produce a very long sword in a black metal scabbard covered with deeply inscribed runes and sigils. From the leather-wrapped hilt to the tip of the scabbard, the sword looked to be a good seven feet long. The Shoppe suddenly felt a lot colder, as though just the sword's presence was enough to chill the soul. Suzie was intrigued. She reached out to take the sword, and Mr Usher fell back a step to keep it out of her reach.

"This sword fell off the back of a passing Timeslip," he said. "And I have a strong feeling it passed through a great many places, and even more hands, before it ended up here. Probably because it had worn out its welcome everywhere else. This is the kind of weapon that gets through a lot of owners, and not in a good way."

He drew the sword from its scabbard. Given the sheer length of the blade, that should have been difficult, even awkward, but the sword seemed almost to leap for its freedom. The long blade glowed with a sick yellow light, like poisoned honey. Suzie could feel her skin crawling, and that didn't happen often. Mr Usher displayed the blade to her, almost sorrowfully. The sword's overwhelming presence seemed to fill the Shoppe, as though a dangerous animal had got out.

"This is an Infernal Device," he said. "The name of the sword is Wulfs-bane."

"Will it cut through Drood armour?" said Suzie.

"This blade is not all that it once was, after so many travels," said Mr Usher. "But trust me; a blade like this could cut through the world."

"And you're ready to sell it to me?" said Suzie. "What's the catch?"

"Wulfsbane is alive," said Mr Usher. "A sentient sword, some would say possessed, with its own needs and motivations. It will seek to corrupt your soul if you hang on to it too long."

Suzie looked at the drawn blade, glowing like something that could poison the whole world just by being in it, and smiled a slow smile.

"I want it. What's the price?"

"How about . . . your first-born child?" said Mr Usher.

Suzie drew her shotgun and jammed both barrels up his nostrils before he could even blink. Mr Usher stood very still and tried again.

"Or alternatively . . . John Taylor, as Walker, must agree never to ban my Shoppes from the Nightside."

Suzie nodded and slipped the shotgun back into its holster. "I can get John to agree to that."

"Then the sword is yours," said Mr Usher.

He slammed Wulfsbane back into its black metal scabbard. There was a feeling of resistance, as though the sword was fighting him because it didn't want to be put away. Mr Usher presented the scabbarded sword to Suzie with a certain sense of ceremony, but she made no move to accept it.

"Don't I get the protective gloves as well?"

"They prevent the sword from bonding with my soul," said Mr Usher. "It has to do that before it will agree to be wielded. The sword is sentient, remember? Once you touch the hilt with your bare flesh, the connection will be made and the covenant entered into. The sword will then serve you, and no other, for as long as you both shall live. Do you agree to this, Suzie, for a chance to kill Droods?"

Suzie didn't even hesitate. She reached out and grabbed hold of the hilt, and it seemed to nestle into her hand as though it belonged there. She hefted the sword, and the great length of the blade in its scabbard seemed almost weightless. She didn't ask for a belt to hang it from. She just put it over her shoulder, and it clung to her back, next to the shotgun in its holster. As though the sword was already a part of her. The hilt peered over her shoulder at Mr Usher, and he looked away, as though to avoid its gaze.

"The deal is made," he said flatly. "And the sooner you get that thing out of my Shoppe, the better. Don't even think about bringing it back, when you inevitably decide you don't want it any more. Disposing of the damned thing is your problem now. It belongs to you, or you belong to it. Feel free to destroy it, if you can."

"Before it destroys me?" said Suzie.

"Before it becomes you," said Mr Usher. "Wulfsbane seduces the soul, then consumes it."

Suzie smiled her cold smile again. "It never met anyone like me."

"You two were made for each other," said Mr Usher.

Back in the deserted Strangefellows, Alex Morrisey poured John Taylor a large wormwood brandy, without having to be asked. He knew a man under pressure when he saw one. John nodded his thanks and knocked half of it back in one go. Alex considered him thoughtfully.

"So," he said. "The Droods have invaded the Nightside, Eddie Drood and Molly Metcalf are on their way here, and Suzie's due to give birth real soon now. What are you going to do?"

"Damned if I know," said John. "When I agreed to take on this job, I thought I'd already come up against the worst the Nightside could throw at me. But I never expected this . . ."

"No one expects a Drood invasion," said Alex. "In fact, that's probably the point. You want to borrow my enchanted baseball bat?"

"Have you got anything bigger?" said John.

Alex surprised John then by thinking about it. "I've got all manner of useful things piled up out back. You'd be surprised what some people will bring to a bar on a night out, then leave behind. And never come back for, probably because they weren't supposed to have it in the first place. But I really can't think of anything that would be much use against an army of Droods. My advice is stop here, have a great many drinks, and not come out again till it's all over. Once the Droods are in charge, they'll still need a Walker to run things for them. I mean . . . Authorities, Droods, what's the difference?"

"No," said John. "I can't do that. As long as I've got this job, I have to do it to the best of my ability. If only for my pride's sake. And the Droods . . . would be a very different kind of boss. Once they take control of the Nightside, they won't be able to resist meddling with things. Laying down the law, enforcing the moral hard-line . . . it's what they do. They'll shut down everything that makes the Nightside what it is. Including this place, probably on moral-health grounds."

"Then get the hell out of my bar and do something to stop the bastards!" said Alex. "And don't come back till you've sorted everything out."

"But that's the problem," said John, not moving. "I don't know of any force, in this world or out of it, that's ever been able to stop the Droods. They've gone to war so many times, they've learned to be really good at it. They've been badly hurt in their time, even crippled . . . but they always come back, and they always triumph. How do you break a winning streak like that?"

"Even the longest winning streak has to come to an end eventually," said Alex. "Use your gift. Find their weak spot."

"If only it was that simple," said John.

"Man up," said Alex, not unkindly. "You're John Taylor. Just as much a legend as the Droods, in your own annoying way, and far more dangerous because you fight dirty." He paused. "You know . . . I could come with you. If you like. Just to watch your back. From a safe distance."

"Thanks for the thought," said John. "But if I'm going to negotiate a deal with Eddie Drood, it might be best not to have any witnesses present during the hard bargaining."

"You sound better," said Alex.

"I've had an idea," said John.

"Good," said Alex. "You're never more dangerous than when you're being devious."

John Taylor took out his gold pocket-watch and disappeared. There was a brief flurry of disturbed air where he'd been standing, then a single piranha fell out of nowhere to land on the bartop.

"Show-off," said Alex.

He tossed the piranha to his pet vulture, Agatha. She snatched it out of mid air, gulped it down, and went back to cooing over her night-dark egg. Alex shook his head. Some nights in Strangefellows were stranger than others. He lifted the glass of wormwood brandy that John had left behind and savoured the aroma of pure rotgut.

"Good luck, old friend. You're going to need it."

Eddie Drood and Molly Metcalf strode down a crowded street, heading for Strangefellows bar, and everyone gave them plenty of room. People might not recognise Eddie, but they sure as hell knew who Molly was. Eddie was still having trouble coming to terms with all the sin and temptation on open display. Book-shop windows full of ghost-written books written by real ghosts, offering spiritual wisdom, new sexual techniques, and cooking tips from beyond the grave. Restaurants that specialised in fine cuisine made from creatures that not only didn't exist any more but were often completely imaginary. Record shops with vinyl delights rare enough to pull in even the most jaded of collectors: music of the spheres, music for robots to dance to, and recent albums by much-loved artists the outside world only thought were dead. Temptation comes in many forms.

Eddie had trouble dealing with just how many people there were, coming and going on the crowded pavements, keen to buy everything on offer. Even though they must have known most of it wasn't necessarily all it appeared to be and that the deal was stacked against them. The crowds were so heavy it was hard for Eddie to see more than a few feet in front of him, but Molly seemed to know where she was going, so he just stuck close to her. Everywhere he looked, Eddie saw faces intent on following their own path, driven on by inner demons and private passions, determined to pursue their dreams no matter where they led.

At least Eddie could feel safely anonymous, out of his armour. Shaman Bond had been to the Nightside now and again, but not enough that his face was known, or remarked upon. And, of course, as long as he was with the infamous wild witch of the woods, he could be pretty sure no one would be looking at him anyway.

"Who, exactly, are you planning on making a deal with?" Molly said finally.

"We're going to Strangefellows," said Eddie. "Everyone goes to Strange-fellows. And you know Alex Morrisey."

Molly looked at him suspiciously. "What's that supposed to mean?"

"You know him well enough that you can persuade him to call John Taylor," said Eddie.

"That won't be necessary," said John.

Eddie and Molly came to an abrupt halt as the legendary Walker stepped out of the crowd to stand right in front of them. The two men looked each other over carefully. Two living legends, face-to-face for the first time and deciding just how impressed they should be. Eddie looked at Walker, poised and elegant in his smart city suit, and his first thought was that John Taylor looked every inch an authority figure. Eddie had never got on well with those, even when he was one. But there was no denying the man had style, and presence, and all the other things Eddie had been trained not to have, as a secret agent out in the field.

John's first thought was that Eddie Drood looked surprisingly ordinary. Just another face in the crowd, nothing like his reputation. Until John looked into the man's eyes and saw a cold determination that could move mountains. Or knock them down and walk through the wreckage. And, of course, he was Molly Metcalf's significant other. Not a position for the faint of heart. John smiled slightly. Perhaps he and the Drood did have something in common, after all.

Molly looked at the two men looking at each other and wondered which of them would blink first.

"Welcome to the Nightside," John said finally. "You might have dropped us a note, to let us know you were coming."

"And spoil the surprise?" said Eddie. "So I'm Eddie Drood. It is good to meet you, at last. How have we managed to put it off for so long?"

"Fear of disappointment?" said John. "One should never meet one's legends."

"Or perhaps, deep-down, we were just worried that we wouldn't be able to resist finding out which of us was the better man," said Eddie.

"Dear God, smell the testosterone," Molly said briskly. "Put them away, boys, before you trip over them."

Both men smiled.

"Suzie's just as bad," said John.

"So I've heard," said Eddie.

"We need to talk," said John.

"Yes," said Eddie. "We do. Is there somewhere nearby where we can do that privately?"

"Of course," said John.

He nodded to the shop beside him, an ice-cream parlour with the unfortunately arch name *Really Cool Ices.* John raised an eyebrow, and Eddie inclined his head slightly in acceptance. Molly sniffed loudly, to make it clear she had no time for such posturing. John opened the door and strode in, followed by Eddie and Molly. John smiled around at the startled customers and staff.

"Everybody out, please. I'm commandeering this over-priced establishment for official Authorities business. At the double; spit spot, hop like a bunny."

The customers immediately rose from their tables, abandoning their ice-creams, and the staff hurried out from behind the counter, not even pausing to take off their aprons and silly hats. They all streamed quickly out the door, being careful to give John Taylor and Molly Metcalf plenty of room. Eddie looked at John.

"I'll just bet you're one of those people who never has any trouble catching the barman's eye."

"Comes with the job," John said easily. "Being Walker should come with a few perks."

"You mean there are drawbacks?" said Eddie.

"Apart from everyone's trying to kill me?" said John.

"I have days like that," said Eddie.

"Shut the hell up and sit down, both of you," said Molly. "You're getting on my nerves."

John seated himself at the nearest table. Eddie and Molly sat down facing him. It was very quiet in the ice-cream parlour, now they had the place all to themselves. Eddie peered around at the cheap and nasty plastic tables, then studied the list of flavours on the wall. THE ARCTIC SELECTION! PENGUIN, WALRUS, KILLER SHARK, SHACKLETON EXPEDITION. Eddie looked at John.

"Any of them any good?"

"Not even a little bit," said John. "It's strictly for the tourists."

"I want an ice-cream," said Molly. "With those little sprinkles on."

"Later," said Eddie.

He looked at John, and John looked back at him, and neither of them knew where to start. They both understood the realities of the situation and what was at stake, but they also knew they had nothing real to offer each other. They might be men of goodwill, but those they served weren't.

"I refuse to believe nothing can be done to stop this," said John.

"As long as we're talking, there's still hope," said Eddie. "You could make a good start by telling me Luther's death was an unfortunate accident."

"Was that his name?" said John. "I never knew."

"Do you often kill people you don't know?" said Eddie.

"It's the Nightside," said John. "That happens all the time. But in this case, Suzie shot Luther while he was trying to kill me."

"Why would he do that?" said Molly.

"He didn't say," said John. "But there can only be one reason: because someone ordered him to."

"The Matriarch sent Luther into the Nightside to talk to the Authorities," said Eddie.

"I can tell you for a fact that he never went anywhere near them," said John. "He just appeared in Strangefellows and attacked me without warning."

Eddie shook his head. "Luther was an experienced field agent. If he'd wanted you dead, you'd be dead."

"Please remember who you're talking to," said John. "I have survived attacks by angels, gods, and members of my own family."

"It's true," Molly said to Eddie. "He has."

Eddie shook his head. "The Matriarch told me . . ."

John raised an eyebrow. "And your Matriarch has never lied to you?"

Eddie didn't answer.

"What if the Sarjeant-at-Arms sent Luther to kill John?" said Molly. "And didn't tell the Matriarch, so she could have deniability? It is the sort of thing he'd do."

Eddie nodded, reluctantly. "But even if he did, he'd never admit it to anyone outside the family. It would be John's word against his, and that wouldn't be enough to stop the invasion." He looked steadily at John. "There's only one way out of this mess that I can see, only one way that will save lives on both sides. You have to persuade the Authorities to surrender. If there's no resistance, there's no need for any bloodshed. We can sort the truth out afterwards."

But John was already shaking his head. "Even if I could convince the Authorities to do that, and I'm not at all sure that I could, no one in the long night would ever accept what your family means to do. They all know the Droods will shut down everything they disapprove of. Droods live to occupy the moral high ground."

"You say that like it's a bad thing," said Eddie.

John leaned forward, fixing Eddie with an earnest stare. "You have to understand; the Nightside exists to be a haven for all the shades of grey. For all the people, good and bad and in between, who wouldn't fit in any-where else. It's not just about satisfying the pleasures of the flesh, or the longings of the heart, or pursuing all the things the rest of the world doesn't want you to have. The long night is where you go when no one else will take you. The last place on Earth where you can be truly free."

"He's got a point, Eddie," said Molly.

"You would say that," said Eddie, not turning his steady gaze away from John. "I'm sorry, Walker, but you must tell the Authorities to stand down. They have no other option. Once the Drood machine has been set in mo-tion, it doesn't stop for anything but complete victory."

"I can't do that," John said bluntly. "And I won't. The one thing that everyone in the Nightside can agree on is that we don't take any crap from the outside world. Not after everything it's done to us and taken from us. This is our refuge, from the tyrannies of Good and Evil, and we'll fight to our last breath to defend it."

"Fight for what?" said Eddie. "The freedom to suffer and die, to be lied to and cheated, to prey on each other and trample the weakest underfoot?"

"The freedom to live as we choose," said John. "And to hell with whether the outside world approves of how we do it."

He pushed back his chair and stood up. Eddie and Molly were quickly on their feet too, facing him.

"I can't let you leave, John," Eddie said flatly. "You're too powerful a player to be left running loose."

"You really think you can stop me?" said John. He sounded honestly curious.

Eddie subvocalised his activating Words, and his armour swept over him in a moment. A golden statue stood in his place, gleaming brightly under the stark fluorescent lighting. John could see his face reflected in the featureless mask and smiled easily to show he wasn't impressed. That he'd seen better and scarier.

Molly glared from one to the other. "Knock it off, both of you! This isn't helping!"

Neither man looked at her. They were locked in their roles, of who they were and had to be. Eddie raised one golden fist, and heavy spikes rose up from the knuckles.

"We don't have to do this the hard way, John."

"Of course we do," said John. "It's the Nightside."

"You're coming with me, Walker. So I can use you to put an end to this madness."

"I really don't think so," said John.

He concentrated, and used his gift to find the activating Words Eddie had just used. They came to him in a moment, and then it was the easiest thing in the world for John to send Eddie's armour shooting back into his torc. Eddie stood before John, just an ordinary man again, too shocked to do anything. Molly opened her mouth. John produced a packet from inside his coat and dashed the contents into Molly's face. Caught by surprise, Molly breathed the pepper in and was immediately seized by a series of violent sneezes. The force of them bent her right over, tears streaming down her face to drip onto the floor. Eddie surged forward, ready to protect Molly even without his armour.

"Hold it!" said John. He pointed a steady finger at the incapacitated Molly. "Back off, Drood. Or I'll use my gift to find a way to make her never have existed, so you never had a chance to meet her."

Eddie stopped where he was. Because this was John Taylor, and he just might be able to do it. John gathered his dignity about him, nodded easily to Eddie, and walked out of the ice-cream parlour. Eddie watched him go, then turned to Molly. She brought her sneezes under control through sheer iron will-power even as tears continued to stream down her cheeks.

"Why did you let him go?" she said fiercely. "He was bluffing!"

"I couldn't risk it," said Eddie.

He offered Molly a handkerchief, and she snatched it from him. She scrubbed fiercely at her face, sneezed explosively one last time, and breathed deeply until she was sure she had everything back under control. She thrust the handkerchief back at Eddie, then smiled wryly.

"So, what did you think of John Taylor?"

"It seems he really is everything people say he is," said Eddie. "But he won't catch me off guard next time."

"Yes, he will," said Molly. "Because that's what he does. Eddie, have you lost your armour permanently?"

Eddie murmured his activating Words, and the armour swept out of his torc to cover him from head to toe. He stretched a few times, as though checking it still fit, then sent it back into his torc.

"No one is supposed to know our activating Words. But now I know he knows, I've set up a safe-guard in my torc to prevent him from doing it again. And I've sent a message to the Sarjeant-at-Arms, so he can tell the rest of the family to do the same."

"John will just come up with another trick," said Molly. "Should we go after him?"

"He'll have disappeared by now," said Eddie. "Let him go. I gave him a chance to do the right thing, so whatever happens next is on him. Let's go to Strangefellows. See what we can learn there."

"And then?" said Molly.

"Depends what we learn," said Eddie.

"I still want an ice-cream," said Molly.

CHAPTER NINE

The Nightside Has No Heart

S till quietly fuming at not having arrived in the heart of the Nightside, the Matriarch led her column of armoured Droods through the bustling streets. They made an impressive sight, dozens of animated golden statues marching in perfect lock-step. People everywhere fell back to let them pass, even stepping off the pavement entirely to make sure they had plenty of room because even the dumbest tourist had at least heard of the Droods. And what they were capable of doing if they got upset.

The Matriarch turned to Ioreth, the Assistant Librarian. She'd made a point of keeping him at her side because he'd read more about the Nightside than anyone else in the family, apart from the Librarian himself.

Ioreth hadn't liked leaving William behind to cope on his own, but he couldn't resist the family summons to war. He'd missed out on the last one, against the Hungry Gods, because he was too young, and he'd always wondered if he had it in him to make a good Drood solider. If he could fight the good fight, when it really mattered, or if he was just a scholar after all. No one was more surprised than him when the Matriarch decided that with the Sarjeant-at-Arms off running his own group, Ioreth would serve as her second in command. Ioreth was pretty sure this was only partly because of his extensive knowledge of the long night and more because she could rely on him not to challenge her authority.

"Where are we now?" said the Matriarch, not for the first time.

"In a business area called Uptown," Ioreth said patiently. "Not far from Victoria House, home to the publishing offices of the *Night Times*."

"Good," said the Matriarch. "Can we rely on Julien Advent to be reasonable, do you think?"

"He's Julien Advent, the legendary Victorian Adventurer," said Ioreth. "So almost certainly not."

Victoria House turned out to be a large and comfortably run-down building, standing amidst sedate and respectable business properties. Though Ioreth knew for a fact that most of those businesses wouldn't even recognise respectability if they fell over it. Victoria House was the largest of the buildings because within its grey stone walls the *Night Times* was written and edited, printed and published, every twenty-four hours without fail. Not forgetting the occasional Special Edition, in times of angel war or the return of a Biblical Myth. The Sunday edition was said to be so heavy you could use it to club a horse to death.

All of this took place under the guardianship of the paper's renowned owner and editor, Julien Advent. He insisted on keeping all the operations under one roof, so he could ensure the safety and independence of the paper and all the people who worked on it. Because there's nothing like telling the truth on a regular basis to make you a whole lot of enemies.

The Matriarch headed straight for the front door. A pair of more than usually grotesque gargoyles leaned out from the roof to peer down at the Droods and shout insults. The Matriarch turned her right hand into a gun and blew both gargoyles apart. Very small pieces of rubble rained down on the Droods and rattled harmlessly off their armour.

"Start as you mean to go on," the Matriarch said briskly. "Tell me about the *Night Times*, Ioreth. In particular, tell me what I need to know before I go in there and beard the lion in his den."

"The paper was founded more than two centuries ago," said Ioreth, dropping automatically into lecture mode. "The newspaper of record for the Nightside, it covers all current events with favour toward none. The paper has as many enemies as admirers, but the last time someone tried to shut it down by interfering with its distribution process, the Little Sisters of the Immaculate Chainsaw made one of their rare public appearances, and made such a mess of the thugs in question that it was several days before the gutters ran freely again."

The Matriarch turned to look at him. "Do you see any supernaturally violent nuns in the vicinity? Then stop looking so twitchy! Droods don't twitch!"

"This is the Nightside," Ioreth said darkly. "Things are different here."

The Matriarch sniffed loudly and turned her attention back to Victoria House. Using the sensors built into his mask, Ioreth could clearly See the many layers of magical defences surrounding the building, laid down over centuries. A subsonic avoidance spell, that worked on the subconscious to persuade people they really should be somewhere else; floating invisible transformation mines, just waiting to turn you into something unfortunate if you got too close; and what looked like the psychic equivalent of barbed wire. All in all, enough to give Ioreth a headache just looking at them.

The Matriarch walked unflinchingly forward, so, of course, Ioreth had no choice but to follow her. He did his best not to slow down as the defences sparked and sputtered, and discharged harmlessly against his armour. The Matriarch reached the front door unharmed, with Ioreth right there at her side, and the building's defences shut down, with a sullen air of having done all that could reasonably be expected of them. The Matriarch looked back at her Droods.

"Stay here. Guard the door and watch the street. No one is to go in or come out till I have finished my little chat with Julien Advent. Ioreth, you're with me. You too, Magnus."

A short and sturdy Drood stepped out of the ranks to join them. Magnus had moulded his armour to resemble that of a medieval knight, complete with helmet, breast-plate, and greaves. He looked solid enough to walk through a wall without slowing. Ioreth didn't know Magnus personally, but he had heard that the Sarjeant-at-Arms was seriously considering appointing Magnus as his second in command. And eventual replacement. Given that Ioreth knew for a fact Magnus had never once worked as a field agent, Ioreth had to wonder just what Magnus could have done to so impress the Sarjeant.

The Matriarch tried the front door. It wasn't locked. She threw the door wide open and marched into Victoria House, and Ioreth and Magnus followed quickly after her.

The lobby turned out to be comfortably spacious and almost completely deserted, apart from a cubicle of bullet-proof glass surrounded by a pentacle of softly glowing blue lines. Ioreth could feel the power emanating from them, even at a distance. The Matriarch studied the single figure sitting quietly inside the cubicle before turning to Ioreth.

"The *Night Times* has many enemies," Ioreth said quietly. "The receptionist is the building's first line of defence. And from what I've heard about her, God help anyone who tries to get past her without an appointment. Please tell me you've arranged an appointment, Matriarch. I'd feel so much safer."

"Man up, Ioreth," said the Matriarch.

She headed straight for the cubicle, with Magnus right beside her, and Ioreth brought up the rear, wishing just a little wistfully that people would listen to him when he warned them about things. The Matriarch tapped loudly on the bullet-proof glass with a golden knuckle, and the little old lady inside put down her knitting, peered at the Matriarch through thick granny glasses, and smiled sweetly.

"I'm afraid no one gets in without an appointment, my dear. And I know for a fact Mr Advent is not seeing any Droods today. I am sure I would remember something like that."

Ioreth studied the receptionist carefully through the sensors built into his mask and hoped the Matriarch was Seeing what he was Seeing. The little old lady was knitting with needles made from human bones, and behind the granny glasses, her faded blue eyes glowed with the same kind of light as the pentacle lines. Her pleasant smile showed sharply pointed teeth.

"I am the Drood Matriarch," said the Matriarch. "I'm here to speak with Julien Advent."

"Oh, he never sees anyone he isn't expecting, dear," said the receptionist. "Would you like me to make you an appointment? I'm sure I could fit you in for a quick word sometime next week."

"Droods don't do appointments," said the Matriarch.

She nodded to Magnus, who smashed a hole clean through the bullet-proof glass with one blow of his golden fist. The glowing blue lines surrounding the cubicle disappeared in a moment, as though they'd been blown out by the simple presence of Magnus' armour. Jagged cracks spread across the front of the cubicle, but somehow the glass still held together. The receptionist looked thoughtfully at Magnus, then picked up her knitting again.

"Go on up, Margaret and Ioreth and Magnus Drood. Mr Advent is expecting you."

At the far end of the lobby, the doors to the elevator slid smoothly open. The Matriarch headed straight for them, not even glancing at the receptionist, and Ioreth and Magnus hurried after her. Magnus made a point of entering the elevator first, to check it out, and only then allowed the other two to join him. There were buttons for several floors, but only the top one was marked EDITORIAL. Magnus hit it with an extended golden finger, and the doors closed.

Even though there was more than enough room in the elevator for three Droods in their armour, Ioreth still felt distinctly uncomfortable and kept looking around for some new threat until the Matriarch told him sharply to cut it out. Magnus didn't seem even a little bit bothered. The elevator took its own sweet time getting to the top floor and played Viennese waltzes at them the whole way. The Matriarch looked at Ioreth, who shrugged.

"Julien Advent's favourite music as a young man. We all have a soft spot for the popular music of our youth."

"I was always very fond of Meat Loaf, and *Bat Out of Hell*," said the Matriarch.

Ioreth said nothing.

The elevator doors finally opened, with a bright and cheerful chiming sound, to reveal a long, empty corridor. There were no doors leading off, just one large and very solid-looking door at the far end marked EDITORIAL, so the Matriarch headed for that. Magnus wanted to lead the way, but the Matriarch was having none of it. Ioreth was quite happy to bring up the rear, so that whatever happened would be sure to hit the others first. The walls were lined with famous front pages from the paper's long history, preserved under glass. *Angel War Ends in Draw. Immortal Griffin Turns Out to Be Just Long-Lived. Walker Missing, Presumed Dead; Nightside*

Celebrates. When they finally reached the end, there was a sign above the door saying ALL THE NEWS, DAMMIT. The door itself was solid steel, deeply etched with protective signs and sigils. The Matriarch nodded to Magnus, who drew back a golden fist. The door opened on its own, and the Matriarch strode on through as if she'd expected nothing less.

Inside Editorial, it was utter bedlam. The long room was packed with people working furiously at their desks, bent over computers and shouting at one another pretty much non-stop. Urgent requests for information filled the air, along with gossip, insults, and some really foul language aimed at the kind of day it had been. Young men and women bolted back and forth between the desks, delivering important memos and updates, dropping off research material, and depositing jumbo-sized mugs of steaming black coffee. Magazines and papers were piled up everywhere, and whole rows of phones never seemed to stop ringing. The sheer volume was deafening and intimidating, but the editorial staff seemed used to it.

Display screens on one wall showed the current locations of new Timeslips, where the most powerful and celebrated personages were hanging out, and quickly changing images of breaking news. One screen showed a building toppled across a road, blocking the traffic. The Matriarch nodded approvingly.

The staff paused just long enough to take a good look at the three Droods in their armour, then went straight back to work again. Their attitude clearly said: *Don't bother us, we're on a deadline.* The Matriarch armoured down and gestured for Ioreth and Magnus to do the same.

"I think they need to see our faces, to be properly impressed," she said.

Ioreth dismissed his armour, feeling quietly grateful that he'd found time to change out of his monk's habit and into something more casual before he left the Hall. He glanced at Magnus and was startled to discover a short and sturdy woman standing next to him. Dark-complexioned and about his age, Magnus was possessed of a broad, pleasant face and a scowl that looked like it could cut through steel.

"You got a problem?" said Magnus, in a voice that sounded like she gargled barbed wire for fun.

"Who, me?" said Ioreth. "No. Almost certainly not. I'm fine. Really. How are you? Okay . . . Why, Magnus?"

"Because being called *Kitty* was holding me back."

Ioreth was saved from further embarrassment by the arrival of a miniature tornado. A whirling cloud of disturbed air came bouncing down the central aisle to bob up and down importantly before them. Ioreth thought he could see something very like eyes deep inside the cloud. A cheerful voice issued from the tornado.

"Hi! I'm Otto! Indentured poltergeist and cub reporter! Always on call; no hands, no waiting. Follow me, and I'll take you to the Editor. And don't get too close to the staff; they bite."

He bounced off down the central aisle, accompanied by raised voices on all sides as his winds blew papers off desks. Otto caught them all, juggled the papers inside himself, and dropped them back where they belonged. Mostly. All without slowing down and while singing snatches of Stephen Sondheim songs in a defiantly minor key.

Ioreth moved in close beside the Matriarch and kept up a running commentary on the various people they passed. Julien Advent had written a book about the *Night Times*, and Ioreth had read every page. Because he'd had a feeling it would come in handy one day and very definitely not just because he was a huge fan of the Victorian Adventurer.

"The semi-transparent manifestation to our left, talking on the memory of an old-fashioned telephone, is in communication with the spirit world. The two ravens perched on the computer monitor screen are called Truth and Memory, moonlighting as fact-checkers. The goblin drag queen in the orange evening dress that really doesn't suit him, never mind the fluffy blonde wig that doesn't even come close to hiding his horns, writes the horoscopes."

The goblin waved cheerfully to them. "Hello, sweeties! I knew you were coming! Is it true what they're saying, about Droods blowing up the Moon? Do you have any idea how that will affect the stars?"

"Just keep walking," said Ioreth.

The Matriarch didn't even glance around. Neither did Magnus. The goblin shrugged easily, then had to adjust one of his shoulder-straps. He was used to being ignored. You got no respect, writing the horoscopes. The Matriarch tapped Ioreth on the arm and nodded to an old Remington Standard typewriter clacking busily away on its own, filling sheet after sheet of paper with never-ending copy.

"Ghost writer," said Ioreth.

They finally came to a sound-proofed room at the far end. Otto opened the door for them and bounced away, singing "Send in the Clowns" at the top of his voice. The Matriarch strode right in, followed by Magnus, and finally Ioreth. The editorial staff waited until the door had closed behind them, then launched into a vigorous betting pool as to the exact time trouble would start.

Julien Advent came out from behind a desk covered with papers to greet his visitors. He didn't seem to mind being interrupted. He nodded pleasantly to all of them and made a point of shaking everyone's hand. The Matriarch gave him her best formal smile.

"An honour to meet you, Mr Advent."

"And you, Matriarch. Please, call me Julien."

"Of course. And you must call me Margaret."

Ioreth and Magnus glanced at each other but thought it best not to say anything.

Julien Advent was a tall and lithely muscular figure, apparently in his early thirties. Impressively graceful, in an entirely masculine way, he had dark hair and eyes and a face handsome as any movie star. His smile seemed genuine enough, but his gaze was serious and reserved. He was wearing the stark black and white formal wear of his Victorian days, which immediately reminded Ioreth of the Sarjeant. The only touch of colour was the purple cravat at Julien's throat, held in place by a silver pin, personally presented to him by Queen Victoria herself. Ioreth had read a great deal about Julien Advent but still wasn't prepared for the sheer impact of the man. Just being in the same room made Ioreth feel as though he'd just walked into King Arthur's Court. The Matriarch introduced Magnus and Ioreth. Ioreth smiled and said how pleased he was to meet Julien and did his best not to gush. Magnus just nodded. Julien went back behind his desk and gestured for the Droods to sit on the visitors' chairs set out before him. He waited for them to sit down before he did. The Matriarch faced Julien, with Ioreth on one side of her and Magnus on the other. Julien started to say something, then gestured to one side.

"I almost forgot! This is Bettie Divine, who's just visiting."

The Droods looked around sharply. Ioreth was frankly baffled as to how they'd missed her. Bettie was sitting in the far corner, tall and athletic and drop-dead gorgeous. Her navy blue cat-suit showed off a remarkable body with magnificent bosoms, and her legs were elegantly crossed to show off her knee-length leather boots. She had frizzy purple hair, a heart-shaped face with high cheek-bones, sparkling eyes, and a sultry mouth. She also had two cute little horns curling up from her forehead. Bettie laughed happily at the look on their faces.

"Bettie is a reporter for the Nightside's very own scabrous tabloid, the *Unnatural Inquirer*," said Julien.

"That's me, darlings!" she said happily. "Bettie Divine, demon girl re-porter. Daddy was a Rolling Stone on one of their Nightside tours, while Mummy was a lust demon on the prowl. No wonder I turned out a journal-ist. Don't mind me, you just chat away! I could leave, but I'm not going to. This is all just too fascinating for words. I smell a story!"

"I could make her leave," Magnus said to the Matriarch.

"Bet you couldn't, sweetie," Bettie said airily.

"She doesn't matter," said the Matriarch.

Bettie pouted. "Well really, darlings . . ."

The Matriarch gave Julien Advent her full attention. "We need to talk."

"Indeed we do, Margaret," said Julien. "So tell me. Why have the Droods come to the Nightside? As an occupying army in defiance of all the Pacts and Agreements."

"You know why," said the Matriarch. "The long night is spreading, overflowing its long-established boundaries. That cannot be allowed to continue. And you must have heard what happened at Strangefellows. One of us was murdered there, shot in the back in cold blood."

"That's not the way I heard it," said Bettie.

The Matriarch ignored her, concentrating on Julien. "The whole Drood family has come to the Nightside to take control of the long night once and for all."

"You can't believe it will be that easy," said Julien.

"Nothing worth doing is ever easy," said the Matriarch. "But it is neces-sary, to make the world safe. We will also be taking over the *Night Times*, as of now. We can use you to get the word out, on the new order of things. What will be expected of everyone and what will no longer be tolerated. You can remain in place as editor, with one of my people at your shoulder. Just to re-mind you of the Drood party line, as and where necessary."

Julien leaned forward across his desk, and his eyes were suddenly very cold. His presence turned in a moment from charming to dangerous. Magnus sat up straight. Ioreth wanted to say something, to stop it all going horribly wrong, but he'd known it was too late for that the moment they'd entered the building. The Matriarch stared steadily at Julien, and he chose his words carefully.

"The *Night Times* has a reputation for telling the truth."

"And you still will," said the Matriarch. "The Droods' truth."

"Censorship?" said Julien. "Propaganda? Not on my watch."

"You have no choice," said the Matriarch, entirely unmoved by the cold anger in his voice. "The Nightside belongs to the Droods now."

"We always have a choice, here," said Julien, settling back in his chair. "That's the point."

The Matriarch considered him carefully. "I would have thought that you of all people, with your background, would appreciate what the Droods stand for."

"I still believe in most of the old-fashioned values," said Julien. "I'm just not convinced you do. The Droods have a long track record for doing whatever they believe is in the best interest of the Droods. Drood law and Drood order, and God help anyone who dares step out of line. Eddie was the only one who ever tried to change that, and he isn't in charge any longer."

"You will do as you're told, Julien," said the Matriarch. "Or I'll have no choice but to replace you with someone who will. You know there's always someone . . ."

"Not on this paper," said Julien. He turned to Bettie Divine. "Buy me some time while I make my escape."

"Love to, darling," said Bettie.

She jumped to her feet. Magnus stood up quickly to face her, and Bettie Maced her. Magnus fell back, wheezing and choking and blinded by tears. Julien Advent was out from behind his desk and racing for the door while Ioreth and the Matriarch were still getting to their feet. Bettie proudly brandished her dinky little spray can.

"Infernal Mace, darlings. With added unholy water!"

"Ioreth, take care of her!" said the Matriarch. "Magnus, come with me!"

The Matriarch ran out the door after Julien. Magnus hurried after her, squinting savagely through puffed-up eyes. Ioreth and Bettie looked at each other.

The Matriarch burst out of the editorial cubicle to see Julien Advent sprinting down the long office, heading for the door. She armoured up and went after him. She didn't manage six paces before Otto the friendly poltergeist materialised out of nowhere and engulfed her in his whirling winds. Buffeted this way and that, the Matriarch quickly lost all sense of direction. She closed her eyes, braced herself, and triggered the exorcism function built into her armour. There was a flash of light and a burst of speeded-up Latin, and Otto cried out shrilly as the forces holding him together were violently dispersed.

The goblin drag queen rose up from behind his desk, produced two heavy machine-pistols, and opened fire on the Matriarch. She stood her ground, her armour soaking up the bullets. Also back in her armour, Magnus picked up a desk and threw it at the goblin. The impact smashed him against a wall. The Matriarch went racing after Julien, only to be tripped by the invisible foot of the ghost writer. Magnus went to blast the ghost with her exorcism function, then realised she had no idea where to aim it. The Matriarch scrambled to her feet, but by the time she looked at the far door, Julien was gone.

"Ioreth!" yelled the Matriarch. "Get out here! Now!"

Ioreth quickly appeared in the cubicle doorway. He glanced back at Bettie Divine, hidden from view, and she blew him a kiss and mimed *Call me!* Ioreth nodded quickly and hurried out to join Magnus and the Matriarch, armouring up as he went.

"No point in chasing after Julien," the Matriarch said savagely. "He could be anywhere in the building by now. I've already contacted my people and told them to guard the front door."

"Bound to be a backdoor," said Magnus.

"Gather up some people and guard that as well," said the Matriarch, and Magnus hurried off. The Matriarch looked around at the *Night Times*' staff, and they stared defiantly back. The Matriarch smiled coldly. "Get back to work. You have a Special Edition to put out. I'll send you an editor to tell you what to put in it."

*   *   *

Down in the lobby, Julien Advent strode quickly over to the receptionist in her cubicle. Despite all his running, he wasn't even out of breath. He was actually smiling, just a little. He always preferred it when the sparring was over, and everyone's cards were on the table.

"Shut down the printing presses, Janet. And tell the printers to sabotage the control systems, so the Droods can't start the machinery up again. Let the Droods write their propaganda; won't do them any good if they can't print it."

"Indeed, Mr Julien," the receptionist said calmly, not even pausing in her knitting of something colourful but shapeless. "And what will you be doing?"

"Organising the resistance," said Julien. "I only held off in the hope reason might somehow still prevail . . . You'd think I'd know better by now. Call my chauffeur, Janet, and have her bring the car around to the rear entrance."

"Already done, Mr Julien," said Janet. "The young lady is waiting for you."

Julien paused and looked at her. "Will you be all right on your own, Janet? The Droods might treat you roughly, for helping me."

Janet smiled, showing her pointed teeth. "Let them try, Mr Julien. Just let them try."

When Julien Advent emerged from the building's back entrance, a 1930s Rolls Royce was already waiting for him. The chauffeur smiled at him from behind the wheel, cool and elegant in her white leather uniform, complete with peaked cap. Julien got into the back, and the chauffeur started the engine. A handful of armoured Droods came charging around the corner, but the Rolls was already pulling out onto the main road and was swiftly lost in traffic.

Eddie and Molly were still on their way to Strangefellows when the Matriarch's angry voice assaulted Eddie's ears through his torc. He stopped to listen, while Molly looked at him impatiently.

"Julien Advent has escaped!" said the Matriarch, in a tone of voice that made it very clear Eddie should not ask questions about that. "Do you have any idea where he might be going?"

"The Authorities?" said Eddie.

"Apart from the obvious!"

"I'll ask Molly," said Eddie, diplomatically. "But Julien knows the Night-side better than any of us. If he decides to go to ground, you can bet he's going to be really hard to find. Why not have the Sarjeant talk to his local agents?"

"I want Advent found!" said the Matriarch. "No excuses!"

"Don't shout at me, Maggie," Eddie said coldly. "I'm not one of your gung ho bully-boys."

There was a pause.

"I'm sorry, Eddie," said the Matriarch. Eddie could hear the strain that went into that. "Talk to Molly, see what she thinks."

"I'll get back to you when I know something," said Eddie.

He broke the connection and brought Molly up to speed on what had just happened. Although neither of them actually said anything, they were both quietly pleased Julien Advent hadn't bowed down to outside author-ity. It was good to know there were some things you could still depend on.

"We need to find Julien," said Eddie. "Before the Sarjeant does."

"You think he'd kill Julien Advent, just for running?" said Molly.

"Don't you?" said Eddie.

And that was when Shotgun Suzie emerged from a side street, cover-ing them both with her double-barrelled shotgun. She looked very preg-nant with her black leather jacket hanging open. Eddie called for his armour, and it shot over him in a moment.

"That won't save you," said Suzie. "You're not the only one with strange-matter bullets. Your family tried to kill my husband. That's a good enough reason to kill you on its own, but killing the famous Eddie Drood should inspire others to rise against your family."

"Is that the same gun you used to shoot Luther in the back?" said Eddie.

"Does it matter?" said Suzie.

Eddie's thoughts raced. Even his armour couldn't move him fast enough to dodge a shotgun loaded with strange-matter bullets. And he didn't have time to draw his Colt Repeater. But . . . why hadn't Suzie al-ready shot him? She was a bounty-hunter, a professional killer, and mercy was not in her. Maybe there were still things she needed to say to him . . . which meant there was still a chance he could talk his way out of this.

"You don't want to kill me," he said, as calmly as he could. "Or you'd have done it by now."

"No," said Suzie. "I just want you to take your armour off. So I can look you in the eyes when I kill you."

Molly turned a cold eye on Suzie. "Get away from my man, bitch."

Eddie stirred uncomfortably. "I really don't think you should call her that, Molly."

Molly looked at him. "Why not?"

"Well . . ." said Eddie. "She's pregnant."

"Your refined sensibilities crop up at the strangest moments," said Molly. She turned back to Suzie. "Lower your gun."

"I wonder what strange-matter bullets will do to a witch," said Suzie.

Molly smiled unpleasantly. "Guess."

Suzie sighed, and thrust the shotgun into its holster on her back. And then she drew Wulfsbane. Eddie and Molly both fell back as the long sword appeared in Suzie's hand. There was a new presence in the street, weighing heavily on the long night, something they could feel in their bones and in their souls. As though a raging animal had burst out of its cage. The bitter yellow glow emanating from the long blade grated on their nerves, as though it were poisoning the world just by existing in it.

"Where the hell did you get that, Suzie?" said Molly. "Put it down. Hell, throw it away. Before it eats you up."

"This is Wulfsbane," said Suzie. She might have been introducing a new friend. "It's not from around here. And it's more than a match for Drood armour."

"Don't let that thing touch you, Eddie," Molly said quickly. "It's cursed. Give it up, Suzie, while you still can."

"Give up a weapon that can scare you and kill a Drood?" said Suzie. "I don't think so."

Molly thrust out a hand, and a bolt of lightning flashed towards Suzie. She hardly seemed to move, but suddenly the long blade was in just the right position to intercept the lightning. The glowing blade soaked up the flaring energies in a moment, and when the night gloom returned, it seemed even darker than before. Eddie drew his Colt Repeater and fired off several shots, using cursed and blessed ammunition, but they all ricocheted harmlessly away from the long, glowing blade. Eddie put away his gun. When in doubt, go with the armour. He grew the long, golden sword out of his hand again and went forward to meet Suzie. She advanced on him, grinning coldly.

The two swords slammed together, and the bitter yellow blade sheared clean through the golden strange matter. Half of Eddie's sword fell to clatter on the ground, and he had to throw himself backwards to avoid a sweeping blow that would have taken his head clean off. The tip of Suzie's sword scored a long thin line across his armoured chest, and smoke rose up from the etched groove, as though the armour had been burned. The fallen part of Eddie's sword leapt up to rejoin his armour, but Eddie was still retreating. Suzie came after him, sweeping the long blade back and forth before her. And Eddie didn't have a clue what to do.

He heard Molly chanting something, in a language he didn't even recognise, and then a vicious storm wind came blasting down the street. It hit Suzie head-on, blowing her off her feet and sending her tumbling all the way down the empty street. But she never let go of Wulfsbane. Eddie looked at Molly.

"What the hell is that sword?"

Molly shook her head grimly. "An Infernal Device. The magic-sword equivalent of a back-pack nuke."

"We're in trouble, aren't we?" said Eddie.

"Oh yes," said Molly.

"What should we do?"

"Run!"

They turned and sprinted out of the side street and back onto the main thoroughfare and kept on running.

In Uptown, not that far from Clubland, lay Wu Fang's Garden of Delights. The gambling-den to beat all gambling-dens, where you could find games of chance to suit even the most jaded of palates. All strictly regulated and entirely honest, of course. And if you believed that, you deserved everything that happened to you at the Garden of Delights.

Dash Oblivion, father to the legendary Oblivion Brothers, Larry and Tommy and Hadleigh, stood outside the highly elegant establishment and looked it over dubiously. Back in the 1930s, Dash had been a private investigator, the Continental Op, and built a hell of a reputation for himself in those hard and unforgiving times. Standing at his side, as always, was his wife, Shirley den Adel, once known as the Lady Phantasm, a costumed adventurer from the same period. They had their own pulp magazines recounting their adventures, and even a few movie serials, but they dropped out of history in 1946, when they pursued that arch-fiend the Demon Claw into a Timeslip. When they came out the other side, it was in the Nightside in 1977.

A whip-thin figure in a smart blue blazer and white slacks, Dash was bald-headed and more than a little hunched over, his heavily lined face dominated by a hook-nose and bushy white eyebrows. Dash was in his late eighties now, but his mouth was firm and his gaze was still sharp. He looked like he could still be dangerous, in the right cause. Shirley was a well-preserved lady in her seventies, with a pleasant face and a great mane of snow-white hair. She looked like she would be only too ready to listen to any problem you might have, as long as you weren't too shocked by her answers. Shirley still carried a gun in a hidden holster on her thigh and a set of brass knuckles in her clutch bag.

"Do we have to go in there?" growled Dash.

"We can't stop the Droods on our own, dear," said Shirley. Her voice still had a faint European accent. "We need support and assistance, and Brilliant Chang says Wu Fang is the only one he can think of who might be able to take on Droods in their armour."

Dash scowled. "Wu Fang . . . He should be dead by now. We should never have let him drink the Dragon's Blood, back in Forty-One."

"Oh hush, dear," said Shirley. "He was dying, and we needed his help. Just like we do now. Let us hope he still thinks he owes us."

Dash snorted loudly. "You really think he'll give a damn?"

"The Droods are coming for him too," said Shirley. "The enemy of our enemy is our ally, if not necessarily our friend."

They headed for the front door. Dash let one hand fall naturally to his blazer pocket, where he still carried his favourite snub-nosed revolver. Shirley let her clutch bag fall open. But the Chinese doorman, in an impeccably tailored tuxedo, just bowed politely to them and opened the door with a flourish.

"Your presence is anticipated, honourable sir and madam. Please to enter."

"Cut the crap," said Dash. "I know a cockney accent when I hear one."

The doorman glanced around quickly to make sure no one was in ear-shot, and shrugged. "All part of the job. The marks expect it. And for the kind of money this place is paying, I'll sound like Charlie Freaking Chan if that's what they want."

Dash and Shirley strode into the Garden of Delights, doing their best to look like they had the kind of money that entitled them to be there. There was no lobby or hallway, just a marvellous indoor jungle of Far Eastern trees and vegetation. The hanging branches were heavy with greenery, and flowers of almost technicolour hues perfumed the air. Tiny birds fluttered overhead, singing their little hearts out. Dash and Shirley followed the narrow path between the trees, past a tumbling miniature waterfall, and did their best not to look impressed by anything. They finally emerged into a clearing packed with gaming-tables. Poker and roulette, craps and vingt-et-un, and other less sophisticated opportunities to throw your money away.

Various items of interest had been set out on display among the trees surrounding the clearing: statues and works of art, suits of medieval armour, and a number of Wu Fang's security people standing still as statues in their trade-mark white tuxedos, watching everything. Because sore losers and bad sports were not tolerated in Wu Fang's Garden of Delights. There were also a number of intriguing trophies, to catch the eye of the discerning gambler. The severed hand of Wild Bill Hickock, complete with the cards he was holding when he was shot in the back. Aces and eights, forever after to be known as the dead man's hand. Howard Hughes' death masque, smiling a disconcerting smile, as though he knew something the viewer didn't. The ball from the roulette wheel that broke the Bank at Monte Carlo; a pair of chaos dice; and a butterfly kept safely imprisoned under glass to keep it from starting storms. Wu Fang liked to celebrate the forces of chance, in all its many forms.

Crowds of gamblers swarmed around the various tables, anxious to lose everything they had as quickly as possible. Artificially loud laughter and forced expressions of bonhomie did their best to fool everyone into thinking they were having a good time, while the air was heavy with the scents of sweat and desperation and losing streaks. Dash and Shirley watched from the edge of the clearing until Brilliant Chang emerged from the crush to greet them. His night-dark tuxedo had been carefully tailored to accommodate all the many weapons he carried concealed about his person.

Dash raised a bushy eyebrow. "You used to be one of Wu Fang's enforcers. Is it safe for you to be here, after you killed so many of his people?"

"That was personal," said Brilliant. "This is business. Wu Fang hasn't lasted this long without being able to separate the two. I have already spoken to him, and he has agreed to meet with you."

Dash nodded slowly. "I wasn't sure he would. It has been a long time."

"And miss a chance to fight alongside my oldest enemies?" said a calm and cultured voice. "How could I refuse?"

They all turned to face a slim and straight-backed Chinese gentleman in a smart Armani suit. Wu Fang could have been any age, with a handsome aristocratic face and jet-black hair, but something in his stance suggested a certain frailty.

"Dash and Shirley. How pleasant to see you both, after all these years."

"The Demon Claw," said Dash. "Criminal master-mind, arch-fiend, and the most diabolical mind of your generation. Reduced to running a gambling den and fleecing the suckers, under a name given you by the old movie serials."

"Time, see what's become of me," said Wu Fang, smiling gently. "You occidentals do so love your descriptive names, and far be it for me to disappoint you. As long as people see the stereotype, they do not see the real me. Is that not why you used the names Continental Op and Lady Phantasm?"

"It was the times," said Shirley. "People expected it of us."

"My point exactly," said Wu Fang. "And now, here you are. It is possible you are the only ones left who still remember the Demon Claw. Though I'm told some of my old pulp adventures now sell for ridiculous amounts to collectors. It doesn't matter. I have reinvented myself. And I make far more money from my Garden of Delights than I ever did as a criminal master-mind and arch-fiend. It's hard for me to remember why I ever adopted the role . . . But still, there was a war on. We all had to play our part."

"We're at war now," said Brilliant Chang. "And we have a common enemy in the Droods. They will close you down and burn your Garden, as a perfect example of the kind of thing they won't tolerate. And you can be sure they haven't forgotten who you used to be. The Droods have files on everyone. But perhaps the three of you can come up with some way to hold their attention and slow them down, while the Authorities work on a plan to stop them."

"What plan?" said Dash.

"I don't know," said Brilliant. "We're still working on it."

Wu Fang considered him thoughtfully. "I have not forgotten the bad blood that lies between us; but as you say, even the most opposed of hearts can find common cause in the face of a mutual enemy. You may leave us now, Brilliant Chang. We shall not be meeting again."

Brilliant bowed formally, turned, and walked away. Wu Fang watched him go and shook his head, as though deciding against something after all. He turned his gaze on Dash and Shirley, who moved a little closer together.

"Come," said Wu Fang, smiling pleasantly. "Let us retire to my private office, have tea together, and plot the destruction of our enemies."

He led Dash and Shirley off the path and through the trees, to a perfectly ordinary-looking door in the middle of the jungle. Wu Fang opened it and waved Dash and Shirley through, into what turned out to be a pleasantly luxurious business office. Wu Fang closed the door behind them and went to sit behind an elegant mahogany desk. Dash and Shirley sat down facing him. A simple silver tea-service was already in place on the desk.

"Earl Grey, I'm afraid," said Wu Fang, as he poured tea into delicate china cups. "I fear I have settled into very British ways since I came here."

"You don't look old," said Dash. "Not your proper age, anyway."

"You look just as I remember, from the last time I saw you," said Shirley. "As though not a day has passed."

"We should never have given you the Dragon's Blood," said Dash.

"I never understood why you did," said Wu Fang. "I would not have done the same for you had our situations been reversed. Still, you both look in remarkably good shape, for your years. Could it be that you took just a sip of the Dragon's Blood for yourselves?"

Dash and Shirley said nothing. They all sipped their tea in silence for a while.

"Well," said Wu Fang. "What are we going to do, about the Droods?"

"You tell us," said Dash. "What can we do? Two antiques like us, and a retired arch-fiend, against an army of Droods?"

"I would suggest we start with these," said Wu Fang.

He held out his hand, and on his palm lay a pair of dice, midnight black with rubies for points. The tiny crimson gems gleamed like unblinking eyes.

"Chaos dice," said Dash.

"Nasty things," said Shirley.

"Tiny calculating machines," said Wu Fang. "Created to undo chance and subvert possibilities. Such as: whether a Drood has his armour on or not. Whether it is completely invulnerable. And other, subtler things . . ."

"When the odds are against us, change the odds in our favour," said Dash. "Good thinking."

"Do the people who come here to gamble know you have these dice and what they can do?" said Shirley.

Wu Fang smiled. "Did you not see the pair I have placed on open display, for all to see? It is not my fault if my guests do not pause to look at them and consider the implications."

"Even chaos dice won't be enough to stop Droods," said Dash. "Not a whole army of them. What have you got in the way of weapons?"

"I have these," said Wu Fang. He opened a drawer in his desk, brought out a pair of handguns, and placed them on the desk-top. He pushed them towards Dash and Shirley.

"Derived from the Droods' Colt Repeaters," said Wu Fang. "My people acquired one from a Drood field agent, whose taste for gambling was not matched by his skill, and my technical staff were able to duplicate some of the gun's remarkable abilities. They aim themselves, they never miss, and they never run out of ammunition. Sadly, the bullets are only ever standard issue. The original gun was reluctant to yield all of its secrets, and we only had so much time before it had to be returned to the field agent. Neither the Drood nor I wanted his family to know it had ever gone missing. So the bullets will not penetrate Drood armour, under normal conditions. You must rely on the chaos dice to give you your chances."

"What weapon will you be using?" said Shirley.

"Something of my own," said Wu Fang.

"Something fiendish," said Dash. "I doubt you've changed that much. Why are you so ready to fight alongside Shirley and me? We were enemies for so many years . . . Chasing each other across roof-tops, and in and out of water-front cellars. We came so close to killing each other so many times . . ."

"I have not forgotten," said Wu Fang. "Why did we spend so much of our lives intent on each other's destruction? Perhaps we realised that only we were worthy of our time and talents. I sometimes wonder if you did win, in the end. With all my marvellous schemes and incredible genius, I should have been a legend in my own right; but you took up so much of my attention, I never could get anything done. And now, when I am remembered at all, it is as just another of the Continental Op's many foes. But . . . I am still going strong, while you have grown old and frail; so perhaps that is my revenge. And yet, I will admit . . . I am bored, being a businessman. The name of Wu Fang is respected throughout the Nightside but not feared. Not feared as the Demon Claw was. I yearn to be what I really am, one more time. Fighting the small-minded and sanctimonious Droods, and sowing terror in their arrogant hearts. It seems to me that a man who could teach the Droods fear . . . would be a legend after all."

"You always did like to talk," said Dash. "But what are you prepared to do?"

"I will show the Droods my chaos dice, then turn you loose with your guns," said Wu Fang. "I think I would enjoy seeing the two of you in action again: the Continental Op and the Lady Phantasm."

Dash picked up one Colt Repeater, and Shirley picked up the other. They checked the guns out, quickly and professionally, looked at each other, and nodded.

"You have a deal," said Dash.

"But I am not wearing the costume," said Shirley.

"Then let us go," said Wu Fang, rising elegantly to his feet. Dash and Shirley stood up, a little more slowly and carefully.

"If this plan of yours doesn't work . . ." said Dash.

"Is there a back way out of this place?" said Shirley.

"Practical as ever," said Wu Fang. "When we enter the clearing, you will see a path leading off, opposite the one that brought you in. You are, of course, free to leave whenever you decide best; but I shall not be going. This is my place, my Garden of Delights, and I will not be driven from it. I have grown old, in years if not in body, and I feel . . . worn out, and worn thin. I shall make my stand here. And show the Droods what fear really is."

"You're right," Shirley said to Dash. "He did always like to talk."

They all laughed, just a little; and then they went out, into the jungle.

The Sarjeant-at-Arms brought his column of Droods to a halt before the Garden of Delights. Along the way he had received word from one of his local agents that Dash Oblivion and his wife could be found there, and the Sarjeant saw possibilities in that.

"I want them," he said bluntly to his people. "As prisoners, they would give us leverage over their sons. And having Larry, Tommy, and Hadleigh Oblivion under our thumb could make a big difference to how quickly the Nightside falls."

His second in command, Anastasia, looked at the Garden of Delights. "Why did you send Conrad, Howard, and Callan away? They're experienced field agents, and we're talking about going up against legends."

"Callan and Howard can be trusted to track down the Authorities on their own," said the Sarjeant. "And I wanted Conrad to catch up with the Matriarch and explain what we're doing. Besides, while they are proven fighters, I'm not convinced they have the stomach for the kind of things we might have to do here."

Anastasia nodded quickly. "We can't trust anyone any more. The only way to win in the Nightside is to shoot first and ask questions of the survivors."

"You're learning," said the Sarjeant.

"Do we armour down again before we go in?" said Anastasia.

"Not this time," said the Sarjeant. "I'm not interested in negotiating."

He headed for the front door, followed by Anastasia, and the tuxedoed doorman moved to block their way.

"So sorry, honoured visitors. You can't come in. You are not on the list."

"Move," said the Sarjeant.

"Or we'll move you," said Anastasia.

"Screw you guys," said the doorman.

He grabbed hold of a bone amulet hanging around his neck, and just like that a Chinese demon was towering over the Droods. Huge and powerful, it was all fangs and claws and long, lashing tongue. The Droods didn't need the Sarjeant's order to open fire; they just blasted the demon with every gun they had. The impact of such massed fire-power threw it back-wards, and it crashed through the door. By the time the Sarjeant walked through the open doorway, the demon was just a doorman again, very human and very dead. The Sarjeant stepped over the body and moved on into the Garden of Delights, and the armoured Droods followed him in.

An alarm was sounding when Dash, Shirley, and Wu Fang emerged out of the office into the jungle. A harsh, strident sound, that sent the tiny birds fluttering back and forth in a panic. Wu Fang smiled.

"The Droods have entered my Garden. The fools."

"Will your people fight to protect you against Droods?" said Dash.

"I would not ask such a thing of them. They will follow their orders and escort my guests out the back door." Wu Fang looked into the shadows between the trees and laughed softly. "After Brilliant Chang killed off my old enforcers, I made a decision not to place my trust in fallible human defenders any more. This jungle is my protection, and like me, it is far more than it appears."

"I don't care if you've stocked it with lions and tigers and velociraptors," said Dash. "It still won't stop Droods in their armour."

"Perhaps not," said Wu Fang. "But it should soften them up for these."

He opened his hand to show them the chaos dice.

The Sarjeant-at-Arms strode purposefully along the jungle path, with Anastasia right beside him. And if he was aware that his column was becoming worryingly strung out and separated behind him, he didn't say anything. Armoured Droods were a match for anything a jungle could throw at them.

He should have kept Conrad with him. The old African hand could have told him different.

The Droods looked suspiciously around them as they made their way deeper into the Garden. Dash and Shirley wouldn't have recognised this part of the jungle now. It had become a dark and sinister place, with danger on every side. The Droods could feel it even if they couldn't see or hear anything specific. The Sarjeant became aware of a growing tension in his ranks and kept them moving. Soldiers work best when you don't give them too much time to think. They all had guns and swords and axes, and the sooner they got a chance to use them, the sooner their confidence would return.

Things stirred in the shadows between the trees. Holding back, staying carefully out of sight and out of range, they moved along with the Droods as they pressed deeper into the jungle. A few Droods fired off shots into the shadows but didn't seem to hit anything. The Sarjeant snarled at them to keep moving and save their shots until they had proper targets.

They finally emerged out of the trees into a brightly lit clearing, full of gaming-tables but no gamblers. Just cards and chips scattered across the tables, and a few crumpled bank-notes. The Droods didn't touch them. Anastasia sniffed loudly.

"The rats have deserted the sinking ship. They must have heard we were coming."

"Wu Fang wouldn't run," said the Sarjeant. "That would be beneath his dignity."

"What about Dash and Shirley Oblivion?" said Anastasia.

"Let us hope they were stupid enough to stay too." The Sarjeant looked around him, and when he spoke again, he kept his voice low. "We're not alone. Something is here with us."

"I say we burn the whole damned jungle down," said Anastasia. "Send a message."

"I like the way you think," said the Sarjeant. "But I need Dash and Shirley alive."

Something was definitely moving on the edge of the clearing now . . . shadows that were more than just shadows. The Sarjeant barked out orders, and the Droods moved quickly to form a circle, facing out and covering the trees with their weapons. Nothing emerged into the light, but the movements were becoming stronger and more openly threatening. The Sarjeant used all the sensors in his face mask, including infra-red heat vision, and still couldn't make out anything. He raised his voice, and his people moved forward, step by step, to get a better view of what was menacing them. Anastasia stuck close to the Sarjeant, holding her golden battle-axe at the ready.

The moment the Droods reached the edge of the clearing, the trees' branches lashed out like bark-covered tentacles. They snapped around the nearest Droods, pinning their arms to their sides and crushing them with inhuman force. More branches picked up Droods and threw them the length of the clearing. Others came hammering down like living bludgeons, slamming Droods to the ground with devastating force. But the Droods' armour didn't crack under the pressure, and falls and blows couldn't hurt them. They were quickly back on their feet again, blasting the trees with every kind of gun they had and hacking and cutting at the twisting branches with golden blades. Strange matter sheared easily through living tissue, and the severed ends fell to writhe and coil angrily on the ground, spouting a thick black sap.

Strange-matter bullets pulverised and shredded the trees, blowing them apart in showers of splinters. The Droods being held broke free and ripped the branches right off the trees. The Sarjeant raked the jungle with a machine-pistol, and even the heaviest tree-trunks exploded into wooden shrapnel. Anastasia advanced steadily into the jungle, hacking and cutting at everything that moved, grunting loudly with the effort of her blows. It felt good, so good, to have something physical to strike out at, and hurt. It would have been even better if the trees had screamed as they died, but then, you can't have everything.

Finally the Sarjeant called out for everyone to stop firing and for Anastasia to come back and join the group. The roar of gun-fire died quickly away, and the Droods lowered their swords and axes, looking around in quiet satisfaction at all the destruction they'd caused. Black sap dripped steadily from their golden blades. Anastasia stalked proudly out of the jungle to rejoin the Sarjeant. And that was when Wu Fang stepped gracefully out of the trees and into the clearing, with Dash and Shirley on either side of him. The Droods froze where they were. After a moment, the Sarjeant stepped forward to face Wu Fang.

"Stand down," he said. "You've seen what we can do. There's no disgrace in being out-gunned. Surrender, and I give you my word you won't be harmed. But give us even the slightest trouble, and I'll have you killed."

"You do not give orders in my Garden," said Wu Fang. "This is my place, and you should not have come here."

He threw the chaos dice lightly onto the ground, and they rolled to a halt at the Sarjeant-at-Arms' feet. Showing snake eyes. And all the possibilities in the clearing ran riot. Droods' armour shot back into their torcs, leaving them revealed and vulnerable. Some armour ran away like liquid gold, pooling around the Droods' feet. Some armour became rigid as steel and imprisoned its wearers. Dash and Shirley raised their Colt Repeaters and targeted the Droods without armour. Steel bullets punched through the hearts and heads of unprotected Droods. Dash and Shirley fired again and again, their old hands steady with long-practised skills, and Droods crashed dead and dying to the blood-soaked ground. Some panicked and ran into the jungle, but it didn't save them. The trees were waiting for them.

The Sarjeant yelled at those Droods who still had their armour to hold their ground, and they did. One by one those with affected armour found it was adjusting to the random energies of the chaos dice, becoming firm and trustworthy again. Dash and Shirley saw what was happening and stopped firing. Wu Fang laughed happily in the sudden quiet.

"This is what I wanted to see. My old enemies in action again, killing my new enemies. Old heroes shooting down new heroes. But now, dear Dash and Shirley, it is time for you to leave. There is nothing more you can do here, and soon enough, the Droods will be dangerous again."

"Come with us," Dash said roughly. "You've had a long run, but it doesn't have to end here. You can't face this many Droods on your own."

"You could come with us," said Shirley. "There are still battles to be fought."

"For you, perhaps," said Wu Fang. "But I am tired . . . so very tired. Far too tired to run. Your guns will no longer kill Droods; so find something else that will. I shall remain here, in my Garden, and show the Droods my last surprise . . . and my last act of defiance."

Shirley leaned in and kissed him on the cheek. "Die well, Demon Claw."

"And take as many of the bastards with you as you can," said Dash.

"My plan entirely," said Wu Fang.

Dash and Shirley hurried off down the path that led to the backdoor. The trees' branches twitched sluggishly as they passed but made no move against them. Wu Fang moved forward into the clearing, to face his foes. He was pleased to see so many Droods dead, but many more were still alive. Once again in control of their armour, they trained their guns on him. The Sarjeant bent down and picked up the chaos dice. He showed them to Wu Fang, then crushed the dice in his golden hand.

Wu Fang just laughed softly.

"Can I kill him?" said Anastasia. "I'd really like to kill that arrogant son of a bitch."

"Be my guest," said the Sarjeant.

Wu Fang opened his mouth, and breathed fire on the Droods. An endless stream of dragonfire, which melted every bit of armour it touched. The last gift of the Dragon's Blood. Anastasia was blown off her feet by the impact of the flames and crashed into the Sarjeant behind her, bearing him to the ground. Wu Fang slowly turned his head back and forth, so that his flames covered the whole clearing, and not one Drood escaped him. They staggered back and forth, crying out in shock and horror as their armour melted and the terrible flames consumed them. Some tried to run, but the flames were faster.

The dragon flames spread to the edges of the clearing, then leapt out into the jungle, the fires jumping from tree to tree. The Garden of Delights burned, and what had been a civilised gambling-den became a raging inferno. Wu Fang glowed with unbearable heat because no man was ever meant to blaze as brightly as a dragon. He was burning himself up to kill his enemies, and he was content with that. His smart Armani suit burst into flames, and his hair caught fire, burning with a blue flame. His old skin charred and cracked, but still he stood tall and proud. Still smiling. Wu Fang burned, as his Garden burned, as the Droods burned; and all was well.

The Sarjeant-at-Arms forced himself to his feet. Anastasia's body had sheltered him from the worst of the flames, but he could feel them even through his armour. Half of Anastasia's armour was gone, revealing burned and blackened flesh. The Sarjeant looked around him, but all he could see was fire. He couldn't even find the way out. And then Anastasia lurched suddenly to her feet. Her mask was gone, her face just a scorched and blackened mask. Her lipless smile showed teeth fixed in a death's-head grin. She grabbed hold of the Sarjeant with her one golden arm, picked him up, and threw him at the jungle with all her remaining armoured strength. He shot through the air, smashing through trees as if they were nothing, until finally he crashed and rolled to a halt on the far side of the jungle, back at the entrance to the Garden. The door stood open before him. He forced himself onto his feet and looked back, but all he could see was flames. He said Anastasia's name once, then turned and stumbled out of the Garden of Delights and into the cool night air.

Conrad caught up with the Matriarch and her people inside the Mammon Emporium, a huge hypermarket packed with shops and businesses offering all kinds of goods from all kinds of Earths and adjoining dimensions. The Droods had slowed down in spite of themselves, fascinated by the contents of the shop-windows. DVDs of the Beatles' second animated film, *Penny Lane Forever*. Stephen King's paranormal romance, *Summer Nights in 'Salem's Lot*. Old vinyl of the Rolling Stones, with Marianne Faithfull as their lead singer; and Wham! featuring Boy George and Luke from the Bros. The Matriarch tried to keep them moving, but she was tempted and just a little distracted herself.

The shops and the corridors were completely deserted. Doors hung open, lights were still on, but the customers and staff were long gone. They'd heard the Droods were coming. The Matriarch looked around sharply as she heard approaching footsteps, only to relax as she recognised Conrad. He had already lowered his armour, so she armoured down too to greet him.

"Something in the Nightside is interfering with our communications," said Conrad. "The Sarjeant has been trying to reach you but couldn't get through, so he sent me to bring you up to speed on what's been happening."

"I wondered why I hadn't heard from him," said the Matriarch. "Whatever it is, it's probably only going to get worse as we go on. Whether it's deliberate jamming or just something about the nature of the Nightside. I've already sent Ioreth and Magnus off on their own, to scout ahead."

"I have . . . concerns, about the Sarjeant," said Conrad. "Some of the tactics he's been using . . ."

The Matriarch nodded grimly. "I know . . . I told him to stop the traffic to make a point, not kill a whole bunch of people. It's the Nightside. It brings out the worst in us. But in the end . . . the Sarjeant will follow his orders. As long as people don't try to fight him, he won't hurt them."

"The streets I walked through to get here were pretty much empty," said Conrad. "People are hiding from us."

"Just like here," said the Matriarch. She indicated the empty mall with a wave of her hand. "You know this isn't what I wanted. I really thought a place as practical as the Nightside would do the sensible thing in the face of overwhelming forces and surrender. No one needed to get hurt. But if parts of the Nightside are determined to defy Drood authority, they have only themselves to blame for what happens."

And then they both looked around sharply, as they were hailed by a loud and cheerful voice. Bounding down the deserted hallway towards them came a young woman in a simple grey suit and a white vicar's collar. A much taller woman strode along beside her, in a brown leather jacket, riding britches, and boots. The vicar crashed to a halt in front of the bemused Matriarch and smiled winningly at her. Barely five feet tall, she looked at first glance as though a strong breeze would blow her away; but she had a presence to her, of someone ready to walk through walls to get to where she had to go. Her sharp face was softened by kind eyes and a ready smile, and her frizzy blonde hair was held in place by a cheap plastic headband.

Her much larger companion was a healthy-looking young woman with a high-boned face, tufty red hair, and bright green eyes. A typical country-set type, all hunting and riding and fishing, with a big appetite for all that life had to offer. She didn't smile.

The vicar looked around at the watching Droods, waved cheerfully to them, then thrust out a tiny hand for the Matriarch to shake. The movement was so emphatic, the Matriarch found herself shaking hands with the vicar before she could stop herself. The young woman smiled brightly.

"Hello there! I'm Tamsin MacReady, rogue vicar. The Christian Church's very unofficial representative in the Nightside."

"We don't answer to Churches," said the Matriarch, struggling to regain the high ground. "We're the Droods. Churches answer to us."

"Gosh," said Tamsin. "How very Drood of you."

"What are you doing here?" said Conrad.

"We save sinners," said Tamsin. "So we have to go where the sinning is. Allow me to present my companion and body-guard, Sharon Pilkington-Smythe."

The big woman just nodded briefly and made no move to shake hands.

"Why does a vicar need a body-guard?" Conrad asked.

"Silly!" Tamsin said brightly. "We are in the Nightside, you know. It can get a bit rough, at times. You must have noticed."

"And Tamsin will insist on trying to see the best in everyone," said Sharon. "So she has me, to be the practical one. No one messes with my beloved."

The two women smiled fondly at each other.

"Not now, darling," said Tamsin. "Working!" She fixed the Matriarch with an earnest stare. "You have to stop the fighting. It's not doing anyone any good. You must know brute force won't win the day here."

"All people have to do is stop resisting us," said the Matriarch. "And then there won't be any trouble. We have come to place the Nightside under Drood control, for the good of the world."

"People are dying," said Tamsin.

"The quicker we win this war, the fewer people will die," said the Matriarch. "Tell your people to stop fighting."

"They won't listen to me," said Tamsin. "I'm just the rogue vicar. It's all I can do to stop them stealing money from the collection plate."

"Then talk to the Authorities," said the Matriarch. "Wherever they're hiding themselves. Help us negotiate a peaceful surrender."

"They might listen to you, Tamsin," said Sharon. "Where they wouldn't, or couldn't, to a Drood."

Tamsin was thinking about that when the Sarjeant-at-Arms arrived. They all looked around as he came staggering down the corridor, one halting step at a time. Half his armour looked as though it had been hit by a blow-torch. Large sections had melted and congealed again. It was starting to repair itself but only slowly. His unsteady footsteps sounded like warning bells in the sudden hush. He finally came to a halt before the Matriarch, and his naked face was full of a terrible loss. The Matriarch had to force herself to meet the cold light in his eyes.

"My people are dead," he said. "All of them. Murdered. Burned alive."

The Droods muttered together, as much at the way he sounded as the news he brought.

"You see!" said Tamsin. "You don't know what you're getting into here! Let me help . . ."

The Matriarch turned on her viciously. "My people are dead! My family! We were ready to accept a peaceful surrender, and this is what they do to us! I will make the Nightside pay for this. Starting with you." She turned to the Sarjeant. "Arrest these women. I want them paraded through the streets as our captives, to show what happens to anyone who gets in our way."

"You can't do that!" said Sharon.

The Matriarch gestured for the Sarjeant to take the two women away. He grabbed Tamsin by the arm. She pulled free and reached out to the Matriarch. The Sarjeant shot her in the back. The rogue vicar crashed to the floor and lay still, blood pouring from her mouth. Sharon cried out in horror and fell to her knees beside the dead woman. Tears streamed down her face.

"Get them out of here!" said the Matriarch.

The Sarjeant hauled Sharon to her feet. She threw him off with inhuman strength, and in a moment the country-set girl was gone, replaced by a huge and awful demon, with bottle-green scales and vicious claws. Her long muzzle opened to reveal rows of jagged teeth, as she howled her shock and grief. Demon wailing for her woman lover. And then she threw herself at the Matriarch.

Conrad went to intercept her, and she slammed him aside with one sweep of her arm. The Sarjeant shot her from behind, and it didn't even slow her down. Other Droods came rushing forward and cut at her with golden swords and axes. She lashed about with appalling strength, and demonic claws cut through golden armour as if it were paper. Flesh tore, and blood flew on the air. Droods fell to the floor, and not all of them got up again. The Sarjeant called up the exorcism function in his armour and hit the demon with a blast of brilliant light and compelling Latin. And the demon turned back into Sharon Pilkington-Smythe.

She hesitated, caught by surprise, and the Sarjeant shot her in the back of the head. The bullet burst out her left eye-socket, and the impact threw Sharon to the floor. She crouched on all fours for a moment, head hanging down, blood spilling onto the floor. She started to crawl towards Tamsin, and the Sarjeant shot her again. She fell forward onto her ruined face and stopped moving. The Sarjeant turned to face the shocked Matriarch.

"That is why we can't go easy on these people. Can't show them any mercy. Because we can never be sure exactly what we're dealing with."

"Go out into the Nightside, Sarjeant," the Matriarch said steadily. "Gather up as many of our people as you need, and bring the Nightside under our control by whatever means you consider necessary. Find the Authorities, and make them kneel to us. Kill them if they won't. They wanted a war; you show them what that means."

Conrad came over to join them and looked at the dead women on the floor.

"None of this would have happened if we'd arrived where we were meant to, in the heart of the Nightside."

"The Nightside has no heart," said the Matriarch.

CHAPTER TEN

Good Deaths and Bad

When a bar is as well-known as Strangefellows, one of the problems is that some people think they can just walk right in. For the most part, much-reported stories about how the regulars behave were enough to make dropping in for a swift drink seem like a really bad idea. But there are people in the Nightside so dangerous in their own right that a little thing like a reputation for appalling behaviour and supernatural menace doesn't even slow them down. People like the Authorities, for example.

Three of them came clattering down the metal stairs into the bar: Jessica Sorrow the Unbeliever, Annie Abattoir the ex-assassin, and Brilliant Chang the ex-enforcer. The expressions on their faces would have been enough to intimidate most people into keeping their heads down and trying not to be noticed, but Alex Morrisey wasn't most people. He glowered at the three Authorities from behind the safety of his bar, secure in the knowledge that he had a great many useful weapons tucked away within easy reach.

"What do you want?" he said loudly. "In case you hadn't noticed, there's a war on. A great many more than usually unpleasant people are roaming the streets, and we are officially closed, for the duration."

"Not any more you're not," said Annie, striding into the bar as though she meant to take it by force of arms.

"We need somewhere to talk where we can be sure the Droods can't listen in," said Brilliant. "And everyone knows Strangefellows has the best protections in the Nightside."

Alex couldn't help but recognise such an obvious appeal to his pride but still couldn't resist it. "All right, since you're here . . . At least have the decency to buy a great many drinks. And choose something expensive!"

Annie and Brilliant studied the long rows of bottles set out behind the bar. Now Alex had brought the subject up, they felt like they could use a drink. In fact, they felt like they deserved one. Jessica drifted down the bar to make friends with Alex's pet vulture. Anyone else, it would have had their eyes out for such effrontery, but Jessica just scratched the nasty creature under the beak, and the vulture cooed happily back at her. Jessica looked at Alex.

"Does your vulture have a name?"

"Agatha," said Alex. "After my ex-wife. May she rest in peace."

"I didn't know your ex was dead," said Brilliant.

"She isn't," said Alex. "It's just wishful thinking."

"I'll have a Bloody Nail," said Annie.

"One large gin with vampire's blood coming right up," said Alex.

"I'll have a Talisker whiskey," said Brilliant. "Double, no ice, no water."

"A man with taste," said Alex, as he busied himself with the drinks. "We don't get many of those in here." He glanced down the bar. "What about Little Miss Scary?"

"I heard that . . ." said Jessica, without looking around.

"Give her a Perrier," said Annie. "It's easier on all our nerves."

"Heard that too . . ." said Jessica.

Everyone looked around as more footsteps descended the metal staircase, then they all relaxed as Julien Advent and Larry Oblivion emerged into view. Annie gave Julien a hard look.

"Didn't take you long to come back after walking out on us. What happened to change your mind?"

"I still had hope then," said Julien, as he and Larry came to the bar. "Hope that the Droods could be reasoned with. I have been proven wrong."

Annie looked like she was about to say something sharp, but Larry got in first.

"The Hawk's Wind Bar and Grill has been destroyed," he said flatly.

"Along with several of its regulars. I turned up just in time to save Julien from a Drood firing squad."

Annie and Brilliant looked honestly shocked. Partly at the loss of a Nightside landmark and partly that the Droods would try to kill one of the Nightside's few real heroes. Julien looked at Larry.

"Tell me, how did you know I needed saving?"

"I'm dead," said Larry. "Which means I hear things the living don't and know things they wouldn't want to."

"You want a drink?" said Brilliant, just to make it clear he wasn't even a little bit impressed. "Annie's in the chair."

"I am?" said Annie.

Larry ordered a glass of formaldehyde, with a crème de violet chaser. Alex didn't even blink. He'd been asked for worse.

Brilliant raised an elegant eyebrow in Larry's direction. "That's a hell of a drink for anyone still moving around. Have you been talking to Dead Boy?"

"I wouldn't lower myself," said Larry. "Just because we're both dead doesn't mean we have anything in common."

"Snob," said Annie, not unkindly.

"Standards have to be maintained," said Larry. "Even if you do happen to be mortally challenged. Julien, what are you drinking?"

"Really not in the mood," said Julien.

"Best time to have a drink," Alex said wisely. "Either it'll help cheer you up, or it'll put you in a mood to go and do something to whichever bastards are responsible for your present mood."

"I'll have an Angel's Tears," said Julien. "Do you still have the bottle with the wing feather in it?"

"If he has, I'm not paying for it," said Annie.

"Give him the bottle, Alex," said Brilliant. "I'm good for it."

Alex produced an unlabelled bottle from beneath the bar. The glass was extra thick to make sure the contents stayed inside. They surged menacingly back and forth as Alex wrestled with the wired-on cork. The pure white feather twitching in the cloudy liquid shone with a supernaturally bright light because Angel's Tears is not a brand name. Alex poured a decent amount into a shot-glass, then stepped back to let Julien deal with it.

Julien glared at the bottle, and the contents grew still. He sipped his drink and nodded.

"Heavenly," he said. He looked at the other Authorities. "The Droods have to be stopped. By whatever means necessary."

"That covers a lot of ground," Brilliant said carefully.

"Fight fire with fire," said Larry, knocking back his drink and gesturing to Alex for another. "If you want to stop something powerful, raise something even more powerful."

"What could possibly go wrong with a plan like that?" said Annie. "Apart from pretty much everything."

"I was thinking about some of the things sleeping under the Nightside, in the World Beneath," said Larry. "Whether they wipe out the Droods or the Droods wipe them out, we'd still come out ahead."

"I was thinking about the Lord of Thorns," said Julien. "He was put here to be Overseer to the Nightside."

"I can't see him listening to us," said Brilliant. "Not after the old Walker pretty much neutered him, on the orders of the old Authorities."

Annie gave Larry a thoughtful look. "Your brother Hadleigh is the Detective Inspectre."

"Seriously?" said Brilliant. "You want to bring Hadleigh into this? Aren't things bad enough without getting him involved?"

"He's a graduate of the Dark Academie," said Annie. "The only ones I know of who are actually scarier than Droods."

"I could talk to Hadleigh," said Larry. "But he goes his own way, you know that."

They all looked around sharply at the sound of yet more footsteps descending the metal stairs. Deliberately loud, as though they wanted everyone to know they were coming.

"What do I have to do to keep people out?" said Alex. "Wasn't a sign saying *We're closed get the hell away from here I have guns and big stabby things* enough? Am I going to have to nail the door shut and put down some land-mines?"

And then a sudden silence fell across the bar as Eddie Drood and Molly Metcalf appeared at the foot of the stairs. They smiled easily about them. No one smiled back. The Authorities might not be sure who Eddie was, but they all had enough Sight to see the torc around his neck. And everyone there knew Molly Metcalf. One way or another. The Authorities turned as one to face Eddie and Molly head-on, even Jessica. Alex ducked down behind the bar, to make it clear he had no intention of getting involved.

"Hello, Authorities!" Eddie said easily. "Please don't be alarmed. I am Eddie Drood, but I'm not like the rest of my family."

"It's true," said Molly. "He really isn't."

Eddie raised his hands above his head. The Authorities stared at him, taken aback. Whatever they'd been expecting from a Drood, that wasn't it. Eddie realised Molly hadn't raised her hands and gave her a hard look.

"We agreed . . ."

"No," said Molly. "I'm not doing it. It's undignified. I have a reputation to maintain!"

"Please," said Eddie. "Just for me."

"Oh, all right," said Molly, ungraciously. "Just for you." She scowled warningly at the Authorities. "No one is to talk about this. Not ever."

She raised her hands in the air.

"She's right," said Annie, after a moment. "On her, it looks unnatural."

"I don't understand," said Julien. "Are you surrendering to us?"

"Not as such," Eddie said carefully, "I just wanted to make it very clear that Molly and I didn't come here looking for trouble."

"That makes a change, in Molly's case," said Larry.

"Don't push your luck, dead man," said Molly.

Eddie moved slowly toward the Authorities, keeping his hands high above his head. Molly stuck close beside him.

"What do you want, Drood?" said Brilliant.

"I want to talk," said Eddie.

"Your Sarjeant-at-Arms destroyed the Hawk's Wind," said Julien. "And killed several of my friends."

"Yeah . . ." said Eddie. "He does things like that. One of the reasons we don't normally let him off the leash. It's just another sign of how far out-of-control things have got. I am nothing like the Sarjeant. I already tried talking to John Taylor, but that didn't work out. He was too inflexible. I'm hoping the Authorities have more room in them for a little give and take."

"You had words with John Taylor?" said Annie. "And you're still among the living?"

"Of course," said Julien Advent. "He's a Drood, and she's Molly Metcalf."

"Who sent you here?" said Brilliant.

"The family Matriarch ordered me to come here and seize control of Strangefellows," said Eddie. "Given that it's such an important symbol of the Nightside."

Alex's head emerged above the bar. "It is?"

"And you wouldn't believe the problems I had getting here," said Eddie. "It's a madhouse out there. But I'm hoping the whole hands-in-the-air thing is helping to convince everyone here that I just want to talk."

"We should talk," said Jessica. Everyone turned to look at her. She shrugged. "This is Eddie Drood. We've all heard of him and the things he's done. For and against his family. If he wants to talk, I say let him. Because I don't think we'd get very far trying to fight him. Or Molly. Hello, Molly."

"Hi, Jess," said Molly. "You look very together."

"You two know each other?" said Eddie. "Of course you do. You know everyone."

"It does feel like that, sometimes," said Molly.

"How did you know the Authorities would be here, right now?" said Julien.

"I'm a witch!" said Molly. "I am also a witch who's arms are beginning to ache . . ."

"Put your hands down," said Brilliant. "You look ridiculous."

"See!" Molly said to Eddie, lowering her hands immediately. "I told you."

Eddie lowered his hands slowly and cautiously, and the tension in the bar eased, just a little. Alex decided that open mayhem and mass destruction might not be about to break out after all and stood up straight. He glowered at Eddie and Molly.

"The last time you were in here you started a riot! It took me hours to clear up the mess. All right, I didn't do it personally; I got Betty and Lucy to do it because they've got muscles, but the principle is the same! You're banned!"

"I can pay for the damages," said Eddie.

"You're not necessarily banned," said Alex. "You want something to drink?"

"I do!" said Molly.

"Later," said Eddie.

Molly gave him a hard look. "You keep saying that."

Alex raised his voice. "Betty! Lucy!"

The two extremely muscular bouncers appeared from somewhere out back, wearing matching T-shirts: NIGHTSIDE ROLLERBALL HELLCAT MUD-WRESTLING CHAMPIONS. Betty was gnawing the meat off what looked very like a human thigh-bone. Lucy had broken hers in half to get at the marrow. They looked at everyone and didn't seem even a little bit impressed.

"Guard the door upstairs," Alex said to them. "I don't want anyone else getting in to see this. Serious enemies, being reasonable, in my bar? I'd never live it down."

Betty and Lucy nodded briskly and clattered up the metal stairs. The Authorities picked out a table and sat down on one side of it, crammed close together. Eddie and Molly sat down facing them. Brilliant and Molly watched each other closely, both ready to kick off big time if either of them even looked like they were starting something. Julien, Larry, and Annie kept their gaze fixed on Eddie. Jessica was already staring off into the distance, at something only she could see, and everyone else left her to it. Because they all felt safer when she wasn't looking at them. Eddie tried his most charming smile on the Authorities, then gave it up as a bad idea when it became clear no one was buying it.

"What do you want, Drood?" said Larry. "Really?"

"An end to the fighting," said Eddie. "An end to the expansion of the Nightside's boundaries, and a way for both sides to withdraw from this mess with honour."

"Do you have any ideas on how this might be achieved?" Julien asked.

"I'm hoping this is a first step," said Eddie.

Brilliant scowled at Molly. "Why aren't you saying anything?"

"Because Eddie is the reasonable one," said Molly, scowling right back at him. "I don't do reasonable."

"We're talking to each other," said Eddie, fixing his attention on Julien. "And not trying to kill each other. That has to be a good starting-place. The next step has to involve your talking to my family. Two of the Matriarch's top people, Howard and Callan, are on their way to the Londinium Club, looking for you. I can talk to them on your behalf. Arrange a meeting, on neutral ground."

"But what would we talk about?" said Larry.

"The need for all of us to work together, to try to find out who or what is behind the Nightside's changing its boundaries," said Eddie. "And then what we can do to put things right."

"You really think your Matriarch will go along with that, now she's got the taste of blood in her mouth?" asked Annie.

"No," said Eddie. "She wants this war too much. I'd have to take control of the family away from her. And the Sarjeant-at-Arms. Getting Callan and Howard on my side would be a good start to bringing that about. My family would listen to them."

"Only a Drood can stop a Drood," said Molly.

"All right," said Julien. "Go talk to them. See how far they're prepared to go. Then report back to us."

"I thought you wanted revenge!" said Larry. "The Droods just slaughtered your friends!"

"I haven't forgotten," Julien said coldly. "I do want revenge. But this isn't about me; it's about the Nightside."

"And that's why you're the best of us," said Jessica. "Welcome back, Julien."

Eddie and Molly got to their feet, slowly and cautiously so as not to spook anybody.

"We'll get back to you," said Eddie.

They backed away from the table, then hurried up the metal stairs. The Authorities waited until they couldn't hear them any more and slowly relaxed, with a series of long sighs.

"That went better than we had any right to expect," said Brilliant.

"How do you work that out?" said Annie. "We're still at war, aren't we?"

"We're still alive, aren't we?" said Brilliant. "Apart from you, Larry, obviously."

"I thought he looked very ordinary, for a Drood," said Jessica. "Almost normal."

Annie gave Julien a hard look. "Do you really believe anything will come of this?"

"I don't know," said Julien. "But we have to try. At least it got those two out of here without bloodshed. And just maybe, a Drood can stop a Drood."

"We can't depend on that," said Larry. "We have to do something! Work out some kind of tactics we can use, to stop an army of Droods!"

Julien looked at him steadily. "I think we need to talk to your brother. Now."

"Tommy?" said Larry. "What's he going to do, confuse them to death?"

"I mean Hadleigh," said Julien. "We need the Detective Inspectre."

Everyone looked at everyone else. Unsettled, and just a bit unnerved. Hadleigh's name and title had that effect on people.

"Are we really back to that?" Brilliant said finally. "Calling on the Detective Inspectre for help is like trying to put out a fire by blowing it up with a nuke."

"I've never met the man," said Annie. "Only heard stories. What's he really like, Larry?"

"Scarier than the stories," said Larry. "I'm dead, and he still creeps the shit out of me. His time in the Dark Academie changed him. Made him more than human, or less."

"But he is a power in his own right," said Julien. "Would he use that power to help us?"

"He might," said Larry.

"Then you need to talk to him right now," said Julien.

"Oh hell . . ." said Larry.

He got out his phone and hit one particular button. "Hadleigh! This is Larry, and yes, it is an emergency. I'm at Strangefellows. The Authorities need to talk to you about stopping the Drood invasion. Can you help? How fast can you get here?" said Larry.

"Look behind you," said Hadleigh.

The Authorities spun around in their chairs, and there was Hadleigh, standing facing them. Without a phone in his hand. Larry looked at his, shrugged, and put it away.

"Show-off."

Wrapped in a long black coat that might have been made from a piece of the night, Hadleigh had a bone-white face, a long mane of jet-black hair, deep-set unblinking eyes, and a cold smile. He appeared starkly black and white because there was no longer any room in him for shades of grey. He looked to be in his twenties, though he had to be much older than that.

"The Detective Inspectre," said Jessica. "He walks in shadows, between Life and Death, Light and Dark, Law and Chaos. The man with responsibility for dealing with crimes against reality itself."

"You know," said Annie, "I think I prefer it when you're not talking."

"A lot of people say that," said Jessica.

"You had to make an appearance, didn't you, Hadleigh?" said Larry.

He was the only one who didn't seem at all shaken by Hadleigh's arrival. But then, he was dead. Hadleigh strolled over to join the Authorities, pulled up a chair, and sat down, all of it with studied calm and elegance. His smile didn't waver once, and his gaze remained unnervingly direct.

"How nice," he said. "To be sitting where Eddie and Molly were sitting, just a moment ago."

"How do you know that?" said Annie, bristling. "Have you been spying on us?"

"No," said Hadleigh. "I just know things. It comes with the job."

"Can you help us stop the Drood invasion?" said Julien.

"I once tried to stop Eddie Drood and Molly Metcalf, in the House of Doors," said Hadleigh. "The Dark Academie wanted a Drood to examine, to learn the secrets of his armour and his body. I failed."

"How is that even possible?" said Larry.

"They cheated," said Hadleigh.

The Authorities looked at each other. None of them knew what to say.

"I never heard that story before," Annie said finally.

"I should hope not," said Hadleigh. "And that was just one Drood . . . And the wild witch, of course. To stop a whole army of Droods, in their armour, in full flow . . . We will need power from the Dark Academie. And that means one of you will have to go there with me to take on that power."

"I'll go," Julien said immediately. "And yes, I understand it will be dangerous. I volunteer."

"I expected as much," said Hadleigh. "But it can't be you, Julien. It has to be Larry."

"What?" said Larry, not unreasonably upset. "Why does it have to be me?"

"Because you are the only one who could survive the experience," said Hadleigh. "Because you're already dead."

"You're not exactly selling this to me," said Larry.

"I wouldn't ask you to carry this burden if I could do it myself," said Hadleigh. "But I'm not sure any living person could contain this kind of power long enough to do any good with it."

Larry looked around at the other Authorities, and they looked steadily, expectantly, back at him. Larry was ready to tell them all to go to Hell, just on general principles. He wouldn't stand for being pressured and bullied into things, even when he was alive. But one of the more unnerving things about the Detective Inspectre was that he always spoke the truth. So if he said this was necessary . . .

"I always knew being dead would come in handy for something," said Larry, resignedly. "All right. When do we go?"

"Now," said Hadleigh.

Larry disappeared from his chair, and the Detective Inspectre vanished with him. The Authorities barely had time to react before both of them were back again. Larry was down on the floor on all fours, shaking and shuddering, his eyes wide with shock. Hadleigh stood over his brother but made no move to help. The Authorities jumped to their feet and gathered around Larry, not sure what to do. In the end, Julien knelt beside him and spoke quietly and reassuringly.

"Larry? What's wrong? What happened to you? You were only gone a moment."

"Years," Larry said hoarsely. "It felt like years. In the dark places, in the cathedrals of bone and horror. There's no light there, even the sun is dark, but I could still see! I was made to see . . ." He turned his head suddenly, to fix Julien with an almost feral stare. "If you could see what I saw in the Dark Academie, if you knew what they do there . . . What they know and what they teach . . . Reality isn't what we think it is, Julien; and it never was."

He started to laugh, then to cry. Julien put a hand on Larry's shoulder, and the dead man flinched away. Annie glared at Hadleigh.

"What did you do to him, you bastard?"

"Nothing he didn't ask for," said Hadleigh. "The Dark Academie offered him power, and he accepted it. He will be very powerful now. For as long as he lasts."

Julien stood up and glared accusingly at Hadleigh.

"He's your brother!"

"Who else could I trust with so much power," said Hadleigh. "Except my own brother?"

Larry finally lurched to his feet. He'd stopped shaking, but his eyes were like a wild thing trapped in a snare. He nodded shakily, as though in agreement to some inner question, and looked at Hadleigh.

"We're going to need Tommy."

"I know," said Hadleigh. "I already talked to him. He's waiting for us to pick him up." He smiled briefly. "Or, he may not be. He is the existential private eye, after all."

"What are you going to do?" said Brilliant.

"Take the fight to Drood Hall," said Hadleigh. "They brought their family home with them, into the Nightside, then abandoned it to go off and fight. There's only a skeleton staff in place to protect the Hall; probably because the Droods didn't think anyone would dare attack it. But we are the Oblivion Brothers, and in our own way, we are all-powerful. We can take Drood Hall. Once you are in control of that, and the very useful things inside it, you should be in a much better position to negotiate a peace."

"These . . . useful things," said Julien. "Are you sure you're not planning to keep some of them for yourself?"

"Well," said Hadleigh, "the Dark Academie did give me a shopping list . . . And the kind of things we're talking about, you people couldn't be trusted with anyway."

"What gives you the right to make that decision?" said Annie.

He looked at her. "I'm the Detective Inspectre."

And even Annie Abattoir had to look away, unable to meet his gaze.

"We have to go," said Larry. "I can feel the power moving inside me. It burns . . ."

"I know," said Hadleigh. "I know."

They both disappeared. The Authorities waited a moment, to see if they might return again, and when that didn't happen, they all sat down. Julien looked at the others.

"Did we just sacrifice one of our own, to stop the Droods?"

"Better Larry than the rest of us," said Brilliant.

"How can you say that?" Annie said angrily.

"Because Larry is dead," said Brilliant, entirely unmoved. "He's already had more time than he was entitled to. Who knows? Being dead might be just what he needs to survive this."

"Hush," said Jessica. "Someone's coming."

They all sat still, listening, but couldn't hear anything.

"I'm not hearing anything!" said Alex from behind the bar, just to remind them he was still there.

"Are you sure, Jessica?" said Brilliant.

He broke off as heavy footsteps descended the metal stairs.

"How does she do that?" said Annie.

"Because she's not all there," said Julien. "So, not surprisingly, sometimes she's somewhere else."

Betty and Lucy Coltrane came down the stairs at a steady pace, bringing with them Charlotte ap Owen and her cameraman Dave. Betty had Dave by an ear, while Lucy had Charlotte in a head-lock. The bouncers stopped at the bottom of the stairs and looked to Alex for instructions. He shook his head disgustedly.

"Just when you think things can't possibly get any worse, that's when the television news turns up." He looked at the Authorities. "What do you want me to do with them? I could always whip up some boiling oil, maybe some tar and feathers . . ."

"Let them go," said Julien. "They are journalists, in their own way. And I am curious as to what brought them here."

Alex nodded reluctantly to the Coltranes, and they released their captives. Dave scuttled away from Betty and checked that his camera was okay. Charlotte straightened up, checked her hair was still in place, then opened her mouth to complain. Julien gave her a look, and she didn't. Alex sniffed loudly.

"You know, I can remember when this used to be my place, and people listened to what I had to say . . ."

"Shut up, Alex," said Annie.

Betty and Lucy disappeared out the back. Charlotte looked after them. "Do they ever talk?"

"Not in public," said Alex. "They're shy."

"*Shy?*" said Brilliant. "Them! They once ate their own dog!"

"Times were hard," said Alex.

Dave started to aim his camera at the Authorities. Brilliant looked at him, and Dave pointed the camera at the floor. Brilliant looked at him some more, and Dave turned the camera off.

"Point that thing at me again," said Brilliant, "and I'll turn you into something."

He didn't specify what. Somehow, that made it worse.

"What are you doing here, Charlotte?" said Julien. "I thought the news was out there on the streets, not in here with us."

"We have a recording to show you," Charlotte said quickly. "It's Droods in action, plus an exclusive interview with their Sarjeant-at-Arms. You really need to see this. If we can agree on a reasonable fee . . ."

"I don't like your shoes," said Jessica.

Charlotte looked down at her suddenly bare feet and swallowed hard. She turned to Dave.

"Play the recording."

Dave checked with Brilliant that this was okay, then turned his camera back on and made some adjustments. A viewscreen appeared, floating on the air before them, and the Authorities watched a complete record of what happened when the Sarjeant led his people into the business area. The toppling of the building, the stopping of the traffic, the Droods killing drivers. And finally, the Sarjeant's words caught on audio, revealing his intentions. Dave shut his camera down, and the Authorities looked at each other.

"I'd heard reports . . ." Julien said slowly. "But I had no idea things had got so out of hand. That wasn't a battle, like the Hawk's Wind. That was just Droods killing people because they could."

"And it's getting worse," said Dave. "You wouldn't believe the kind of things we saw on the way here . . ."

"What else would you expect, from Droods?" said Annie.

"No," said Julien. "I've worked with some of them. Sat drinking with some of them, right here in Strangefellows. They were never this bad."

"It's the Nightside," said Jessica. "The long night has its effect on everyone."

"We have to strike back!" said Annie. "Before they kill someone we care about."

"Oh God," said Charlotte. "You don't know. I'm so sorry."

Annie looked at her. "Know what?"

Charlotte swallowed hard. "It happened in the Mammon Emporium. Everyone's talking about it. The Sarjeant-at-Arms killed the rogue vicar Tamsin MacReady and her friend."

Annie lurched to her feet, swaying unsteadily, and looked around as though she didn't recognise anyone. "My daughter is dead?"

Julien stood up to comfort her, and she turned on him savagely.

"The Droods murdered my daughter! I'll see them all dead for this!" She stopped for a moment, breathing hard, and when she spoke again, her voice was almost inhumanly cold. "I will make them pay, and I will make them suffer, and when I am done, there will not be a single Drood left alive to poison this world with their presence."

She turned her back on the Authorities and stamped heavily up the metal stairs. Running away from her pain and towards her revenge. Brilliant Chang got to his feet and went after her. The ex-enforcer going to support the ex-assassin because he knew all about revenge and what it could do to you. Charlotte looked at Julien and Jessica, then at her cameraman. He nodded reluctantly.

"We have to be going," said Charlotte. "We still have a story to cover."

"Do a good job," said Julien. "Be a real reporter, for once."

"I can do that," said Charlotte.

She hurried up the stairs, with Dave right behind her. Julien looked at Jessica.

"Why didn't you go with Annie?"

"Because I don't do the revenge thing any more," said Jessica. "Or the Nightside wouldn't be here. Find me something better to do, Julien."

"I'll think of something," he said.

They got to their feet and made their way steadily up the metal stairs. The bar was suddenly very quiet. Alex let out a breath he hadn't realised he was holding.

"I thought they'd never go. Betty! Lucy! I want all the entrances and exits sealed and barricaded. And make sure all the defences and protections are still operating. I don't want anyone else getting in. Oh, this is going to be a really long night, I can tell . . ."

John Taylor walked down a deserted street, his footsteps eerily loud in the quiet. Most of the buildings around him had been smashed in or burned out. Thick twists of smoke still hung on the air. The fighting had moved on, but the destruction and the bodies remained. John would have liked to stop and check the fallen, to see if he recognised anyone, but he had to keep moving. He had to do something even if he hadn't worked out what. He finally decided on Strangefellows. He'd heard the Authorities were there.

He took out his gold pocket-watch, but when he tried to use it, nothing happened. He looked at the watch, blinked a few times, then gave it a good hard shake. He'd never known it to fail him before, ever since the previous Walker gave it to him. He concentrated and called on his gift for finding things. He needed an answer. His gift squirmed uneasily in his mental grasp; then a vision appeared before him. Of a large and mysterious machine surrounded by people in white lab coats. Knowledge came to John that he was looking at the dimensional engine Alpha Red Alpha, deep under Drood Hall. The machine that brought the Droods into the Nightside. It was broadcasting a signal to shut down all Timeslips in the long night and make sure no one could get in or out. And that included the Timeslip in his watch.

John let the vision go. His head ached. He put the watch away and got out his phone; but when he called Suzie, no one answered. John swore briefly. She must be working. He called on his gift again, to find Suzie. This time the vision showed him Suzie facing two Droods in their armour, in the corridors of the Mammon Emporium. A fierce pain stabbed through his head, and he lost his concentration and the vision. John swore some more and went running down the street, looking for some traffic he could commandeer.

It took him three streets before he could find anything moving. An ambulance sailed right past him, sirens wailing. An articulated rig didn't even slow down when he hailed it, and a taxi actually growled at him for getting too close. He tried to flag down a motor-cycle courier, and when the man just drove straight at him, John gritted his teeth and used his gift to find the bike's ignition and shut it down. He stepped aside as the motor-cycle skidded to a halt, then strode over to it. The courier, a beefy young man in shocking pink Lycra and steampunk goggles, started to yell at John, then saw who he was. He shut up immediately and got off the bike.

"I'm taking this," said John.

"Of course! Go right ahead! Please don't kill me!" said the courier, backing away. He watched John get on the motor-cycle and study the controls dubiously. "Excuse me, Walker, sir, but . . . do you actually know how to ride a motor-bike?"

"I'm in a hurry," said John. "I'll work it out as I go."

"Stop fighting me," the bike said inside John's head. "I'll get you there. Where to?"

"The Mammon Emporium," said John. "And don't stop for anything."

"That's what I like to hear!" said the bike.

It started itself and roared off down the road, with John hanging on grimly for dear life. The bike accelerated through the streets, dodging around the patchy traffic, singing loudly *Here I come to save the day!*

Ioreth and Magnus returned to the Mammon Emporium with one of the Sarjeant's local contacts, Harry Fabulous. He hadn't been hard to find; he'd been looking for a Drood to report to. A shabby man in shabby clothes, Harry had a hard-worn face, unreadable eyes, and a professional smile that meant nothing at all. After a lifetime of being everyone's Go To Guy for absolutely everything that was bad for you, Harry finally made a deal too far in the back room of a Members-Only Club in a really bad part of town. He never talked about what had happened that night, but afterwards he led a life of desperate penance, trying to atone for something through a great many good deeds.

While still making a profit on every deal, of course.

Ioreth and Magnus wanted to introduce Harry to the Matriarch, so he could tell her what he'd told them, about the Droods' blocked communications. Apparently they were doing it to themselves. Harry had talked to people who understood such things, and they said it was a side-effect of what Alpha Red Alpha was doing to the Timeslips. And only the Matriarch had the authority to decide whether or not to stop doing it. But as Ioreth and Magnus led Harry deeper into the mall's corridors, it quickly became clear the Matriarch and the rest of the Droods had moved on. All they'd left behind were two bodies, in a large pool of drying blood. Harry shook his head sadly.

"Tamsin MacReady, the rogue vicar; and her girl-friend, Sharon. Your family shouldn't have done this. These young ladies were well-known as good people."

"I don't understand," said Ioreth. "Why would we kill a vicar?"

"Something must have happened here," said Magnus.

"Like what?" said Ioreth. "How could a vicar pose a threat to us?"

"By disagreeing with you," said a cold voice behind them. Ioreth and Magnus turned around quickly and found themselves facing a very pregnant woman in black leathers, covering them with a double-barrelled pump-action shotgun. Ioreth sucked in a sharp breath.

"Oh shit . . ."

"What?" said Magnus. "Ioreth? What are you hyperventilating for, it's only a gun!"

"Don't you know who that is?" said Ioreth. "Didn't you read the briefing or at least look at the photos? That's Shotgun Suzie!"

"Really?" said Magnus. "I didn't think she'd be so . . . pregnant."

"I think I'll be going now," said Harry Fabulous.

"You stay right where you are, Harry," said Suzie. "How long have you been working for the Droods?"

He shrugged quickly, which was his default response to most questions. "You know how it is, Suzie. I work for anyone. Just like you."

"I haven't betrayed the Nightside," said Suzie.

"It's only a matter of time," said Harry. "As long as you have that sword on your back."

Suzie didn't take her eyes off the two Droods, but when she spoke, there was a certain caution in her voice.

"You know about Wulfsbane?"

"I know of it," said Harry. "Enough to be properly scared. That thing is dangerous."

Suzie smiled slowly at Ioreth and Magnus. "Yes, it is. A blade sharp enough to cut through Drood armour. And Droods."

Magnus smiled right back at her. "Good. I love a challenge."

"Are you crazy?" said Ioreth, his voice rising. *"This is Shotgun Suzie!"*

"And we're Droods!" Magnus said fiercely. "Man up, Ioreth! You need to get out of the Library more."

"And you need to read the damn briefings!" said Ioreth, just as fiercely. "Suzie Shooter is a bounty-hunter in the Nightside, which means she makes a living tracking down people and things even a Drood field agent would think twice about bothering. She's killed more people than you've ever met, and you can bet good money she's killed worse things than Droods. And as if all that wasn't enough, she's John Taylor's wife."

"Good," said Magnus. "She'll make a fine hostage. Once he finds out we've got his wife, he won't dare give us any more trouble."

Ioreth looked at Harry. "You talk to her. She won't listen to me."

"Ioreth!" said Magnus. "Stop talking and armour up! We can take one woman with a shotgun!"

"That gun is what killed Luther Drood," said Harry.

Ioreth and Magnus looked at Suzie, and even Ioreth's gaze grew colder. Suzie stared back at them unflinchingly.

"How were you able to kill a Drood with a shotgun?" said Magnus.

"Strange-matter bullets," said Suzie. "You can find anything in the Nightside. Don't worry. I have enough left for both of you."

Magnus and Ioreth armoured up in a moment and dived in different directions. Suzie's reactions were fast enough for her to get off two separate shots, but she still couldn't match the speed of Droods in their armour. She missed both times, and before she could fire again, Ioreth and Magnus surged forward and hit her from different directions. Ioreth grabbed hold of the shotgun, jerked it out of Suzie's hands, and threw it away. Magnus hit Suzie with a lowered shoulder. The impact slammed Suzie back against the wall, and she cried out despite herself. The blow broke her left arm and stove in most of her rib-cage. She fell to her knees, pain screaming all through her left side. She gritted her teeth, brought her head up, and looked for her shotgun. It was lying on the floor some distance away. Ioreth saw her look and kicked the gun even farther out of reach.

"Bastard," said Suzie.

The effort made her cough, and blood sprayed from her mouth. Pain stabbed through her, suggesting at least one rib had pierced her lung. Her left arm hung uselessly at her side. She thought about the other weapons scattered about her person, but none of them were any use against a Drood in armour. She spat out a mouthful of blood and raised her head to smile coldly at the Droods standing before her. Suzie's teeth were slick with blood, and more of it spilled down her chin as her smile widened. Magnus smiled back at her.

"One for Luther. You can surrender now or die. It's up to you, bounty-hunter."

"I have a better idea," said Suzie.

304 ◦ Simon R. Green

She forced herself up on her feet, with an effort that made her head swim, and drew Wulfsbane from the long scabbard on her back. That took no effort; the sword seemed to leap into her hand. Just holding the Infernal Device made her feel stronger. Ioreth and Magnus glanced quickly at each other, as their armour picked up on the power blazing in the long blade. It glowed a poisonous yellow in the flat mall light, and the sword had a terrible presence all its own. Harry Fabulous stumbled backwards, then turned and ran for his life.

"Do you know what that is, Ioreth?" said Magnus.

"I've read about things like it," said Ioreth, just a bit breathlessly, "but I never thought I'd see one. That . . . is an Infernal Device."

"It's spooking the shit out of my armour," said Magnus. "How dangerous is it?"

"Very," said Ioreth.

"Could it really cut through our armour?"

"Yes! That sword was made to cut through the world."

"We can still take her!" said Magnus. "Look at the state of her."

"We have to take her," said Ioreth. "Or the sword will kill us both."

They moved apart again, to split Suzie's attention and come at her from different sides again. Suzie kept her back against the wall, sweeping the long blade back and forth in steady arcs, ready to take on whichever Drood came within reach first. Her face was deathly pale and slick with sweat, and pain stabbed through her with every breath, but the sword in her hand was perfectly steady. Wulfsbane made her strong, so it could use her to kill.

Magnus formed her hand into a gun and shot Suzie twice in the heart. But Wulfsbane moved impossibly fast, so that it was in just the right place to block and absorb the strange-matter bullets. The yellow blade swallowed them up, and the bullets screamed as the Infernal Device devoured them. For the first time, Magnus was shaken. She'd never heard her armour scream before. She dismissed the gun; grew a long, golden sword from her hand; and charged Suzie, trusting to her armour's strength and speed to make her unstoppable. Ioreth attacked with his own blade from the other side. Wulfsbane beat Magnus' blade aside and then swept back to shoot past Ioreth's sword and run him through. Wulfsbane punched through his stomach and out his back, and the golden armour didn't even slow it down.

Ioreth cried out and fell to his knees, his sword collapsing back into his hand as he lost concentration. As Suzie jerked the blade out of his body, he cried out and fell onto his side in a spreading pool of his own blood. His armour retreated back into his torc, leaving him exposed and vulnerable, as though it couldn't bear to be anywhere near the awful wound Wulfsbane had made.

Magnus screamed something foul and threw herself at Suzie. The two women slammed together, and Wulfsbane sheared clean through the golden blade. The broken piece fell to clatter on the floor, while Wulfsbane came sweeping around in a vicious arc that would have taken Magnus' head off if she hadn't thrown herself desperately to one side. Her armour's speed was still faster than Suzie's reflexes. Magnus hit the floor hard, soaked up the impact in a roll, and was quickly back on her feet again. The broken piece of her sword leapt up to rejoin her armour, and her sword reformed itself.

While Magnus was concentrating on that, Suzie went after Ioreth. He saw her coming and tried to crawl away, but he could barely move. It wasn't just the pain; Wulfsbane had put something in his wound. He could feel it, eating away at his insides. Suzie quickly caught up with Ioreth, and drew back her sword for the killing thrust. Ioreth rolled over onto his back, so at least he could look his death in the face.

And that was when Bettie Divine appeared out of nowhere, to stand between Suzie and Ioreth. Suzie hesitated, and Bettie hit her with a face full of unholy Mace. Suzie stumbled backwards, tears streaming down her cheeks from puffed-up eyes. She swept her sword back and forth to keep her enemies at bay, but Bettie only had eyes for Ioreth. She knelt beside him, her face slack with shock as she took in the terrible wound in his gut.

"Oh, sweetie . . . What has she done to you?"

"I didn't know you could teleport," said Ioreth, trying to smile for her.

"A girl doesn't tell everything on a first date. What can I do?"

"Know any good healing spells?"

"Not really my line, darling."

"Then we're both out of luck," said Ioreth. "Hold my hand, Bettie. I think I'm dying."

"There must be something I can do!" said Bettie. Tears dripped from her face onto his as she leaned over him.

"Get me home," said Ioreth. "Back to Drood Hall. I don't want to die here."

Bettie took hold of both his hands, and they disappeared.

Magnus attacked Suzie while she was still trying to knuckle the Mace out of her eyes, but Wulfsbane seemed to have eyes of its own, moving always to intercept Magnus' blows and block her attacks. Magnus knew better than to try to meet Wulfsbane full on, for fear her blade would shatter again on the Infernal Device, so she constantly changed her angle of attack, using her armour's strength and speed to try to power her sword past Wulfsbane's defences. She cut Suzie again and again, and the bounty-hunter's blood fell to the floor. Magnus smiled coldly behind her featureless golden mask.

For you, Ioreth.

And then Magnus hesitated, as she heard an engine approaching. It seemed to be coming from somewhere inside the mall. She backed away from Suzie and looked around just in time to see John Taylor come racing down the corridor on a motor-cycle. She turned to face him, and John aimed the bike straight at her. He waited until the last moment, then threw himself off the bike. He hit the ground rolling and was back on his feet in time to see the motor-cycle crash into Magnus. The bike exploded, and they both disappeared in a cloud of flames and black smoke.

John started toward Suzie, then stopped as Magnus walked out of the smoke and flames, entirely unharmed, and headed straight for him. His hands started towards his pockets, but he knew he didn't have anything that could get past a Drood's armour. So he called on his gift again, to find a way out; and a vision came to him of a shop full of clocks, and one time-piece in particular. He sprinted in the direction his vision showed him. And Magnus left Suzie to go after him.

John pounded down the corridor, with Magnus right behind him, her armoured feet thundering on the floor. She was catching up fast. He forced himself to run faster, gasping for breath, and finally plunged through the open door of a deserted shop. It was packed full of all kinds of clocks, and John looked desperately around for the one he needed. Magnus appeared in the doorway, blocking off the light with her armoured form. And then John saw it: the Stop Watch, set out on display. He grabbed hold of the

Watch and turned to face Magnus as she advanced on him, no longer hurrying now he had nowhere left to run. She held up her golden sword, and
blood dripped thickly from the blade. A slow anger moved through John,
as he realised he was looking at Suzie's blood.

He hit the button on the Stop Watch, and Time stopped, for Magnus.
She froze in place, a golden statue caught between one moment and the
next by the power of the Watch. John sat down hard on a nearby chair, his
heart racing, and took a moment to get his breathing back under control.
That had been close. He put the Stop Watch in his pocket, for later, and
forced himself back onto his feet. He walked up to Magnus, put one hand
on her face, and gave her a good hard shove. She toppled over backwards
and landed with a satisfyingly loud crash. John stepped over her and left
the shop in search of Suzie.

She came stumbling down the corridor towards him, her teeth clenched
against the pain that hammered through her with every step. Wulfsbane
was back in its scabbard, and she held her broken arm to her side with her
good hand. Sweat dripped off her face, and she could only just see out of
her puffed-up eyes. Whatever the demon had sprayed her with was vicious
stuff. John called out to her, and she turned her head slowly to look at him.
John stopped abruptly, as he saw there was nothing in her face to show she
recognised him. She let go of her broken arm and drew Wulfsbane. The
long blade glowed horribly yellow, like a corpse-fire on a cairn. John called
out to Suzie, and she ran straight at him.

The Infernal Device shot forward, in a blow that would have punched
right through John if he hadn't dived to one side at the last moment. Suzie
cut and hacked at him, and he kept ducking and dodging, calling out her
name and his, but she didn't react at all. So John chose his moment carefully, took a packet of pepper out of his pocket, and dashed the whole
contents into her face. She stopped dead, her abused eyes squeezed shut;
and then she sneezed explosively. And the sheer violence of it shocked her
awake. She forced her eyes open to look at John, then at Wulfsbane in
her hand. She threw the sword away from her, and it clattered loudly on
the floor, as though reproaching her.

"John?" said Suzie. "I almost . . . I'm sorry. I didn't know you. The sword
got inside my head."

She stumbled and almost fell, but John was there to catch her and hold her up. He was careful of her left arm, but she still cried out as he touched her. He helped her lean back against the nearest wall, then checked her out as gently as he could.

"Your arm is broken in three places," he said finally. "And your whole left rib-cage is a mess. What happened to you?"

"I thought I could take two Droods," said Suzie. She smiled bloodily. "Came pretty close."

"You need a hospital," said John.

She looked at him sharply. "The baby?"

"Seems fine," John said quickly. "But we need to get you properly looked at. Just in case."

"We don't have time for that," said Suzie.

She fished in her jacket pocket with her good hand and brought out a pulsing grey blob. John looked at it dubiously, and Suzie managed another small smile.

"Medical-repair blob. Black-market Drood rip-off. The Gun Shoppes of Usher don't just sell guns."

She pressed the blob carefully in between her left arm and her ribs, and the blob swelled up until it covered the whole of her left arm and side in a gently pulsing cocoon. Suzie sighed with relief as the pain shut off. The cocoon wrinkled, then shrivelled, and finally detached itself from Suzie and fell to the floor, all used up. Suzie flexed her arm and slapped her ribs and smiled at John.

"All done," she said. "Droods aren't the only ones with the best toys. Speaking of which, where's the one I didn't kill?"

"She's taking a timeout," said John.

"Show me," said Suzie.

"You can kill her later," John said patiently. "Trust me, she isn't going anywhere. We need to get to the Londinium Club. I got a message from Alex; two high-ranking Droods are on their way there, looking for the Authorities. If we could take two major Droods captive, that should give us some real bargaining power."

"Sounds like a plan to me," said Suzie. She looked at Wulfsbane, lying on the floor some distance away.

"Leave it," said John. "You don't need it."

"I'd have been killed without that sword," said Suzie. "And we haven't a hope in hell of stopping the Drood invasion without it."

"That sword nearly made you kill me," said John.

"Don't take it personally," said Suzie. "Wulfsbane wants to kill everyone."

"But if it can overpower you . . ."

"Then I'll just have to be stronger," said Suzie.

She strode over to the Infernal Device and picked it up, grimacing as she felt its presence in her head again. Like a soft voice whispering constantly in her ear. She slammed the sword back into its scabbard, and the voice retreated.

John Taylor and Suzie Shooter left the Mammon Emporium together and went looking for Droods.

The Drood advance had been forced almost to a halt by the sheer pressure of Nightside resistance. They couldn't kill people fast enough to make any progress. They were winning all the battles, but the Nightsiders were throwing everything they had at the Droods, and some of it was working.

They blew up their own buildings, so the wreckage would bury Droods. It didn't take the Droods long to dig themselves out, entirely unharmed, but it did take them out of the fight. And clearing the blockage slowed them down. People threw increasingly strange things at the Droods, trying to find something that would get past their armour. Guns didn't work, and magics discharged harmlessly on the air, so the Nightsiders turned to more lateral thinking. They set up invisible dimensional doorways all along the street, so that Droods who passed unknowingly through them ended up back at the start again. People teleported in and out, sticking around just long enough to try out a new weapon, watch the result, then disappear to report back. The hit-and-run tactics might not be hurting the Droods, but they were holding the Droods' attention and slowing them down even more.

Big flying creatures soared overhead and crapped on the Droods. Some of it was radioactive. Fizzing fluorescent fairies dive-bombed the Droods with sparkling clouds of pixie dust that made all their luck turn bad. It couldn't affect the Drood armour, which had learned and adapted after the Garden of Delights, but the dust still worked on their surroundings. The ground cracked open under Drood feet, sending them stumbling this way and that, or melted into quicksand that swallowed Droods up.

310 ∘ Simon R. Green

Some Droods became confused as to who the enemy was and attacked one another. Some became horribly ill and had to pull the armour back from their faces so they could vomit, while others became so turned-around they just sat down on the street and refused to move until someone they trusted could tell them where the hell they were.

The Sarjeant summoned guns into his hands and used the flying fairies for target practice. But even a full-on hit did little more than throw the nasty creatures around, and they swooped back and forth over his head, giggling happily and calling him awful names in fluty, high-pitched voices. The Sarjeant had to settle for holding their attention and keeping them from dive-bombing anyone else.

An earthquake generator cracked the street open from end to end, and Droods fell through to find all kinds of subterranean monsters waiting for them. Huge, segmented things, with armoured bodies and limbs like bludgeons. The Droods tore them apart with their golden hands, happy to have something solid and uncomplicated to fight.

The Matriarch finally ordered a retreat, over-ruling the Sarjeant's objections.

"We must keep going, Matriarch! We have to keep up the momentum!"

"We're not going anywhere, Sarjeant! We need to pull back and re-group. The family is exhausting itself on fights that don't matter. At this rate, they'll be worn-out long before we get to the real threats."

The Sarjeant looked at the crowds blocking the street ahead and nodded reluctantly. The Droods were fighting fiercely, but their armour could only do so much for them.

"You're right," he said. "This is just a distraction."

He called for the Droods to break off, and they quickly retreated to take up defensive positions at the other end of the street. The Nightsiders held their ground, wary of pursuing their enemy in case it was a trap. The Matriarch called Conrad over to join her. He'd been fighting at the front, and his armour was soaked in blood. It streamed down the slick golden surface and left a bloody trail behind him. The Matriarch, the Sarjeant, and Conrad move off to one side and pulled their golden masks back, so they could see one another's faces as they talked.

"I value your long experience in the field, Conrad," said the Matriarch. "These tactics aren't working. What am I doing wrong?"

"Stop trying to hit the crowds head-on," Conrad said immediately. "Break the family up into smaller groups and advance on several fronts at once. The resistance will have to break into smaller groups to stop us, and we can overpower them more easily."

The Matriarch nodded. "See to it, Sarjeant. No, wait a moment; have either of you seen Ioreth or Magnus? They should have caught up with us by now."

"We don't have time to worry about a missing Librarian," said the Sarjeant. "And Magnus can look after herself."

"I was wondering what had happened to Howard and Callan," said Conrad. "If they ever got to the Londinium Club, and the Authorities."

"If they had negotiated a surrender, I think we would have heard about it by now," said the Sarjeant.

"Would we?" said Conrad. "Our communications are getting worse."

"This is just another distraction," the Sarjeant said forcefully. "Matriarch, you need to give me full command over all military matters. Only I have the knowledge and experience to win this war. It's your job to set policy, mine to see it is carried out."

The Matriarch didn't answer for a moment, thinking it through. Things had not gone as she had anticipated.

"We came here to conquer these people," she said finally. "Not slaughter them. This isn't what I wanted."

"They're not giving us any choice," said the Sarjeant. "They'd kill all of us if they could."

"We're in danger of forgetting the object of this mission," Conrad said carefully. "Control of the Nightside; not its destruction."

"I never expected these people to put up such a fight," said the Matriarch. "Or be so good at it." She scowled at the Sarjeant. "You said they'd be soft and decadent!"

"Well," said the Sarjeant. "I was right about the decadent. Have you looked in some of these shop-windows?"

"We need reinforcements," said the Matriarch. "People who understand how to fight Nightsiders."

"Who can we ask for help?" said Conrad. "You already tried calling a summit, and no one wanted to know."

"They told us to go to Hell," said the Sarjeant.

"Things are different now," said the Matriarch. "They thought they could pressure us into calling off the invasion by withholding their support; but now we've committed ourselves to this war . . . They either help us or watch us fall. We have to try again."

"How?" said the Sarjeant. "Conrad is right; our communications have been failing us ever since we entered the long night."

"We could always try in there," said Conrad.

They looked to where he was pointing. On the other side of the street was a shop called Happy Talk, its window crammed full of all kinds of comm tech. The Matriarch clapped her hands delightedly.

"Well spotted, Conrad! Lead the way."

The shop-door turned out to be locked, so the Sarjeant kicked it in. The door was blasted right off its hinges and flew half-way across the shop. Inside, all kinds of weird communications gear had been set out on display. A conch-shell with an antenna, the ghost of an early telephone, and a television set with severed rabbit ears piled on top.

"For better reception," Conrad explained.

And then they all stopped as they saw something they hadn't expected to see. They advanced slowly on the glass display-case in the centre of the shop, inside of which was a silver-backed hand-mirror. The sign on the case said: *The legendary Merlin Glass, sent back through Time from the Thirtieth Century. Serious offers only. Do not attempt to touch if you like having fingers or your soul securely attached.*

The three Droods looked at the Merlin Glass, then at each other.

"Is that even possible?" the Matriarch said finally. "Could this really be a future version of our Merlin Glass?"

"If I understand Time travel theory," Conrad said slowly, "and I'm perfectly prepared to be told that I don't, there are supposed to be any number of different futures. So I suppose anything is possible . . ."

"All that matters," said the Sarjeant, "is will it work for us?"

"Find out," said the Matriarch.

The Sarjeant smashed the glass display-case with an armoured fist, reached in, and grabbed the hand-mirror. No alarms sounded. The Sarjeant handed the Merlin Glass to the Matriarch, who identified herself to it. The Glass didn't do anything, but it did seem to be listening.

"Contact the London Knights," said the Matriarch.

The mirror jerked itself out of her hand and grew rapidly to door size, hanging on the air before them. At first all they could see was their own reflection, then that was replaced by a face they all knew. A large and blocky man in an expertly cut grey suit, with a square and brutal face, marked with scars that had healed crookedly a very long time ago. Kae, stepbrother to King Arthur. Sole survivor of Camelot and the only immortal Knight. Grand Master of the London Knights, the last defenders of the dream of Camelot. He looked coldly out of the Glass.

"I've been waiting for you to try me again, Matriarch. My people kept you at arm's length before so I wouldn't have to say no to your face. But things have changed."

"Are you ready to help us now?" said the Matriarch.

"No," said Kae. "We have our own problems. While you've been wasting your time in the Nightside, a real problem has arisen that threatens the entire world. The London Knights are preparing to ride out and deal with it. But I will send you some of my younger, more headstrong Knights. They're inexperienced, and too ill-disciplined to be trusted in my army, but they're brave enough and ready for action . . . and desperate for a chance to prove themselves. Sir Bors, Sir Allain, Sir Gawaine . . . Maybe a dozen others. If you want them, they're yours. They'll make good shock-and-awe troops if nothing else."

"We'll take them," said the Sarjeant.

"Thought you would," said Kae. "I've got them waiting. Send the survivors back when you're done with them."

"Thank you, Kae," said the Matriarch.

"It is quite literally the least I can do," said Kae. He studied her soberly for a moment. "You know this can only end badly, don't you?"

His image disappeared from the Merlin Glass, which then shot out of the shop and into the street. The Droods hurried out after it, just as a company of Knights in full medieval armour came bursting through the Glass on huge, powerful horses. The Sarjeant went to meet them, subtly shifting his armour to look a little more like theirs, so they would take him seriously. The huge war-horses stamped their feet and tossed their heads. They didn't like the feel of the place they'd come to. The leading Knight leaned forward in the saddle of his brightly caparisoned charger.

"Where is the enemy, Drood?"

Behind his square, steel helmet, with only a narrow slit for the eyes, the Knight sounded very young. The Sarjeant pointed down the street.

"That way. You can't miss them. Anyone not in Drood armour should be considered a threat. Show them no mercy because they won't show you any."

"We don't do mercy," said the young Knight.

He drew his sword and set off down the street, and the whole company of Knights surged forward after him, quickly accelerating to full gallop. The Knights had broadswords, axes, and morning stars, and looked very eager to use them. Some were already singing victory songs. The Sarjeant watched them go, pulled his armour away from his face, and went back inside the shop.

"Well . . ." said Conrad. "They all sounded very keen, I suppose."

"Children," the Sarjeant said disgustedly. "He sent us children. They won't last long, but they should keep the Nightsiders occupied for a while. Give us a chance to think."

"They're London Knights!" said the Matriarch. "The pride of Camelot!"

"They might be, one day," said the Sarjeant. "If they survive being thrown in the deep end, where the sharks are. If they were any good, Kae wouldn't have been able to spare them. From the sound of it, he's facing a serious problem of his own."

"I wonder why he didn't tell us what the threat was," said Conrad.

"Because if he had put a name to it, I might have felt obliged to leave the Nightside to help him," said the Matriarch. "He was being kind, in his way."

"Is there anyone else we can ask for help?" said Conrad.

"There's always the Spawn of Frankenstein," said the Sarjeant. "The Baron's surviving creations are indebted to us. And maybe . . . we need monsters to fight monsters."

The Matriarch marched out of the shop and into the street, to stand before the hovering Merlin Glass. The Sarjeant and Conrad hurried after her. The Matriarch called out to the Spawn of Frankenstein, and the Glass showed her another familiar face.

The Bride was seven feet tall and very well-built. In his early days the Baron made all his creations extra large, so he could be sure of having enough room to fit everything in. The Bride's face was deathly pale, with taut skin and huge dark eyes that didn't blink often enough. Prominent scars showed on her chin and neck, and she wore her long black hair piled on top of her head in a towering beehive. A low-cut blouse showed off even more scar tissue over skin-tight leather jeans. The Bride would never be beautiful, but she was attractive, in a frightening sort of way.

"None of us will fight for you," the Bride said flatly, before the Matriarch could say anything. "Yes, we owe the Droods. But not enough to get involved in the mess you've made. You have no business being in the Nightside. You deserve everything that happens to you for as long as you're dumb enough to stay there."

Her image disappeared from the Glass.

Next, the Matriarch tried the Soulhunters. Strange sights came and went in the Merlin Glass, as though it was having trouble making a connection, then yet another familiar face appeared. All three Droods winced.

"Oh hell," said the Sarjeant. "We've got Demonbane again."

The figure in the Glass smiled happily on them. "That's because no one else here wants to talk to you."

Unhealthily slender in his pale lavender suit with padded shoulders, Demonbane's grey skin looked like it could use a trip through a car wash, with extra detergent. His face was sunken and hollowed, as though he were burning up from some spiritual fever. He had the look of someone who had seen many things, none of which any sane person would want to hear about. He stepped out of the Glass and onto the street, and all of the Droods flinched, just a little.

"Everyone else is busy," said Demonbane. "Don't ask what with. You wouldn't understand. So I'm all you're getting! I'm only here because I fancied a trip to the Nightside. I don't play well with others, so I won't be joining your army. I'll just wander around and look for some trouble to get into, on your behalf."

"How can we be sure you're on our side?" said the Sarjeant.

"You can't!" Demonbane said cheerfully. "However, to put your minds at ease, I brought someone with me. Someone you know."

And out of the Merlin Glass stepped the current Head of the Carnacki Institute, JC Chance himself, in his marvellous white suit, rock-star hair, and very dark sun-glasses. He nodded easily to one and all.

"And I'm all you're getting from the Ghost Finders, so don't go bothering them. I felt a need to be here, to see what's happening. But basically, I'm just along for the ride."

The Matriarch gave Demonbane a hard look. "You already contacted JC? How did you know I was going to contact you? I hadn't decided that till a moment ago!"

"Time is just another direction to look in," Demonbane said grandly.

"Don't ask," said JC. "I don't, and I find I'm a lot happier that way."

"You two are friends?" said the Sarjeant.

"Not sure if I'd go that far," said JC. "More like colleagues, with interests in common. And you really don't want to ask about them, either."

"He deals with death," said Demonbane. "And I deal with what comes after." He nodded to JC. "Shall we sally forth and see what this place has to offer in the way of entertainment?"

"Why not," said JC.

The two of them strolled off down the street, calm and casual, two young gentlemen on a night out. The Droods they passed fell back to give them plenty of room.

"You know," said Conrad. "We were probably better off before they arrived."

The Sarjeant gestured at the Merlin Glass, still hovering patiently in mid air. "You want to ask anyone else, Matriarch? We haven't done too well so far."

"No," said the Matriarch. "It's our job to do, so let's do it."

"At least we got some Knights out of it," said Conrad.

They looked down to the end of the street, where the company of London Knights were cutting a bloody path through the packed Nightsiders, with an excess of enthusiasm and bloody slaughter. Their charge had been slowed almost to a halt, but their weapons were still rising and falling.

"If nothing else, they're holding the Nightsiders' attention," said the Sarjeant. "What do you want to do with the Merlin Glass, Matriarch?"

"It comes with us," the Matriarch said immediately. "I'm not leaving it in the Nightside. I can't believe no one here has tried to use it."

"Maybe they did," said Conrad. "No doubt it has all kind of protections."

"The Glass is ours," said the Matriarch. "Wherever it comes from."

She thrust out her hand, and the Glass shrank back down to hand-mirror size, flew through the air, and nestled comfortably into her hand. The Matriarch slipped the Glass through her armoured side and into a dimensional pocket.

"When we get back to the Hall, we're going to have two versions of the Merlin Glass," said the Sarjeant. "That could mean problems . . ."

"I'm really not thinking that far ahead, for the moment," said the Matriarch.

"I suppose it's always possible some future Drood sent the Glass back to help us," said Conrad. "Because they read in the family records that somebody did."

The three Droods thought about that.

"I hate Time travel," said the Sarjeant. "It makes my head hurt."

Bettie Divine appeared outside Drood Hall, holding up a dying Ioreth. She started toward the front door, but Ioreth made her stop and listen to him.

"You can't just go barging in, Bettie. The Hall is protected."

"I'm half demon, darling, remember?" said Bettie. "I can handle this."

"No, you really can't," said Ioreth.

Scarecrows stepped out of the shadows to block their way. Ranks of raggedy things that looked like they'd just come down off their crosses in a really bad mood. They stood before the front door, wrapped in the tattered remains of what had once been fashionable and even elegant clothes. Because they used to be people. Their faces were horribly weather-beaten, the skin taut and brown as parchment, and tufts of straw jutted from ears and mouths. Their eyes were still present, alive and endlessly suffering.

"What the hell are they?" said Bettie.

"The Hall's first line of defence," said Ioreth. "Guardians, fashioned from the bodies of my family's greatest enemies. Hollowed out and filled with straw, animated by unnatural energies, bound by unbreakable pacts to defend the family from all threats. I'm told if you listen in on the right spiritual frequency at night, you can hear them screaming."

"Why would your family do that?" said Bettie.

"Because no one bears a grudge like a Drood," said Ioreth.

"Anywhen else I'd be impressed," said Bettie, "but we are in just a bit of a hurry right now, sweetie. We've got to get you to a doctor. Isn't there a password you can use to shut them down, or at least make them stand aside?"

"If there is such a thing, I never knew it," said Ioreth.

"I recognise some of them," said Bettie. "That's Laura Lye, the Liquidator! And Mad Frankie Phantasm . . . I always wondered what happened to him."

"My family happened to him," said Ioreth.

"Just as well, he was a complete bastard," said Bettie. She lowered Ioreth to the ground, and he wrapped his arms around himself tightly, because it felt like his guts might fall out of the hole Wulfsbane had made. He was shuddering, and not from the cold. Bettie put a hand on his forehead and winced. "You sit tight, sweetie. I'll deal with this. Now close your eyes."

"Why?" said Ioreth.

"Because I'm going to have to let out my inner bad girl," said Bettie. "And I don't want you to see that."

She kissed him on the forehead, and he closed his eyes. So he never saw her change into the image of her mother. Suddenly all fangs and claws, with goat-horns curling up from her brow, Bettie Divine launched herself at the scarecrows and tore them to pieces, ripping off arms and tearing torsos apart. Decapitated heads rolled along the street, their eyes still suffering and hating. And still Bettie raged among the scarecrows, reducing them to ragged bits and pieces and trampling the remains under her cloven hooves. Ioreth heard it all and kept his eyes squeezed shut. After a while, it all went quiet.

"It's all right, sweetie," said Bettie. "You can open your eyes now."

He did, and she was crouching before him, herself again. The scarecrows were just ragged bits and pieces. Some were still twitching.

"Impressive," said Ioreth, trying to find the strength to smile at her.

"Sorry about the mess," said Bettie.

"Don't worry," said Ioreth. "My family will put them back together again. Waste not, want not."

Bettie helped Ioreth back onto his feet. His legs trembled under him, and the whole front of his clothes was soaked in blood. Bettie steered him toward the front door, and Ioreth gritted his teeth so he wouldn't make any noise. He didn't want her to know she was hurting him.

*　　*　　*

Once they were inside the main hallway, Bettie looked quickly around her. Any other time she would have taken a moment to admire all the valuable things out on open display and calculate the best way of liberating a few for herself, but all she cared about now was finding help for Ioreth. She raised her voice, calling out his name, but no one answered. Her voice echoed on the quiet, then died away. She looked at Ioreth.

"Where is everyone?"

"Most of the family went to war," said Ioreth. He had to fight to focus his drifting thoughts. He was feeling increasingly numb and distant, and part of him wondered if he ought to be worried about that. He realised Bettie was waiting for him to continue. "There are only a few of us left here. The old, the young, and the sick. Locked up in the Redoubt, the Drood equivalent of a panic room. You couldn't get past that door with a tactical nuke. But we can't just stand around, Bettie; the Hall's internal defences will start kicking in soon."

"More defences?" asked Bettie, glaring around her. "Like the scare-crows?"

"No," said Ioreth. "Much worse than the scarecrows." His voice faded away. His eyes had almost closed. He forced himself awake again. "Get me to the Old Library, Bettie."

"You need a doctor!"

"All gone, with the army," said Ioreth. "And I don't think they could have helped with this anyway. I want William. The Librarian knows things that no one else knows."

"Where do I find him?" said Bettie. "Where is this Old Library?"

. It took Ioreth a while, but he finally made her understand about the painting that wasn't a painting but a door. Bettie locked onto it with her teleport, and just like that they were inside the Library. Ioreth smiled at the familiar setting, with its warm and comforting lighting.

"Home . . ." he said.

"I don't see anyone!" said Bettie. She looked at Ioreth, but his eyes had closed. She was having to support most of his weight now, and the colour in his face was really bad. She raised her voice. "William! Librarian! I have Ioreth with me! He's hurt! He needs you!"

The Librarian emerged from the stacks, took one look at Ioreth, and hurried forward. He helped Bettie lower Ioreth onto a nearby chair and looked him over quickly. Ioreth opened his eyes and smiled at the Librarian. William did his best to smile reassuringly back. He turned to Bettie, and his eyes were dangerously cold.

"Who did this to him?"

"He was stabbed with a cursed sword," said Bettie. "An Infernal Device."

William flinched. "Damned things."

"Told you," Ioreth said proudly to Bettie. "The Librarian knows everything. William, this is Bettie Divine."

William glanced at the horns on her forehead, then smiled at Bettie. "About time he brought a girl-friend home to meet the family."

"Don't you have one of those medical blob things?" said Bettie. "I thought they were standard issue for Droods?"

"They wouldn't help," said William. "Not with a wound made by an Infernal Device. Help me get him on his feet again, Bettie."

Between the two of them, they half led and half carried Ioreth deeper into the stacks, until they reached the Librarian's personal area. They laid Ioreth down on William's cot, and he sighed happily at being off his feet at last. William put a blanket over him, then found a cloth, so he and Bettie could wipe Ioreth's blood off their hands.

"How did you get past the scarecrows?" said William.

"I'm half demon," said Bettie.

"Isn't she lovely?" said Ioreth, not opening his eyes.

"Get some rest, Ioreth," said William. "Conserve your strength while I work out what to do." He looked at the endless stacks of books, thinking hard. "I need books on healing magical wounds, and everything we have on the Infernal Devices. And I want them right now!"

His voice crackled with authority, and a whole bunch of books jumped off their shelves and flew through the air to hover around him. William grabbed the nearest and slammed it down on a reading-stand. He leafed quickly through the massive leather-bound volume, while the other books waited patiently. He couldn't find anything he needed so he threw the book to the floor and grabbed the next. He searched through one book after another, and discarded volumes piled up on the floor around him.

"If you're part demon, you must be magical," he said to Bettie, not looking up. "Can't you do anything to help him?"

"It's not in my nature," she said miserably. "I never wanted to help anyone before . . . He told me to bring him here! He said you could help him!"

William threw a book away with extra force and reached out for another. "I'm trying!"

An alarm-bell rang: a harsh and strident sound. Bettie looked quickly around her. William didn't look up from his book. Ioreth didn't open his eyes.

"What is that?" said Bettie.

"Drood Hall has been invaded," said William. "Don't worry. The Hall can look after itself."

Hadleigh, Larry, and Tommy Oblivion appeared outside Drood Hall. The Detective Inspectre, the dead detective, and the existential private eye. (Who specialised in cases that might or might not have actually happened.) Tommy had limp hair, a horsey face with a toothy smile, and long-fingered hands he liked to flap around while he was talking. A studiedly effete young fellow, in brightly coloured New Romantic silks, Tommy was far more dangerous than he looked. He was an Oblivion Brother, after all.

"Why do I have to be here?" he said peevishly. "You're the ones built for fighting; I just reason with people."

"You're here because we've tried everything else against the Droods," said Hadleigh.

"And because we're desperate," said Larry.

Tommy sniffed loudly. "Typical."

They looked at the scattered remains of the scarecrows. Some of the hands were crawling around like oversized spiders.

"What the hell happened here?" said Larry.

"Someone got here before us," said Hadleigh. "And made our job that little bit easier. One less defence for us to get past. Now, Tommy . . . Tommy!"

"What?" said Tommy, staring raptly at the front of Drood Hall. "Look at the size of this place! Isn't it magnificent?"

"Yes," said Hadleigh. "And we're here to seize it on behalf of the Nightside."

Tommy turned to look at him, and not in a good way. "You really think we can do that?"

"With the power the Dark Academie put in Larry, and the three of us working together . . . Maybe," said Hadleigh.

Tommy looked dubiously at Larry. "I don't know what they did to you, Lar, but you really don't look good. Even for a dead man."

"We can do this," said Larry.

"Of course we can!" Tommy said proudly. "The Oblivion Brothers, together again for the first time!"

Larry winced. "Must you?"

"Almost certainly," said Tommy. "What's the matter with you? I mean, yes, you've been grim and depressed and downright grumpy ever since you were murdered by your own partner and brought back from the dead as a zombie, though you don't need to eat brains, so I can't help feeling you dodged a bullet there, but . . ."

"Breathe, Tommy," said Hadleigh.

"But you've never been this bad!"

"I took him with me, to see where I work," said Hadleigh.

"You took him down to the Deep School?" said Tommy. "But that's not fair! You know I've always wanted to see that!"

"No, you don't," said Larry. "Trust me. There's nothing there you'd want to see."

"You wouldn't have survived the trip, Tommy," said Hadleigh.

"Larry did!"

"No," said Larry. "I didn't."

"If we could please get a move on," said Hadleigh. "Drood Hall isn't going to conquer itself."

They studied the huge expanse of the Hall, with its towering walls and hundreds of windows. There were no lights on anywhere. Nothing to show anyone was home.

"How many Droods do you think are in there?" Tommy said finally.

"Not many," said Larry. "According to our informants, most of the family is out in the streets. Killing people for the sin of not being Droods."

Tommy frowned. "Did something happen to them? They're not usually like that."

"It'll just be a few really old people, looking after the children," said Hadleigh. "We can handle them."

"They're still Droods," said Larry. "Which means they'll have armour. And they won't surrender."

"Then we'll just have to play hardball," said Hadleigh.

Tommy stirred uncomfortably. "Are you talking about killing them? Even the children?"

"Hopefully, a strong enough show of force will be enough to help them see reason," said Hadleigh. "If not, we've got you to help persuade them to see our side of things."

"If I'm your secret weapon, we're in real trouble," said Tommy. "I'm not hurting children!"

"Even if they're in armour and trying to kill you?" said Larry.

Tommy scowled. "There has to be another way."

"The Droods have already killed hundreds of people in the Nightside!" said Larry. "Who knows how many by now."

"We'll do what we have to, Tommy," said Hadleigh. "Hopefully, with the power the Dark Academie gave Larry . . ."

"What power?" said Tommy.

"The Black Fire," said Hadleigh.

"It burns . . ." said Larry, not looking at anything.

Hadleigh strode forward into the Hall, and the others followed him in. They stopped just inside the great entrance-hall, awed despite themselves by the sheer scale of the place, and its opulence. Tommy oohed and aahed as he pointed out valuable paintings and statues that should have been in museums. He almost went into ecstasies over the antique furniture. Hadleigh studied the lay-out, and looked around for guards or protections. Larry got out his elven wand.

"This should give us the advantage . . ."

And then he stopped and looked at the wand. He shook it a few times.

"What's wrong?" said Tommy.

"It's not working," said Larry. "I just tried it, to make sure I could stop Time inside Drood Hall, and nothing happened."

"Wait just a minute!" said Tommy. "You tested it on us?"

"There was no one else here," said Larry. "The point is, I was relying on the wand to freeze the Droods in place, so we wouldn't have to fight them. So I wouldn't have to use the Black Fire."

"The Hall's defences must have shut the wand down," said Hadleigh. "I can feel them churning on the air around us. The only reason they haven't killed all three of us is that they're confused by our various natures. You're dead, Tommy's existential, and I . . ."

"Yes," said Tommy. "What are you, exactly?"

"Complicated," said Hadleigh. "Let's get moving."

"Fine," said Tommy. "Any idea where we should go? It's a hell of a big place."

"You're not going anywhere," said a calm, steady voice.

The Oblivion Brothers moved quickly to stand together and looked down the hallway to find an old man and a young man staring back at them. The old man had to be in his late seventies, wearing a battered dressing-gown and carpet slippers. The young man was barely into his twenties, wearing a Black Sabbath T-shirt, faded jeans, and sneakers. He was clearly not well. His face was flushed with a fever, and he was trembling all over just from the strain of standing upright.

Tommy turned to Hadleigh. "Are they Droods? They don't look very scary."

"Of course they're Droods," said Larry. "Can't you See their torcs?"

Tommy looked closely. "No."

"The dead see many things that are hidden from the living," said Hadleigh.

Tommy glared at him. "Can you See them?"

"Of course," said Hadleigh. "I'm the Detective Inspectre."

"I'm Maurice," said the old man, his calm voice breaking across theirs. "I used to work on the accounting side before I retired. And this is David, from Operations. He's not well, which is why he didn't get to go with the others."

"I'm still a Drood!" David said loudly. "And I've still got my armour! What are you people doing here, inside our home?"

"Are you the only guards?" said Hadleigh.

"We're just the first to get here," said Maurice. "More are on their way."

"I was worried I was going to miss out on the action," said David. "But now the Nightside has sent people into the Hall, just so I can have the fun of throwing them out!"

"Cocky, isn't he?" said Tommy.

"He's a Drood," said Larry.

"There doesn't need to be any unpleasantness," said Maurice, looking severely at David. "All these gentlemen have to do is turn around and leave, and we can all pretend they were never here. Which is probably best for everyone."

"That's not going to happen," said Hadleigh. "Your family have brought war to the Nightside. Did you really think it wouldn't come home to haunt you? We're here to take control of Drood Hall. Stand down, and you won't be hurt."

"No one speaks like that to a Drood," said David. His eyes were over-bright from the fever, and his hands were shaking, but his voice was steady.

"You shouldn't have brought your home into the Nightside," said Hadleigh. "That made it vulnerable. And now it's ours. Along with any useful weapons or devices you might have that we can use to put a stop to what your family is doing."

"Really not going to happen," said Maurice.

"Who the hell are you people?" said David.

"The Oblivion Brothers!" Tommy said proudly.

Maurice and David looked at each other.

"You've heard of us!" said Tommy.

"Run," David said to Maurice. "You can't fight these people. Have the others lock down the Armoury and the Old Library, then hole up inside the Redoubt. Let these bastards wander around the Hall, looking for something to steal. We can wait them out."

"I can't leave you here, on your own," said Maurice. "You're in no condition to fight monsters like these."

"Neither are you," said David. "But I can slow them down, buy you some time. Go on, get out of here. Before I come to my senses. Anything, for the family."

Maurice nodded jerkily and squeezed David's shoulder once. And then he armoured, turned, and sprinted down the long hallway at incredible speed. In just a few moments he was lost to sight. Tommy stepped forward and smiled at David.

"Come," he said, smiling. "Let us reason together."

"Let's not," said David.

He armoured up, and golden strange matter covered him from head to toe in a moment. Tommy scowled and looked at his brothers.

"I can't reach him through that stuff. It's unnatural. It's doing something to my mind. Or his."

"Then we do this the hard way," said Hadleigh.

David surged forward, inhumanly fast and strong in his armour despite his illness. Black flames burst up around Larry. Fires dark and deep as midnight, and so fiercely hot Tommy and Hadleigh flinched back from them. The floor-boards under Larry's feet scorched and charred, but though the Black Fire burned hot enough to burn the world, it didn't touch the man who carried it. Larry thrust out a hand, and the black flames shot forward to engulf David from head to toe. The midnight fire hit his armour so hard it cracked and broke open, shattered by a force greater than it could stand. The golden strange matter melted and ran away, and David burned alive. He didn't even have time to scream. His body crashed to the floor, already blackening and curling up as the flames consumed it. Larry lowered his hand, and the Black Fire shut off. A few crackling flames still burned where the floor-boards had caught alight around the body. Smoke rose up, to curl lazily on the air.

Tommy looked at his brother.

"Don't look at me like that," said Larry. "Like I'm the monster. You haven't seen what the Droods have been doing."

"No," said Tommy. "But I saw what you did. And I saw that you didn't care." He turned to Hadleigh. "What did they do to him in the Deep School?"

"He asked for power, and they gave it to him," said Hadleigh.

Tommy looked back at the body. "We just killed a Drood in cold blood. They'll never forgive us for this. They'll never stop coming after us."

"Then we'd better take control of the Hall," said Hadleigh. "That will give us all the bargaining power we need."

"I never thought it would be so easy to kill a Drood," said Larry.

Tommy looked at him again. "You don't sound at all well, Larry."

"I'm dead," said Larry. "And the Black Fire is burning me up inside. Just like the Drood. So let's do this while we still can." He pointed down the Hall. "We need to go this way."

"How can you be so sure?" said Tommy. "Don't tell me; the dead see many things."

"I didn't see what the Black Fire would do to me," said Larry. "Or what it would make me do."

"You asked for it," said Hadleigh.

"Yes," said Larry. "I did, didn't I?"

He led the way deeper into the Hall, and the others followed.

In the Old Library, William had found a book of healing spells for magical wounds. He ran through one chant after another until his voice grew hoarse, but none of them worked. Ioreth's wound refused to heal. Fortunately, Ioreth was so out of it by now, he didn't realise what was happening. William finally threw the book away and went back to a volume dealing with Infernal Devices. Bettie sat beside the cot, holding Ioreth's hand. She wasn't even sure he could feel it.

"I think I've identified the sword in question," said William. "It's called Wulfsbane. It has the power to corrupt its owners, body and soul. Any wound the sword makes will rot till the body dies. Nothing can stop the process once it's begun. The sword has travelled through many worlds for many years, and isn't as powerful as it once was. But it's still strong enough to cut through Drood armour. Ioreth's torc is fighting the corruption, or he'd be dead by now; but it can't save him. And neither can I."

"He can't die!" said Bettie. "I only just found him. He said if I got him here, you could help him!"

William closed his book and came over to crouch beside the cot. He said Ioreth's name several times until finally Ioreth opened his eyes.

"I need you to put on your armour, Ioreth," said William. "That should help keep you stable. For a while."

"It's hard to concentrate," said Ioreth. His voice was little more than a whisper.

"I know," said William. "But you have to try, boy."

"Do it for me," said Bettie. "Please, sweetie . . ."

Ioreth smiled. "Anything, for you."

He frowned, slowly mouthing the activating Words, and the armour crept out of his torc, unnaturally slow. It took awhile, but eventually the strange matter covered him completely, sealing him in. A golden statue, lying unmoving on the cot. Like a carving on a tomb. Bettie couldn't even hold his hand any more. She rose to her feet, and William got slowly to his.

"He is going to die, isn't he?" said Bettie. "All the books in this Library, all the knowledge in the world, and you can't save him."

"I still have more books to check," said William. "I won't stop trying. I'll never stop trying."

"Yes, you will," said Bettie, fighting to keep her voice steady. "Because eventually, there'll be no point."

"Don't cry," said William, helplessly.

"What else is there?" said Bettie, turning her head away.

Maurice returned with over twenty Droods in their armour, everyone who could still fight. They could have been young or old behind their faceless golden masks. It didn't matter. Their armour made them strong. They could have remained safe inside the Redoubt, but they were Droods, and they were needed, so they locked the door on everyone else and came to face the enemy. They saw the Oblivion Brothers at the end of the corridor and started towards them.

"We can't go easy on them," said Larry. "They must know by now that we've killed a Drood. They'll tear us to pieces."

"Please," said Tommy. "Let me try. I'm sure I can persuade them to stand down. Isn't that why you brought me, because I can talk anyone into anything?"

"Go ahead," said Hadleigh. "Try."

He didn't look at Larry, to tell him to be ready. He didn't have to. Tommy strode down the corridor to meet the on-coming Droods, trying hard to look like a man without a care in the world because he just knew things would work out for everyone.

"Come," he said. "Let us reason together."

He gave it his best shot. He tried to persuade the Droods that they had no quarrel with the Oblivion Brothers. That there would be no shame in surrendering Drood Hall to the Nightside because of all the lives that would save. When that didn't work, he tried to persuade them they weren't really in Drood Hall. He used the full force of his existential nature to confuse them as to whether they were in their armour or out of it, and even whether they were really Droods at all. None of it worked. In their armour, in the Hall, the Droods were strong and certain.

Hadleigh grabbed hold of Tommy's shoulder and pulled him back out of the way, and Larry hit the Droods with Black Fire. The terrible flames surged forward, turning the whole corridor into a blast-furnace, in which Drood armour melted and all the Droods inside burned. When Larry finally stopped, and pulled the Black Fire back into him, all that remained were cracked and blackened bones. Steam rose thickly on the superheated air. The floor and both walls were scorched and blackened from the intense heat, for as far as the eye could see. Tommy and Hadleigh moved over to join Larry. Their faces and hands smarted from exposure to the scorching air. Larry looked cold as death, cold as what comes after death. Tommy looked at him as if he were a stranger.

"What did they do to you in the Dark Academie?"

"They gave me a gift," said Larry. "Something only a dead man could carry. So I could do what needed doing."

"The Black Fire is burning away your Humanity," said Tommy. "It's destroying you!"

"I died years ago, little brother. I'm looking forward to lying down, at last." He smiled briefly at Tommy. "Look on the bright side. At least you won't have to pay for a cremation."

Tommy looked at the blackened bones, and the scorched corridor, and the fires still burning. "The Droods will never forgive us for this."

"Then we'd better make sure we win, hadn't we?" said Larry.

"We should have kept a few alive," said Hadleigh, "to tell us how to find the things that matter. It's a big place."

"The Drood mentioned an Armoury," said Larry. "What better place to look for weapons?"

"Why would Droods need weapons?" said Tommy. "When they already have that marvellous armour?"

"Because there's a limit to the destruction one man can do," said Larry. "For bigger things, you need bigger weapons. Like the Armageddon Codex."

"Okay . . ." said Tommy. "That does not sound like something we should be messing with."

"The Codex contains the Forbidden Weapons," said Hadleigh. "Powerful enough to save reality from any threat. Exactly what we need to persuade the Droods to surrender."

"You stand right where you are," said Tommy. "I am not going anywhere near something called Forbidden Weapons till I know a lot more about them."

"He has a point," said Larry. "There are bound to be all kinds of booby-traps in place, to protect the Codex from outsiders. We need more information . . . The Drood also mentioned a library. I think we need to go there first and do some research."

He looked at Hadleigh, who shrugged. "I suppose there could be all kinds of interesting things in a Drood library. How are we supposed to find it?"

Larry looked around, with eyes that blazed so fiercely they looked like they could burn through walls. "I can see it, but not how to get to it. There's some kind of barrier . . ."

Hadleigh turned to Tommy. "Give me your hand."

Tommy raised an eyebrow. "I didn't know you cared."

"Shut up and give me your hand."

Hadleigh and Tommy Oblivion clasped hands. Hadleigh focused his power through Tommy's uncertainty principle, then reached out to take Larry's hand and draw on his power. Together they found the painting that was not a painting, and just like that, they were standing inside the Old Library.

William and Bettie looked around, startled, as the three men materialised.

"Who the hell are you?" said William. "What are you doing here? Get out of my Library!"

"Easy, William," Bettie said quickly. "I know them. Hadleigh, Larry, and Tommy. The Oblivion Brothers."

"Oh . . . them," said William. He fixed Hadleigh with a heavy scowl. "Will you please tell the Deep School to stop sending me invitations. I have no interest in being a Guest Lecturer at the Dark Academie. Now, what do you want? I'm busy."

"We want information," said Hadleigh.

"Tough," said William. "This isn't a lending Library."

"Then we'll just have to take what we need," said Larry.

"Unless you just happen to feel like telling us where we can find a book that will tell us all we need to know about the Forbidden Weapons of the

Armageddon Codex," said Tommy, smiling winningly. "Come, let us reason together."

William smiled unpleasantly. "I'm married to a telepath, you idiot. She put so many protections in my head, God himself couldn't get through. Now get the hell out of here. This is my place, and I don't have to be reasonable."

Tommy turned to Hadleigh. "He's right. I can't get to him. And the girl is a demon."

"Part demon!" said Bettie.

"Either way, the inside of her head is a real mess."

"What do you want with the Forbidden Weapons?" said William. "They're only to be used when reality itself is under threat."

"Isn't it?" said Larry. "What your family is doing in the Nightside threatens everything."

"You can't be allowed access to the Forbidden Weapons," William said flatly. "You're not worthy of them."

"And you think you are?" said Larry. "Have you seen what your family is doing in the Nightside? The blood and the slaughter?"

"But we'll always be more worthy than you," said Ioreth. He rose to his feet in one smooth motion, his armour gleaming in the warm Library light. He looked at Bettie. "I had a bad dream, then woke up to find it was real. Get behind me, love. William, go to the Armoury. Protect the Lion's Jaws. I'll deal with the Oblivion Brothers."

"No, sweetie!" said Bettie. "They'll kill you!"

"I'm dying anyway," said Ioreth.

"No one is going anywhere," said Hadleigh.

"That's what you think," said William. "Pook!"

Time slowed and stopped, and a giant white humanoid rabbit emerged from the stacks, wearing a stylish dinner jacket with the Playboy logo on the breast. He fixed William with fierce pink eyes.

"I told you, I'm not getting involved in this. You people are no fun any more."

"This isn't for the family; it's for me," said William. "I need one last favour."

The Pook studied him thoughtfully. "It would be the last."

"Take me to the Lion's Jaws," said William.

The Pook smiled. "Why not?"

And just like that, William and the Pook were standing before the statue of a lion's head in the Armoury, the only entrance to the Armageddon Codex. Twenty feet tall and almost as wide, carved from dark blue-veined stone, the lion's head came complete with mane and was perfect in every detail. Its eyes seemed to gleam dangerously, and the open jaws seemed to roar. The whole thing looked ready to pounce on anyone dumb enough to upset it.

"And that's it," said the Pook. "Hello, William, I must be going."

"Wait. Why did you follow me here, from the insane asylum?" said William.

"Because you had such an interesting mind," said the Pook. "Till you started getting sane again. And because you needed me. You don't need me any more, William; you've got Ammonia now. It's time I was going."

"Thank you," said William. "For all your help. For your company, in the bad times. Tell me one last thing. Are you really what I think you are?"

The Pook grinned. "I'll never tell."

He disappeared down a rabbit-hole that closed after him, and was gone.

Back in the Old Library, it was as though the Librarian had just vanished. Ioreth took advantage of the Oblivion Brothers' surprise to pick up one of the heavy wooden stacks and throw it at Hadleigh. The weight smashed him to the floor and held him there. And while Hadleigh struggled with that, Ioreth charged Larry and Tommy. Driven on by the armour's strength and speed, even though he had none of his own. Bettie went full demon, all teeth and claws. Larry hit Ioreth with the Black Fire, but even as his armour cracked and burst apart, Ioreth kept pressing forward. He grew a golden sword from one hand, and swung it in a short vicious arc. He cut off Larry's head, and the midnight flames snapped off. Larry's head fell to the floor and rolled away, the mouth still working soundlessly. The headless body stumbled after it, arms outstretched.

Bettie kicked Tommy so hard in the groin that his voice disappeared completely. He dropped to the floor, and curled into a ball around his pain. Bettie went after Larry's headless body and tore it to pieces with her demonic strength. And then she stamped on the head until it was just a crushed and broken mess.

Ioreth turned slowly, in what was left of his melting armour, and went after Tommy; but he couldn't seem to find him. Even in the midst of his pain, Tommy's nature still protected him. As Ioreth stumbled blindly around, Tommy forced himself up onto his feet and produced a small, glowing dagger. Just a little something, for emergencies. He moved in close, and Ioreth couldn't even see him coming. But Bettie could, with her demon's eyes. She snatched up Larry's head and threw it at Tommy with all her strength. It slammed into the back of Tommy's head, destroying his concentration. Ioreth turned around, saw that Tommy was right on top of him, and stabbed him through the heart with his sword. Tommy fell to the floor, a last look of surprise on his face.

Ioreth and Bettie turned to face Hadleigh, as he finally threw the heavy wooden stack off him and rose to his feet. He wasn't injured. Bettie snarled, and threw herself at him. Hadleigh reached out and touched her once, and she was dead before she hit the floor. Because she was just a demon girl reporter, and he was the Detective Inspectre. Ioreth made a low, wounded sound, stumbled forward, and sank to his knees beside Bettie. He armoured down and took her in his arms, rocking her slowly like a sleeping child. He didn't cry. He didn't have any tears left in him. He looked up at Hadleigh.

"Go on. Kill me. You know you want to."

"You're already dying," said Hadleigh. "I can see the rot inside you. But there's still some mercy left in me. So, go be with your demon girl-friend."

He laid his hand on Ioreth's head. The last of Ioreth's life went out of him, and he slumped to the floor, to lie beside his beloved. Hadleigh looked at them, then at his dead brothers.

"We should never have come here. Nothing good ever comes of taking on the Droods. But . . . I had to try. Be seeing you."

He looked at the spot where the Librarian disappeared, found the way to where he'd gone, and went after him.

Hadleigh appeared standing before the Lion's Jaws, right next to William, who didn't even jump, as though he'd been expecting him.

"Where are your brothers?" said William.

"Dead," said Hadleigh. "Your friends killed them. And I killed your friends."

"They weren't friends; they were family," said William. "At least Ioreth got a chance to be the kind of Drood he thought he ought to be. While I, it seems, am now the only Drood left to stand between you and what you want." He gestured at the Lion's Jaws. "Beyond this point lie the Forbidden Weapons. Oath Breaker and Time Hammer, Sunwrack and Winter's Sorrow. You have no idea how powerful they are. Any one of them could blow up worlds or put out suns. It doesn't matter. You can't have them. Only a Drood can open the Jaws. I could open them. I could take out the Forbidden Weapons and go walking in the Nightside and kill every living thing I saw. And you have no idea how much I want to do that.

"But I won't. Because I know my duty. To protect Humanity, not destroy it. Some of my family may have forgotten that, for the moment, but I have not. And besides, Ioreth wouldn't want me to do it."

"You Droods do love to talk," said Hadleigh. "I can open the Jaws with a touch. You have no idea what my time in the Dark Academie did to me. I am the Detective Inspectre, with responsibility for judging crimes against reality."

"I am a Drood," said William. "I may have forgotten much of who and what I used to be, but I never forgot that."

"I am the guardian of this world!" said Hadleigh. "I have jurisdiction here!"

"What does that mean?" said William.

"It means I can do anything I decide is necessary," said Hadleigh.

"Who decided that?" said William.

"It was decided where all the things that matter are decided," said Hadleigh. "In the Courts of the Holy, on the Shimmering Plains. I am powerful because what I do in Heaven's sight has Heaven's strength."

"But are you sure you're still on the side of the angels?" said William. "After everything you've done, and everything you want to do? If you're so very powerful, why did you need to bring your brothers with you? Why did you need Larry to take on the Black Fire? You have strayed from your path, Hadleigh, and you know it. You are not what you were."

"Enough talking," said Hadleigh.

"More than enough," said William.

He put on his armour, grew a sword from his hand, and went to meet Hadleigh. The Detective Inspectre thrust out a hand and William stopped dead, as though he'd crashed into an invisible wall. And then he smashed it with one blow of his arm and moved forward again. Hadleigh surged forward and punched William in the chest. The Librarian slammed to a halt again. Slow ripples moved across the surface of his armour, which sounded like a struck gong. But the ripples quickly died away. Hadleigh grabbed hold of William's shoulders with his killing hands.

"Die, damn you! Why won't you die?"

"Because I was blessed by a rabbit," said William.

He thrust his sword all the way through Hadleigh's body. The golden blade punched out his back in a flurry of blood. Hadleigh cried out briefly, as much in surprise as anything. William jerked his blade back, and Hadleigh fell to his knees. He looked down at the blood soaking the front of his coat.

"That's not possible . . ."

And then he fell forward and died. William looked at the bloody sword in his hand, and drew it back into his hand. It left a thick smear of blood on the glove. He looked down at Hadleigh's body.

"You lost your way. I know what that feels like."

He looked at the Lion's Jaws.

"I should destroy you. Smash you to rubble, so no one could ever threaten the world with the Forbidden Weapons. But I won't. Because there's always a chance my family might need you someday, to save the world. After they come to their senses again."

Ammonia's voice rang suddenly inside his head. "William? Are you all right? I had this dream about a white rabbit, and when I woke up I had this terrible feeling you were in danger. What's happening?"

"I'm fine," said William. "The Hall still stands."

CHAPTER ELEVEN

Things Worth Defending

S tuck in the middle of the Nightside and going nowhere fast, the Droods split into several smaller groups, to force the resisting Nightsiders to do the same. The Sarjeant-at-Arms placed his most trusted people in charge, people he thought he could depend on to follow his methods. The Matriarch wasn't a part of those decisions. She had moved away to be on her own, to think about tactics and losses and why everything had gone so horribly wrong. Her dream of a bloodless coup had turned into a blood-soaked nightmare. And the more she thought about it, the more she blamed the Nightside. Just being in the long night brought out the worst in everyone. The Matriarch sighed heavily and wished she could blame everything on that. But she was too honest to allow herself such an easy way out.

The Droods set off again, under their new leaders, and because it took time for the Nightsiders to adapt to the new tactics, the Droods made swift progress on several fronts. But it was only as they pressed deeper into the Nightside that they began to comprehend just how much territory the long night covered. The Nightside might be the secret heart of London, but down the centuries it had grown to be much bigger than the city that surrounded it. The boundaries stayed the same, but the space within expanded to contain all the sins and secrets the long night made possible. The Nightside thrived on such paradoxes.

That was why the Sarjeant-at-Arms had taken pains to explain how important it was to seize and control important key locations: places of symbolic significance. Just knowing the Droods held places like Strangefellows, St Jude's, and the Street of the Gods would help convince the Nightsiders that the Droods were in control. He didn't convince everyone, but no one else had any better ideas. Most just wanted to get this unpleasant job over and done with, so they could get the hell out of the long night and go home. Back to sunshine and sanity and wars that made sense. Of all the hard campaigns the family had fought, this one seemed the most lacking in moral clarity. One of the Droods' main strengths had always been the conviction that in any fight, they were always going to be the good guys. But given some of the things they had been forced to do, just to survive in the long night, they weren't so sure of that any more.

It wouldn't stop them fighting, or winning. They were Droods, after all. But a lot of them were wondering what shape the family would be in afterwards. And whether they would still be so ready to say *Anything, for the family.*

Angela Drood led her armoured company toward the ancient church known as St Jude's. She strolled along, head up and shoulders back. She was enjoying herself. As part of the Operations Room team, she didn't normally get to leave Drood Hall and go out into the world. Now she was in the Nightside and facing appalling people on all sides, Angela had discovered in herself unsuspected capacities for extreme violence. It felt good to be able to strike down the bad guys in person instead of spending all her time sitting at a desk, sending other people out to do all the fun stuff. But still, of all the missions the Sarjeant could have sent her on, she wished it hadn't been this one.

The legend of St Jude's had spread far beyond the Nightside. It would probably have been a tourist attraction if not for its fearsome reputation. Supposedly, someone had been turned into a pillar of salt just for taking a selfie inside the church. But Angela had her orders, to take control of St Jude's, and Angela always followed orders. Particularly if there was a chance she would get to beat someone's head in for getting in her way.

She'd been following her special compass for some time and was starting to wonder why it insisted on leading her away from all the more civilised parts of the Nightside. The streets were increasingly empty, the buildings deserted, and there were no traces of resistance anywhere. Almost as though the Nightside didn't think St Jude's needed protecting. Angela marched along, concentrating on all the wonderfully violent things she would do when she got to the church; so the sudden ambush by heavily armed nuns caught her completely by surprise.

They came swarming out of the shadows from all sides at once, surrounding the Droods in a matter of moments. Dozens of nuns, in traditional black robes and starched wimples, carrying all sorts of guns. Angela yelled for her people to stand still and, above all, not start anything. She lowered her armour, smiled encouragingly at the nuns, and looked around for someone in charge.

"Hello? I'm Angela Drood. What's going on here, please?"

A burly figure in billowing robes stepped forward. The face under the wimple was entirely unsmiling.

"I am Sister Josephine. I lead the Salvation Army Sisterhood. The only order of nuns committed enough to tackle the long night on its own terms."

"Nuns with guns?" said Angela.

"First, you have to get people's attention," said Sister Josephine. "We're all about saving sinners, but we have to stay alive long enough to do it."

"Why are you stopping us?" asked Angela, very politely. "I would have thought you of all people would support our mission to bring the Nightside under control and put an end to all the evils here."

"The Salvation Army Sisterhood exists to save sinners, not slaughter them," said Sister Josephine. "Except under extreme conditions. We've heard about what you've been doing."

"Only what's necessary!" said Angela.

"You murdered the rogue vicar Tamsin MacReady as she tried to argue for peace," said Sister Josephine. "She wasn't one of us, but we admired her courage and her faith."

"I don't know what happened there," Angela said carefully. "I wasn't at the Mammon Emporium. But I'm sure there was a good reason . . ."

"Sinners always have excuses," said Sister Josephine. "You will make a fine example, to show your family there is a line which must never be crossed." She stepped back and looked at the other nuns. "Kill them."

"No!" said Angela.

The nuns opened fire. Blessed and cursed bullets tore through Drood armour, punching through golden chests and gleaming face masks, and the Droods crashed to the ground like toppled statues. Until only Angela was left. She stood trembling, wide-eyed and trying not to cry, in the middle of the carnage. She couldn't believe it had all happened so quickly. She hadn't even had time to put on her armour. She jumped, startled, as Sister Josephine spoke to her. The nun was holding up a withered human hand whose fingers had been made into candles. Blue flames blossomed from the fingertips.

"A Hand of Glory," said Sister Josephine. "Made from the severed hand of a martyred Saint. Powerful enough to hold even a Drood in place."

Angela tried to move and found she couldn't. She whimpered for a moment, then reminded herself she was still a Drood, and made herself face the nuns steadily.

"I don't understand," she said. "Do you want me to take a message to my family? Is that it?"

"You will be the message," said Sister Josephine. "When they see what we have done to you, they will know to stop their excesses."

"But I didn't kill the vicar!" said Angela. "I'm not responsible for her death! Please, don't hurt me. I'm a good Christian."

"Then you should be ashamed of what you've done," said Sister Josephine. "You might not have killed Tamsin MacReady, but how many others died at your hand? People who knew they had no hope of defending themselves against your armour but fought anyway, to defend their homes?"

"Please," said Angela. "I'm sorry!"

"Well," said Sister Josephine. "That's a good start."

She spoke a Word, and the Hand of Glory clenched like a fist and crushed the life out of Angela Drood. All her bones broke at the same moment, and blood spurted thickly. Sister Josephine looked at the human wreckage hanging on the air before her, and said another Word. The body fell to the ground, to lie with the others, and Sister Josephine said a prayer over them. Then she put the Hand of Glory away and led her sisters out into the Nightside, to look for more Droods.

The main body of Droods was still under the command of the Sarjeant-at-Arms. He was heading for Strangefellows when word reached him of what had happened to Angela and her people. He quickly changed direction and headed for St Jude's. Because no one killed Droods and got away with it. He made sure his people knew exactly what had happened, of what the Nightside was capable of if you showed weakness even for a moment.

They found the dead Droods lying just where the informants said they'd be. Bullet-ridden golden bodies left piled together, without respect or dignity. The Sarjeant armoured down and knelt beside Angela's crushed and broken body. He knew her: one of Howard's people, from Operations. He'd put her in charge of the group despite her youth and inexperience because he admired her enthusiasm. He should have known better. The Nightside was an unforgiving place to learn how to be a soldier.

He got to his feet and used one of his security Words to send the dead Droods' armour back into their torcs. Then he had his people absorb the torcs into their own armour. After that was done, the Sarjeant dropped molecular-acid bombs on the bodies, destroying them right down to their DNA, so that absolutely nothing was left behind to betray Drood secrets to the enemy. Standard procedure for Droods who fell in the field. There would be a funeral in their names on the Drood grounds, when the war was over.

"This is why you can never show mercy," the Sarjeant said to his people. "Now move on."

But the Droods were looking past him, staring down the street. The Sarjeant turned and found himself facing two very familiar figures: Julien Advent and Jessica Sorrow the Unbeliever. The Sarjeant looked back at his people.

"Hold your ground. Yes, I know who she is; now hold your damned ground!"

Down the street, Julien turned to Jessica.

"I didn't think there'd be so many of them."

"Numbers don't matter," said Jessica.

"I came here hoping to negotiate," said Julien. "To make some kind of deal, to save St Jude's, but . . ."

"The Sarjeant-at-Arms will not negotiate," said Jessica. "And he will not be turned away from what he sees as his duty. You should leave now, Julien. Leave this to me."

"Jessica . . ."

"I will show the Droods the full force of my Unbelief," she said calmly. "But since I have never tried it on Drood armour, there's always a chance you could be hurt. So off you go, Julien. I believe I'm about to be very busy."

Julien looked at her, then at the Droods. He turned away and hurried down the street, and didn't stop until he was around the corner and half-way down the next. Because one way or another, something really bad was about to happen. He would have liked to see it, after what the Droods had done at the Hawk's Wind, but it was never safe to be around Jessica when she really cut loose. The whole street could disappear.

Jessica walked unhurriedly forward to confront the Droods. She was quietly surprised they weren't already running. The Sarjeant summoned a gun into his hand and shot her. Jessica didn't believe the bullet would hit her, and it disappeared in mid-flight. She smiled easily at the Sarjeant and let loose her Unbelief on all the Droods standing before her. Her power shot down the street like a tidal wave, an unrelenting power stronger than the building-blocks of reality itself. Everything apart from the ground and the walls disappeared, dismissed by her disbelief. And then it hit the gleaming golden armour, rebounded and flew back and hit Jessica; and just like that, she was gone.

The universe didn't believe in her any more.

The Droods whooped and cheered. The Sarjeant let them get it out of their system, then raised his voice.

"Move out."

Julien heard the cheering, and the heavy tramp of armoured feet coming his way, and set off down the street. He had to get to St Jude's and warn them what was coming. And say a quiet prayer for a fallen friend. He didn't have far to go when his phone rang. He was tempted to just shut it off, but very few people had his number, and none of them would use it unless it was important. He answered the phone without slow-ing down.

"What?"

"This is Brilliant Chang, Julien. You need to get to the Hospice of the Blessed Saint Margaret right now. They need you."

"I have to get to St Jude's," said Julien. "The Sarjeant-at-Arms is leading his Droods there."

"A hospital full of wounded needs you more. St Jude's can take care of itself."

"Why can't you help the hospital?" said Julien.

"Because I'm busy," said Brilliant. And the phone went dead.

Julien sighed heavily, put away his phone, and changed direction.

Harry Fabulous, the man who could get you anything, for a price, went walking through Uptown. The very best part of the Nightside, Uptown was home to all the most exclusive and expensive night-clubs, where the show never ends and you can dance until your feet bleed. Where parties go on forever, and the piper is never paid. And in some of Uptown's special Members-Only Clubs, there are very private back rooms, where you can find everything that's hot, everything that's cool, and absolutely anything that's bad for you . . . but oh so delicious. There was a time when Uptown had been Harry's stalking ground and second home, making deals and taking chances and always coming out on top. Harry Fabulous had been *the* Go To Guy, and everyone knew it.

The Droods hadn't penetrated this far, but even so, most of the clubs were closed. The owners and club members were off in the wind, keeping their heads down and waiting for the storm to pass. The street was wide open and utterly deserted. Harry had never known the area to be so quiet. It looked cheap and tawdry, without its customary glamour, like a working girl without her war-paint.

He stopped before one particular night-club. Heaven's Doorway had been infamous in its day as the very best place to find pleasures beyond belief. But that wasn't why Harry remembered the club. This was where it had all gone wrong for him. Back when Heaven's Doorway had been the club everyone went to, to get the kind of highs no one else could deliver. Taduka and tanna leaves, Martian red weed, and the Really Deep Fix; and the kind of mushrooms that only grow on supernatural corpses. Now it was just another deserted building. They hadn't even bothered to lock the door, just left it hanging open. The madder music had been stilled, the dance was over, and the party had moved on. But Harry was pretty sure that what he was looking for would still be there, in the back room only a few people knew existed.

He went inside, walking steadily down a corridor full of memories and on into the empty ball-room. The great open space was disturbingly still and silent, the floor scattered with the kind of things people leave behind when they're in a hurry to get away. There was a spattering of dried blood on the dance floor, but that was just business as usual. The ball-room smelled of old smoke and perfume that had gone off, and the need to have a good time no matter what. The atmosphere was dead, the illusion shattered. Harry thought it was like looking at a corpse's face before the mortician slapped on the make-up.

He strode quickly across the ball-room, his footsteps loud and impatient in the quiet, shouldering aside the ghosts of good times past, and made his way out the back and up the narrow stairs to the top floor. It was darker there, but then, it always was. He stopped before one particular closed door and took a deep breath to steady himself. The door had no number, no description or warning; you either knew what lay in wait or you had no business being there. Harry stood very still, remembering.

The last time he'd been here, all those years ago, it had been because the room was such a great secret; and he prided himself that no one kept secrets from Harry Fabulous. He made his way up here without telling anyone, or seeking anyone's permission, and just opened the door and strolled in. To find himself facing an angel with broken wings, trapped inside a pentacle with glowing red lines. Just the sight of her took his breath away.

The angel could have been male or female, both or neither, but was really too beautiful for that to matter. Harry chose to think of the angel as female because of the effect she had on him. She looked like a work of art come to life, like a dream walking, like everyone you ever loved that you just knew you weren't worthy of. Locked in a cage and suffering.

Harry took awhile to find his voice, then asked the angel why she was being kept prisoner. She answered him in a voice like liquid gold, like birds of paradise singing, telling him she had been imprisoned because there was a market for angel's blood, wing feathers, and tears. And because there were always those who would pay good money for the chance to have sex with an angel. For the first time in his life, Harry's heart had been touched. He'd asked what he could do to free the angel. And she told him the only way to break the prison was to spill the heart's blood of one of the people who had made it. Harry asked the angel for a name, and she provided one. It was a woman Harry knew, but that didn't stop him.

He tracked the woman down and killed her, then went running back to the angel to tell her she was free. The angel laughed in his face. He'd been conned. She was a Fallen angel, and she had just tricked Harry into murdering a perfectly innocent person. He'd damned his soul to Hell, just to amuse the angel. She was in the pentacle because she chose to be, so she could destroy all those who came to her.

Harry ran away with the angel's laughter still ringing in his ears and never went back. He spent the rest of his life doing penance, while always knowing it could never be enough.

And now here he was, back again. Come to make a deal with the Fallen angel because that was what he did. He opened the door and went in, and she was still sitting in her pentacle of glowing red lines, magnificent as ever. She didn't look in the least surprised to see him, just smiled slowly, and when she spoke, her voice was like a razor blade in an apple, like the pain of a loved one.

"Hello, Harry. I always knew you'd come back to me."

Harry looked at the angel, saying nothing, controlling himself. This would be the most important deal of his life if he could pull it off.

"Why are you still here?" he said finally.

"Why would I want to leave?" said the angel. "As long as I remain, there will always be fools like you to play with."

"But the Droods are on their way," said Harry.

"I know," said the angel. "I've been watching their progress and delighting in the slaughter. There's nothing Hell enjoys more than good people doing bad things for what they think are good reasons. One of them is bound to come here, eventually. I shall enjoy seducing a Drood and teaching them all the ways of corruption."

"I have a better idea," Harry said steadily. "How would you like to kill some of those notoriously worthy and morally inflexible Droods? How would you like to kill a whole bunch of them and teach that family the true meaning of terror?"

The angel looked at him. "Are you tempting me, Harry?"

"Here is my offer," said Harry. "The last deal I'll ever make. I will allow you to possess me, in return for enough strength to fight Droods and strike them down with my bare hands. I need to hurt them, to stop them, but I can't do it on my own."

"I thought you worked for them, Harry?"

"They betrayed me by not being what they claimed," said Harry. "They're just as bad as everyone else. They tricked me, and I will have my revenge. Well, what do you say? Wouldn't you like to leave that pentacle and walk up and down the Nightside in my body? I'm offering to sell you my soul in return for power."

"You're already damned, Harry," said the angel, smiling happily. "You murdered an innocent."

"Yes," said Harry. "I did. But I've spent years doing penance. I could have redeemed myself. Do you want to risk that? I could still go out into the streets and die heroically."

"Enough strength to fight Droods, for the duration of the invasion," said the angel. "Release me, and we have a deal. Dear sweet Harry."

He produced a stoppered phial from inside his coat. Holy water from St Jude's; acquired through several removes, so no one would know it was him. He opened the phial and poured the contents across the glowing red lines, and they vanished as though they'd never been there. The angel rose to her feet, smiled dazzlingly at Harry, and launched herself forward. She dived inside him, like a swimmer plunging into a deep pool. Harry cried out in shock as the Fallen angel took up residence inside him. He hadn't expected Hell to burn so cold. But he also felt strong and powerful enough to do anything . . .

"Better get a move on, Harry," said the voice inside his head. "Do what you can, while you can. The clock is ticking."

Harry turned his back on the room, and walked back down the stairs.

He hurried along Uptown's empty streets, and all the time the angel murmured suggestions of terrible things he could do. Harry closed his mind and his heart to the angel and kept going. He might be possessed, but he was in control. Because he had been careful to drink half the holy water from St Jude's before he went anywhere near the club. The angel could say what she liked, but he would do what he would do.

He went looking for people. The angel wanted him to find Droods, but he didn't listen. Instead, he found a place where the Droods had already passed through, leaving behind buildings on fire, wreckage and rubble, and any number of wounded people. They sat in the street beside the dead and the dying, sobbing and traumatised, unable to help themselves or anyone else. So Harry walked among them and did his best to help.

He did what he could for the wounded and comforted the distressed with words of hope. He dug down through collapsed buildings to rescue people trapped underneath. He cleared wreckage out of the road, so people could leave and ambulances could get through. He worked tirelessly, and through his actions inspired others to do what they could. They dug people out of the wreckage, put out fires, and worked alongside Harry without ever knowing who and what he was. He liked that. He did his good works anonymously, using his new strength to do the things no one else could. And all the time the angel screamed and raged helplessly within him.

Harry smiled to himself and kept working.

But eventually, as the hours wore on, even though Harry's body didn't grow tired, his will did. The angel's voice grew louder and louder, until he could barely hear his own thoughts. He knew that eventually the angel would take control of him and use the strength in his body to do terrible things. So he excused himself to the people around him, saying he needed a break. Everyone nodded understandingly because he had done more than all of them put together.

Harry moved off down a side street, made sure no one was watching, and produced a simple black capsule. Guaranteed to provide a way out, for people who'd had enough of life. He'd been assured it was powerful enough to drop a T Rex in its tracks. Harry dry-swallowed the capsule with only a little difficulty, then sat down in the street and put his back to the wall. Because he didn't want to look undignified, at the end.

"What are you doing?" the angel screamed inside his head.

"Killing myself," Harry said calmly. "Rather than let you hurt anyone. That was always my plan. To use the strength you gave me to help people I'd put in danger because I helped the Droods. And then to deny you any triumph, through one last willing sacrifice. How does it feel to be conned, the way you conned me?"

The Fallen angel burst out of him and was immediately sucked down into Hell, screaming all the way. It couldn't stay inside a dying body, but there was no pentacle to protect it any more. And Hell could be very hard on those who failed it. Harry allowed himself a small smile. It had been a good con, a good last deal to go out on. He hoped he'd finally done enough to atone for what he did.

A new light filled the alley as an angel appeared before him. Not the Fallen kind, this time. She stood before him, winged and shining, glorious and magnificent, smiling benevolently.

"We have met before," she said, in a voice like all the music Harry had ever loved in his youth. "Though you wouldn't know me in this form. I was called Pretty Poison then, but like you, I did penance and found a better way."

"I remember the name," Harry said slowly. "But you've left it a bit late to look me up. I'm dying."

"No, Harry," the angel said kindly. "You're dead. But you mustn't worry. You're not damned; you never were. There is no sin without intent, and you thought you were doing a good thing. The Fallen angel lied to you. It's what they do. And all your years of penance have wiped the slate clean for everything else you did. So I'm here to take you home. Come with me, Harry. To Paradise."

Harry realised he was standing up, facing the angel. He looked back and saw his body sitting slumped against the wall. It looked very small now, without him in it. He turned back to the angel.

"I'm ready."

Sometime later, when people came looking for him, they weren't that surprised to find him dead. Because he had worked so very hard for so long. But they did wonder at the contented smile on his face.

John Taylor and Suzie Shooter were on their way to Strangefellows when John's phone rang. He stopped to answer it. Listened, nodded reluctantly, scowled, and put it away. He chose another direction and strode off. Suzie went with him.

"Brilliant Chang has a mission for us," said John. "He wants us to go to Shadow Deep."

"I'm sort of hoping there's another Shadow Deep that isn't the one I'm thinking of," said Suzie. "Apart from the really nasty prison where the Nightside dumps its most dangerous prisoners."

"No," said John. "That's the one. That's where we're going."

"I've spent most of my life trying to stay out of Shadow Deep," said Suzie. "I'd hate to spoil my record now."

John looked at her. "You must know I would never have let them hold you there. I would have come and got you."

"You would have defied the Authorities, for me?"

"Of course."

"Well," said Suzie. "That's good to know. And I would have come for you, of course."

"Of course," said John. "It should be an interesting visit. I've always wondered if Shadow Deep really is as bad as it's supposed to be."

"You are sure you can get us out again, afterwards?" said Suzie.

"Don't worry. Brilliant Chang's arranged everything."

"Why are we going?" asked Suzie. "Are the Authorities planning to use it as a last hiding-place, where even the Droods wouldn't dare come looking?"

"A nice idea, but no. Brilliant Chang has given us a very special mission. Which I'm not going to tell you about now because if I did, you wouldn't come with me."

"Oh, this can only go well," said Suzie.

Sunk deep beneath the bed-rock of the Nightside, far away from civilisation and half-way to Hell, lies the awful prison known as Shadow Deep. Constructed specifically to hold all the really dangerous prisoners that the Authorities can't kill, for one reason or another. The only way to get down there is through the single official transport circle, maintained and operated by three witches in a small room over a really rough bar, the Jolly Cripple. John found the place easily enough: a shabby hole-in-the-wall establishment in a really down-market neighbourhood. The few people still out and about took one look at John and Suzie and slunk quickly off to hide. Because small predators can always recognise bigger ones.

The door to the Jolly Cripple was locked, so John kicked it in. He strode into the bar with Suzie at his side, only to find the gesture had been wasted on an empty room. The place was deserted, with half-empty glasses still standing around. The occupants must have heard that the Droods were coming. Or that John Taylor and Shotgun Suzie were on their way.

John led the way to the back of the inn, then up the gloomy and decidedly sub-standard stairs to the next floor.

"I suppose the witches will still be here?" said Suzie. "Given that everyone else has run away."

"They'll be here," said John. "Their presence is required, to make sure no one can get in or out of Shadow Deep without official permission. And even the Droods would think twice about messing with these particular witches. They're old school."

"You've been here before," said Suzie.

"Just the once," said John. "Henry brought me, back when he was preparing me to take over from him as Walker. He thought I should know about this in case I ever needed to send somebody down."

He found the right door on the top floor and strode in without knocking. The three witches were waiting for him, striking traditional witchy poses around the great circle marked out on the floor. Three bent-over hags in tattered clothes with hooked noses, clawed hands, and a sprinkling of warts. They cackled loudly as John and Suzie came to a halt before them.

"Knock it off!" said John. "We're not tourists."

One of the witches straightened up. "Well, pardon us for breathing. Someone has to keep up the old traditions. I mean, people expect it of us, darling. We are professionals, after all."

"Why haven't you left?" Suzie said bluntly. "Don't you know that the Droods are on their way?"

The witch sniffed haughtily. "Let them come. We'll send them on their way with a flea in their ear. Or possibly somewhere much worse. We are here because the Higher Powers require it. The Droods would have better luck arguing with the force of gravity. Now, what do you want, darlings?"

"We have been authorised by Brilliant Chang to access Shadow Deep," said John.

"Well, we didn't think you'd come here to admire the ambience," said the witch. "Just show us the proper paper-work, and . . ."

"Papers? We don't need no stinking papers!" Suzie said loudly.

"Right," said John. "I'm Walker. So get on with it."

"No one cares about proper procedure any more," said the witch. She turned to the others. "Oh well . . . hubble bubble, girls, and all that."

The three witches went through a series of surprisingly spry limbering-up exercises. Suzie looked at the circle on the floor and turned up her nose.

"What is that smell . . ."

"The circle is laid down fresh every day, in a mixture of chalk, sulphur, and semen," said John.

Suzie looked at him. "And you know this how?"

"Henry told me. He liked knowing details like that."

"I'll bet he did."

The three witches finally did the business, with a minimum of chanting and arcane gestures, and the circle began to glow. John and Suzie stepped inside and were sent down, all the way down, to Shadow Deep.

They arrived in complete and utter darkness. John and Suzie reached out to each other automatically and linked hands. Not because they were frightened but to reassure each other they were still there. Slow, heavy footsteps approached out of the dark, drawing steadily closer, until a pair of night-vision goggles were suddenly thrust into each of their hands. When John and Suzie finally fumbled the goggles into place, Shadow Deep appeared before them as dim green images and impenetrable shadows. They were in a circular stone chamber, with an uncomfortably low roof and only the one exit. Before them stood a clay golem, rough and bulky, with a completely smooth face.

"Prison staff," John explained. "Set to follow simple preprogrammed routines."

Suzie scowled at the golem. "Why doesn't it have a face? I don't trust anything that doesn't have a face."

"Down here it doesn't need one," said John.

The golem turned abruptly and stomped away. John and Suzie followed it out of the chamber and through a series of featureless stone tunnels, until finally the golem lurched to a halt in front of a closed door. The golem knocked once, so hard the door shuddered in its frame, then turned and stomped away. Suzie looked at John.

"Governor's office," he said. "The only human staff down here. He's serving time, just like the prisoners. Only under somewhat better conditions. Brace yourself; he's the only one allowed light in this place."

He pushed open the door, and dazzlingly bright light spilled out into the corridor, overwhelming the night-vision goggles. John and Suzie tore them off and hurried inside. John slammed the door shut, and they looked around them, blinking into the pleasant glow. The large room was packed with all of life's necessities and quite a few comforts because the Governor rarely got to leave it. He was already hurrying forward to greet his guests, a large well-padded fellow in an old-fashioned suit that looked more than a little scruffy because he had no reason to look good for anyone. He stuck out his hand to John, beaming all over his round face.

"Hello, hello! So good to see you! Good to see anyone, really; I don't get many visitors down here."

John and Suzie suffered their hands to be shaken, then gave the Governor a hard look to make it clear they were there on business. He just shrugged and went on smiling.

"Sorry, sorry . . . It's just that I've been down here so long, I've forgotten most of the social niceties. If Brilliant Chang hadn't warned me you were on the way, I'd still be in my dressing-gown . . ."

"How long have you been here?" said Suzie.

"Since Walker put me here? The previous Walker, I mean . . . I stopped counting. It was starting to obsess me. It's not like I've got a release date to look forward to. It's been years. Years and years and years . . ."

"Don't start feeling sorry for him," John said to Suzie. "If you knew why Henry put him here, you'd think he was being merciful."

"Oh, he was!" said the Governor. "Don't think I'm not grateful! Mostly."

"I didn't think Henry did mercy," said Suzie.

"He certainly had his own definition," said John. He looked sternly at the Governor. "Brilliant did tell you why we're here? We need to see the prisoners."

The Governor stopped smiling. "You really think that's a good idea? You do know what happens to people when they get sent here? The moment a prisoner arrives in the reception area, he is marched to his waiting cell by a golem, without benefit of night-vision goggles, then pushed inside. Some try to fight, but the golem is always stronger. The door to the cell is then nailed shut. Because Shadow Deep is forever. They're left to sit in the dark, and the quiet, on their own. Food and water are shoved through a narrow gap at the bottom of the door by the golems, so they never have anyone to talk with. No visitors, no care packages, no time off for good behaviour. They're here till they die."

Suzie frowned. "What about . . ."

"There's a grille in the floor," said the Governor.

"Makes you wonder why any of them are still alive," said John.

"Most aren't," the Governor said blithely. "Of course, there are some who just won't die. Like Shock Headed Peter. Nasty bastard. The Authorities executed him three times, but it wouldn't take, so they sent him down here and washed their hands of him. Now, to what do I owe the pleasure of this visit?"

"Brilliant Chang didn't tell you?" said John.

"No one tells me anything they don't have to," said the Governor.

"The Authorities have decided to open Shadow Deep," said John. "Release all the inmates and set them against the Droods. Freedom, in return for service. For those who survive the war."

The Governor stared at him, shocked. "Are things really that bad?"

"Yes," said John. "How many prisoners do you have here?"

"Well . . . At the moment, just two."

John and Suzie looked at the Governor.

"All this, for just two prisoners?" said Suzie.

"We don't get many," the Governor said defensively. "I mean, you have to be really bad, even for the Nightside, to qualify for Shadow Deep. And most of those who do end up here don't tend to last long. In the dark and the silence. I think it's the lack of hope that does it for most of them. They hear their door being nailed shut and immediately start thinking about the only sure way out of here. We only know who's alive by keeping track of the meals we provide. And we don't check them that often.

"So! At the moment we only have two prisoners. An ex-detective, Sam Warren, who killed a bunch of people and ate them, to acquire their special abilities."

"A detective?" said John. "How . . ."

The Governor shrugged. "I didn't ask. I never do. And then, of course, we have Shock Headed Peter. Do people still talk about him in the Nightside? He killed three hundred and forty-seven people. We think. They never did find any of the victims' bodies, just their clothes. Sam and Peter. If you want them, they're yours."

"We'll take them," said John. "Then throw them at the Droods and hope for the best. And, Brilliant told me that you are also free to go, Governor. Your time is up."

The Governor was so surprised he burst into tears of pure joy. He threw his arms around John and hugged him tightly, looked at Suzie, and thought better of it, then danced around his room shouting, "Thank you, thank you!" After a while he calmed down and wiped the tears from his eyes.

"Walker promised me this wouldn't be forever, and that kept me going, but I've been here for so long . . . It's hard to think of living anywhere else. Though I'm damned if I'll let that stop me . . ."

"Do you want to take anything with you?" said John.

"There's nothing here I'll miss," said the Governor. "Nothing that wouldn't bring back memories. So . . . to hell with all of it. Come on; let's go free the prisoners, then we can all get the hell out of here." He stopped, and looked thoughtfully at John. "You are sure you can handle them? I mean, Sam Warren does have powers, and Shock Headed Peter . . ."

"This is Shotgun Suzie," said John.

"Fair enough," said the Governor. He smiled at her briefly. "I always thought I'd see you down here one day."

They all put their night-vision goggles on, left the office, and followed a golem through the narrow stone tunnels. They passed a great many doors, all firmly shut. The Governor banged on a few with his fist and called out, just in case, but there was never any response. John thought about a life spent in the dark cells and shuddered.

"They say Sam Warren used to be a first-rate detective," the Governor said chattily. "Till they talked about retiring him. He's supposed to have killed a werewolf, a minor Greek godling, a farseer, an immortal, and a chat-show radio host. I don't know why that last one apart from the obvious. Ms Fate identified Sam Warren as the murderer and brought him down, and he's been here ever since."

They finally stopped before one particular door, and the Governor gestured to the golem. It laid its rough clay hands on the door and tore it away from the cell. There was a loud rending of breaking wood, and broken nails flew through the air. An appalling stench wafted out of the cell, enough to make all of them turn their heads away: an accumulation of human filth. John braced himself and stepped forward to peer into a cell that couldn't have been more than eight foot square. An old man sat huddled in the far corner, wrapped in the foul and ragged remains of the clothes he'd been wearing when he was nailed into his cell. He didn't move, didn't say anything. John threw him a pair of night-vision goggles, and the old man jumped as they fell into his lap.

"Put the goggles on," said John. "The good news is, you're being released. The bad news is, you have to fight Droods. But even that has to be better than this."

Sam Warren slowly put the goggles on and looked at John. He rose cautiously to his feet and stumbled forward. Out in the corridor, he looked around him. At the first new thing he'd seen in years.

"How long was I in there?" he said finally. His voice was rough from disuse.

"Not quite nine years," said the Governor.

Sam shook his head slowly. "Is that all . . ."

"I'm the new Walker," said John. "You agree to fight the Droods who've invaded the Nightside, and you get to walk out of here. Any problems with that?"

"No," said Sam. "I didn't go mad in the dark. Though I came close, several times. I'll fight your war for you, Walker. How many Droods are we talking about?"

"All of them," said Suzie.

Sam surprised them then with a smile. "No wonder you needed me. Who else is being released?"

"There is only one other surviving prisoner," said the Governor. "Your neighbour, Shock Headed Peter."

"No!" Sam said immediately. "You can't let him out! Not after everything he did. Not after all the trouble I went through to find him and drag him down here. Don't you know how dangerous he is?"

"That's why we want him," said John. "A lot of Droods will take a lot of killing."

The Governor had the golem rip the door off the next cell. They braced themselves for the smell, but there was just dry, stale air. The Governor peered into the cell and made a low, surprised sound. The others quickly moved in beside him. The cell was empty, apart from a small pile of clothes on the floor.

"He can't have escaped!" said the Governor. "It's not possible!"

"He didn't," said Sam. "He just couldn't take it any more and turned his power on himself. All the years I spent, convinced he'd find some way of getting to me . . . and he was never there at all."

"But then . . . who's been eating all his meals?" said the Governor.

"That's Shock Headed Peter for you," said Sam. "Determined to be a mystery, to the last. Well, good riddance to the man. Let's get out of here."

Back on the streets of the Nightside, the Governor shed more happy tears. He was so pleased to see the neon-lit streets after so long away, he ran back and forth, touching buildings and kissing street-lamps as though to make sure they were real. Finally he shook everybody's hand and went dancing off down the street, singing happily.

"Let's just hope he doesn't run into a Drood," said John. He turned to Sam Warren, who shrugged.

"I don't know how much use I'm going to be, even with my stolen abilities . . . But I know my duty. I was a detective, you know. The first real detective in the Nightside. I lost my way for a while . . . But I know a second chance when I see one. Point me at the nearest Droods, and I'll show them how dangerous a real lawman can be."

There was the roar of a powerful engine, and a long, low-slung impressively styled car came racing down the street and screeched to a halt in front of them. It was the shocking-pink Fatemobile, with Ms Fate herself behind the wheel. She shut down the mighty engine, pushed up the door, and emerged from the Fatemobile to stand before them. Ms Fate, the Nightside's very own costumed adventurer. A man who dressed up as a super-heroine to fight crime. She looked very impressive in her black leather outfit, complete with cowl and cape. It didn't look like a costume on her; it looked like work-clothes. She even had a utility belt strapped around her narrow waist, packed full of useful items. Though the high heels on the boots were a bit much.

"Hello, Sam," she said, in her low, smoky voice. "I heard you were being released to fight the Droods. I thought I should be here since I was the one who put you away. I always respected the work you did as a detective . . . and I could use a partner when I go to face the Droods. What do you say, Sam?"

"I can't think of anyone I'd rather have at my side," said Sam. "Old friend, old enemy."

Ms Fate climbed back into the Fatemobile, and Sam got in beside her. John and Suzie walked off and left them to it. They hadn't got far when John's phone rang. He took it out and glared at it.

"It's getting so I wince every time the damn thing rings. Yes! Hello! What do you want?"

"You need to get back to Strangefellows right now," said Alex. "You would not believe what's happening here."

Sam peered out his side-window as the Fatemobile roared through the long night. He knew how bad he must smell, but Ms Fate hadn't said anything. He wasn't used to making conversation after so long in a cell on his own, but he thought he should say something.

"I can't believe how empty the streets are. What happened to all the traffic?"

"The Droods happened," said Ms Fate, slamming through the gears in an expert racing shift. "They've killed a lot of people."

Sam shook his head slowly. "What brought the whole Drood family to the Nightside?"

Ms Fate filled him in as best she could. Sam sat and thought for a while.

"How did John Taylor end up as Walker?" he said finally.

Ms Fate smiled. "The long night is still full of mysteries, Sam."

"Then let's start with you," said Sam. "If we're to be partners. Your secret identity came as something of a surprise to me. Who are you really?"

"I have no secret identity," Ms Fate said steadily. "The whole point of the Nightside is that you can live your dream full time. I am Ms Fate, now and forever."

"Even when you take off the mask?"

"What makes you think it comes off?"

"All right, how did you become Ms Fate?"

"Shirley den Adel took me under her wing and trained me. She used to be a costumed adventurer, the Lady Phantasm. She helped me understand the importance of being true to the role. But even so . . . Even after everything I've done as Ms Fate, I still sometimes wonder if I'm the real thing. A real hero. But now we're going to fight Droods, and I don't suppose it gets any realer than that." She glanced across at Sam. "I have to ask: How is it you're not batshit crazy after all those years in solitude?"

"My powers helped," said Sam. "Particularly the one I took from the farseer. I could see occasional visions of the Nightside, in my cell."

"What other powers do you have?"

"Strength, speed, some healing. Nothing else took. Let's hope that's enough. How far to the nearest Droods?"

"According to the television news team broadcasting live, not far at all," said Ms Fate.

She brought the Fatemobile roaring around a corner and stamped on the brakes. A small group of Nightsiders were fighting desperately against a much larger company of Droods, with improvised incendiaries. Liquid flames slid down the golden armour without making any impression. Ms Fate and Sam Warren got out of the car.

One Drood stopped when he saw the Fatemobile. He ordered his people to stay where they were and headed straight for Ms Fate and Sam Warren. He lowered his armour as he got closer, revealing the Sarjeant-at-Arms.

"Hello, Cedric," said Ms Fate. "Been awhile since we last had a drink together in Strangefellows."

"You don't need to get mixed up in this," said the Sarjeant. "We're not here for people like you."

"This is my home," said Ms Fate. "I belong here. When did the Droods decide to just kill anyone who didn't agree with them?"

The Sarjeant didn't answer her, staring at Sam. "Who's your smelly companion?"

"This is Detective Sam Warren," said Ms Fate. "He's the law in the Nightside."

"I thought that was you," said the Sarjeant.

"No, I'm justice. Tell your people to stand down, Cedric."

"Not going to happen," said the Sarjeant. "I know my duty."

"So do I," said Sam.

Ms Fate fixed the Sarjeant with her coldest glare. "You're killing people! I thought a Drood's duty was to protect Humanity!"

"We are," said the Sarjeant. "We're protecting Humanity from the Nightside."

"People don't stop being people just because they live in the Nightside," said Ms Fate.

"But they stop acting like people," said the Sarjeant. "We have learned, at our cost, not to trust anyone here."

"Typical Drood," said Sam. "Always convinced you know what's best for everyone else."

"Drive away," the Sarjeant said to Ms Fate. "If you stay, I can't guarantee your safety."

"I'm not going anywhere," said Ms Fate. "This is my home. And you should not have come here."

She kicked the Sarjeant in the groin, so hard he couldn't even make a sound. He bent right over, and Ms Fate punched him in the head with her weighted leather glove, so hard just the sound of it made Sam wince. The Sarjeant dropped to the ground. The rest of the Droods came charging forward. Ms Fate produced a handful of shuriken from her utility belt. She threw the razor-edged throwing stars with uncanny aim, and they sliced through Drood armour to bury themselves in the flesh beneath. Droods cried out in shock and pain, as the armour healed around the throwing stars and held them in place, sunk deep in arm and leg muscles. The Droods staggered to a halt, trying to tear the shuriken free.

"What the hell are those things?" said Sam. "I didn't think anything could get through Drood armour."

"Strange matter, courtesy of the Gun Shoppes of Usher," said Ms Fate. "Unfortunately, they only had a few in stock, and I just used them all up. But they also had these."

She produced two golden fighting sticks from her boots.

"The last strange matter in the shop. Keep an eye on the Sarjeant, Sam, while I go and pound some sense into Drood heads."

She marched right into the midst of the Droods, and struck viciously about her. Her speed and fighting skills made her a match for anything a Drood could do, and her fighting sticks slammed into the side of one golden head after another, dropping Droods to the ground like they'd been struck by lightning. She danced among the Droods, evading their outstretched hands and flashing swords and ducking the occasional gun.

But after a while she started to grow tired because she was only a costumed adventurer and not a real super-heroine. The Droods crowded in around her, denying her room to manoeuvre, then clubbed her to the ground with brutal golden fists. She went down fighting, until one set of spiked golden knuckles ripped half her cowl away, and another slammed into the exposed side of her face. She dropped to the ground, hardly moving, and a Drood rammed his sword right through her.

Sam Warren was already running forward at incredible speed and was in and among the Droods before they knew what was happening. He quickly discovered he wasn't strong enough to break Drood armour, so he settled for picking them up and throwing them down the street. They landed heavily and took their time getting to their feet again. Sam picked up one Drood and used him to club down another, and the two clashing armours sounded like a bell tolling at a funeral. Armoured fists and swords hit Sam from every side as he raged among the Droods, and even his healing ability couldn't cope with all the damage he was taking. He slowed down, despite himself, but fought on doggedly.

The Droods finally fought him to a halt as he stood over the fallen body of his partner, refusing to be moved. Because she had been a real hero at the end, and he wanted to be one too, for her. He struck out with all his strength, sending Droods staggering this way and that, but they always came back. They beat him viciously from all sides with their spiked fists. Bones broke and shattered, and blood splashed onto the ground, but still he wouldn't fall. The Droods stopped abruptly and fell back. Sam stood swaying, his face pulped, one eye ruined.

"What's the matter, you bastards?" he said thickly. "Haven't you got the guts to finish off one old lawman?"

The Sarjeant-at-Arms stepped forward and shot him twice in the head. Sam Warren fell to the ground, dying as the hero he always should have been.

The Sarjeant stood over the two dead bodies for a while, thinking his own thoughts, then turned abruptly and pointed at Charlotte ap Owen and her cameraman Dave, who'd broadcast it all live to the Nightside.

"They were warned," said the Sarjeant. "Kill them."

The Droods advanced on Charlotte and Dave. The cameraman didn't lower his camera.

"We could run," he said.

"Keep filming," Charlotte said steadily. "Show the people what's happening. That's our job."

"It is?" said Dave.

"That's what Julien Advent said, and I'm not going to argue with him."

"They'd only catch us if we did run," said Dave. "So why not? Hey, boss, sorry now you never slept with me while you had the chance?"

"No," said Charlotte. "Not even a little bit."

After they were dead, the Droods smashed their camera.

Eddie and Molly went hurrying through the streets, on their way to St Jude's. Hearing that the ancient church was to be seized by the Droods, or destroyed if necessary, had been a step too far for Eddie. When they finally reached St Jude's, they were surprised and a little relieved to discover that somehow they'd got there first. Eddie and Molly looked the church over. The squat, solid shape looked as strong and steadfast as ever.

"I can't let my family do this," said Eddie. "I've heard stories about St Jude's all my life. It's important. It matters."

"It's one of the few places in the Nightside that really is everything people say it is," said Molly.

"This whole invasion has gone seriously off mission," said Eddie. "If I make a stand here, maybe I can make my family stop and think about what they're doing . . ."

"They won't stop," said Molly.

"Then I'll stop them," said Eddie. "By force, if necessary."

"Are you sure about this?" Molly asked. "I mean, obviously I'm all for it, but the last time you went up against your entire family, you almost got killed."

Eddie smiled briefly. "That's happened so often I'm getting used to it."

"Just like old times!" said Molly. "You and me against the Droods."

"Someone has to save the family from itself," said Eddie.

"And who better than you?" said a familiar voice.

Charles and Emily, Eddie's father and mother, stepped out of the shadows at the side of the church. Eddie laughed out loud and hugged them both, then his parents made a point of hugging Molly too. Just to make it clear that as far as they were concerned, she was family. A middle-aged man in a rumpled sports jacket and grey slacks, Charles was completely bald but boasted a heavy salt-and-pepper beard. He had the look of a man who could fix things, one way or another. Emily was a cool and poised middle-aged lady in a cream silk dress and a Panama hat crammed down on her long grey hair.

"We heard what was happening," said Charles. "The Department of Uncanny has been forbidden to interfere, by the highest levels of Government; so we decided we'd use some of our vacation time to pay a visit to the Nightside. Isn't that right, dear?"

"Of course, dear," said Emily. "Just tourists, that's us. Here to help."

"Help who?" said Eddie.

"You, of course," said Emily.

"Even if it means taking on the whole Drood family?" said Molly.

Emily smiled. "It wouldn't be the first time."

"Just like old times," Charles said happily.

"I said that!" said Molly.

"I know," said Charles. "I heard you."

Eddie led the way into St Jude's. The only truly neutral place in the Nightside was now a refuge for the spiritually wounded. People with shattered nerves, who'd seen their homes and businesses destroyed, who'd lost loved ones, or who simply had nowhere else left to go. They sat huddled together on the rough wooden pews, shaking and shuddering and comforting each other as best they could. Because no one else was going to do it. St Jude's was there to give you something to lean on, to help you find your strength, not tell you everything was going to be all right.

Everywhere Eddie looked, he saw broken hearts and thousand-yard stares. These weren't just people who'd lost everything; these were people who'd had it torn away, then crushed. *My family did this*, Eddie thought. *How could we have lost our way so quickly? Or were we always like this, and I just wouldn't let myself see it?* He looked around sharply as the Lord of Thorns came over to join them.

"Everyone here is under my protection," he said, in his voice like old stones rasping together. "No one will threaten them again, without going through me first."

Eddie went to introduce his parents, but the Lord of Thorns stopped him with an upraised hand.

"I know who everyone is," he said. "Comes with the job. Just as I know that the Droods are almost upon us. What I don't know . . . is whether I have the power to stop them. I have fallen a long way from what I was meant to be."

"How close are they?" said Molly.

"I can hear them," said the Lord of Thorns.

Eddie hurried out of the church. Molly fell in beside him, and his parents brought up the rear. They didn't say anything. There was nothing that needed saying.

Out in the night, the street was empty, but Eddie could hear the heavy tramp of armoured feet, drawing steadily closer. Eddie started toward the sound, and the others went with him. They'd only made it half-way down the street when a large company of Droods in their armour came into view at the far end. Dozens of golden figures, as implacable and unstoppable as an on-coming storm. The leader saw who was waiting for them and stopped her people where they were. She came forward alone and armoured down, revealing the Matriarch. She looked at Eddie and Molly, then at Charles and Emily, before fixing her gaze on Eddie.

"What are you doing here, Eddie? You weren't supposed to be here."

"What are you doing here?" said Eddie. "St Jude's was never supposed to be one of our targets. This church is older, and arguably more important, than our entire family. It was a force for good before we even existed; and you want to destroy it?"

"Of course I don't want to destroy St Jude's!" said the Matriarch. "I'm just here to take control of an important location, to make it clear to the Nightside who's really in charge."

"What about the people sheltering inside the church?" said Molly.

"They'll find somewhere else to go," said the Matriarch, keeping her gazed fixed on Eddie. "We'll just occupy the church, to make our point, then leave a few Droods on guard while we move on. Access to the church will be allowed, for truly deserving people, after the war is over. No one needs to get hurt. All they have to do is stand aside and let us do our job."

"Listen to yourself," said Eddie. "Who are we, to decide who should be allowed sanctuary in St Jude's? Are you really ready to kill the people sheltering here if they won't leave, just to make a point? There's been too much killing, Matriarch."

"I make the decisions for this family!" the Matriarch said sharply. "You owe me a duty of obedience!"

"Please," said Eddie. "Remember who you're talking to. I took control of the family once before, to save it from itself. I can do it again if I have to."

"Damn right," said Charles.

"For a family to lose its soul once is bad enough," said Emily, "but twice . . ."

The Matriarch glared at them. "We should never have allowed you to come back. Once a traitor, always a traitor!"

"Oh . . . You really shouldn't have said that," murmured Molly.

Eddie armoured up, and so did the Matriarch. The two of them stood face-to-face in the middle of the street. The Matriarch grew a long sword from her hand, and so did Eddie. Their blades slammed together, and just like that the fight was on.

The rest of the Droods came surging forward. Charles suddenly had a glowing quarterstaff in his hands. He ran forward into the midst of them, striking about him with a speed and skill they couldn't match. He couldn't hurt the Droods in their armour, so he knocked them this way and that, tripped them up, and ran them ragged trying to keep up with him. Emily produced an elven wand and pointed it sharply at this Drood and that. Their armour seized up, holding them in place like golden statues. The effect didn't last long, but Emily just kept pointing the wand, and Droods kept crashing to a halt. Molly conjured up a raging storm wind that howled down the street, picking up Droods and sending them tumbling helplessly.

And then the Matriarch stepped back from Eddie, made her sword disappear, and yelled at her people to stand down. She armoured down, and so did Eddie.

"This is just a distraction," she said flatly. "I don't have time to waste on this; I have a war to win."

Eddie just nodded. He was ready to let the Matriarch save face in front of her people as long as she left St Jude's alone. Emily unfroze the few Droods still held in place by her wand, and Charles strolled back through the Droods, leaning just a little heavily on his quarterstaff. Molly stood ready to go again. The Matriarch looked at Eddie.

"The Sarjeant is on his way, with the main body of Droods," she said. "I'll have to tell him about this, and you know how he'll react."

"Let him come," said Eddie. "Even better, I'll go and meet him. Where is he?"

"Just walk down the street," said the Matriarch. "He's closer than you think."

"Isn't he always," said Eddie. "Okay, we'll go this way, you choose another. But, Maggie . . . this isn't over. If you don't change your tactics, if you don't stop killing people just because they're in your way . . . I will stop you."

"You'd turn on your own family?" said the Matriarch. "Again?"

"Maybe if I'd hung around long enough to fix it properly, this wouldn't have happened," said Eddie.

"You were lucky, last time," said the Matriarch. "And you're in the place where luck runs out."

She led her people away. Eddie took his people off to have a word with the Sarjeant-at-Arms.

Meanwhile, St Jude's had another visitor: the Soulhunter known as Demonbane. He refused to go inside the church, just stood at the doorway and yelled for the Lord of Thorns to come out and play. Demonbane looked very out of place in his lavender jacket, with his relentless smile and haunted eyes, but then, he always did. The Lord of Thorns came to the doorway and nodded to him.

"Demonbane . . . You told me you'd never come back to the Nightside after what happened last time."

"That was then, this is somewhat not then," Demonbane said cheerfully. "I'm here to help!"

The Lord of Thorns looked at him. "You?"

"I'm a Soulhunter. Saving souls is what we do. Normally that involves me sending my mind into the Up and Out to find them after they've been taken, then fighting Dragons and Wolves and Hags to get them back, so I can take them home again. But hey, I'm flexible."

"You're used to fighting demons," said the Lord of Thorns. "These are Droods. They're different."

"So am I!" said Demonbane. "The Droods called me here to help them, but having seen how badly they're messing things up . . . I don't think so. I've never seen so many souls ripped loose and running around screaming. That's the kind of thing that attracts attention from the Outer Reaches. No, it's obvious which side I should be on."

"The Nightside?" said the Lord of Thorns.

"No, silly! Yours. I can't defend the Nightside, I'm not even sure I'd want to; but St Jude's . . . I can do that."

"Then stand your ground here," said the Lord of Thorns. "The Sarjeant-at-Arms and his people will be arriving soon. It's up to you to hold them off."

"Got it!" said Demonbane. "They shall not pass! Oh, this is going to be fun!"

"You have a strange definition of fun," said the Lord of Thorns. "But, then, you always did."

He went back inside. Demonbane put his back to the open doorway and faced the street. He rubbed his hands together eagerly and hummed a merry tune, looking forward to something as simple as human enemies. For someone who spent most of his time throwing his mind out to the dark places between the stars to fight eaters of souls, taking on a few Droods seemed like a nice change of pace. His ears pricked up as he heard the sound of armoured feet approaching, and he smiled a truly unpleasant smile. He leaned on the door-frame, adopting a deliberately and even offensively louche pose, and waited for the Droods to come to him. Dozens of armoured figures came marching down the street. Demonbane looked at them and raised a single eyebrow. The Drood leader brought his people crashing to a halt. The Sarjeant lowered his armour, walked forward, and frowned at Demonbane.

"How did you get here before us?"

"Partly because I haven't been running around the Nightside cutting people down and stamping on their heads," said Demonbane. "But mostly because I'm a Soulhunter, and you're not. Now, I have drawn a line in the sand, and you're on the other side of it. In fact, you're so far on the other side you probably can't even see the line from where you are. So it's just as well I'm here to point it out for you. I have sworn to defend St Jude's against all comers. And most especially from the likes of you. None shall pass!"

"Have you lost your sanity?" said the Sarjeant.

"What, that old thing? I threw it away years ago. It just got in the way," said Demonbane.

"I don't have time for this," said the Sarjeant. "St Jude's is a designated target. Move, or we'll move you."

"Not on the best day you ever had," said Demonbane. And he reached out and tweaked the Sarjeant's nose.

The Sarjeant stumbled backwards, pulled on his armour, and yelled for his people to attack. They came storming forward, and Demonbane straightened up in the doorway. His smile disappeared. Demonbane opened his mind and threw it at the Droods like a weapon. And the mind that walked among the stars, in the farthest reaches of the longest night of all, to fight far worse things than Droods . . . slammed into their minds like a wrecking ball.

The Droods cried out and stumbled this way and that, holding their armoured heads with their armoured hands, as Demonbane went rampaging through their thoughts and trampling over their souls. He could see into all of them, as though they were made of glass. He confronted the Droods with memories of their past sins and raised up the faces of all those they'd killed, to condemn their killers. Demonbane stirred his barbed mental fingers in Drood psyches and hit them where they lived. Droods fell to their knees, helpless in the grip of despair and self-loathing. Even the Sarjeant-at-Arms; or perhaps especially him.

And then Sir Bors arrived. The last surviving London Knight in the Nightside came marching steadily down the street. He'd lost his marvellous war-horse, along with all the good companions who'd followed him into the long night. One by one they had fallen to the forces of the long night, and now only he remained to fight the good fight.

His armour was cracked and dented, but he still carried his battered sword in his hand, dripping with blood. He'd come to St Jude's for comfort and reassurance, and the first thing he saw was Droods under attack by one smiling figure. Sir Bors didn't understand the nature of the attack, but then, he didn't need to. He strode through the ranks of stricken Droods and felt nothing, nothing at all. Because he was a young Knight, pure in thought and word and deed. He walked right up to Demonbane and thrust his sword through the man's heart. The Soulhunter looked at his killer with quiet surprise, as though to say *Where did you come from?* And then Sir Bors drew back his sword, and Demonbane fell dead inside the church. Still blocking the way with his body.

The Droods slowly regained control of themselves, forcing the memories of what they'd just experienced out of their minds. The Lord of Thorns appeared in the church, to face Sir Bors. The London Knight bowed to him.

"What have you done, Bors?" said the Lord of Thorns.

"You have nothing to fear," said the Knight. "I have saved you from the danger."

"The man you killed was defending this church," said the Lord of Thorns.

Sir Bors looked at the Droods, then at the Lord of Thorns. "I don't understand. I did my duty."

"You killed a good man," said the Lord of Thorns. "How is this possible, sir Knight?"

Sir Bors put away his sword and took off his steel helmet, so he could look the Lord of Thorns in the eyes.

"I have become . . . confused, by much I have encountered here. This has not been the great adventure I expected. I came here to stamp out evil, not men and women fighting to protect their homes. I have seen horrors, on both sides. I fear . . . that I have lost my way." He looked past the Lord of Thorns, at the man he had just killed, and then back again. "But in you, and in this place, I still have faith. So instruct me, I beg you; what must I do to put this right?"

"Take his place," said the Lord of Thorns. "Defend this church from those who would destroy everything it stands for."

Sir Bors nodded, put his helmet back on, drew his sword again, and turned to face the Droods. The Lord of Thorns went back into the church. The Sarjeant-at-Arms strode back and forth among his people, encouraging those who needed it and shouting at those who needed that, until he had them back in shape again. He turned to Sir Bors, armoured down, and approached him to give his thanks. Only to stop as the young Knight raised his sword threateningly.

"Sir Bors? What's wrong?"

"It seems I have made a terrible mistake," said Sir Bors. "Take your people away, Sarjeant. None shall pass, as long as I draw breath."

The Sarjeant started to shout at him, then controlled himself with an effort. He couldn't afford to make an enemy of the London Knights by attacking one of the few people they'd sent to help. Not without good reason. He adopted his most reasonable tone and tried again.

"Kae sent you to support us."

"The Grand Master sent me here to do right," said Sir Bors. "And for the first time since I got here, I am sure of what that means."

"I order you stand aside, in Kae's name!" said the Sarjeant.

"You do not speak in his name," said Sir Bors. "No Drood does, or ever could. I will defend this church, as Kae would want me to. For that is the legacy of Camelot: the strong defending those who cannot defend themselves."

"Have you forgotten why we're here?" said the Sarjeant. "We came to this awful place to save the world!"

"You can't save the world by killing people just because they don't agree with you," said Sir Bors. "I forgot that, for a while. In my determination to have an adventure. Thank you, Sarjeant, for helping me see the error of my ways."

The Sarjeant turned to the waiting Droods. "Drag him out of there. Try not to damage him more than necessary."

"Stand away from the only real Knight in the Nightside!" said Eddie Drood.

The Sarjeant looked around sharply, then fell back to stand with his people as Eddie and Molly came running down the street. Eddie had got a little turned around, looking for the Sarjeant. Charles and Emily had decided to stay with the Matriarch and keep talking to her, in the hope they could change her mind. Because somebody had to. The Sarjeant looked steadily at Eddie as he approached.

"Have you forgotten whose side you're on, Eddie?"

"We're here to defend St Jude's, from anyone who threatens it," said Eddie. "And if you were in your right mind, you'd be doing the same thing."

The Sarjeant shook his head, too angry for a moment even to speak.

"What is it about this place that drives everybody crazy? Why can't everyone just do what they're told, so we can save the world?"

"Because you're doing more harm than good," said Molly.

The Sarjeant ignored her to stab an accusing finger at Eddie. "I always knew you'd betray your family again!"

"From where I'm standing, you're the one betraying everything our family is supposed to stand for," said Eddie. "I told Maggie, and now I'm telling you; I will not allow the family to become the very thing we have always existed to fight."

"Kill him!" shouted the Sarjeant, almost spitting out the words in his fury. "Kill all three of them! And then kill all the vermin infesting this church!"

Eddie armoured up. Molly wrapped herself in bark from the trees of her wild woods, to make armour of her own. And then both of them moved to stand on either side of Sir Bors, to defend St Jude's. The Knight nodded approvingly.

"I have heard many stories of both of you. It pleases me to learn that most of them are probably true. You do realise the odds are stacked against us?"

"Given that there's only three of us, and over a hundred of them, yes, I had worked that out," said Molly.

"Then allow me to do something to change the odds in our favour," said Sir Bors.

He ran forward, his sword held high, yelling his battle-cry. He headed straight for the Sarjeant-at-Arms, trusting one strike from his enchanted blade to leave the Droods leaderless and confused. The Sarjeant summoned a gun and shot Sir Bors through the eye-slit of his helmet. Sir Bors crashed to the ground and lay still. And the Sarjeant's only regret was that he wasn't sure how he was going to explain that to Kae. But no doubt he would find someone to blame it on. This was the Nightside, after all. He looked at Eddie and Molly, standing shocked and silent in the church doorway.

"Kill them both," the Sarjeant said tiredly to his people. "And when you're done, cut off their heads and stick them on spikes. So everyone can see what happens to traitors."

And then they all looked around sharply, as Isabella Metcalf came racing down the street on her mystical motor-bike in her blood-red biker leathers, with Louisa Metcalf riding pillion in a billowing white gown. The motor-bike floated some two feet above the ground, defying gravity on general principles. The Sarjeant opened fire, but his bullets just burned up against the bike's flaring force screens. And then he had to throw himself to one side as the motor-cycle smashed head-on into the Droods, sending them flying in all directions. Isabella brought her bike screeching around in a tight circle and slammed to a halt before Eddie and Molly.

"Somebody call for a rescue?"

"About time you got around to checking your messages," said Molly.

Isabella jumped off her motor-bike, and it stood happily upright on its own. Louisa put out a delicate hand to Eddie, and he helped her off. She didn't need the assistance; she just liked to be made a fuss of. Isabella looked thoughtfully at the Droods, already heading her way with a great many weapons in their hands, and produced a Hand of Glory from inside her jacket. She used its power to freeze them all where they stood, but only for a moment. The armour was learning and adapting. So Isabella put the Hand away, slipped on a pair of knuckle-dusters personally cursed by the Anti-Pope, and went striding among the Droods, punching them in the face and cracking their armour.

Isabella had always been the most direct of the Metcalf sisters.

Louisa went tripping lightly among the Droods, like a fairy-tale princess with feral eyes. She laughed at one Drood, and he started laughing and couldn't stop. Louisa moved on to another Drood and cried real tears, and he sobbed like his heart would break. Wherever she went, people felt what she felt, until it wracked their souls and broke their hearts. Because she could make people feel anything, anything at all.

Louisa had always been the scariest of the Metcalf sisters.

The Droods turned and ran because there are some things no one can face and stay sane. The Sarjeant was forced to retreat with them, to keep it from becoming a rout. Isabella and Louisa went back to rejoin Eddie and Molly at the church doorway.

"What took you so long?" said Molly, sending away her bark armour.

"We were busy," said Isabella.

"We were!" Louisa said brightly. "Really. Ever so busy." She looked hopefully after the retreating Droods, now regrouping at the far end of the street. "Do you think they'll come back, so we can play some more?"

Eddie looked at the two dead bodies. One lying on the ground before them, the other just inside the church.

"The one in the medieval armour is a London Knight. The Sarjeant called him Sir Bors."

"And that's Demonbane!" said Molly. "I didn't think anything could kill him. What was he doing here, anyway?"

She broke off as the Sarjeant came walking back down the street. He'd lowered his armour as a sign of trust. Eddie did the same, so as not to be outdone. Isabella leaned against her motor-bike and looked thoughtfully at the Sarjeant. Louisa smiled dazzlingly. The Sarjeant stopped a respectful distance away and nodded to Isabella.

"Hello, Iz. It's been awhile."

"Hello, Cedric. Yes, it has."

"They used to go out," Molly said to Eddie.

"I know!" said Eddie. "I keep up with the family gossip."

"Well, this is awkward," said the Sarjeant.

"Why?" said Isabella. "Just because we used to be an item? If I got awkward around all my excs, I'd never be able to leave the house."

"I'm sure that sounded so much better while it was still in your head," said Molly.

Isabella ignored her. "Why did you kill the London Knight, Cedric?"

"Because he got in the way," said the Sarjeant. "It was necessary. I've always been able to do the hard, necessary things. That's why they made me Sarjeant-at-Arms."

"You once gave me a weapon to use against you," said Isabella. "In case you ever got out-of-control."

She held up her hand, and in it was a small plastic clicker in the shape of a green frog. Eddie tensed. He'd seen one of those before. The old Armourer made them as a defence against Droods gone bad. The clicker could force a Drood's armour back into their torc and hold it there. Eddie hadn't known the Armourer had given a clicker to the Sarjeant, and he certainly hadn't known the Sarjeant had given his to Isabella.

"I have new protections in place," said the Sarjeant.

"And I upgraded the clicker," said Isabella.

The Lord of Thorns came to join Eddie and Molly in the doorway and fixed the Sarjeant with his coldest stare. "Why are you still here?"

"I have more people on the way," said the Sarjeant. "Enough Droods to dismantle this church stone by stone if need be. But I'm still hoping I can persuade you to surrender peacefully. Your defiance has already cost good lives."

"You would have to kill everyone here to take St Jude's," said the Lord of Thorns. "Not just those standing before you but all the innocents within that I have given sanctuary to. You would have to bathe these ancient stones in blood. And given that this is a church where prayers are heard and sometimes answered, do you really want to attract God's attention with a massacre?"

The Sarjeant sighed. "I don't need St Jude's. There are more important places that will serve equally well as significant victories. And after the Authorities have been forced to surrender, and the Nightside has fallen . . . I'll have St Jude's anyway."

He turned and walked away, his back stiff and unyielding. Isabella made a rude noise after him. Eddie looked at the Lord of Thorns.

"Were you bluffing, just then?"

"No," said the Lord of Thorns.

"Would you admit it if you were?" said Molly.

"No," said the Lord of Thorns. And he went back into his church.

Conrad Drood had never wanted the responsibility of leading Droods. He was used to working on his own, as a field agent. But since it was his idea to break the invading army up into smaller groups, he didn't see how he could refuse when the Matriarch ordered him to lead one of those groups to the Street of the Gods and take control of it. He didn't expect that to take long. The Street was certainly valuable territory, but since it had already been deserted by its inhabitants, he couldn't see any problems. So he led his people through the largely deserted streets, going out of his way to avoid confrontations with any resisting Nightsiders because he had been trained to get the job done with a minimum of trouble.

He'd killed people when he'd had to, as a field agent. It had never bothered him. But he always liked to think he'd never killed anyone who didn't need killing.

When the Armourer's compass finally brought Conrad to the Street of the Gods, his people slowed right down as they gawped about them, dazzled and baffled by the weird and wonderful edifices on all sides. Churches and temples, with stained-glass windows and flaring neon, steeped in sanctity or blatant as a whore's come-on. The Droods chattered loudly together, awed and occasionally spooked by their surroundings. They'd all heard stories about the Beings and Forces that manifested on the Street of the Gods. The miracle workers and the wonder makers, the strange and the sinister, the divine and the damned and pretty much everything else Humanity has ever worshipped, at one time or another. Or if not worshipped . . . feared, with good reason. Conrad finally stopped, turned, and lowered his armour so he could glare properly at his people.

"What is wrong with you? We are Droods; we don't do impressed."

His people stirred unhappily, and there was a lot of looking back and forth before one Drood stepped forward and lowered his armour. Conrad didn't know him, but then, it was a large family, and he didn't get home much. The Drood looked very young and very troubled.

"We came here to fight people, not gods," he said. "What use is armour against a plague of boils?"

"The gods ran away when they heard we were coming," said Conrad. "What does that tell you about them? This is just another market-place, selling lies and false hopes to the spiritually gullible. Now put your armour back on."

"Why?" said the Drood. "If there's no one here to threaten us . . ."

"Because I will punch you in the head if you don't stop annoying me!" said Conrad.

The Drood nodded and armoured up. He'd worked with the Sarjeant, and this was the kind of pep talk he understood. And then Conrad realised most of his people had stopped looking at him and were staring past him, at something farther down the Street. Conrad turned to look and swore silently as he saw the two figures blocking the way. Conrad knew Dead Boy, if only by reputation, but he didn't recognise what appeared to be a homeless person standing next to him. Whoever he was, if he palled around with the infamous Dead Boy, he was bound to be trouble. Conrad ordered his people to stay put and went forward to confront the new arrivals. He deliberately didn't put his armour on, to suggest he didn't feel in any danger. He finally came to a halt before Dead Boy and nodded briefly.

"I know you, but who's your scruffy-looking friend?"

Dead Boy grinned. "This is Razor Eddie, Punk God of the Straight Razor."

Conrad frowned. "I thought all the gods had left the Street?"

"This isn't my Street," said Razor Eddie, in his ghostly grey voice.

"Then why are the two of you here?" said Conrad.

"Someone has to show up when the barbarians are at the gates," said Dead Boy.

"This is sacred ground," said Razor Eddie. "In its own appalling way."

"Stand aside," said Conrad. "This doesn't have to get unpleasant."

"From what I hear, that ship has already sailed," said Dead Boy. "You people have crapped all over some of my favourite places. I'd never be able to show my dead face in this town again if I let you get away with that."

"We're only doing what we feel is right," said Conrad.

"Did no one tell you, before you came here?" said Razor Eddie. "The long night brings out the worst in everyone."

"Besides," said Dead Boy, "according to the Authorities, the gods bailed out of here in such a hurry they left behind all kinds of things people like you shouldn't be allowed to get your hands on. I know! I couldn't believe it either! It was news to me that there had ever been anything here worth the taking, or I'd have ransacked a few likely places myself. But anyway, it's hands off everything as far as you're concerned. And I have always wanted to know whether I could take a Drood."

"I just thought this was the right thing to do," said Razor Eddie.

"Yes," said Dead Boy. "But that's you."

Conrad had started breathing through his mouth because the Punk God's stench was really starting to get to him. And he couldn't help noticing how the flies buzzing listlessly around Razor Eddie dropped dead out of the air if they got too close.

"Why are you so ready to defend a Street that all the other gods abandoned?" he said finally.

"I never had a church here," said Razor Eddie. "I never wanted to be worshipped, only feared, by the right kind of people. But it seems to me that the Street belongs to the worshippers, not the gods. It matters to them. And you would destroy that." He smiled slowly, showing grey teeth. "And I always wondered whether I could take a Drood."

"You really think you can stop us?" said Conrad. "A zombie with appalling dress sense and a homeless person with delusions of godhood, defending empty churches deserted by celestial con men . . ."

"You see it your way," said Dead Boy, "and we'll see it ours. So, get out of our playground, Drood, while you still can. The Street of the Gods, every last little tasteless bit of it, is under our protection."

"I have thirty armoured Droods under my command," said Conrad. "Be sensible!"

"This is the Nightside," said Razor Eddie. "We do things differently here."

Conrad armoured up and stood before them, splendid in his golden armour. Just the sight of that was usually enough to make the point that Droods were not to be messed with. The power of the armour and the eerily featureless face mask made it perfectly clear who was in charge. But Razor Eddie and Dead Boy just stared at him politely, as if to say *Is that all you've got?* Conrad called back to his people to come and join him. And while he was busy doing that, Dead Boy picked him up bodily and heaved him at the nearest church. Conrad sailed through the air, arms and legs waving wildly, and smashed through the wall. The other Droods stopped to watch Dead Boy do this, and he ran straight at them, laughing out loud.

"Come on, then! Give me your best shot! I can take it!"

Razor Eddie followed after him, shaking his head. There were good reasons why so few people were willing to fight alongside Dead Boy.

The Droods moved closer together to meet Dead Boy's charge, but his sheer momentum was enough to slam some of the Droods right off their feet. Dead Boy waded into the Droods, picking them up and throwing them around as if they were weightless. He punched one of them in the face mask and broke every bone in his hand. Dead Boy just shrugged and carried on fighting. He didn't feel pain any more; in fact, he had to take some fairly heavy-duty pills in order to feel anything. He ducked and dodged most of the Droods' blows, despite their armoured speed, because for all his bravado he wasn't stupid, and did his best to roll with the few that landed. He heard more bones break but decided he'd worry about that later.

Razor Eddie produced his supernaturally sharp straight razors and went to work among the Droods. The first few just put up armoured arms to block the blows, but Razor Eddie's blades were sharp enough to cut clean through Drood armour, and sink deep into the flesh beneath. The strange matter repaired itself almost immediately, but the wounds didn't.

Droods cried out in shock as much as pain, as blood ran inside their armour. Razor Eddie darted among the Droods with godly speed. Come and gone in a moment, he was never where they thought he was going to be, his straight razors flashing out to cut throats with grim precision. Droods crashed to the ground, making hideous sounds, bleeding out inside their armour.

Conrad dug himself out of the church he'd been thrown into and bellowed orders to his people. They swarmed all over Dead Boy, hanging on to his arms and legs, and dragged him down by sheer weight of numbers. Razor Eddie had to stop slaughtering Droods to go save his friend. His razors dug deep into armoured backs and shoulders, until the Droods were forced to release their prey and retreat. Dead Boy tried to get up, and couldn't. Razor Eddie hauled him up onto his feet. The Droods had done a job on Dead Boy. More of his bones were broken than not, the edges protruding jaggedly through torn skin, though no blood flowed. His deep-purple greatcoat had been ripped to tatters, and he'd lost his slouch hat. But he still had enough strength to laugh at the look of concern on Razor Eddie's face.

"Nothing some hard work, an industrial stapler, and a fair amount of duct tape won't put right," he said. "There are times when being dead has its advantages."

The two men stood side by side in the middle of the Street of the Gods. Dead Droods lay scattered all around them. Conrad walked forward on his own, and Razor Eddie moved to place himself in front of Dead Boy. Conrad grew a gun, and shot Razor Eddie's straight razors out of his hands. The broken pieces fell to the ground at his feet.

"You're just a god," said Conrad. "I'm a Drood."

Two new blades appeared in Razor Eddie's hands, shining unnaturally bright. He smiled coldly.

"I am the Punk God of the Straight Razor. And I have faith in myself."

Conrad shot Razor Eddie in the face. One razor moved too quickly to follow, and two pieces of bullet fell to the ground. They rattled around for a moment, then shot back to be reabsorbed by Conrad's armour. Some way down the Street, the other Droods moved a little closer together.

Dead Boy leaned in close to Razor Eddie. "Nice trick, but there's no way we can win this. There are too many of them. Sooner or later they will bring me down, and even you can't stop a bullet to the back of the head. So get out of here while I hold their attention."

"You're being very heroic," said Razor Eddie. "It doesn't suit you."

Dead Boy shrugged as best he could, with one shoulder smashed to pieces. "Like the man said, no point in dying over an empty Street."

"Where would I go?" said Razor Eddie.

"There are other people fighting," said Dead Boy. "Join up with them and find a way to fight Droods that works. Allow me my pride. It's all I've got."

Razor Eddie nodded. "You know . . ."

"I know," Dead Boy said kindly. "Now get the hell out of here before you say something that will embarrass both of us. Come on, I'm dead! What more can they do to me?"

Razor Eddie cut a hole in Space, stepped through it, and disappeared. The hole slammed shut behind him. Dead Boy turned to face the Droods, who were advancing on him with more confidence now Razor Eddie was gone. Dead Boy laughed happily and went lurching forward to meet them.

"Come on, then! Is that all you've got? I'm Dead Boy! I'm a legend, a dead man walking, the nightmare in the long night; and I am scarier than all of you put together!"

The Droods swarmed all over him and pulled him down, despite everything he could do. They forced him onto his knees and held him there. Conrad grew a golden sword from his hand, raised it, and cut off Dead Boy's head. It rolled away down the Street, and the body collapsed. The Droods let go and stood back, murmuring in relief. And then they all looked around sharply as a futuristic car came screaming down the Street toward them.

The moment it was within range it opened up with front-mounted machine-guns, and the sheer impact of so much fire-power blasted the Droods right off their feet. The car screeched to a halt beside Dead Boy's body, and transformed into the sex droid from the future, Silicon Lily. She picked up Dead Boy's severed head and hugged it to her chest for a long moment before holding it up before her face; and it winked at her. The mouth moved soundlessly, saying, *Think you could find some needle and thread?*

"I'm so sorry, lover," said Silicon Lily. "I got here as fast as I could. But now I think you should come home with me. I've had enough of this place. Trust me; you're going to love the Twenty-Third Century."

She disappeared in a flurry of discharging tachyons, taking Dead Boy's head and body with her. Back to her future.

The Nightside's main hospital, the Hospice of the Blessed Saint Margaret, had declared itself neutral ground and opened its doors to the Nightside's wounded. The Droods tacitly accepted this by ignoring it. The wounded and the dying were brought in from all over the long night, in ambulances and taxis and any other vehicle that would carry them, bearing terrible wounds and unspeakable injuries because the Droods weren't built to do small damage. Soon enough, every Ward and room in the hospital was full, and the injured spilled over into the corridors. The hospital staff worked themselves to exhaustion trying to cope, while the floors grew slick with blood, and the antiseptic on the air was overpowered by the stench of opened bodies. Other hospitals were doing what they could, but Saint Margaret's took the main load.

Not that far away, the Sarjeant-at-Arms listened as his local informants told him the hospital was being used as an organising point for the resistance. Behind the cover of treating the wounded, they were stockpiling weapons to use against the Droods. The Sarjeant wasn't sure he believed that, but he had to check it out. He led his main group of Droods to Saint Margaret's, to shut the hospital down. After everything that had been done to them, the Droods were in no mood to show mercy.

Saint Margaret's soon got word that Droods were on their way. They'd done too good a job, giving aid and comfort to the enemy, and now the Droods were coming to punish them. Julien Advent was already there, organising defences and inspiring people, when JC Chance turned up to help. Julien went outside to meet him.

"I thought you came here with Demonbane to help the Droods?" he said, too tired to be anything but blunt.

"I find a little of that man's company goes a long way," said JC. "So I wandered off on my own to see what there was to see. This place really has gone to hell in a hurry, and the Droods have completely lost their minds. Anyway, once I heard Saint Margaret's was in trouble, I bustled right over. I even brought a couple of old friends with me. Do you know the Bride of Frankenstein and her companion, the current Spring-heeled Jack?"

"We're here to help," said the Bride, crushing Julien's hand in a power-

ful grip. Up close, she smelled of attar of roses with a hint of formaldehyde. "The Spawn of Frankenstein voted not to get involved because they
owe so much to both sides, but I couldn't live with that. So here I am."

"And I go where she goes," murmured Jack.

The latest inheritor of the Spring-heeled Jack meme was tall and slim,
with a dignified bearing. Handsome enough in a sinister way, with dark
hair and darker eyes, he wore an old-fashioned tuxedo, a gleaming top
hat, and an opera cape that flapped around him like bat-wings. He looked
dandy and debonair, if somewhat dated.

"I like the outfit," said Julien. "It reminds me of my younger days."

"The look is imposed by the incarnation," said Jack. "I am, after all,
just an idea that manifests itself by possessing people."

Julien nodded. He'd heard stranger things. "You two stay out here and
guard the front entrance. Do what you can to hold off the Droods. I'll give
orders for the wounded to be dropped off at the back to give you a clear
field of play. JC, you come with me. Help organise some defences inside."

"Suits me," said JC. "I'm trained to deal with the dead, not the living."

Julien and JC went inside, while Spring-heeled Jack and the Bride took
up positions guarding the front entrance. The car-park stretched away before them, almost empty for once. The ambulances never hung around,
and no one had any time for visitors. The night was clear, and the air was
cool. Up above, the sea of stars and the oversized full moon looked down
impartially. The Bride slipped on two pairs of spiked silver knuckle-dusters:
one blessed and one cursed. Spring-heeled Jack produced his traditional
straight razor. Its blade shone supernaturally bright in the gloom, not unlike Razor Eddie's. There had been a lot of comment about that in the
Nightside, but never where Razor Eddie or Spring-heeled Jack might hear it.

"You really think we can take on an army of Droods?" Jack asked, after
a while.

"Stranger things have happened," said the Bride. "Hell, we are stranger
things."

"It does feel strange, to be fighting Droods," Jack said carefully.
"They've done so much for the Spawn of Frankenstein."

"Some of them have," said the Bride. "If Eddie were here, I'd talk to
him, find another way. I trust Eddie. But the Sarjeant-at-Arms is in charge
now, and by all accounts, he's a complete bastard."

"I notice you haven't answered my question," said Jack. "Do you believe we can fight an army of Droods in their armour?"

"Of course not, darling," said the Bride. "I'd have to say such a thing was impossible, wouldn't you? But we are both of us impossible, in our own ways, so who knows?"

Spring-heeled Jack laughed softly. "Give them hell, my love."

"With both hands," said the Bride.

The Sarjeant led his people into the hospital car-park, then stopped when he saw who was waiting for him. His Droods looked to him for orders, carefully quiet behind their anonymous golden masks. The Sarjeant had been losing his temper more and more easily of late, as events and people appeared to conspire against him. But in the end he just armoured down, told his people to wait where they were, and went to meet Jack and the Bride.

"More people I thought I could trust as allies," he said heavily. "What are you doing here?"

"Protecting the innocent," said the Bride. "Like you should be. This is a hospital!"

"That's not all it is," said the Sarjeant. "Why can't you people understand? The Nightside is the real danger here! We have to bring it under control before it breaks its boundaries and sweeps out to cover the whole world in a night that never ends!"

"I don't see much control in what you've been doing," said the Bride. "I don't see any attempts to understand why the boundaries have changed or to work with people here to try to stabilise them."

"Because we're too busy fighting the Nightsiders!" said the Sarjeant. "They won't listen to us. Won't let us do what's necessary."

"Maybe if you stopped killing them," Jack suggested.

"They've killed my people," said the Sarjeant. "Murdered members of my family, who only came here to save the world."

"You're so busy concentrating on the big picture, you can't see what you're doing," said the Bride. "You have to concentrate on what's in front of you. Like this hospital, full of the wounded and the dying."

"So take your stupid war somewhere else," said Jack.

"There are no innocents here," said the Sarjeant. "Only murderers we haven't dealt, with yet." He turned to his people. "Kill these two traitors, then deal with the hospital. Whatever it takes."

He shouldn't have turned away from the Bride. Her fist came sweeping around in a vicious arc and punched him in the side of the head. The spiked knuckle-duster tore open half his face. He fell to one knee but had his armour up before Spring-heeled Jack could get to him. A glowing razor flashed toward the Sarjeant's throat, and he automatically raised an armoured arm to block it. The vicious edge cut sliced in and out of the golden strange matter, cutting deep into the flesh beneath. The armour sealed over immediately, but the Sarjeant could feel blood streaming down his arm, under the armour. He summoned a machine-pistol and sprayed bullets wildly about him. The Bride and Spring-heeled Jack dived out of the way, and the Sarjeant took advantage of that to scramble back out of range.

The other Droods arrived, and Spring-heeled Jack went dancing among them, moving too swiftly to be stopped. His razor gleamed impossibly bright as it cut through armour and flesh. The Bride strode right into the midst of the Droods and struck out powerfully with her blessed and cursed knuckle-dusters. Her punches cracked armour and sent Droods staggering, but the armour repaired itself, and the Droods always came back. The Bride just kept fighting, making no attempt to defend herself. Death held no horrors for her.

One extraordinary man and one woman raised from the dead took on a small army of Droods and held them back from their objective. But both sides knew that wouldn't last.

Inside Saint Margaret's, Julien ran himself ragged organising barricades and inspiring the walking wounded to take up arms to defend the hospital because the staff were just too busy. Or exhausted. JC did what he could. Julien finally paused for a moment, leaning against a wall, his eyes drooping with fatigue.

"I'd much rather be outside, fighting the Droods with Jack and the Bride. But I learned the hard way; I'm no match for Droods in their armour."

"There are all kinds of ways to fight," JC said thoughtfully. "Excuse me, while I wander off and have a little ponder about that."

He walked away, humming a merry tune. Leaving Julien to get back to organising defences he knew wouldn't even slow the Droods down. Because he had to do something.

Outside in the car-park, the Bride and Spring-heeled Jack had been forced back-to-back, surrounded by Droods. The two of them held their ground before the front entrance, refusing to be moved. Blood dripped thickly from Jack's razor and from the Bride's spiked knuckle-dusters. The Sarjeant summoned a really powerful gun and aimed it at the Bride's head. She glared back at him unflinchingly. And then the door behind them opened, and JC Chance came strolling out.

"Fall back," he said calmly to Jack and the Bride. "I've got this."

They almost collapsed through the door, leaning on each other for support, happy for someone else to take over. JC smiled easily at the Sarjeant.

"Hello, Cedric. That is you under the armour, isn't it? The stance and the really big gun are a bit of a give-away."

"It just goes to show," the Sarjeant said disgustedly. "You can't trust anyone. Walk away, Ghost Finder. While you still can."

"Really?" said JC. "You know, that's just what I was about to say to you."

The Sarjeant raised his gun. JC took off his sun-glasses, and a golden light blazed from his eyes, so unbearably otherworldly, the Sarjeant and all the other Droods had no choice but to turn their heads aside. JC looked around the empty car-park and saw a door standing on its own that hadn't been there a moment before. Just an ordinary, everyday door, standing entirely unsupported, with a large EXIT sign glowing above it. JC smiled at the door and snapped his fingers commandingly.

"Come out, all you dead and dearly departed! Come forth, all you who died here at Saint Margaret's. Come to me, all of you who lost loved ones here, or had your loved ones saved by those who work within. Come back because the hospital needs you."

The door to the after-life swung open, and an unearthly light spilled out across the car-park. And through that door, the dead returned. An endless stream of ghosts, shining in the night like so many candles in church. More and more of them came through, transparent figures with solemn faces full of reproach and condemnation. They made no move to attack the armoured Droods, just strode endlessly forward to stand in shimmering ranks before the hospital. Hundreds of them, men and women and children, come back to defend the last place that had cared for them. The Sarjeant looked around at his Droods and saw at once there were no orders he could give that they would follow against such protectors. He turned his back on the hospital and stalked out of the car-park. The other Droods went with him.

JC put his sun-glasses back on. He nodded easily to the ranks of standing ghosts and went back inside the hospital, to give them the good news.

John Taylor and Suzie Shooter arrived at Strangefellows in a taxi. They'd commandeered it by the simple expedient of Suzie's stepping out in front of the taxi and aiming her shotgun at the driver. She'd then kept the barrel of the gun pressed against the back of the driver's head all the way to the bar. He had enough sense not to ask for a tip and drove off the moment John and Suzie were out of his cab. They hurried down the back alley-way and were immediately confronted by Betty and Lucy Coltrane, armed with sledge-hammers. They nodded John and Suzie past and took up their positions again, looking hopefully for someone to come and challenge them. John and Suzie went inside.

They could hear the noise even as they descended the metal stairs: an uproar of raised voices, screams and shouts and foul language. But this wasn't just another night at Strangefellows. When they got to the bottom of the stairs, they discovered the bar had been turned into a field hospital. The furniture had been cleared away and the injured laid out in rows on the floor. Volunteers moved among the wounded and the dying, doing what they could with what they had. Persecution Psmith, the Puritan Adventurer, moved among the worst off, praying over them and offering what comfort he could. Rather unfairly, his black garb made him look like a gorecrow on a battle-field.

John stood at the bottom of the stairs, lost for anything to say. He'd known things were bad; he'd seen the Droods ploughing through Nightside defenders, but still the blood and pain and death laid out before him hit him hard. He wanted to do something but had no idea what. In the end, Suzie put a hand on his arm and urged him forward. They headed for the bar, where Alex was dispensing endless hard liquor as an alternative to pain-killers and anæsthetics. He nodded grimly to John and Suzie.

"Brilliant Chang's idea," he said. "I didn't get a say in the matter. Not that I objected. It makes me feel as though I'm contributing something."

"Why did he choose Strangefellows?" said John.

"Because we have the best protections in the Nightside," said Alex. "To hide this from the Droods. Word is, they're already attacking Saint Margaret's. That's why I wanted you here, John. You saw Betty and Lucy in the alley-way?"

"They looked very keen," said John.

"Oh, they are," said Alex. "You have no idea how keen. But just one Drood would walk right over them."

"Someone will talk about what's happening here," said Suzie. "Because someone always does." She looked at John. "See what you can do. I'll go outside and support the Coltranes."

She walked off. Alex looked at John.

"You haven't told her yet, have you? About the young man who appeared here before the invasion, claiming to be your son from the future. He said the whole world was going to be destroyed because of something you were going to do."

"And I killed him," said John. "Because if I hadn't, he would have killed me. How could I tell Suzie something like that? I've been trying to find the right moment, but we've been so busy . . ."

"I think you should tell her right now," said Alex, looking over John's shoulder.

John sighed. "She's standing right behind me, isn't she?"

"I had to come back to use the toilet," said Suzie. "One of the problems with being this pregnant is that your bladder contracts to the size of a pea. Yes, I heard everything. So talk to me, John. Right now."

"Don't you need to . . ."

"It can wait."

He told her the whole story, and when he was done, Suzie looked down at her bump, protruding from her leather jacket.

"You really think that was our son?"

"No," said John. "He couldn't be. I made sure that future timeline could never happen. You know I did."

"But you never foresaw the Drood invasion," said Suzie. "Who knows what you might feel compelled to do to stop it?"

And that was when the future Suzie appeared, stepping out of nowhere to stand before them. She looked old and hard-used, her straggly grey hair packed with dirt. Inside her torn and battered leathers, she was painfully thin. Half her face had been savagely burned, long ago, the skin blackened and crisped, twisted around the seared-shut eye. One side of her mouth was turned up in a permanent caustic smile. Her right forearm was missing. The last time John had seen her, right here in Strangefellows, her arm had been replaced by the Speaking Gun, grafted directly onto her elbow. Merlin had torn it off, and she had vanished.

"I sent our son back through Time to stop you," said the future Suzie, in a harsh cracked voice. "And you murdered him."

"You're not my Suzie," said John. "And he wasn't our son."

"You look just like I remember you, John," said the future Suzie. "And you still have that same arrogance that will damn the whole world to Hell."

Suzie drew Wulfsbane. The future Suzie smiled at her. "And that, right there, is where I was born."

She disappeared. Suzie stared at the empty space for a long moment, then put the sword away.

"I really don't see the point of that visit," said John, keeping his voice carefully steady. "I mean, she didn't try to do anything to stop me. Didn't tell me anything I could use, didn't so much as threaten me . . . So what was the point?"

"She sounded like me," said Suzie.

"But she had an injured face!" said John. "And yours was healed long ago. So she can't be your future."

"Who knows what might happen between now and then," said Suzie. "I'm going outside for a while. To think."

"Before that, don't you need to . . . ?" said Alex.

"More than ever," said Suzie.

Sometime later, she was standing in the back alley, some distance away from Betty and Lucy Coltrane, who wanted nothing to do with the sword on her back . . . when two Droods came walking down the alley in their armour. Betty and Lucy hefted their sledge-hammers and did their best to look confident. Suzie put a hand on Wulfshead's hilt, then stopped as the Droods came to a halt and lowered their armour. Revealing a middle-aged blonde and a younger woman with dark skin. They stood together, doing their best to look not at all threatening.

"I am Dr Mary Drood," said the older woman. "This is my colleague, Dr Indira Drood. We're here because we can't support what our family is doing."

"The Matriarch isn't in charge any more," said Indira. "The Sarjeant-at-Arms has taken control, and I honestly think he's lost his mind. All he wants to do is kill people."

"But we are doctors," said Mary. "So we walked away."

"We couldn't fight our own family," said Indira. "So we came here to offer our assistance."

"How did you find this place?" said Suzie.

"We just followed the injured," said Mary. "And if we could do that, you can bet it won't be long before someone else does the same thing."

Suzie's hand closed around Wulfsbane's hilt. The sword was murmuring in her head, reminding her how many people were dead and dying because of the Droods, and how good it would feel to make some Droods pay for that. So Suzie took her hand away from the sword, just to make it clear she was in charge.

"Go down into the bar," she said. "See what you can do."

The two Drood doctors made their way down the metal stairs and quietly introduced themselves to John Taylor. He took them to see Persecution Psmith. The old Puritan Adventurer had been around so long he could look into anyone's heart and see the truth there, which was why he so rarely got invited to parties. Not that he would have gone, anyway. He took one look at the two Droods and vouched for both of them, so John just left them to it.

Dr Mary and Dr Indira rolled up their sleeves and got to work. Not letting the extent of the carnage and suffering get to them. They'd feel guilty later, when they had time. They quickly used up the half-dozen medical blobs they had on the worst cases. They weren't used to working without their usual medicines and support tech, but they'd both had field training, where you learned to make do with what you had. And it helped that they could quietly shape their armour into all kinds of surgical instruments. They concentrated on saving lives and didn't think about anything else. It got in the way of doing the job.

* * *

Augusta and Agatha Moon were the next notable faces to arrive at Strangefellows. Augusta, the middle-aged supernatural trouble-shooter, was still wearing her tweed suit from the Adventurers Club, even though much of it was spattered with other people's blood. She'd lost her monocle, and the silver top of her heavy walking-stick was caked with dried blood and matted hairs. She strode up to the bar with her sister, Agatha, at her side, and Alex immediately found a reason to be very busy at the other end. John Taylor felt like running away too but made himself stand his ground. Because Augusta would only chase after him, tackle him, then sit on him while she told him what she wanted.

"Hello, Augusta," he said resignedly. "What are you doing here?"

"I had to walk out of the Adventurers Club," she said briskly. "Damn fools still can't make up their minds as to which side they should be on. It all got a bit loud, and the next thing you know, there are blood and teeth flying on the air. I don't mind a bit of boisterousness in the bar, but you can't beat good sense into someone else's head, no matter how big a stick you use. I know, I've tried. So I decided to come here. Only other decent bar in the Nightside. And what I saw on the way here was enough to convince me that the Droods have lost it, big time. I called my sister and told her to meet me here. So we could decide what to do about it."

"I thought I was being invited out for a quiet drink," said Agatha. "Not a trip to a slaughter-house."

A renowned business woman in an elegantly tailored suit, Agatha had short dark hair, a striking face, and a superior expression. Which she was having a hard time maintaining in the face of so much death and suffering.

"Hello, Agatha," John said politely. "Looking for Alex?"

"You know better than that." She scowled around her. "This used to be my favourite drinking-place when I was younger. Augusta and I came here all the time. Look at what the Droods have made of it."

"This is where you met Alex," said Augusta. "I introduced you."

"And I still haven't forgiven you," said Agatha. "Hold everything. What is *that*?"

John looked. "That is Alex's pet vulture. And next to her is the egg she laid, sometime back. Most of us are still having trouble coming to terms with the idea that anything was willing to have sex with the scabby-looking thing, and there is quite a lot of betting going on as to what will eventually emerge from the egg."

"But the egg is bigger than the bird!" said Agatha.

"I know," said John. "It grew. Intriguing, isn't it?"

"Does the bird have a name?" said Augusta. "Would it like a cracker or something?"

"Don't try to feed her," John said quickly. "She'll have your hand off. Her name is Agatha."

"What?" said Agatha Moon. "Alex named his pet vulture after me?"

Augusta almost doubled over, she was laughing so hard. When she finally straightened up, she had to wipe tears from her eyes before she could say anything.

"Guess you really shouldn't have cheated on him, Agatha. And definitely not with Merlin Satanspawn, who had to possess Alex's body so he could do it."

Agatha shrugged. "I always did have a thing for older men."

"Talk to Alex," Augusta said firmly. "Go on, girl. Make your peace with him. We may not have much time left."

Agatha sighed and went down the bar to join Alex. He nodded to her.

"Relax," he said. "I'm too tired to be properly mad at you. And our small problems don't seem that important compared to what's covering the floor of my bar."

"Where's your young bit of stuff?" said Agatha.

"Cathy Barrett is on her way here," said Alex. "I just hope she's being sensible and avoiding the trouble spots. Have you got anyone in your life?"

"No one who stayed," said Agatha.

"Well," said Alex. "I am a hard act to follow."

And that was when the Sarjeant-at-Arms came stamping down the metal stairs into the bar, followed by half his remaining troops. The other half were still trapped in the alley-way, fighting Suzie Shooter and the Coltranes. The Sarjeant had come to Strangefellows because everyone else he'd sent had got diverted and because he felt the need to achieve at least one clear victory.

He stepped away from the bottom of the stairs and gestured for his

Droods to spread out on either side of him. And then he armoured down so everyone could see his face. Half of it was torn apart, only held together by dried blood, and his gaze was very cold. If it bothered him at all to be confronted by so much suffering and death that he was responsible for, it didn't show. Dr Mary and Dr Indira Drood stood up to face him, quietly defiant. The Sarjeant dismissed them with a glance and fixed his attention on John Taylor at the bar. Augusta Moon moved to stand beside John, hefting her stick. Alex produced his glowing baseball bat from behind the bar. And still more golden figures came hurrying down the metal stairs to join the Sarjeant and fan out across the bar.

John took a step forward, and everyone looked to him, to see what he would say and do.

"How did you know I was here, Cedric?" he said finally.

"I didn't," said the Sarjeant. "I'm just here to take control of the bar. Your death will be a fortunate bonus."

"This is a hospital," said John.

"I don't care any more," said the Sarjeant. "All I care about now is winning. After everything I've been through, everything I've seen and had to do . . . I have to win. Or all of it will have been for nothing."

He looked around sharply, at the sound of a single set of footsteps descending the metal stairs. Everyone turned to look as Suzie Shooter descended into the bar. She had Wulfsbane in her hand. Blood dripped thickly from the long blade. The Droods fell back to give her room. She stopped at the bottom of the stairs.

"Where are the rest of my people?" the Sarjeant asked.

"Dead," said Suzie.

The Sarjeant shook his head slowly and turned to his remaining troops.

"Kill them all," he said. "Kill everyone in this God-forsaken place."

And that was when the great black egg on the bar cracked open, and a miniature dragon blasted its way out. Bright green, with a proud head and wide membranous wings, it flew across the bar and breathed flames on the Droods. Dragonfire washed across golden armour in endless streams until it melted and ran away. The Droods struggled to get back up the metal staircase, and the dragon swept back and forth above them, bathing them in its fiery breath. One by one the Droods fell and did not move again.

Only those nearest the foot of the stairs were able to escape, pushing the Sarjeant ahead of them because he didn't want to go.

The dragon flew back to settle on the bar, where the vulture cooed maternally over it. And everyone else went back to work, helping those they could.

CHAPTER TWELVE

Who's Missing from This Photograph?

T he war raged on, devastating the Nightside, and the bodies piled up. Blood and horror filled the long night, and still neither side seemed any closer to winning. So, unbeknownst to each other, both sides decided it was time for extreme measures. In order to finally put a stop to the fighting, they would do the unspeakable, the unthinkable. In their own way, and for their own reasons, both sides decided it was time to bring back the dead.

The Matriarch called for a meeting with the Sarjeant-at-Arms. The Droods were still having problems with torc-to-torc communication, so the Matriarch chose one of her most reliable messengers, a young man named Ruan, and sent him off to find the Sarjeant. The Matriarch waited with her people, resisting all attempts to continue the fighting, until Ruan finally returned with word from the Sarjeant. The word was that the Sarjeant was far too busy to come to her. He had ground to hold and attacks to organise, so if she wanted to speak with him, she would have to follow the messenger back to the Sarjeant.

The Matriarch took pains to nod calmly, as though this was only reasonable and nothing more than she'd expected, and seethed inwardly. She couldn't afford to let her people see how angry she was at having her authority thrown back in her face. She would go to the Sarjeant and make him pay for his defiance. She nodded stiffly to Ruan, who had delivered the Sarjeant's words with a definite air of *Please don't shoot the messenger for the message,* and he set off quickly, with the Matriarch striding along behind. Silently rehearsing all the many pointed things she meant to say to her Sarjeant-at-Arms to remind him which one of them was in charge.

Ruan led her through burned-out ruins and blood-spattered streets, and she wouldn't let herself look away from all the corpses. The stench of blood and slaughter hung on the night air like a ground mist that refused to dissipate. None of it was her intention, none of it what she'd wanted.

The Sarjeant's words had been the closest he'd come so far to open defiance. She was the Matriarch; her word was law. He lived only to serve her, and through her, the family. That was the way it had always been. So what the hell did the man think he was doing? Yes, she'd put him in charge of the invasion, with responsibility for all practical matters, but she was still the Matriarch.

Ruan led her through wrecked streets, full of deserted buildings with smashed windows and kicked-in doors. There was no sign of resisting Nightsiders anywhere. They'd learned that tackling the Droods head-on rarely got them anywhere. The Matriarch kept a careful eye out for hidden attacks and ambushes, but no one moved in the dark alley-ways. A thought struck the Matriarch and chilled her to the bone. The Sarjeant couldn't have killed everyone in the area, could he? She followed Ruan through places where all the street-lights had been smashed, the ever-present neon signs were dull or broken, and only a shimmering blue-white illumination from the oversized moon was left to light their way. The Matriarch moved in close beside Ruan, who seemed grateful for the company.

"Why has the Sarjeant put so much effort into destroying everything?" said the Matriarch. "I haven't seen any evidence of real resistance for some time: no bloodstains, no bodies . . . So what happened here?"

"The Sarjeant disapproved of this entire area," said Ruan, staring straight ahead. "We are in Rotten Row, Matriarch, where people go to have sex with gods and monsters, aliens and computers, ghosts and demons and some of the livelier versions of the walking dead. Rotten Row, where sex isn't just a sin and a sacrament, it's an obsession."

"I see," said the Matriarch. "That was rather more information than I needed . . ."

"The Sarjeant had a lot to say on the subject," said Ruan. "And I really didn't feel like interrupting him. Should I continue?"

"There's more?" said the Matriarch. "More importantly, is it relevant?"

"It is, if you want to understand why the Sarjeant ordered all of this," said Ruan. He waited for her to nod stiffly and carried on. "When the Sarjeant came here he didn't like what he saw, so he had his troops drag people out of the buildings. And when he found out what they did here, and about some of the people and things they did it with . . . He said Rotten Row was an affront to everything the Droods believed in."

"How many people died here?" said the Matriarch.

"All of them," said Ruan.

They continued on in silence. The long street stretched away before them, as empty and silent as the dark side of the moon. When they finally reached the end, it widened out to form a great open square, and there was the Sarjeant and his troops. Rows and ranks of golden figures, the largest remaining part of the Drood invasion force, waiting patiently while the Sarjeant argued with his advisors over where to go next. Apparently the Droods were now so far off what few maps they had that even the Armourer's compasses didn't work. No one seemed too sure of where anywhere else was in relation to where they were now. The Sarjeant wanted to know where he could find the Authorities, because once he had them, he'd have control of the Nightside. But no one had anything useful to offer. The Sarjeant was growing angrier by the moment, while the people standing before him looked increasingly nervous.

Ruan led the Matriarch through the standing Droods, and row by row they armoured down. Normally she would have taken that as a sign of respect, but what she saw in their revealed faces wasn't so much an acknowledgment of her authority as simple curiosity. Their main reaction seemed to be: *What is she doing here?* As though she had no right to interrupt the Sarjeant, or the important work they were doing. The Sarjeant waited until the Matriarch had almost reached him before he turned abruptly to face her. Ruan stopped dead and let the Matriarch continue on her own.

The Matriarch was shocked to discover that half of the Sarjeant's face was a bloody mess; dark dried blood crusted over deep and nasty wounds. It looked like some animal had tried to claw his face off. He didn't even nod to the Matriarch, just waited to see what she had to say. She kept her voice carefully calm and business-like.

"What happened to you, Sarjeant?"

"I let a traitor get too close," he said flatly. "Where were you, Matriarch? We were supposed to meet at St Jude's, but when I got there, you'd already moved on."

"Is that where . . . ?"

"No. Where were you?"

"I had business elsewhere," she said steadily. "People I needed to talk to."

"You were talking. I should have known." The Sarjeant made a sharp, dismissive gesture. "What do you want, Matriarch?"

His voice was flat, openly disinterested. The Matriarch met his cold stare with an even colder glare of her own.

"What have you been doing here, Sarjeant? I didn't order any of this."

"Just what needed doing."

The Matriarch pressed on. "I have been talking with Charles and Emily. As Heads of the Department of Uncanny, they have been able to provide an outside view, and it's clear to me that my plan for the invasion has failed. I wanted a bloodless coup, or at the very least, an absolute minimum of death and destruction. This mass butchery is not what I intended. More importantly, it isn't helping us win. And we did come here to win, Sarjeant, not just stamp out everything you disapprove of. We came here to solve the problem of the expanding boundaries!"

"You have some other course of action in mind?" said the Sarjeant.

"Charles and Emily believe they can arrange a meeting with the surviving members of the Authorities," the Matriarch said steadily. "Brilliant Chang, Annie Abattoir, and Julien Advent. So we can work together on how to put the Nightside boundaries back where they belong."

The Sarjeant stopped her with an impatient gesture. "I know Jessica Sorrow is dead. I was there when she overreached herself. What happened to Hadleigh Oblivion?"

"All three Oblivion Brothers invaded Drood Hall in our absence," said the Matriarch. "None of them survived. Apparently the Librarian killed Hadleigh personally."

The Sarjeant smiled for the first time. "I always knew Uncle William still had it in him."

"The important thing is to put an end to the fighting and concentrate on what really matters," said the Matriarch.

The Sarjeant looked around him, at all the things he'd done, and smiled again. "This is what really matters."

"We have to make a deal, Sarjeant! We're not winning this war!"

The Sarjeant leaned forward suddenly, thrusting his injured face right into hers. "No deals! The Bride of Frankenstein ripped my face apart. One of our own allies. This is what being in the Nightside does to people. We can't trust anyone. How can you talk about stopping the fighting when so many of the family are dead or injured? We paid a high price for the ground we've taken, and I will not allow it to be for nothing."

The Matriarch met his gaze with cold authority. "And what have we gained that was worth all this blood and suffering, Sarjeant?"

"I always knew you were too weak to lead the Droods into battle," said the Sarjeant. He didn't sound pleased to have his suspicions confirmed, only terribly tired. "I knew you didn't have the guts to do what needed doing. And I always knew it would come to this. So I will take charge of the family now."

He gestured to half-a-dozen of his people, and they quickly moved forward, as though they'd only been waiting for orders. They armoured up and surrounded the Matriarch. They made no move against her, but from the way they looked to the Sarjeant, it was clear they were ready to do anything he wanted. The Matriarch stood very still.

"Don't put on your armour, Maggie," said the Sarjeant, quite calmly. "Or I will have them subdue you. By any means necessary. I can't afford another traitor with a knife at my back. Surrender, and you'll live to go back to your precious gardens when all of this is over."

The Matriarch looked to her messenger, Ruan. He was looking at the Sarjeant with something very like hero-worship, and she knew she'd lost him. She was on her own. The Matriarch nodded stiffly to the Sarjeant, not so much surrendering to him as to the inevitable. The family had decided it belonged to the Sarjeant, body and soul. All she could do was bide her time and wait for a chance.

"Find somewhere secure and lock her up," said the Sarjeant. "Don't hurt her unless you have to. When the war is over, we'll find someone more suited to be Matriarch."

One of the armoured Droods surrounding the Matriarch gestured at a nearby building, and they all moved forward at once, herding her in that direction. She kept her face cool and calm as she went, though inside she was ice-cold with fury. She'd never wanted to be Matriarch; she was perfectly happy as head gardener, but they told her she had to do it, so she'd done everything in her power to be the Matriarch the family needed. And now they'd turned on her. She smiled sourly. She should have seen this coming. Ever since they entered the long night, the Sarjeant hadn't been the same. Maybe he was right; maybe just being here did things to people.

They'd almost reached the scorched and scarred building when Emily and Charles suddenly stepped out of the shadows to block their way. Charles held up a small green plastic clicker in the shape of a frog, and all the Droods surrounding the Matriarch cried out in shock and horror as their armour was forced back into their torcs. Emily took the Matriarch by the arm, and the three of them disappeared into the shadows.

The unarmoured Droods ran back to tell the Sarjeant what had happened. They stood stiffly before him, ready to accept whatever punishment he deemed necessary, but he just nodded, as though he should have expected it. This was the Nightside, after all. And then everyone looked around sharply as a very familiar figure came striding down the street toward them, the steady clacking of her heels disturbingly loud on the hush. It was Martha Drood, the previous Matriarch. Martha, who'd been murdered inside Drood Hall.

Tall and elegant and more regal-looking than the Queen, Martha strode right through the ranks of the shocked and startled Droods. A grey-haired woman in her seventies, dressed like country-side aristocracy in tweeds, twin-set, and pearls. She had been a famous beauty in her day, and her strong bone structure meant she was still striking. The Droods fell back to give her plenty of room as she passed, murmuring agitatedly among themselves. Because this was the Nightside. Everyone knew the dead walked here, sometimes. Martha finally came to a halt, directly before the Sarjeant, who looked steadily back at her.

"You're not her," he said flatly. "Not Martha. Give me one good reason why I shouldn't just kill you now, for such effrontery."

"Because I'm here to give you what you need, to win this war," said Martha.

And just like that she was gone. In her place stood Puck, the only elf who was not perfect. With the glamour dismissed, he was a short and compact figure, his body smooth and supple as a dancer's. But the hump on his back pushed one shoulder forward and down, and the hand on that arm had withered into a claw. His hair was grey, and his skin was the colour of yellowed bone. Two raised nubs on his forehead might have been horns. He wore a pelt of animal fur, which blended seamlessly into his own hairy lower body. His legs ended in cloven hooves.

Puck: trickster, spy, and joyful killer. Who hated humans almost as much as he hated his own kind.

"Well?" he said, smiling an unpleasantly knowing smile. "Aren't you pleased to see me, Cedric?"

"Is anyone ever pleased to see you?" said the Sarjeant. "How were you able to duplicate Martha? You never even met her."

"You'd be surprised who I've met," Puck said easily. "Martha had contacts with all kinds of surprising people. That's what made her such a successful Matriarch. She always was a very pragmatic person. You'd be surprised at some of the people who wanted to meet me when it suited them."

"I might if I cared," said the Sarjeant.

"Then let us talk of something you will care about," said Puck. "I am here to supply you with the troops you need, to make up for the Droods you've lost. I have an army waiting in the wings, enough trained fighters for you to put down any resistance the Nightside can set against you. More than enough to bring this war to a satisfying conclusion."

"Where could you find such an army?" said the Sarjeant.

"I offer you elves," said Puck. "Fighters who will sink themselves in slaughter for the sheer delight it brings. Elves with enchanted armour and cruel weapons, who are not scared of anything in the long night because they're always going to be the scariest things in it. Not all of us left this world, to go to Shadows Fall and the Sundered Lands. I offer you an army that will fight under your orders in return for a fair share of the loot to be found in a conquered Nightside."

The Sarjeant frowncd. "You'd fight for money?"

"Not for gold, Sarjeant," said Puck. "For ancient weapons and Objects of Power, for lost secrets and forbidden knowledge. The Nightside has those in abundance."

"And why should we give up any of those things to you?" said the Sarjeant.

"Because your family already has more of that than you know what to do with," said Puck.

"True," said the Sarjeant. "You have your deal. Bring me your army, and we'll raze the Nightside to the ground."

Molly, Isabella, and Louisa were talking together outside St Jude's. Because they disturbed the hell out of the people inside the church. They were busy playing catch-up, when they weren't arguing over who'd done most against the Droods. Eddie stood back and let them get on with it. He was worried about the Matriarch. She should have made contact with the Sarjeant and come back to tell him about it long ago. He'd sent Charles and Emily travelling through the shadows to check for him, and they hadn't come back either. He was just getting ready to interrupt the Metcalf sisters, by force if necessary, when Molly turned suddenly to face him.

"Stop worrying about the Matriarch. You must have known making a deal with the Sarjeant was going to take time."

"I should never have let her go," said Eddie. "The Sarjeant has the taste of blood in his mouth now, and I think he likes it. But she was so sure she could convince him . . ."

"You always were an optimist," said Molly. "Which is frankly odd for someone who grew up with your family."

"I'm fed up just standing around!" Isabella said loudly. "I came to the Nightside for a little action."

Louisa laughed and clapped her hands together delightedly. "Oh, me too! Do let's go! I want to break some more hearts and listen to people scream. I want to tear the spirit out of people and dance with the dead!"

Molly looked at Isabella. "You know . . . sometimes she even scares me."

"That's why I keep her close, as much as I can," said Isabella. "I keep hoping some of my sanity will rub off on her."

"I think I see a flaw in your scheme . . ." said Eddie.

Molly looked at him, and he stopped talking. And that was when Emily, Charles, and the Matriarch burst out of the shadows at the side of the church. Eddie's first thought was relief, until he saw the look on the Matriarch's face. It took awhile to get the whole story out of them, including some things they'd observed while hiding in the shadows; and then everyone stood around and thought about it.

"Puck?" Molly said finally. "What the hell is that twisted little troublemaker doing in the Nightside?"

"Taking advantage of the situation," said Eddie. "So he can play his games and stamp on human faces. But what's he doing here on his own? Usually, he only follows along behind Oberon and Titania."

"It sounded like he's struck out on his own," said the Matriarch. "He has his own army now."

"I can't believe the Sarjeant would put us in league with elves," said Eddie.

"I can," said Molly. "He's desperate, ready to grab at any chance that will let him win. And the Droods have taken so many losses, you can bet the rank and file won't have any problems going along with it. Your family isn't used to losing; they don't like the taste."

"They'll do it," the Matriarch said grimly. "Even my most trusted messenger threw in with the Sarjeant. The Droods have always admired fighters more than leaders. Which means . . . if I want to take back control of the family, I need something to make me stronger than the Sarjeant. I have to get back to Drood Hall, Eddie; talk to the Armourer and hope they can provide me with something powerful enough to overthrow the Sarjeant and an army of elves."

"Molly and I will go with you," said Eddie. "Isabella, you and Louisa stay here, with my mother and father. Protect St Jude's."

"But I want to go with you!" said Louisa, pouting.

"Yeah," said Isabella. "Why don't we get to go to Drood Hall?"

"Because St Jude's is important," said Eddie. "It matters."

The others nodded. They couldn't argue with that.

"I don't want to risk using the Merlin Glass," said Eddie. "The Sarjeant will have set some of his people to watch for its distinctive energies."

He looked at Molly, but she shook her head firmly.

"No, I can't just teleport us there. I've used up most of my magics, and the few I've got left I'm hanging on to for when I need them."

"Then use this," said the Matriarch. And she showed them the Merlin Glass from the future.

It took her awhile to explain what it was and when it had come from, but in the end Eddie just shrugged.

"It's the Nightside . . ."

The future Merlin Glass took Eddie, Molly, and the Matriarch straight to Blaiston Street, outside Drood Hall. The moment they stepped through the Glass, they were struck by how much conditions had deteriorated since they'd left. Half the buildings had collapsed, the brick and stone just crumbled away, as though centuries had passed. Eddie remembered a story he'd once been told, of a future Nightside where everything was ruins, and everyone was dead but the insects. The Matriarch reached out to the Merlin Glass, and it shrank down and shot through the air to nestle into her hand. The Matriarch looked at the Glass, then at the street.

"Has something gone wrong? Has the future Glass brought us to Blaiston Street's future?"

"No," Molly said immediately. "We're exactly where and when we're supposed to be."

"She knows about these things," said Eddie.

The Matriarch gave them both a hard look but went along. She put the hand-mirror away, while Molly scowled around the deserted street.

"This street is centuries older than it should be. The changed boundary must be stretching the fabric of the Nightside dangerously thin, maybe to breaking-point. So . . . if the long night keeps expanding into the outside world, the whole fabric of reality could be dangerously weakened."

"This war is just a distraction," said Eddie. "To keep us from noticing the real problem. I think someone deliberately arranged all of this."

"You mean we've been played?" The Matriarch glared around her, outraged. "Someone set the Droods and the Nightside at each other's throats, so they could put the whole world at risk? Who would do that?"

"When we find out who, that should give us the why," said Eddie. "For now, we need to concentrate on doing whatever it takes to stop the war. So we can get to the real problem."

"We need the Armourer," said the Matriarch.

She started toward the Hall, then stopped, as she took in the remains of the Droods' scarecrows, lying scattered across the road. Eddie recognised them immediately. He'd fought the scarecrows before. He knelt to study some of the pieces and frowned. They were desiccated, almost mummified, centuries old. Like the street.

"Something killed all the scarecrows?" said Molly, peering over Eddie's shoulder. "What kind of power could do that?"

"The Oblivion Brothers," said the Matriarch, as Eddie got to his feet again. "They came here to invade our home. Oh, don't worry; they're all dead. But we need to get inside the Hall and see what's happened in our absence."

She broke off as two figures emerged from the shadows to block the way. Dash Oblivion and Shirley den Adel, who long ago had been the Continental Op and the Lady Phantasm. They both looked their age now, tired and worn-down, faces drawn and haggard from tears and loss. But the old hands pointing guns at Eddie and Molly and the Matriarch were still perfectly steady. Eddie stood very still, wondering how Dash and Shirley could have got their hands on weapons specially designed for Drood field agents.

"Careful," he said quietly to Molly and the Matriarch. "Those are Colt Repeaters. They can call on whatever kind of ammunition they need to get the job done."

"Including strange-matter bullets?" asked the Matriarch, just as quietly.

"Theoretically, yes," said Eddie.

"Terrific . . ." said Molly.

"Our sons went into your Hall," Dash said loudly. "Hadleigh and Larry and Tommy. And none of them came out again. The Dark Academie says they're all dead."

"Your family murdered them!" said Shirley.

The Matriarch stepped forward to talk to them, and they opened fire. Eddie and the Matriarch armoured up, their golden armour closing over them before the bullets could get anywhere near them. Molly was already standing behind Eddie, using him as a shield. But the guns were only knock-offs, firing regular ammunition, and the golden armour just soaked that up. Eddie and the Matriarch stood their ground and let the old people shoot at them until finally Dash and Shirley accepted their guns were no good against Drood armour. They slowly lowered their weapons, and Eddie lowered his armour, to show them the sympathy on his face.

"I'm sorry about your sons," he said. "We've all lost people in this stupid war. We're trying to put an end to it."

"Why did you have to come here?" said Dash.

"You even killed my adopted daughter," said Shirley. "Ms Fate is dead."

"Oh no . . ." said Molly.

Dash and Shirley turned and walked away, leaning on each other. Two broken old heroes who had outlived their children.

"They're right," said the Matriarch, armouring down. "I should never have brought the family here. This isn't what Droods are supposed to do. If someone did trick us into this, for their own purposes, I will have their heart's blood."

She headed for the Hall, and Eddie and Molly hurried after her.

"How did you know the Oblivion Brothers were dead?" said Eddie.

"William got word to me after they'd been dealt with," said the Matriarch, not looking around. "He killed one of them himself."

Eddie wasn't sure how he felt about that. It sounded like the Librarian had saved the day, as well as the family, but it didn't sound like the William he thought he knew.

"How was he able to contact you?" he said, as much to distract himself as anything. "When we've been having such trouble with communications?"

"I never got a chance to ask him," said the Matriarch. "Presumably just being so close to Alpha Red Alpha was enough to boost his signal. I still don't see how the Oblivion Brothers were able to get in, past all our protections."

"You saw what they did to the scarecrows," said Molly.

"It's the Nightside," said Eddie.

"I am getting really tired of hearing that," said the Matriarch.

She slammed the front door open and strode into the entrance-hall, followed by Eddie and Molly. And the first thing they saw was the body of a man who'd been burned alive, curled up inside the half-melted remains of Drood armour. Eddie gestured sharply for the Matriarch to stay where she was, while he moved slowly forward for a closer look. He was remembering the dead Droods he'd found in the Other Hall, in the Other dimension Edmund came from.

Eddie knelt beside the twisted body, surrounded by thrown-off pools of melted armour. What kind of heat could have done such a thing? He looked for clues to the Drood's identity, but the face was just a skull with crisped and blackened remnants of skin clinging to it. The eyes and the nose were gone, and the teeth gleamed in a mirthless grin. There was no way of knowing who had laid down their life to defend the family.

After a while, Molly came over and patted Eddie comfortingly on the shoulder. He got to his feet, saying nothing, and led the way deeper into the Hall. The sound of three sets of footsteps was disturbingly loud on the hush. It didn't take them long to find more signs of damage. Blackened woodwork and scorched walls, and signs of fires that had burned for a while, then put themselves out, because there was no one to come and see to them. And finally, a great pile of fire-blackened bones and the remains of melted armour. More dead Droods, but no way of telling how many.

"What the hell happened here?" Molly said quietly.

"The Oblivion Brothers," said William.

They all looked around, as the Librarian emerged from a side corridor. His face was grim, and his gaze was cold, but Eddie had to admit he'd never seen the Librarian look so focused. The Matriarch started to question William, but he talked right across her.

"Ammonia is watching over the Hall, from a distance. She looked inside your head when you arrived and told me what you know. I'll take you down to the Armoury, so you can find what you need."

"The rest of the family in the Redoubt," said the Matriarch. "Are they all right?"

"Most of them," said William. "Some came out to fight the Oblivion Brothers. You've seen what happened to them. Ioreth is dead too. And his new girl-friend."

Eddie shook his head slowly. He'd liked Ioreth.

"You're sure all the Oblivion Brothers are dead?" said Molly. "They can be tricky . . ."

"They're dead," said William. "I killed Hadleigh to keep him from getting to the Armageddon Codex."

"How could so much have happened here in such a short time?" Eddie asked.

William smiled. "It's the Nightside."

Eddie didn't think he liked this new version of the Librarian.

"Did anyone else get into the Hall?" said the Matriarch. "Are there any other enemies still at large?"

"No," said William. "I had the Armourer run a full interior scan and reinforce all the shields and protections. And, of course, Ammonia is keeping an eye on everything. The Hall is secure."

The Librarian led them down into the Armoury. He didn't have anything else to say, and no one felt like asking him any more questions. There was something about this new William, the air of a man who had remembered when he used to be dangerous. The Armoury was full of lab assistants bustling around in their white coats or struggling with exotic new pieces of high-tech, all talking at the same time and at the top of their voices. It made Eddie feel briefly nostalgic for the way the Armoury used to be under his uncle Jack. The Armourer were fiercely intent on Alpha Red Alpha, so much so that Maxwell and Victoria didn't even notice the Matriarch was there until she said their names really loudly. They didn't seem surprised she was back and didn't even ask how the invasion was going. As always, they'd become so immersed in their work, they'd lost interest in everything else.

Alpha Red Alpha was surrounded by all kinds of diagnostic equipment, set up a cautious distance from the great dimensional engine.

"We tried attaching all kinds of sensors," said Max.

"But nothing would stick," said Vicky.

"We're not actually sure what the surface of Alpha Red Alpha is," said Max. "It only looks like crystal."

"Just one of the many secrets the engine's creator never got around to putting down on paper," said Vicky. "He kept it all in his head."

"Which is probably what drove him crazy," said Max. "Though, of course, it's always possible he never wrote anything down because he knew that if the family ever found out what he'd used to make Alpha Red Alpha, they definitely wouldn't approve."

"So we're using remote scanners and sensors," said Vicky. "They're telling us all kinds of things."

"Not terribly useful things as yet," said Max. "But we are starting to get a sense of why Alpha Red Alpha dropped the Hall here instead of in the centre of the Nightside, as intended."

"At first we thought the centre must be more heavily protected," said Vicky. "To make invasion more difficult."

"But now the evidence is suggesting that something from outside interfered in the transition," said Max. "And deliberately dumped us here, so the family would have to fight its way into the Nightside."

"Making my plan for a bloodless coup untenable," said the Matriarch. "Doomed from the start." And then she stopped and looked sharply at the Armourer. "Why didn't you take your people up into the Hall when the Oblivion Brothers broke in? Why did you leave it to the Librarian to defend the family home?"

The Armourer looked at each other, genuinely surprised.

"Someone got in?" said Max.

"We didn't hear a thing!" said Vicky.

"But then, behind the Armoury's shields, we wouldn't," said Max. He looked at William. "You never told us . . ."

"You were busy," said William.

"We would have helped," said Max.

"You know we would," said Vicky.

"Yes," said William. "I know. It's all right. I took care of everything."

The Matriarch looked steadily at the Armourer. "You said something interfered with Alpha Red Alpha. What could be powerful enough to do that?"

"We're still working on the problem," Max said carefully, "but we have been able to identify the nature of the energies involved."

"We've encountered them before," said Vicky. "It was the elves."

"Puck!" said Eddie. "That's why he turned up here to meet with the Sarjeant!"

"But why would he want to interfere?" said the Matriarch.

"Because it's been him all along," said Eddie. "Everything that's happened here has been down to Puck. That devious, twisted little . . . He wanted a war between the Droods and the Nightside, to weaken both of us."

"But what would he get out of it?" said Molly. "Most of the elves are gone now, to Shadows Fall or the Sundered Lands. Whatever grudges they might have had they took with them."

"Maybe he thinks if he can weaken the Droods enough, the elves will come back," said Eddie.

"And a depopulated Nightside could make a fine new home for the elves," said William.

"We have to talk to the Sarjeant," said the Matriarch. "Tell him what we know."

"You really think he'll care?" said Eddie.

Razor Eddie came to Strangefellows to talk with John Taylor. He walked steadily between the wounded and the dying laid out on the floor, not even looking at them because he knew there was nothing he could do to help. Razor Eddie wasn't there for the good things in life. He nodded easily to John at the bar, and his ghostly grey voice was entirely calm as he told him Dead Boy was finally dead, and that the Street of the Gods now belonged to the Droods.

"Let them have it," Razor Eddie said finally. "It's not like there's anyone left for them to kill."

"You couldn't help Dead Boy," John said kindly. "But maybe you can help us. We're trying to think of something powerful enough to stop the Drood invasion."

"Have you tried the Gun Shoppes of Usher?" said Razor Eddie.

"Closed," said John. "For the duration."

"Use your gift," said Razor Eddie.

"It's not that simple," said John. "My gift needs a specific question before it can provide a specific answer."

"I'm not sure anything can stop the Droods now," said Razor Eddie. "They can die; I've killed my share. But there are just so many of them."

Brilliant Chang was suddenly standing right next to them. No one flinched or jumped; sudden appearances were business as usual at Strangefellows. But John thought Brilliant looked tired and drawn, even haggard. He nodded to Alex, who poured Brilliant a large whiskey. Brilliant knocked it back in one gulp, and Alex looked at him reproachfully.

"If I'd known you were just thirsty, I wouldn't have wasted the good stuff on you."

"I've just been to Saint Margaret's," said Brilliant. "I asked Julien Advent to come with me, to broker a peace deal with the Droods. But he wouldn't leave the hospital as long as it needed defending. And Annie Abattoir has lost her mind since her daughter died. So that just leaves me, the last of the Authorities, to make whatever kind of deal will stop the fighting. I was hoping you'd come with me, Walker. Just to make it clear I can speak for the Nightside."

"Traitor!" said an angry voice behind them.

They looked around, and there was Annie Abattoir, her face flushed with rage.

"You're ready to betray the Nightside to the Droods!"

"Take it easy, Annie," John said carefully. "We're just talking. Working out our options. We're all friends here."

"She won't listen," said Brilliant. "She lost her mind when Tamsin died."

"You're not fit to mention her name!" said Annie.

She stabbed her elven wand at him. Brilliant's hands moved impossibly fast, raising a screen of protective magics that howled and coruscated on the air before him. But the elven magics punched right through and exploded him where he stood. Bloody pieces of Brilliant spattered across the front of the bar, only narrowly missing John. Annie turned to face him.

"And you, John Taylor. You're just as bad. Just as ready to make a deal with the Droods."

Suzie Shooter was immediately there at John's side, Wulfsbane in her hand, shedding its terrible light across the scene. Razor Eddie's straight razors gleamed supernaturally bright in his hands as he stepped forward. Annie looked quickly back and forth between them, then stabbed the elven wand at the Punk God. One of his hands moved too quickly to follow, and his razor cut the magic out of the air before it could reach him. And while Annie was distracted by that, John raised his gift and used it to find the connection between the wand and the elves who provided its power. And then it was the easiest thing in the world for him to break the link, leaving Annie with nothing but a piece of carved bone in her hand. She felt the power go out of it and dropped the wand to the floor.

"What have I done?" she said slowly. "I never meant to hurt so many people."

"It was the wand," said John, kindly. "Affecting the mind. There's a reason why people say never trust elves offering gifts."

"This wasn't even why I came to Strangefellows," said Annie. She struggled to bring her thoughts back together. "I came here to tell you there is a way to stop the Droods. Something I was told about when I first joined the

Authorities. Something so dangerous only the Authorities could be allowed to know it even existed."

"Then why didn't Brilliant tell us?" said Suzie. She'd sheathed the Infernal Device but was still watching Annie carefully.

"Probably because he was afraid to use it," said Annie. "And with good reason. I came here to tell you where to find it, John. If you're ready to risk everything to stop the Droods."

"After what they've done, I'll do whatever it takes," said John.

"Under the Nightside, in the deepest part of the World Beneath, there is a Door," said Annie. "A very special Door, made long ago to give us access to realities beyond our own. Created so the Authorities would always be able to find whoever or whatever they needed to protect the long night."

"You have someone in mind, don't you?" said John. "Someone you think we should call on . . . You want to bring back Merlin Satanspawn, don't you?"

"No," said Annie, meeting his gaze steadily. "We need your mother, John. We need Lilith, the creator of the Nightside."

John said nothing, his thoughts racing. At the end of the war against Lilith, when she'd tried to destroy all of her creation and every living thing in it for the sin of not being what she'd intended, John had helped push his mother outside reality. With the help of his father, Charles, who went with Lilith to make sure she could never return. His mother and his father, fighting forever, to keep this world safe.

"My father sacrificed himself to make sure Lilith could never threaten us again," John said finally. "It wasn't what I wanted, but that's how it worked out. And now you want to bring her back?"

"Can you think of anyone more suited," asked Annie, "to destroy an army of Droods?"

Everyone looked at everyone else. No one wanted to be the first to say anything. In the end, Alex cleared his throat.

"Allow me to be the first to say that this sounds like a really bad idea. And as someone who's had more than his fair share, trust me when I say I know one when I hear one. I don't think anyone here doubts Lilith could stop the Droods. Hell, she'd probably eat them up on toast. But how would we stop Lilith, afterwards?"

"You defeated her once, John," said Annie. "You could do it again."

"We got lucky," said John. "You have no idea how lucky. This time, Lilith would be forewarned. I'm not sure anyone could stop her a second time."

"Are we really that desperate?" said Suzie.

"You can ask that?" said Annie. "With an Infernal Device on your back?"

"We have to think of something else," said Alex. "Right, John?" And then he stopped because he really didn't like the look on John's face. "Oh, come on! Are you seriously considering this? Why don't we just have Suzie shoot us all in the face; it'll probably hurt less!"

"I don't like the idea," said John. "But what else is there?"

"Maybe this is why the gods left the Street of the Gods," Razor Eddie said quietly. "Not because of the Droods but because they saw Lilith coming back."

"She did kill a lot of them," said Alex. "Even though some were her children." They all looked at him, and he shrugged. "I keep up with things . . . John, you can't bring your mother back. You just can't."

"We're losing the war!" said John. "The Droods will kill us all and burn the Nightside to the ground before they stop, and I can't think of anything else to do! Suzie, we have to go to the World Beneath. Just to see if this Door can do everything it's supposed to."

"I'll bring Wulfsbane," said Suzie.

"You do that," said Alex. "Lilith could probably use a snack."

"I won't have anything to do with this," Razor Eddie said flatly. "I will stay here and protect Strangefellows."

"Me too," Alex said quickly.

"You'll need me, John," said Annie. "Only one of the Authorities can open the Door. And besides, I feel the need to make amends for some of the things I've done."

"Lot of that going around," said Razor Eddie.

At Drood Hall, down in the Armoury, the Matriarch fixed the Armourer with a cold, unwavering stare.

"I need something powerful enough to stop the Sarjeant and everyone with him. What have you got?"

"Are you asking for a weapon?" Max said carefully.

"Something that would kill the Sarjeant?" said Vicky. "Are we really talking about Droods killing Droods?"

The Matriarch made an exasperated gesture. "Not necessarily . . . What about Alpha Red Alpha? Could we just grab hold of the Sarjeant and his people and transport them out of the Nightside? Send them home to cool off and buy us some time?"

"The dimensional engine is linked to the Hall," said Max, still choosing his words very carefully. "Because that has always been its main function, to protect the Hall."

"We were only able to bring the family here because they were assembled right outside the Hall," said Vicky. "If you could lure the Sarjeant and his people back here, then perhaps . . ."

"Not a chance," said Eddie. "The Sarjeant would never give up the territory he's fought so hard to take."

"And you know he'd smell a trap," said Molly.

"Then, yes, I want a weapon," the Matriarch said steadily. "Something so appallingly powerful even the Sarjeant would have to surrender rather than face it. Then the family would follow me again, and I could bring this war to an end."

The Armourer looked at each other, then around the Armoury. The lab assistants had all stopped what they were doing to see what the Armourer would do. It was suddenly very quiet.

"We have all kinds of prototypes here," said Max. "And even more things ready for testing. But they were designed to take down our enemies, not members of our own family."

"The armour has always been our best weapon," said Vicky.

"Then why have so many things been able to get through it?" the Matriarch said sharply. "Ever since we came to this place, I've seen all manner of weapons and magics get past the armour and kill the Droods inside! That isn't supposed to be possible!"

"This is the Nightside," Max said simply. "All kinds of things are possible in the long night; that's the point. It wouldn't surprise me if some of reality's rules had been bent, just a little, specifically to weaken our armour. Just in case we ever put aside the Pacts and Agreements."

"It seems likely," said Vicky.

"Then maybe we can make our armour stronger than the Sarjeant's," said the Matriarch. "Ethel! I need to talk to you!"

The other-dimensional presence immediately manifested, suffusing the Armoury with her rose-red glow, a quiet reminder of gentle sanity and heart's-ease.

"No need to shout," Ethel said calmly. "I'm not deaf. And no, I can't change your armour. Strange matter is what it is. Max and Vicky are perfectly correct, though; the armour is weaker inside the Nightside. I can't change that without changing the very nature of reality in this place."

"Could you do that?" said the Matriarch.

There was a long pause as Ethel thought about it. Eddie and Molly exchanged a look; it was a worrying question, with even more worrying implications.

"Well, yes," Ethel said finally. "I could do it . . . But I'm not going to. That would be a very bad precedent to set. If I start making decisions like that, allowing myself the right to do things like that, where would it end? This is the kind of thinking that made the Heart what it was. You wouldn't want me to turn into another Heart, would you?"

The Matriarch made a loud, exasperated sound. "Every time I want you to do something, you always find a reason to say no! There's always some excuse! What are you here for if not to help us when we need it?"

"You really want to know?" said Ethel.

Something in her voice sent a chill down everyone's spine, but the Matriarch was too angry to care.

"Yes!" she said defiantly. "I want to know!"

"Very well," said Ethel. "I stay because I see such potential in you. To perform wonders, without the need for armour. I am here to teach you and care for you, to reward you when you do well and hold you back when necessary . . . Till the day comes when you don't need me any more."

"Oh my God . . ." said Eddie. "I get it. I finally get it. You're raising Droods! We're your pets!"

"Yes," said Ethel. "That's the word. I told you that you didn't want to know . . ."

Her voice fell silent, and the rose-red presence disappeared. She wouldn't answer them any more, no matter how loudly the Matriarch shouted. The Matriarch finally took a-hold of herself and turned back to the Armourer.

"If Ethel won't help us, then I definitely need a weapon. What is there?"

"There's always the Forbidden Weapons in the Armageddon Codex," said Max.

"No," William said immediately. "They're too powerful. There's a reason why they're only to be used when reality itself is under threat. Because just using them could be enough to damage reality."

"He's right," said Eddie. "You can't use them, Maggie."

She rounded on him. "How can you be so sure?"

"Because I've seen them," said Eddie. And the sound of his voice and the look in his eye was enough to convince the Matriarch.

"It seems like anything powerful enough to stop the Droods is going to be too powerful for us to use," said Molly.

"That is one of the reasons why we've survived this long," said William.

"But I have to do something!" said the Matriarch.

William frowned thoughtfully. "There is something you could try . . . Something the Armourer might not know about."

Max's ears pricked up. "If it's a weapon, Vicky and I should know about it. Weapons are our business."

"Quite right, dear," said Vicky. "You tell them, Max."

"I am telling them, dear."

William looked at the Armourer, and they both fell silent. Because this new William was not a man to be trifled with.

"As Librarian, I know many things I'm not supposed to," he said slowly. "Things the family have forgotten, or don't like to talk about. We do have one very special, very secret Door, hidden away. A Door too dangerous to be used except under the most extreme circumstances."

The Matriarch was already shaking her head. "If there was such a Door, I'd know about it."

"Not necessarily," said Eddie. "There were all kinds of things I wasn't told when I was running the family. Things certain people thought I didn't need to know."

William looked at the Armourer. "You know the Door I'm talking about, don't you?"

They nodded, reluctantly.

"We're not supposed to talk about it," said Max.

"To anyone," said Vicky.

"But I'm in charge of the family!" said the Matriarch.

"The Sarjeant was very clear on the matter," said Vicky.

"And the Sarjeant isn't someone you argue with," said Max.

"Not that we're frightened of him, you understand," said Vicky.

"Of course not," said Max.

"We're just careful."

"Very careful."

"Why didn't he want the Matriarch to know?" said Eddie.

"Because," Max said reluctantly, "theoretically . . . this particular Door can open onto the Hereafter."

There was a long pause. No one wanted to be the first to say anything.

"I remember seeing Doors marked Heaven and Hell, in the Doormouse's House of Doors," Eddie said finally.

Molly nodded. "He seemed quite certain they would work. Though he swore he'd never tried them."

"I can't believe we're taking this seriously," said the Matriarch.

"It's the Nightside," said William.

"Stop saying that!" said the Matriarch.

"You weren't involved when we had to deal with the Apocalypse Door," said Eddie. "That was real enough." He turned to the Armourer. "How did we come to acquire a Door that could give us access to the Hereafter?"

"The Sarjeant ordered the Doormouse to make it for the family," said Max. "As a special commission."

"Because after your experience with the Apocalypse Door, he felt we needed to have something like that for ourselves," said Vicky.

"He didn't like the idea of anyone's having something we didn't have," said Max.

"The Doormouse delivered it some time ago," said Vicky. "But as far as I know, no one has ever tried it to see if it would work."

"For fear of what might come through," said Max.

"Why would we want to use it now?" said Eddie.

"To bring back the dead," said William. "To bring back the only Droods everyone in the family would listen to, even the Sarjeant. I mean your uncles, Eddie . . . James and Jack. The greatest field agents this family has ever known. If anyone would know how to bring the family together again, it would be them."

There then followed a spirited discussion as to whether this was a good idea, involving quite a few raised voices. Would James and Jack want to return, and if they did, what might they say or do? Would they want to remain and run the family afterwards? And most of all; if the family did start bringing back the dead . . . where would they stop? Who else would they bring back? In the end, the reluctant consensus was that they should at least try the Door. Because no one had any better ideas. The Matriarch fixed the Armourer with a cold look.

"Where exactly is this Hereafter Door that I was never supposed to know about?"

"In the one place that has become a permanently soft spot between this world and the next," said Max.

"Because of who was there for so long," said Vicky.

"Wait a minute!" said Eddie. "You're talking about the ghost of Jacob and the old chapel!"

"Exactly," said William. "If you're going to hide something, put it where no one wants to look."

"But . . . I used the old chapel as my office for a while!" said the Matriarch. "I never noticed anything!"

"You wouldn't," said Max.

"It was designed that way," said Vicky.

Molly looked at Eddie and shook her head. "Your family . . ."

"Finding the Door isn't the problem," said Max. "We don't know how to open it."

"The Sarjeant never told us," said Vicky. "Never even allowed us to examine it."

"Not that we really wanted to," said Max.

"Not really," said Vicky.

"Some things are better left undisturbed," said Max.

"Though we were interested," said Vicky.

"Oh yes, very interested," said Max.

"The Sarjeant must have known how to open it," said Eddie.

"He had a key," said Max. "But knowing him, he still has it on him."

Eddie looked at Molly. "You've always been good with locks . . ."

"Loath as I am to admit it, this sounds seriously out of my league," said

Molly. "Fortunately, I think I know someone who could open it. The Door-mouse! He created the Hereafter Door, after all."

"Then we'd better go talk to him," said Eddie.

"You know where he is?" said the Matriarch.

"Of course," said Molly. "He'll be where he always is, in his House of Doors."

"And one of the main access points is in the Nightside," said Eddie. "Of course, the last time we were there, we did make rather a mess of the place, fighting Hadleigh Oblivion."

"At least you don't have to worry about him this time," said William.

They all looked at him. He didn't appear to be joking.

"I'm sure the Doormouse will be only too happy to help us out," said Molly. "And if he isn't, I'll just kick his hairy arse till he is."

"Molly and I will be back with the Doormouse as soon as possible," said Eddie. "Everyone else, guard the Hall."

"I can do that," said William.

Eddie used his Merlin Glass because he didn't think it mattered any more whether anyone tracked them, and the Glass dropped them off just out-side the House of Doors because there were some protections even it couldn't get through. The street was deserted, but there was enough gen-eral destruction around to show that the Droods had passed through. Some of the fires were still burning. The House of Doors appeared un-touched, but the front entrance was locked, and the windows were covered with steel shutters.

Eddie gave the door a good rattle with an armoured hand, but it wouldn't budge. So he hit it with his fist. The door didn't give an inch even though there was enough strength in the blow to punch a hole through a mountain. Eddie stepped back to let Molly have a look at the lock, but she just shook her head quickly.

"We are talking serious security. I'm not sure I could pick that even if I had my full kit of supernatural burglary tools with me. I suppose we could knock, very politely . . ."

"Would you answer the door right now?" said Eddie. "No, I've got a bet-ter idea. Set a Door to open a Door."

The Merlin Glass was hanging on the air in the middle of the street, in case they felt like doing the sensible thing and getting the hell out in a hurry. Eddie gestured to the Glass, and it floated reluctantly over to join them. He pressed the Merlin Glass up against the closed door, and its ancient magics overpowered the protections put in place by the Doormouse. The Glass replaced the door, Eddie and Molly strode quickly through, then Eddie pulled the Glass away, and the door returned. Eddie shook the Glass down and put it away in his pocket dimension.

"The things we take for granted," said Molly. "You ever think about that, Eddie?"

"No," said Eddie.

He looked around the reception area. It didn't seem to have changed since their last visit except that someone had cleaned up the mess they'd made. A huge open space of quite staggering style and elegance, with thick carpeting and walls of a white so pure they were practically luminous, the reception area boasted abstract paintings, futuristic furnishings, and a few low tables covered with recent magazines. There was no reception desk and no receptionist. Molly raised her voice.

"Hey, Mouse! Shop!"

There was a pause, followed by the sound of scurrying feet, before the Doormouse burst through the door at the far end. A six-foot-tall, vaguely humanoid mouse, with dark-chocolate-coloured fur, under a white lab coat that reminded Eddie irresistibly of the Armourer. Right down to the pocket protector and many-coloured pens. The Doormouse had laid-back ears; long, twitching whiskers; and very human eyes. He looked cute in a disturbing way. Mice aren't supposed to be that big. He sighed deeply as he recognised his visitors and came reluctantly forward to join them, addressing them in a high-pitched, almost human voice.

"What are you doing in here? Haven't your family done enough damage?"

"I'm not with them," said Eddie. "We need your help to bring this war to an end. I'm pretty sure both sides have been played."

"Who by?" said the Doormouse. "I mean, who would dare?"

"Puck," said Molly.

"Oh, him . . ." said the Doormouse. "Yes, he'd dare. Shifty little bastard. All right, come with me to the Storeroom. We can talk privately there. Watch where you're stepping, and *don't touch anything!*"

They followed him out the back and into the Storeroom. Eddie raised the subject of the Hereafter Door, and the Doormouse nodded quickly.

"I wasn't terribly keen on making it, but the Sarjeant came here in person to order it; and he's not the kind of person you say no to. If you like having your organs on the inside."

The Storeroom was almost unbelievably vast. Eddie and Molly couldn't even see the sides, never mind the end. Packed with row upon row of Doors, standing upright and unsupported, hovering a few inches above the colourless floor, under a ceiling so high there wasn't any sign of it. The Doors stretched away farther than the human eye could comfortably cope with, and then just a bit farther than that. Doors to Anywhere and Anywhen, made from wood and metal, glass and crystal. Some blazed with their own inner light, while others were so dark they might have been spaces between the stars. Each Door had its own special handwritten card, spelling out its particular destination. Eddie spotted a few familiar names: *Shadows Fall, Sinister Albion, Carcosa.*

"Why are you still here, Mouse?" said Molly. "Anyone with any sense would have sprinted for the horizon long ago."

"I've been putting my Doors to good use," said the Doormouse. "Providing a way out for people who just don't want to fight any more. The homeless and the wounded, the refugees and the lost souls. Don't look around; they're not anywhere you can see."

"I'm not here for them," said Eddie. "I just need the Hereafter Door. What can you tell me about it?"

The Doormouse sighed heavily. "I always knew that one would come back to haunt me. It was a tricky commission, and I always said no good would come of it. But I couldn't resist the challenge."

"There are Doors here marked Heaven and Hell," said Molly.

"And they should work!" said the Doormouse. "The mathematics are perfectly sound!"

"But you never tried them?" said Molly.

"Would you?" said the Doormouse.

"So where does the Hereafter Door open onto?" said Molly. "Heaven or Hell?"

"Both, neither, who knows?" the Doormouse said briskly. "It was designed to provide access to the Fields Beyond Those We Know. That was the commission, and that was what I created."

"And you never even tested it before you handed it over to the Sarjeant?" said Eddie.

"No," said the Doormouse. "Because I'm not crazy. Wherever it opens onto, those are not places you want to be caught trespassing." He stopped and looked steadily at Eddie and Molly. "Tell me you're not thinking about using it. Things aren't that bad!"

"Aren't they?" said Molly.

The Doormouse sniffed loudly. "They might be if you open the Hereafter Door. By their very nature, all Doors are exits as well as entrances."

"That's why we need you to come with us to Drood Hall," said Eddie. "To open the Hereafter Door for us and make sure nothing goes wrong."

"Any money in it?" said the Doormouse.

"No," said Eddie.

"But you do want to be there to see what happens, don't you?" said Molly.

"Temptress," said the Doormouse.

"Oh, you have no idea," said Eddie.

"All right, I'll go with you," said the Doormouse. "But only because I just know you'll try to force it open if I don't, then blame me for everything that goes wrong. Someone sensible needs to be there. In case of emergencies."

Molly looked around her. "So many Doors, going to so many places . . . How did you ever get started in this?"

"Because I'm not just a graduate of the Deep School," said the Doormouse. "I'm a teacher there."

Eddie and Molly looked at the Doormouse with new respect.

"Creating Doors is just a hobby, really," said the Doormouse.

"You do know . . . that Hadleigh Oblivion is dead?" said Eddie.

"Yes," said the Doormouse. "Everyone knows. There's a lot of discussion going on right now, down in the Dark Academie, as to how anyone in your family could do that."

"He should have known better than to invade our home," said Eddie. "Will there be consequences over his death? In the future?"

"Oh, almost certainly," the Doormouse said cheerfully. "But you don't need to worry about that. Not when you have so many other things to worry about right now."

"Are you sure this Hereafter Door will work?" said Molly. "As in do what it says on the lid?"

"I don't see why not," said the Doormouse. "Of course, you can't just stand in front of it and yell for someone to come out. That's not how it works. Someone is going to have to go through the Door, into the Fields Beyond, whatever they turn out to be, and find who you're looking for. And then persuade them to come back with you. All the time being very careful that something else doesn't slip past you and make a break for the opening." He looked at Eddie. "You're really thinking about doing this, aren't you?"

"I spent a lot of time keeping company with the ghost of Jacob," said Eddie. "Dead people don't bother me. And anyway, the people I'm going after are family. They'll understand."

"I wouldn't count on it," said the Doormouse. "Death changes people."

"Anything, for the family," said Eddie. "Some things don't change."

He reached inside his pocket dimension for the Merlin Glass, but the Doormouse dropped a furry paw on his arm.

"Don't you dare try and use that thing in here! It'll override all my coordinates. We'll use one of my Doors."

"Hold it," said Eddie. "You have a Door that can transport us straight to Drood Hall, past all our shields and protections?"

The Doormouse smirked. "I can go anywhere that has accepted one of my Doors."

"Because you always build a back door into them," said Molly.

"Of course! Just a little safety feature. In case I have to be called in to do some repair work."

"We will talk about that later," said Eddie.

"Looking forward to it immensely," lied the Doormouse.

There are no advertised entrance points to the World Beneath, the dark underworld of the Nightside. John Taylor knew of one because he'd used it before. A small private garden, inviolate behind heavy stone walls and a securely locked iron gate. Annie snapped her fingers in Strangefellows, and suddenly John and Suzie were standing with her outside the garden. John looked at Annie.

"How long have you known about this place?"

"I didn't just steal state secrets when I was a spy," said Annie.

John tried the gate, but as he expected, it was still locked. He stepped back and nodded to Suzie, and she gave it both barrels from her shotgun. The gate didn't even shudder in its frame. Suzie put away the gun and drew Wulfsbane. The gate slowly swung open before them.

"Smart gate," said John.

"I thought so," said Suzie.

She led the way into the garden, with John and Annie following close behind. It was a pleasant enough setting, lit by a pleasant butter-yellow illumination from flaring gas-jets. There were trees and shrubs, and flower-beds providing a thick, heady perfume on the night air. But as Suzie strode down the path with the Infernal Device in her hand, the nearest vegetation started to wither and die. John had a quiet word with her, along the lines of *Let's not make any enemies we don't have to*, and Suzie put the sword away.

"This is where I came to find the Lord of Thorns and wake him from his long sleep," said John. "I'm still not sure whether that was a kindness or not. It didn't turn out too well for anyone."

"That's what happens when you go somewhere without me," said Suzie.

The trees were unnaturally tall, and the wide swathes of night-blooming flowers were strange and unhealthy shades. Everything in the garden was moving slightly, though there wasn't a breath of breeze. John and Suzie stuck close together. Annie trudged along behind them, paying no attention to the garden, thinking her own thoughts. The path finally ended before the statue of an angel, kneeling weeping over its torn-off wings.

"What's that supposed to be?" said Suzie. "A monument to the angel war?"

"No," said Annie. "It's much older than that. Some say this is all that remains of an actual angel."

"What could do something like that, to an angel?" said John.

"Another angel," said Annie.

The statue's face was almost completely worn away, by wind and rain, or possibly tears. Beside the angel stood a chunky stone moon-dial. John turned the pointing gnomon through one hundred and eighty degrees, and the moon-dial slid jerkily to one side, revealing a dark shaft falling away into the earth. A black metal ladder had been clumsily bolted onto one side. Annie conjured up a ball of light and sent it bobbing down the shaft to illuminate the way. John set off down the ladder without hesitating, Suzie went after him, and Annie brought up the rear.

The rungs had been set uncomfortably far apart, as though never intended for human use, and John's arms and legs were aching long before he reached the bottom of the shaft. When he ran out of rungs, he just let go and dropped, and ended up on a narrow stone platform beside a canal. Dark waters in a dark place. The glowing ball shot this way and that, as though checking out the territory, then came back to bob impatiently beside John as first Suzie, then Annie, dropped out of the shaft to join him. Suzie glowered around her and wrinkled her nose.

"What is this place? I thought I'd chased bounties through every part of the Nightside, but this is new to me."

"Not many come down here," said John. "The World Beneath is a refuge for those who feel the long night isn't dark enough. A whole system of underground tunnels, catacombs, and secret galleries, spread out under the Nightside. Inhabited by people, and others, with more reason than most to seek the comfort of the dark. The subterraneans who left the world above to hide from their enemies. Or their friends. It's that kind of place. There are some who use the World Beneath as a way of getting back and forth in the Nightside without being observed, though that's not without risk. The subterraneans have a tendency to kill and eat anyone who disturbs them. Not necessarily in that order."

"You take me to the nicest places," said Suzie.

She might have meant it. John could never tell. He looked at Annie.

"Where now? The World Beneath is a big place. Do I need to summon a barge to take us to the Door? That's how I got around last time."

"We're not tourists," said Annie. "We're going off the beaten track. This way."

She strode down the platform, the ball of light bobbing happily along at her shoulder. John and Suzie had to hurry after her, to keep from being left behind in the dark. Annie kept leaning in close to study the wall until finally she located a door only she could see. She identified herself as one of the Authorities, and the door opened to her voice, revealing a narrow tunnel. Annie led the way in, and John and Suzie followed after in single file. Moisture ran down the cracked and pock-marked walls and splashed underfoot. The smell was really bad. The light from the floating ball didn't travel far, as though something in the darkness resented its efforts. John thought the ball's movements looked rather subdued, but that might just have been the confined space. Suzie moved in behind John, so she could murmur in his ear.

"I knew Annie was a killer and a spy, but did you know she could work these kind of magics?"

"Annie's always kept a lot to herself," John said quietly. "I mean, I knew Tamsin was her daughter, but who was the father? And how did Annie's daughter end up a vicar?"

"I can hear you," said Annie, not even glancing back. "And my secrets are mine to keep. Till I choose to sell them."

They finally emerged onto a deserted tube station. The ball's light flared up to illuminate a platform thick with dust and rails thick with rust. The walls were pitted and stained, and only scraps and tatters remained from what had once been colourful posters. John could just make out the station's name on the far wall: DOWNSIDE.

"I never heard of any such station," he said.

"Not many remember it these days," said Annie. "But the World Beneath wasn't always as separate as it is now."

"Why leave the Door down here?" said Suzie.

"Because the underground rail system is protected by extremely powerful forces," said Annie. "So that people can travel safely. This may be a disused station, but the protections are still working."

"Could trains still come here?" John asked.

"They could," said Annie. "But they won't. They're afraid."

"I just know I'm going to regret asking this," said John, "but what, exactly, are the trains so afraid of, and might it still be here somewhere?"

"Another reason why the old Authorities chose this location for the Door," said Annie. "Downside may be disused, but it's far from deserted.

Things live here, more than powerful enough to protect the Door. And they're always hungry."

John and Suzie looked around. The shadows outside the circle of light were very dark and deep enough to hide any number of dangerous things.

"I don't have time for this," said John. He raised his voice. "Listen up! I am John Taylor, and this is Shotgun Suzie. I don't care how long you've been down here, you know those names. For the moment, we're just passing through. But if you give us any trouble, I promise we will make a point of sticking around long enough to ruin your entire existence. Is that clear?"

There wasn't any answer, but there was something about the surrounding shadows that suggested they were listening carefully and thinking hard. Nothing moved or showed any signs of thinking of moving. John turned to Annie.

"Find the Door."

"Why didn't you include my name?" said Annie. "I have a reputation too, you know."

"Find the Door," said John. "We have a war to stop."

Annie led the way down the platform until she came to an unobtrusive door marked MAINTENANCE. She nodded quickly.

"Standard misdirection." She gestured at the Door, being careful not to get too close. "The Door is open now. My presence was enough to do that. But you have to talk to it because you're the one who wants something from it. Just call out to who you want, and they'll come to you. Or they won't. You can never be sure in situations like this."

"Are you sure this is a good idea, John?" Suzie said quietly. "Lilith tried to destroy the long night and everyone who lived in it. Even if you could bring her back, what makes you think she'd want to help save the Nightside from the Droods?"

"Because she wouldn't want someone else taking control of her creation," said John. "Because I'm her son. And . . . because she wants to get out of wherever she is. I'm happy to go along with any of those reasons. We stopped Lilith before, and I don't see any way of stopping the Droods; so we have to roll the dice and go with the lesser of two evils." He smiled, briefly. "Though that is almost certainly the first time anyone has ever said that about Lilith."

"She's your mother," said Suzie.

"Keep your gun handy," said John.

"Not Wulfsbane?"

"Not unless you absolutely have to."

"Get on with it," said Annie. "Some of those shadows are starting to look a bit restless."

Suzie drew her shotgun. Light gleamed almost caressingly along the twin barrels. John pushed the Door back, and the opening was full of Light. A bright and glorious Light, that spilled out onto the platform and forced back the darkness. John stared unblinkingly into the Light, not feeling in any way threatened. He felt as though he knew it. Perhaps from before he was born.

"Call out to Lilith! Quickly!" Annie said urgently. She had her head turned away from the Light, her eyes squeezed shut. "Before something else senses the opening and comes to investigate."

"Lilith!" said John. "This is your son, John. Come back to the Nightside. We need you."

And then he stumbled backwards, almost falling over his own feet, as Lilith stepped out of the Light and onto the platform. She stood before John, smiling calmly. Disturbingly tall and almost supernaturally slender, the lines of her body were so smooth they looked as if they'd been streamlined for greater efficiency. Her hair and eyes and lips were jet-black, and her skin was so pale as to be colourless. She looked like a black and white photo superimposed on reality.

She was naked, and she had no navel. Her face was sharp and pointed, with a prominent bone structure and a hawk-nose. Her dark mouth was thin-lipped and far too wide. She looked wild, elemental, something from when the world was new. And she looked strong enough to break the present world just by walking up and down in it.

John's mother: the Biblical Myth.

And then someone else stepped out of the Light, to stand beside Lilith. John's father, Charles. He looked a lot like John and not much older. Tall and dark and handsome enough, with a calm, quiet presence to him. He was wearing the same casual clothes as the last time John had seen him just before he sacrificed himself to force Lilith out of the world and keep her out. And then, to John's utter astonishment, he put out a hand to Lilith, and she took hold of it. And they both smiled easily at him. Suzie was so thrown she actually lowered her shotgun for a moment.

"It's all right, John," said Lilith, in her low, sultry voice. "Charles and I aren't fighting any more. It's only been a few years for you, but a lot longer where we were. We've had time to make our peace with each other."

"How did that happen?" said John, too astonished to be polite.

"It turned out he still loved me," said Lilith. "Even after everything. Isn't that sweet?"

"What can I tell you?" said Charles. "There was a reason I fell for her in the first place. Some people are just made for each other."

"You shouldn't have called me back, John," said Lilith. "We have no reason to return to this world. We've moved on. The Nightside has changed so much since its creation. It's not at all what I meant it to be."

"Our time here is over," said Charles. "It's your time now, John. Your Nightside. Do what you want with it."

They started to turn away, to go back through the Door and into the Light, but Annie yelled at them to stop. They looked back at her, curiously.

"You can't go!" Annie said fiercely. "We need you. You have to stop the Droods!"

"We don't do that any longer," said Lilith.

"Then at least give me my Tamsin back!" said Annie. "That's why I came here. I want my daughter."

"I'm sorry," said Charles. "But you've come to the wrong Door for that."

"If you won't help me, I'll make you!" said Annie.

She pointed a finger at Suzie and spoke a Word of Power, and all the expression dropped out of Suzie's face as Annie's will got inside her head and took over. Suzie put away her shotgun and drew Wulfsbane. Her movements were slow and strained as she fought against Annie's possession and lost. She advanced slowly on Lilith and Charles, the long sword held out before her, glowing with its poisonous light.

"That sword has killed gods, in its time," said Annie. "If you won't give me what I want, we'll see if it can kill a Biblical Myth."

"Don't hurt Suzie!" John shouted desperately to Lilith. "She's not in control!"

"Of course I won't hurt her," said Lilith. "She's carrying my grandchild." She looked at Annie. "You, on the other hand . . ."

"I want my daughter!" said Annie.

"Then go and be with her," said Lilith.

Annie's eyes rolled up in her head, and she collapsed. Dead before she hit the platform. Lilith smiled.

"No one threatens my family. I haven't changed that much."

Suzie groaned out loud, swaying on her feet. With Annie dead, the compulsion was gone, but now the voice of the Infernal Device roared inside her head. Wulfsbane wanted to kill Lilith. It tried to drive Suzie on, to make her do it, but she fought the sword off, forcing the voice to the back of her head. The sword subsided, reluctantly. Suzie sheathed the sword and nodded quickly to John to show she was all right.

"This is why we didn't want to come back," said Charles. "Your world is bad for us. It reminds us of what we used to be."

"So we're going back," said Lilith. "To where we belong. You don't need me, John."

"This is your time, son," said Charles. "Be happy. We are."

"Wait!" said Suzie. "Before you go . . . The boundaries of the Nightside have changed. How do we restore them?"

"Find whoever changed them," said Lilith. "And make them do it."

Lilith and Charles walked back into the Light, still hand in hand, and the Door closed silently behind them.

Suddenly, it was utterly dark. When Annie died, her magic light died with her. John and Suzie stood very still. Slow, heavy movements in the darkness around them suggested certain things were no longer content to remain still. John reached into his pocket and brought out a salamander ball. He shook it hard and it generated a soft blue glow, just enough to see by. The surrounding shadows looked darker and deeper now and quite a bit closer.

"Time we were leaving," said John. "I'd hate to think we've outstayed our welcome."

"Then use your portable Timeslip and get us out of here," said Suzie, covering the shadows with her shotgun.

"It doesn't work any more," said John.

"What? Why not?"

"Because something doesn't want it to."

"Why didn't you tell me this before?"

"You didn't ask."

"Do you at least remember the way out of here?" said Suzie, looking about her for something she could make a nasty example of.

"I can find the way out," said John. "I can find anything."

Suzie looked dubiously at the salamander ball. "Will that thing last long enough? It's not very big."

"Well," said John. "You only get two to a salamander."

He set off back down the platform, with Suzie sticking close beside him.

"This was a wasted journey," said Suzie.

"Not entirely," said John. "At least now I know my parents are happy together."

Eddie, Molly, and the Doormouse appeared inside the old chapel, set just outside Drood Hall. Close enough that it had been brought along when Alpha Red Alpha deposited the Hall in the Nightside. The chapel's interior was no longer the shabby mess Eddie remembered so fondly from the old days. The Matriarch had had it all cleaned up when she decided to use it as her office. Eddie preferred the chapel how it used to look; it had character. Even if it wasn't a particularly nice character. Now everything was clean and tidy, spick and span. Apart from a pile of old wooden pews and other fittings and furnishings stacked up against the far wall. Eddie looked at them thoughtfully. He was certain they hadn't been there the last time he'd visited the chapel to meet with the Matriarch. Right in the middle of the pile stood a tall wooden door, and standing before that was the Matriarch, studying it intently. She suddenly realised she had company and turned to glare at them.

"Took you long enough. Is that the Doormouse?" She smiled briefly. "You look just the way I thought you would."

"Lots of people say that," said the Doormouse. "Please don't try and hug me. Everyone always wants to hug me, and I am not the hugging type."

"The thought never occurred to me," said the Matriarch.

"Trust me," Eddie said to the Doormouse. "It really didn't."

The Matriarch gestured at the door leaning against the wall. "I am assured that this shabby-looking thing is the Hereafter Door. Hard though that is to believe. Can it really do what the name implies?"

"Of course," said the Doormouse, bristling. "Or I wouldn't have given it that name. I do have my reputation to think of."

"Can you open it?" said the Matriarch.

"Naturally," said the Doormouse. He scurried over to stand before the Door, not quite crowding the Matriarch out of the way. The Doormouse peered near-sightedly at the Hereafter Door, as though checking for signs it had been maltreated or misused since he'd dropped it off, then nodded quickly and raised his voice.

"Open!"

The Door swung slowly backwards, apparently through and past the solid stone wall behind it, revealing an opening full of Light. The Doormouse smirked.

"His Master's Voice . . ."

He scurried back out of the way as the Matriarch planted herself firmly in front of the open Door. She stared unflinchingly into the bright and glorious Light and raised her voice.

"James Drood! Jack Drood! Grey Fox and Armourer! You must return to us! Your family needs you!"

There was a long pause. Nothing happened. The Doormouse cleared his throat meaningfully and looked at Eddie.

"I told you. You can yell all you like, but if they don't want to come, one of us is going to have to go in there and get them. Please note that *one of us* very definitely does not include me."

"What's in there?" said Molly, staring unblinkingly into the Light.

The Doormouse managed a very human shrug. "The Fields Beyond Those We Know means beyond anything we know. That is what I was asked for, and that is what I delivered."

"Heaven or Hell?" said Eddie.

"Both, neither, I don't know," said the Doormouse.

"I can't go in there," said the Matriarch. "I can't risk myself because that would leave the Sarjeant in charge."

"I'll do it," said Eddie.

"Why does it always have to be you?" said Molly.

"Because that's the job," said Eddie.

"You are not going in there without me," Molly said flatly.

"I have to," said Eddie. "This is family business." He smiled at her. "It's all right. It's James and Jack. My uncles. What could I have to fear, from them?"

"You heard the oversized rodent," said Molly. "Being dead changes people. And besides . . ." She scowled into the Light, as though it might be trying to hide something from her. "Who knows what else might be in there?"

"You must hurry!" the Doormouse said urgently. "It's not wise to leave the Door open too long. It calls . . ."

He didn't say to what, and no one felt like pressing him. Eddie squeezed Molly's hand reassuringly and strode forward into the Light.

It was like plunging into an ocean without end. The Light was so overpowering, it was all Eddie could see, wherever he looked. A Light so pure as to be without colours or shadings, a perfect thing that had no place in the material world. And yet it didn't feel unfriendly. It felt like coming home after a long journey.

But even though Eddie couldn't see anything but the Light, he could tell he wasn't alone. It felt like he was surrounded by crowds of people, endlessly coming and going on unknowable business of their own. Bustling around him, invisibly and silently. He moved cautiously forward, hands stretched out before him, but they didn't find anything. He couldn't even feel the ground under his feet.

And then he got the feeling that there was something else: a destination, far off in the distance. Somewhere he belonged . . . and even though he couldn't put a name to what it might be, he wanted desperately to go there. He started towards it, moving faster and faster, until he was running full out. A deep contentment swept through him and an almost exultant sense of belonging. And then a voice called out to him to stop, and he stumbled to a halt despite everything he was feeling because it was a voice he knew he could trust. Jack Drood appeared out of the Light to stand before him, with his brother James at his side.

They stood together, smiling easily, and Eddie's heart leapt at the sight of them. James, the legendary Grey Fox, was tall and darkly handsome, effortlessly elegant and sardonic, dressed in the finest three-piece suit the mind could imagine. His smile was broad and genuine. He looked a lot younger than the well-preserved middle-aged man Eddie remembered.

It took Eddie a moment to accept that the man standing beside James really was his uncle Jack, the old Armourer. He was young again too, not much older than Eddie. The stained and battered lab coat was gone, replaced by a suit every bit as fine as his brother's. He grinned broadly at Eddie.

"You never knew me when I had hair, did you?"

Eddie was smiling so hard he could feel it, and tears stung his eyes. His two favourite uncles, young again and in their prime, when they were the greatest secret agents in the world. Eddie lurched forward and hugged Jack hard, and his uncle patted him on the back and murmured reassuring things. He felt properly real and solid. Eddie finally let go of him and stepped back.

"I'm so sorry . . ."

"We've been through that," Jack said easily. "You have nothing to feel sorry for. It's good to see you again, Eddie."

"And you, Uncle Jack."

Eddie turned to look at James, who raised a single eyebrow.

"Don't I get a hug?"

"I killed you, Uncle James . . ."

"It was the right thing to do," said James. He opened his arms, and Eddie hugged him too. It was a very manly hug.

Eventually Eddie stepped back and looked his two uncles over carefully. They looked very alive, very real, even though he knew they couldn't be. James gave him a stern look.

"Where did you think you were running to, Eddie?"

Eddie still couldn't put a name to it, so he just pointed off into the distance. The only word he could think of was *home*, and that seemed far too small. Certainly it had nothing at all to do with Drood Hall. Jack shook his head firmly.

"You're not ready for that, Eddie. Not yet."

"That's the end of the line," said James. "No way back."

"We know why you're here," said Jack.

"We know everything now," said James. "All the answers to all the questions we ever had."

"Though some of them turned out to be a bit of a surprise," said Jack.

The two men smiled easily together.

"Then you must know why I came here," said Eddie. "And why you have to come back with me. The family needs you. The Nightside needs you."

"We can't," said James. "All is forgiven, no hard feelings and all that, but we can't go with you."

"Why not?" said Eddie.

"Because we're busy," said Jack. "And don't ask what with because you wouldn't understand if we told you. Just trust me when I say it's important."

"We're doing good work," said James. "Which is all I ever really wanted."

"The world is in danger!" said Eddie. "What could be more important than that?"

"You'd be surprised," said James.

"One day you'll understand," said Jack.

"I can't do this without you!" said Eddie. "It's too big for me . . ."

"Of course you can do it," said James. "We trust you."

And they both nodded calmly, the Grey Fox and the Armourer.

"You don't owe me anything," Eddie said steadily. "I owe you everything. But I'm still asking. Not for myself but for the family."

"Oh well," said James. "If you put it like that . . ."

"We can spare a few moments," said Jack.

"For the family," said James.

"Damn right," said Jack.

Eddie started to turn around, to go back the way he'd come, and only then realised he had no idea which way led back to the Door. James and Jack moved in on either side of him and linked their arms companionably through his. And together, the three Droods walked back into the world.

They stepped out of the Hereafter Door and into the old chapel, and it was like leaving a cathedral to enter a small back room. The Hereafter Door closed quietly behind them, cutting off the Light. Molly gaped at the young James and Jack, then applauded delightedly. The Matriarch looked like she wanted to but held on to her Matriarchal dignity. She nodded her thanks to Eddie, then bowed to James and Jack. They just nodded easily in return.

Eddie went over to Molly, who checked quickly to make sure he was all right, then punched him hard in the arm.

"What was that for?" said Eddie.

"For worrying me!" said Molly. And then she hugged him like she'd never let him go. Eddie wanted to tell her everything he'd seen and heard and felt, but he didn't have the words. He was already forgetting most of it, and he couldn't help feeling that was for the best.

The Doormouse hovered at the back of the chapel, fascinated and dying to ask all sorts of questions but knowing better than to intrude on Drood family business.

"You honour us with your presence, James and Jack," said the Matriarch.

"Cut it out, Maggie," Jack said kindly. "It's just me. And he's just him."

"We're here to do a job," said James. "So let's go talk to the Sarjeant."

"Because we've got a lot to say," said the Armourer.

"And not a lot of time to say it in," said the Grey Fox.

"Let's go save the world," said Jack.

"One last time," said James.

They used the Merlin Glass to return to the Nightside, pausing only to drop the Doormouse off at his House of Doors. He rushed inside without waiting to be thanked for his help, as though worried they might change their mind. He didn't look back once. At least partly because just being around James and Jack made all his fur stand on end. He slammed the front door behind him, and the whole establishment disappeared.

The Doormouse was taking no chances.

Eddie instructed the Merlin Glass to take the rest of them straight to wherever the Sarjeant-at-Arms was. It showed them a great open square where the Sarjeant was haranguing his army, along with an equally large gathering of elves. Eddie stepped through, followed by Molly and the Matriarch, James and Jack.

The Sarjeant broke off from exhorting his troops to kill every living thing in the Nightside, as the only sure way of winning, and turned to face the new-comers. The Droods looked at the new arrivals and crashed to attention. The elves looked on curiously, as Eddie and his people came forward. The Sarjeant glared at the Matriarch.

"I can't believe you were foolish enough to come back. You must know I can't risk letting you escape again." And then he looked past her at Eddie and Molly and thought he understood. "Reinforcements . . . As though that will make any difference against such superior numbers. We have no time for traitors here."

And then he saw James and Jack and just stopped talking. The undamaged half of his face went white with shock. The famous names were already moving swiftly among the watching Droods, sweeping through the rows like a quiet prayer that the Grey Fox and the old Armourer had come to rescue them from the authority of the Sarjeant. They'd only followed him because the Matriarch had disappointed them and because most Droods always needed someone to tell them what to do. But a war of extinction . . . was just too much. One by one, the Droods knelt and bowed their head to James and Jack.

The elves didn't kneel. They stood a little closer together, behind Puck, while he struck a casual pose and studied the new-comers with wary, watchful eyes.

James and Jack strolled through the ranks of kneeling Droods, heading straight for the Sarjeant. He stood his ground because there was nowhere left for him to go. Eddie and Molly and the Matriarch hung back, letting James and Jack have their moment with the Sarjeant. They finally came to a halt before him, and he met their gaze defiantly. James and Jack just nodded easily.

"Hello, Cedric," said James.

"It's been awhile," said Jack.

"It is you," said the Sarjeant. "It really is you . . . But that's not allowed! Family ghosts are never permitted to return . . . No. Wait. They used the Hereafter Door, didn't they? I always knew that thing would come back to haunt me. The Grey Fox and the old Armourer . . . the Matriarch chose well. The only Droods no one in the family would argue with. But I won't kneel to you."

"We never wanted you to kneel to us," said James. "That's not why we're here."

"We just want you to listen," said Jack.

"The invasion is out-of-control," said James.

"You are out-of-control, Cedric," said Jack. "Dammit, man, you're allying the family with elves!"

"You're endangering the family," said James.

"Everything I've done, I've done for the family!" said the Sarjeant.

"You're supposed to be doing this for Humanity," said James.

"Anything, for Humanity," said Jack. "To keep the world safe."

"That's what this is all about!" said the Sarjeant. He looked at them pleadingly, desperate to make them understand because he respected them more than anyone. "We have to put an end to the Nightside, destroy it completely! It's always been a knife at our back, but now it's become a danger to the whole world!"

"More than an army of elves?" said Eddie, unable to keep silent any longer. "When have we ever trusted elves, let alone tied our honour to them? Elves never do anything that doesn't serve their own best interests. Come on, Sarjeant, this isn't what we came here to do."

"It's what I came here to do," said the Sarjeant, his attention still fixed on James and Jack. "We should have done this long ago. The Nightside has always been an unexploded bomb, just waiting to blow up in our faces. We should never have allowed things to become this bad."

"Stand down, Sarjeant," said the Matriarch, letting her voice ring out over the listening Drood army. "You have no authority to deal with elves or to order the execution of every living thing in the Nightside."

"I took the authority because you didn't have the guts to use it!" said the Sarjeant. "Because you wouldn't do what was necessary!" He looked at Eddie for the first time. "You of all people should understand that."

"I took control of the family to save it from itself," said Eddie. "Not to kill everyone who disagreed with me."

The Sarjeant glared around him. At James and Jack, at Eddie and the Matriarch, at Molly standing on her own at the edge of things because this was family business. He glared around at the silently watching Droods . . . and some of the strength went out of him as he realised no one was on his side.

"I'll never stand down," he said flatly. "I know my duty. Even if you take my people away from me, I still have the elves."

"Listen to what you're saying!" said the Matriarch. "You'd set the elves against your own family?"

"I won't be stopped!" said the Sarjeant. Shaking with rage and frustration, his voice rose unsteadily. "I won't be beaten! This is too important. I'll kill all of you rather than fail in my duty. I have to. It's all I've got."

A gun appeared in each of his hands, aimed at James and Jack. The two dead men stared steadily back at him.

"It's over, Cedric," said James.

"You need to come with us now," said Jack.

The Sarjeant dropped to his knees. The guns disappeared from his hands. He sighed once, as though he were very tired, and fell forward to lie on his face. He didn't move again. The watching Droods stood very still. The elves moved a little closer together. Molly came forward to stand with Eddie as he stared unbelievingly at James and Jack.

"You killed him. That isn't what I brought you back to do!"

"You brought us back to do what needed doing," said James.

"To do the one thing you could never do," said Jack.

"And now, it's time for us to go," said James. "We've already stayed longer than we should and done more than we should have."

"But you always were our favourite nephew," said Jack.

The Hereafter Door was suddenly standing behind them. The ranks of watching Droods made a soft sound of surprise, then awe, as the Door opened to reveal it was full of Light. The elves murmured among themselves. James and Jack walked back through the Door. And at the very last moment, just before they disappeared into the Light, Eddie saw the ghost of Cedric walking between them, shaking his head at how wrong he'd been. The three of them laughed silently together, and then they were gone. The Door closed and disappeared. Eddie wondered if it had gone back to the old chapel, or whether James and Jack had taken it with them. He rather hoped they had. Some things were just too powerful, even for Droods. Perhaps especially for Droods.

The Matriarch addressed the waiting family, her voice full of her old authority. "The war is over. I will talk to the Authorities, and we will work together on how to solve the problem of the Nightside's shifting boundaries. No recriminations, no crime or punishment on either side. You will all return to the Hall and wait there till I come for you."

The Droods rose to their feet and bowed briefly to her. Because how could they argue with a Matriarch who could bring back the trusted dead to shame them? The Matriarch had her future Merlin Glass open a Door back to the Hall and nodded to Conrad, the only surviving troop leader. He led the Droods back through the Glass in a steady stream. It was going to take awhile, given how narrow the opening was. They took the Sarjeant's body with them.

While all that was going on, the Matriarch turned to Eddie and Molly.

"Where can I find the Authorities? Tell me you know where they are."

"We've been hearing things," said Eddie. "Or at least Molly has; she still has connections here. All the Authorities are dead now except one. Julien Advent. You'll find him at the Hospice of the Blessed Saint Margaret."

"Julien . . . good," said the Matriarch. "He always was the sanest of them. You think he'll bear a grudge, after everything that's happened?"

"Almost certainly," said Molly. "But he won't let that get in the way of stopping the fighting. It will help that the Sarjeant, the author of all this death and destruction, is dead."

"But before we can go there, we have business here," said Eddie.

They all turned to look at Puck and his elves. Puck stared unflinchingly back at them. His usual meaningless smile didn't waver once as they moved over to stand before him.

"Save your talk of peace," he said. "I came here for a war, and I will have one."

"You started this war," said Eddie. "Didn't you?"

"Well," said Puck, "I might have had a little help . . ." He laughed softly, mockingly. "Now you're sending your army away, how are you going to stop my elves? There's more than enough of us to conquer what remains of the Nightside."

"My army is resting, not disbanded," said the Matriarch. "I can still ally it with the Nightside, against you. Do you really believe you can take both of us, working together?"

"You'd be surprised at what I'm capable of," said Puck.

He vanished, along with all his elves, leaving just an empty open square. Molly blasted lightning bolts through the space where the elves had been, vivid energies that crackled viciously on the air. Molly lowered her hands, looked at Eddie and the Matriarch, and shrugged.

"Just checking, in case they were still there, hiding behind a glamour. But no; they're gone."

"Where have they gone?" said the Matriarch. "Are we still going to have to fight them?"

"I shouldn't think so," said Eddie. "Puck promised his people an easy victory, and that's just blown up in his face. I think the plan was . . . they take the Nightside, with the help of the Droods, then turn on the weakened Droods. But now . . . I think Puck's army will just slink back to wherever it came from. They were just the dregs, after all. The real warriors went to Shadows Fall and the Sundered Lands."

"Why did Puck want this war in the first place?" said the Matriarch.

"Something I plan on asking him at the first opportunity," said Eddie. "Preferably with my foot on his throat, to make sure he tells the truth."

"He made it sound like he had help," said Molly. "Of course, that could have just been him messing with our heads, but . . ."

"But maybe we have been missing something all along," said Eddie. "If Puck does have a partner, who could it be? Who is there left that we haven't heard from? Who's missing from this photograph?"

Eddie and Molly went straight to Saint Margaret's Hospice, via the Merlin Glass, to speak to Julien Advent. At the last moment, the Matriarch decided not to go with them. Partly because she believed the Droods needed her, back at the Hall, but mostly because she felt it would be a lot easier for Julien to speak to someone who hadn't smashed up his *Night Times* offices. Eddie and Molly appeared in the car-park outside the hospital. Eddie put the Glass away, and Molly grabbed his arm, painfully hard.

"What?" said Eddie, looking around quickly. "What is it? There's no one else here!"

"We are not alone," said Molly, staring fixedly before her. "My Sight is showing me rows and rows of ghosts, standing between us and the hospital. And they do not look at all happy to see us."

Eddie focused his Sight through his torc and jumped despite himself as an army of shimmering forms appeared before him.

"Okay . . ." he said quietly to Molly. "What should we do now?"

"Well, I plan on standing very still and not doing anything that might upset them."

"They're just ghosts," said Eddie. "What could they do to hurt us?"

"You really want to find out?"

"I am going to stand extremely still," Eddie decided. "And hope there's a second part to this plan of yours."

"I was thinking . . . maybe sneak around the back?" said Molly. "And then knock, very politely."

The front door to the hospital opened, and Julien Advent came out.

He walked right through the rows of ghosts and didn't flinch any more than they did. He stopped before Eddie and Molly and nodded curtly.

"I thought it must be you. The ghosts told JC Chance, and he told me, that a Drood and a very scary witch had just appeared in the car-park. So what do you want?"

"We're here to negotiate an end to hostilities," said Eddie. "No, wait a minute. *Very scary witch?* The ghosts are afraid of Molly?"

She beamed happily at the shimmering ranks. "I am so proud."

"And JC Chance?" said Eddie. "What the hell is a Ghost Finder doing here?"

"Helping protect this hospital from your family," said Julien. "When he isn't sitting around stuffing his face with free food. An end to hostilities . . . Really?"

"Really," said Eddie. "The Sarjeant is dead now, and the Matriarch has given me full authority in this matter. We should never have gone to war in the first place. Both sides were tricked into this by Puck."

"And possibly someone else," said Molly. "We're still working on that."

Julien nodded, tiredly. "The elves . . . I should have known. Very well. You agree to whatever terms I want, and I'll agree to whatever terms you want. But officially this war is over right now. I'll have to get the other Authorities to confirm it . . ."

Eddie and Molly looked at each other. They'd really hoped he would have heard, by now.

"I'm sorry," said Eddie. "The others are dead. You're the only Authority left."

Eddie ran quickly through what he'd heard about the true situation, including the threat posed to the Nightside by the changed boundaries, and Julien nodded.

"All right. Let it go. I have enough personal authority to stop any more fighting by the Nightsiders as long as you Droods stay away from them. And get the hell out of the long night as soon as possible."

"That's the plan," said Eddie. "We'll stay long enough to help you put the boundaries back where they should be . . . and then we're out of here."

"I have to get back to the *Night Times*," said Julien. "We need to put out a new edition, telling everyone the truth about what's happened." He looked steadily at Eddie. "You're sure the elves are gone?"

"They have no reason to stay," said Eddie. "Though I would be the first to admit that there's a lot to this situation I don't properly understand yet."

"You should talk to John Taylor," said Julien. "He's had dealings with the elves, and Puck in particular."

Eddie pulled a face. "John and I didn't get on too well the last time we tried talking."

"Testosterone," Molly said airily. "It's a curse."

"Hopefully, things have changed now," said Eddie.

"I'll write you a note," said Julien.

"That would help," said Eddie.

John Taylor and Suzie Shooter came up from the World Beneath and walked back through the private garden to find Eddie Drood and Molly Metcalf waiting for them at the gate. They all looked at each other for a long moment.

"How did you know to find us here?" said John.

"I told the Merlin Glass to take us straight to you," said Eddie. "The war is over. The Droods have made a truce with Julien Advent. I have a note."

"Why would he agree to that?" said Suzie, scowling suspiciously.

Eddie took a deep breath and launched into his explanation of everything that had happened one more time. When he finally got to the end, John just looked at him.

"Read the note," said Eddie. "Julien vouches for me."

"No need," said John. "Puck . . . I should have known."

And then John and Eddie looked at Suzie and Molly, who were glowering fiercely at each other. Eddie and John shared a smile. Suzie and Molly caught the smile and immediately calmed down. If only because they refused to be predictable. The four of them talked together for a while, cautiously searching out common ground. They were pleasantly surprised at how many friends, and enemies, they had in common. There was still a lot of work to be done, cleaning up the mess on both sides, as well as dealing with the Nightside boundaries, but none of them doubted it could be done, now they weren't distracted by the war. It wasn't going to be easy. They'd all lost too many people.

And then Suzie cried out suddenly, clutched at her head, and swayed on her feet.

"Suzie?" said John. "What is it?"

He reached out to her, but she staggered backwards, gesturing for him to stay away. "The sword is in my head! Wulfsbane doesn't want this to be over; it doesn't want the killing to end. Its voice is so loud I can't hear myself think . . . It's taking control, and I'm not strong enough to stop it any more!"

John looked quickly at Eddie and Molly. "Wulfsbane is an Infernal Device. It's trying to possess her."

"That's what she's got on her back?" said Molly. "I've heard of them, but I never thought I'd get to see one . . . We have to get it away from her."

"You can't!" said Suzie. She showed her teeth in a death's-head grin. "It won't let you."

And then all expression disappeared from her face as something else looked out from behind her eyes. Wulfsbane leapt out of the scabbard on Suzie's back and dropped into her waiting hand. The long blade glowed bitter yellow, poisoning the night with its presence. Suzie laughed breathlessly, sweeping the Infernal Device back and forth before her.

"The war isn't over till I say it's over. Not while there's still so much killing to be done. I'll start with you. The murder of three such famous names should be enough to get the war going again. I will stoke the flames of fear and hatred, and walk back and forth in the Nightside, killing and killing till there's no one left; and then . . . I will walk out into the world and soak it in blood and suffering. It's what I was made for."

Eddie armoured up. Molly's hands closed into fists, and magics sparked and coruscated around her. John stared helplessly at Suzie.

"Fight it!" he said.

"She can't," said the sword.

"Don't let the blade touch you," John said to Eddie and Molly. "I've seen it cut through Drood armour, and even the smallest wound would be enough to kill you. But you can't fight Suzie; she's due to give birth anytime now!"

"Then think of something," said Eddie. "Because I am all out of other options."

John thought frantically, then stepped forward to face Suzie, putting himself in front of Eddie and Molly.

"I won't fight you, Suzie," he said. "And I won't let them fight you. I'm just standing here before you, with empty hands and no defences. So it's up to you. Either you fight off the sword, or I'm a dead man. You can do it, Suzie. I have faith in you."

The thing in Suzie's head smiled at him and drew back the sword for a killing thrust. And then her hand opened, and Wulfsbane dropped from her fingers. The long blade clattered heavily on the ground. Suzie looked at it, as though she couldn't understand what had just happened, and reached down to pick up the sword. But one leg bent suddenly, and she stumbled sideways. Her face convulsed, and she fought to get back to the sword, but something inside wouldn't let her. She cried out loud as forces within her went to war in her head and in her heart. Her need to kill against her need for John, but in the end perhaps it was just that Suzie had always been her own woman, and always would. She stood very still, breathing hard, her face pale and drawn and slick with sweat. But her eyes were her own again. She slowly straightened up and nodded to John.

"I'm back . . ."

The Infernal Device leapt up and hung upon the air before them, supported by its own malevolent power and implacable will. The long blade glowed brighter than ever, an unearthly light that sickened them just to look at. A voice rang inside all their heads, a sound that was not a sound, a voice within nothing human in it. *If I can't have you, Suzie, I'll take your baby. Poor defenceless little thing. I'll curl up inside its head, like a worm in an apple, and you'll never get me out. Your child will be my child, and oh the things I'll make it do . . . Unless you take me back, Suzie. And let me do what I was made to do.*

Suzie's face was cold and utterly focused as she drew her shotgun and placed the barrels firmly under her chin. "Get out of me. All the way out. Or I will pull the trigger. I'll kill us both before I let my child be a slave to something like you."

John started forward, then stopped himself. He had no doubt she'd do it.

"No need to be so dramatic," said Molly.

She had wrapped herself in the bark of trees from her wood between the worlds, ancient primeval trees from when the world was young and magic and nature walked hand in hand. The bark sealed her in from head to toe, like living armour, insulating her from all outside influences. Molly grabbed hold of Wulfsbane, the hilt and the blade, with her armoured hands. The sword fought to possess her, to take control, but it couldn't reach her past the protection of the trees. Molly broke the sword in two with one convulsive effort, and they all heard the Infernal Device scream horribly as it died. The two pieces of the sword stopped glowing, and suddenly it looked like just another sword. Molly threw the pieces away, and they clattered harmlessly on the ground. The bark of the living armour disappeared, back to where it came from, and Molly nodded easily to Suzie.

"I'm not just here for the bad things in life."

Suzie lowered her shotgun, breathed steadily, and put the gun away. She patted her bump.

"Back to sleep. False alarm."

She nodded her thanks to Molly, and Molly nodded back. Which was as far as either of them would go.

"I swear, living in the Nightside puts years on you," said John.

"I had noticed," said Eddie. "But we still have work to do. We need to find Puck and get the truth out of him."

"Finding things is what I do," said John. "My mother told me that if I wanted to put the Nightside boundaries back to what they were, I needed to talk to whoever changed them."

Eddie looked at him. "You spoke to your mother? Recently?"

"Only briefly," said John.

He raised his gift and reached out, but the elf had serious protections in place. John struggled, trying to focus in on what he needed to know, but it felt like someone else was there, standing between him and Puck. Hiding the elf from John's gift.

"Someone's with Puck," he said to Eddie. "I can't get past them . . ."

Eddie placed his armoured hands on John's shoulders. The power of Drood armour boosted the power of John's gift . . . and it dashed suddenly away in a different direction. If it couldn't find who it was looking for, it would find someone else who could. And just like that, Gaea was standing before them. Mother Earth herself, manifesting as just a good-looking woman in a business suit. She wasn't smiling.

"There had better be a really good reason as to why I suddenly felt I should be here," said Gaea.

Eddie pulled his armoured hands back from John. "Someone has been working with the elf Puck to set the Droods and the Nightside at each other's throats. And what they've done is endangering the whole world."

"We can't get past their protections to find them," said John. "Do you know who's working with Puck?"

"Of course," said Gaea. "Nothing is hidden from me."

"Who is it?" said Eddie.

"I think . . . This is something you need to do for yourselves," said Gaea.

She gestured briefly, and sent John Taylor and Eddie Drood to where they needed to be.

They appeared standing on top of Griffin Hill, looking out over the Nightside. The hill stood high and lonely, under the star-speckled sky and the oversized full moon, and the whole of the Nightside lay spread out below them, its lights blazing fiercely against the dark. A cold wind was blowing, spiritually cold, because of what this place was and what had happened here. John glanced behind him at the great hole in the ground: a pit full of darkness, a drop so deep it seemed bottomless. Even the shimmering moonlight couldn't penetrate far beyond the torn and ragged edges. John and Eddie moved cautiously over to look into the pit, and what they could see of the interior was scorched and blackened by incredible, impossible heat. John made a low, sad sound.

"This is Griffin Hill, where Griffin Hall once stood till the Hall and everyone inside it was dragged down to Hell by the Devil himself."

"Damn," said Eddie. He peered into the depths of the pit and shuddered, not at all from the cold. "I always knew there was a good reason why my family stayed out of the Nightside. You're too weird, even for us. So what are we doing here?"

"Gaea must have sent us here for a reason," said John. "It can't be the Griffins; they're not coming back."

"Did anything else happen here?" said Eddie.

"Yes . . . This was where the previous Walker, Henry, died."

"I never did get the full story on that," said Eddie.

"It was no one else's business," said John.

"But what does that have to do with anything?" said Eddie.

John looked at him pityingly. "What do you think? I should have known . . ."

"Of course you should," said a calm, cultured, and very familiar voice. "I can't believe you never even suspected it was me."

They both looked around to see Henry, the man who was Walker, standing just a few feet away. Smiling easily, the perfect city gentleman, sharp and stylish and sophisticated, in the finest suit Savile Row had to offer. Right down to the bowler hat and neatly furled umbrella. He was handsome enough, if a little on the heavy side, as befitted a man well into middle age. His smile was cold, and his eyes were colder; and he was in surprisingly good shape for a man who was supposed to have died years ago.

"I should have known because there was no body," said John. He looked at Eddie. "Henry and I fought here. He fell into the bottomless pit, and we all assumed he was dead and gone."

"What did I always tell you, John?" said Henry. "If there isn't a body, you can never be sure they're dead."

"Perhaps I just wanted you to be dead," said John.

"How hurtful," murmured Henry.

"The truth," said John. "Tell me the truth. I think I deserve it."

"I faked my death so you could take over as Walker," said Henry. "I was never ill, never dying; I was just feeling old and tired and more than ready to put down my burden and retire. The Nightside had changed so much, and I hadn't. I couldn't just walk away, not after all the things I'd done as Walker; too many people might come after me. So I worked out a plausible scenario, made you the hero of the hour, and disappeared."

"Was that you I saw in the Winter Hall?" said Eddie. "When I was trapped in Limbo?"

"No," said Henry. "Though I did hear about it from the person masquerading as me. Puck, of course, hidden behind one of his glamours. He has been so many people in his time. But then, he has been playing a very long game."

"And what about you, Henry?" said John. "How long have you been playing a game?"

"I retired to spend more time with my family and take it easy at last," said Henry. "Only to find my family didn't need me. My wife had made her own life, and my two boys . . . were always busy. So I pottered around on my own for a while, trying to find things to do . . . Till I realised I just couldn't let it go.

"I always knew the Nightside was a danger to Humanity. I always said I would happily nuke the whole damned freak show, if it were up to me. And the thought of its still persisting, a knife at Humanity's throat, long after I was gone . . . became intolerable. Unacceptable. So I decided to do something about it while I still could. Of course, I couldn't do it on my own. I reached out, through some of my old contacts, to the elves who stayed behind after the others left, and through them I found Puck. Who was more than ready for a little murderous mischief. Between us, we planned a war to take down my enemies and his.

"It turned out that Oberon and Titania knew of many ancient and mysterious Objects of Power, scattered across the world, that they couldn't be bothered to take with them when they left. And Puck knew all about them. We finally settled on the one we needed, and he went and got it. I think you know it, Eddie. The Soul of Albion."

Henry held up a small, polished crystal, hardly bigger than his thumb. It boiled and blazed with unearthly fires, impossibly, heart-stoppingly beautiful, like the Platonic ideal behind every gem or jewel that ever was.

"You shouldn't have that," said Eddie, so angry he could barely get the words out. "No one is supposed to have that!"

"I hate to admit it," said John, "but even I can't keep up with all the Objects of Power and what they do. What's so special about this one?"

"It's supposed to have fallen to Earth thousands of years ago," said Eddie.

"Oh, it's much older than that," said Henry. "Or so Puck assures me."

"The Soul of Albion guarantees the borders of Great Britain," said Eddie. "It protects us from invasion. As long as it stays where it's supposed to: under the stones of Stonehenge! You've put everyone in this country in danger just by removing it!"

"I'll put it back when I don't need it any more," said Henry, slipping the crystal into his waistcoat pocket. "Puck stole it, without anyone's noticing, because that's what elves do. Since the Soul of Albion is all about boundaries, it was easy enough to pervert its function and use it to expand the Nightside's boundaries. Exactly what Puck and I needed, to set the ball rolling.

"We made one small change in the nature of things, and the Droods and the Nightside walked themselves into war. Protesting all the way that none of them wanted it. All so the power of the Nightside would be broken and the Droods fatally weakened. Puck would have the emptied long night for his elves to live in, and I would have a world safe from the horrors of the Nightside and the arrogant authority of the Droods. Isn't it nice when everyone gets what they want?"

"But the changes in the boundaries have destabilised the Nightside!" said John. "There won't be anywhere for the elves to live!"

"Yes . . ." said Henry, smiling modestly. "I made one small change in the way we used the Soul of Albion, and Puck never even noticed. I didn't go through all of this just so the Nightside could continue as a threat, under new management. And yes, I know the changes I made in the boundaries also threaten the outside world. I'll use the Soul of Albion to put everything right once the Nightside has become so damaged the elves won't want it any more."

"Did you know changing the boundaries would destroy the Wulfshead Club and kill everyone in it?" said Eddie.

"Of course," said Henry. "I put the predatory house in just the right position to ensure that would happen. I needed to make an impact, you see. I needed what I'd done to be noticed."

"Good friends of mine died in the Club!" said John. "People you knew!"

"Yes, that was regrettable," said Henry. "But sometimes you can't make an omelette unless you use a really big hammer."

"You killed all those people, just to bring a Drood into the Nightside," said Eddie. "And you used a predatory house to do it, so you could be sure the Drood would have to use their armour."

"I needed an inciting incident," said Henry. "Something guaranteed to outrage the Nightside. And you performed your function admirably, Eddie."

"You stole the Nightside's copy of the Pacts and Agreements," John said suddenly. "Because you still had access from when you were Walker."

"Exactly!" said Henry. "There was always the chance there might be something in them you could use to defend the Nightside, and I couldn't have that."

"You had Puck interfere with the Hall's arrival in the Nightside," said Eddie. "Keeping us well away from the centre, so we'd have to fight our way in. And start your damned war for you."

"The devil is always in the details," Henry said modestly.

"So many dead because of you and Puck," said John. "I can understand it from him; he's an elf, and they live to mess with mankind. But you . . ."

"I have always been able to do the cold, hard, necessary things, to serve the greater good," said Henry. "That's why they made me Walker. It's why I chose you, John."

"I'm nothing like you!" said John.

"I know," said Henry. "That's why I chose you."

"Don't argue with him, John," said Eddie. "His kind always has an answer for everything."

"Not always," said Henry. "I have to say, I am surprised to see the two of you here. I was convinced I'd covered my tracks quite thoroughly. How did you know to come to Griffin Hill?"

"My gift for finding things," said John.

"Ah, yes," said Henry. "Your very inconvenient gift."

"Enough talk," said Eddie. "Give me the Soul of Albion, or I'll take it from you. First to repair what you've done to the Nightside boundaries, then to put it back under Stonehenge. I don't care who you used to be, Henry; I don't even care that we worked well together once, and were almost friends. I will do whatever's necessary. And you must know you can't stop a Drood in his armour."

"Especially with me here to help him," said John. "I never did show you all my tricks, Henry."

"Unfortunately . . . the situation is a little more complicated than that," said Henry.

The Suzie from the future appeared out of nowhere, standing next to Henry. Still battered and disfigured, and weighed down by long years of surviving against impossible odds. Still old and haggard, with only half a face, but this time the Speaking Gun was attached to her elbow, replacing her missing right forearm. That terrible weapon from prehistory that could uncreate anything. Made from flesh and bone and dark-veined gristle, held together with strips of cartilage and pale skin, living tissues shaped into a killing tool. The Speaking Gun had a hot and sweaty look, and it smelled like a mad dog. John swallowed hard at the sight of it on Suzie's arm.

"Who is that?" Eddie said quietly to John. "I mean, I know who she looks like . . ."

"It's Suzie," said John. "From a future timeline."

"Your life is almost as complicated as mine," said Eddie.

"I warned you, John," said the future Suzie, in her harsh grating voice. "Soon you and the Droods will go to war with the elves, and what you will do to win that war will destroy everything. Nothing will remain but ruins and monsters. You know that; you've seen it. But I came back to give you a chance to do the right thing. Let me kill you now, with this." She pointed the Speaking Gun at John, and he stood very still. Suzie tried to smile at him with her half a face. "Die now, John, and save everyone. I don't want to have to lead the life that made me this."

Eddie remembered Old Father Time saying that the Nightside could be saved if one good man would just do the right thing. But this was the Nightside, and Eddie didn't trust anything in it. He focused his Sight through his torc. John started to say something to the future Suzie, and Eddie cut quickly across him.

"According to my torc, that thing on her arm isn't the Speaking Gun," he said flatly. "There's a power in it, but nothing like what you'd expect from such an infamous weapon."

John smiled, as a great many things suddenly became clear to him. "Of course. It's not real; and neither are you, Suzie. You just couldn't resist over-playing your hand, could you . . . Puck?"

Future Suzie disappeared, gone in a moment, to be replaced by the crooked elf. With nothing in his right hand but a glowing dagger. John recognised it as the weapon his future son had tried to kill him with. Puck nodded easily to John.

"Well, it was worth a try."

"That was you in Strangefellows, pretending to be the future Suzie," said John. "And even before that, you pretended to be my future son. Why? To rattle me, so I wouldn't be in a proper frame of mind when it came to dealing with what was happening in the Nightside? So you could have your stupid war? That's how the body disappeared from Strangefellows! You just walked away, hidden behind another glamour."

Puck took a bow, as though these were all compliments. He realised he still had the glowing dagger in his hand and slipped it into his belt.

"Why involve the Droods?" said Eddie. "We went out of our way to help the elves."

"You shouldn't have won that last Big Game against us," said Puck. "It was my idea, and you shamed me in front of Oberon and Titania."

"You petty-minded little shit," said Eddie.

"Why did you want the Nightside?" said John. "You had a place of your own beside Oberon and Titania, in Shadows Fall."

"I never really had a place with them!" said Puck. He wasn't smiling any more. "Because I was always Puck, the elf who was not perfect. Forced to play the jester and the fool, to amuse Oberon and Titania . . . So I could at least remain close to the source of power. I should have been King of the elves! My mother was Mab, First Queen of the Fae; but my father was the mortal Tam O'Shanter. Just like in the old stories. And his genes collided with hers to make me the mis-shapen thing I am.

"I attached myself to Oberon and Titania because they had ambition, and when they overthrew Mab, I rose along with them. Then they got old and decided to retire to Shadows Fall . . . But I wasn't ready to leave the world. I hadn't finished playing with you mortals yet. So I decided to make a new kingdom for myself, here in the Nightside. After I'd cleaned out all the trash, of course. And brought down the only family who might have opposed me." He turned suddenly, to glare at Henry. "But you meddled with the Soul of Albion! You betrayed me! You spoiled everything!"

"You're an elf," said Henry. "You should have seen that one coming."

Puck's hand dropped to the glowing dagger at his belt, then stopped as Henry held up one hand. In it . . . was a simple brass door-knob. He smiled pleasantly.

"Surrounded by my enemies, with all my plans revealed and endangered, I still have this. The final answer to all our problems."

It was quite definitely just a door-knob. But because Henry was who he was, John and Eddie and Puck watched him carefully and waited for him to explain himself.

"This," Henry said easily, "is a potential Door. A Door in waiting, if you will. Not actually real till it's opened. I had the Doormouse make it for me, some time back. As a possible solution to the problem of the Nightside.

And then I made him forget all about it, so he wouldn't know what he'd done and couldn't warn anyone about it. This is my fall-back position in case all my plans should fail me. You see, this potential Door opens inside the heart of the Sun. If I turn this knob, the Door will open, and from it will issue a heat beyond your imagination. Enough to scorch the whole Nightside clean. How fitting, I thought, that the Sun should bring an end to the long night."

"But you'd die too!" said Puck.

"Which is why I never used it," said Henry. "I always had some other plan in mind. But now . . . my war is over; John and Eddie are ready to take the Soul of Albion away from me, and I don't think I care any more. What better way to go out than by taking all my closest friends and enemies with me? All I have to do is open this Door, and the Nightside will be destroyed. And I will have done my duty, one last time."

Before any of them could stop him, he turned the door-knob. A great Door of beaten brass appeared hovering beside him and swung open. They all braced themselves for a blast of fire they'd never even feel, but there was nothing inside the open Door but a Light that John and Eddie had already encountered. And out of that Light stepped Charles Taylor, John's father, and Mark Robinson, who grew up to be the Collector. Henry's oldest friends. They smiled at him, and he stared blankly back at them, lost for anything to say.

Charles looked just as he had in the World Beneath. Like John, only younger. Mark looked as he had in his younger days. He had the whole young Elvis thing down pat: a black leather jacket with far too many zips and chains, and a great quiff of greasy black hair. John murmured to Eddie, explaining who everyone was, while Puck snarled at everyone, trying to work out what it all meant.

"The Doormouse is sharper and stronger than you ever gave him credit for, Henry," Charles said calmly. "He is a graduate of the Dark Academie, after all. He didn't make you what you wanted; he made you what you needed. And then just went along with the whole amnesia bit. This is a Destiny Door, made to save the day. To bring me and Mark to you, in your hour of need."

"Give it up, Henry," said Mark. "It's over. Your time is up. You knew that once; it's why you retired. Come with us, old friend."

"But you're dead," said Henry.

"So are you," said Charles. "You really did die when you fell into that pit. It's only your stored magics and your own stubborn will that's kept you going all this time."

"That's why you couldn't settle into retirement," said Mark. "And why your family barely noticed you. Deep-down, you all knew the truth."

"Well," said Henry. "That does explain a lot." He smiled at John, then at Eddie, before producing the Soul of Albion from his waistcoat pocket and tossing it lightly to Eddie.

"Let's go," said Mark.

"The Hereafter isn't what you think it is, Henry," said Charles. "There's still lots of good work to be done."

"That's all I ever wanted," said Henry.

The three old friends strode through the Door and into the Light. The Door closed behind them, and disappeared.

Eddie and John were left standing together on top of Griffin Hill, facing Puck. His hand dropped to the glowing dagger again.

"Give me the crystal, Drood."

Eddie put it in his pocket dimension.

"Don't think I can't take it from you!" said Puck.

"If you could, you'd have done it by now," said Eddie.

"What are we going to do with you, Puck?" said John. "So many deaths to lay at your door . . ."

"Don't you look at me like that," said Puck. "Don't you dare! You were all happy enough to kill each other till you found out it wasn't your own idea. And you don't dare kill me, despite everything I've done! The elves would return from Shadows Fall and the Sundered Lands and go to war with all Humanity to avenge me. For honour's sake."

"Even after we tell Oberon and Titania how you went behind their backs to set up your own kingdom?" said Eddie.

Puck laughed in his face. "You never did understand elves. They would be proud of my ambition. And with your family so weakened, and the Nightside only a shadow of its former self . . ."

John looked at Eddie. "He may be a petty-minded little shit, but he has a point. However . . . there is one person who could punish him as he deserves. Someone even the elves wouldn't go against."

Eddie grinned. "Of course. Go ahead. Call her."

John reached out with his gift to find Gaea; and she appeared on Griffin Hill, looking coldly at Puck.

"I've been watching, and listening," said Gaea. "I know everything that's happened. The elves were my first children, and my first real disappointment. But I think I can still make something useful out of you, Puck. After a millennium or two in my service."

Puck turned to John and Eddie, real horror in his eyes. "Don't let her take me! Please! Kill me!"

Gaea snapped her fingers, and Puck vanished; the air rushing in to fill the space where he'd been. Gaea nodded easily to Eddie and John.

"I think I've interfered enough. You can do all the clearing up."

"Wait!" said John. "Before you go, can you please explain why the Nightside is so important?"

"Yes," said Eddie. "I'd really like to know the answer to that one."

"If you must," said Gaea. "The idea behind the Nightside is that Good and Evil aren't always opposites. Rather, they are two sides of the same coin because you can't have one without the other. The Nightside is an attempt to see what happens when people embrace them both at the same time. To see if that might produce a whole greater than the sum of its parts. Lilith didn't know that when she created the Nightside, but that is why the long night has been allowed to survive as long as it has." She smiled briefly. "Think of it as God's Little Experiment."

And then she disappeared too.

"Damn!" said John. "I never thought to ask her why the moon is so big!"

"I'm sure you'll get another chance," said Eddie. "She's bound to be back."

"You're just saying that to depress me," said John.

"Let's get out of here," said Eddie. "It's cold, and the girls are waiting."

"Never let them hear you call them that," said John.

"Perish the thought," said Eddie.

"Come on," said John. "Lots to do."

"Isn't there always," said Eddie.

EPILOGUE

Afterwards, a great many things happened.

The Soul of Albion returned the Nightside boundaries to where they were supposed to be, and the long night became stable again. The war was over, so the Droods took their Hall back to where it belonged, and the Nightsiders set about rebuilding and burying their dead. The gods returned to the Street of the Gods, but no one gave much of a damn.

Suzie gave birth to a lovely little girl, which eased John's mind, just a little. Maggie gave up being Matriarch and went back to heading the gardening staff, which was where she'd always been happiest. And Cathy Barrett became the new Ms Fate.

After a certain amount of cautious discussion, it was decided that both sides needed to learn from each other, to make sure nothing like this could ever happen again. So Eddie went to the Nightside to become the new Walker, with Molly at his side, while John and Suzie took their new daughter and went to Drood Hall, to run things there.

None of them lived happily ever after, because that doesn't happen.
But life went on.

ACKNOWLEDGMENTS

I don't normally do these, but this feels like a special occasion, so pay attention at the back there; I have a few words to say.

Basically, this book is me saying good-bye. I've finally written the last chapter in a very-long-running story, bringing together a lot of characters and even more loose ends. So it's good-bye to a world of Droods and Ghost Finders, to men who find things and the women who love shotguns, to the Forest Kingdom and Shadows Fall and the land of Mysterie. The story is over, so let's ring down the curtain, pass the hat around, and move on.

I'm still going to be writing novels, but there are other worlds waiting for me to explore.

It's time for me to make a few acknowledgments to all the people who helped me on my way.

First, I have to thank my agent, Joshua Bilmes, who has been with me from the beginning. I wouldn't be where I am today if it weren't for him. These days he runs his own literary agency, JABberwocky. So thanks to Joshua, and all at JABberwocky, especially the ones who send me money.

I have to thank the three most important editors in my life: Ginjer Buchanan in the US, and Richard Evans and Jo Fletcher in the UK. They found and nurtured me and loved what I wrote. What more can you ask, from an editor.

And my current editor, Rebecca Brewer, who has always been very supportive.

I'd like to talk about my parents, Stan and Nancy Green, who were always there for me.

My dad started out as an engineer. During World War II, he was a fireman. Afterwards, he ran a small family business, and I worked there on and off from an early age. When I was about eight, I found a stack of old *Galaxy Science Fiction* magazines from the Fifties; and when he saw how much I enjoyed them, my dad introduced me to his collection of Edgar Rice Burroughs . . . Tarzan and Mars and Pellucidar. And then to Thorne Smith and Leslie Charteris.

He taught me the value of hard work and believing in your dreams.

My mum started out as a printer's devil, a type setter. An unusual occupation for a woman in the Thirties, but no one ever stopped my mum from doing anything she set out to do. During the war, she joined the fire service, which is where she met my dad. Afterwards, she helped him run the family business, in between raising my brother and me.

She taught me the value of stubbornness and never giving up.

I have to thank my oldest friend, Steve Lovett, who has spent a great many years listening to some of my wilder ideas. He believed in me long before anyone else did. Even when I wasn't sure myself.

And finally I have to thank you, my readers. I may be moving on to pastures new, but I hope you'll stick with me . . . Because the view promises to be spectacular.

One story ends; another begins.

The work goes ever on.